ROB
DUGONI

A Novel

WRONGFUL
DEATH

NEW YORK TIMES
BESTSELLING AUTHOR
ROBERT DUGONI
is
"A DISTINCTIVE NEW VOICE."
—Stephen White,
New York Times bestselling author

**DON'T MISS HIS
IMPOSSIBLE-TO-PUT-DOWN NEW
THRILLER FEATURING FEARLESS
ATTORNEY DAVID SLOANE**

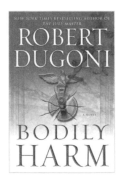

Coming soon in
hardcover from Touchstone!

ISBN 978-1-4165-9297-6

50799

EAN

"An entertaining thriller. . . . Good guys to like, villains to hiss, windmills to attack. . . . Dugoni plots deftly."

—*Kirkus Reviews*

"An interesting, contemporary plot."

—*Library Journal*

"Dugoni has earned a slot on the A-list. . . . [He] is a master at explaining complex legal concepts in an understandable, readable way and in an exciting, riveting context."

—Bookreporter.com

THE JURY MASTER

"A smart and savvy story with more muscle than the average legal thriller. Combining an astonishingly good plot, perfectly drawn characters and intensely sharp writing, Robert Dugoni has put the thrills back in the genre."

—Nelson DeMille

"John Grisham move over. . . . Dugoni explodes from the tired pack of Grisham wannabes with a riveting tale of murder, treachery and skullduggery at the highest levels."

—*The Seattle Times*

"Dugoni is well out in front. . . . A writer to watch."

—*Kirkus Reviews*

"Impressive. . . . Plenty of action. . . . A gripping legal thriller."

—*Publishers Weekly*

"This thriller is reminiscent of the early John Grisham and should easily find its way onto the bestsellers list."

—*Library Journal*

ALSO BY ROBERT DUGONI

ROBERT DUGONI

WRONGFUL DEATH

Pocket Books
New York London Toronto Sydney

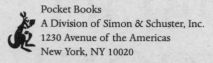

Pocket Books
A Division of Simon & Schuster, Inc.
1230 Avenue of the Americas
New York, NY 10020

First Pocket Books paperback edition March 2010

POCKET and colophon are registered trademarks of
Simon & Schuster, Inc.

For information about special discounts for bulk purchases,
please contact Simon & Schuster Special Sales at 1-866-506-1949 or
business@simonandschuster.com.

The Simon & Schuster Speakers Bureau can bring authors to your live event. For more information or to book an event, contact the Simon & Schuster Speakers Bureau at 1-866-248-3049 or visit our website at www.simonspeakers.com.

Cover design and photo illustration by Jae Song

Manufactured in the United States of America

10   9   8   7   6   5   4   3   2   1

ISBN 978-1-4165-9297-6
ISBN 978-1-4391-0060-8 (ebook)

For Chris, the Irishman, who pointed me in the right direction and encouraged me to dream. For my mother and father, whose sacrifices gave me the opportunity to pursue my dream, and for all those men and women who wear the uniform and serve so we are free to dream.

Wisdom too often never comes, and so one ought not to reject it merely because it comes late.

Justice Felix Frankfurter
Henslee v. Union Planters Bank, 1949

PROLOGUE

Phillip Ferguson set his Ruger over-under shotgun on the kitchen table and felt for the stock of the Remington Wingmaster. He racked back the fore end, stuck his finger into the receiver to ensure the gun was not loaded, unscrewed the magazine cap, and removed the barrel.

So far, so good.

He had cleaned his shotguns so many times he had once bragged he could do it with his eyes closed.

"Here's your chance," he said to the darkness.

He put down the barrel and felt along the tabletop for the can of Hoppe's No. 9 cleaning solvent, held a wet patch over the top, and turned the can over to saturate the swab. He sensed that he spilled a few drops of solvent, but he'd covered the table with newspaper to protect it. He'd never professed to being neat. The familiar pungent chemical odor made him reconsider slipping on a pair of rubber gloves, but he dismissed the thought; he needed the dexterity to feel what his eyes could no longer see.

He picked up a cleaning rod, found the end of the barrel, and pushed the wet patch through the tube. Then he set the barrel down to give the solvent time to loosen the powder. He couldn't rush the process, though anxious to get finished and lock the guns back in the cabinet; if Katherine were to walk in at that moment and see him sitting with his shotguns, she'd likely scream. His wife wouldn't admit it, but Ferguson knew she harbored doubts about his ability to cope with being blind. Hell, so did he. Living in the dark wasn't exactly how he'd expected to spend the rest of his life, but at forty-three he also wasn't ready to check out. He had moments of self-pity, but he would never abandon his wife and kids. Getting the shotguns ready for duck season would prove he intended to stick around. He might not be able to shoot anymore, but that didn't mean PJ had to give up the sport. Come the fall, they'd go out together with his brother, Joe, and bring home some duck.

Using the cleaning rod, he alternately ran wet and dry patches through the tube. After several passes he brought a dry patch to his nose to try and detect the amount of residual powder, since he could no longer see when the patch came through clean.

The dogs began to bark out front.

Ferguson froze, listening for the sound of an approaching car. When he did not detect the crunch of tire on gravel, he sighed in relief and went back to work. Given the ferocity of the dogs' yapping, they had likely treed another raccoon, or squirrel.

He set down the barrel, about to oil it, when he heard the front door open. "Damn." He stood quickly, bumped the table, and knocked over the can of Hoppe's. Fumbling to find it, he righted the can, and called out, "Katherine?"

He'd purposely waited until she went to work. What was she doing home?

Ferguson grabbed his cane and tapped the linoleum to the doorway, stumbling over something on the floor. He reached for the door frame to regain his balance. "What are you doing home?"

He stepped into the hall to block her access to the kitchen and give himself a chance to explain. A breeze brushed cool against his skin and he heard the weight sewn into the fabric of the lace curtains that covered the sidelight knock against the wainscoting.

"You left the door open. Katherine?"

A floorboard creaked to his left. Ferguson turned. "Joe?"

The front door latch clicked closed across the door-plate. The breeze stilled. "Who's there?" he asked, no longer certain.

Sensing someone behind him, Ferguson spun and whipped the cane, but the tip struck the wall, knocking a picture frame to the floor, glass shattering. He drew the cane back and coiled to strike again when something thick and solid struck him across the calves, knocking his feet out from under him. He fell backward, his head hitting the floor with a dull thud. Before he could recover, the intruders had flipped him onto his stomach. A knee pressed between his shoulder blades, driving his sternum into the hardwood. They yanked his left wrist behind his back, then his right, binding them.

"Get off me!"

One on each side lifted him to his feet. He heard noise coming from the kitchen, a third person in the house.

"What do you want? Just take it and leave."

The front door shuddered open. The breeze again blew stiffly in his face. They tugged and pulled him toward the door. This was not a burglary. There was a familiarity to the swiftness and efficiency of the assault. Snatch and grab, they had called it.

He planted his feet, fighting for traction, but his heels slipped on the hardwood, offering little resistance. Using the men on each side for leverage, he reared back and kicked out, wedging a foot against the doorjamb. A blow to his shin knocked it free, sending needles of pain radiating up his leg.

The men pulled him across the threshold onto the porch and down the steps, the boards creaking beneath their weight. The dogs continued to bark. From the direction of the sound, Ferguson realized they had been penned. Gravel jabbed the soles of his feet. Behind him shoes crunched rocks, the third person following.

He yelled over his shoulder, "Just tell me what you—"

A jab to the lower back, the butt of a rifle, silenced him. The sharp pain flared down both legs, but Ferguson knew the force had been tempered, a warning to shut up and cooperate. Not that yelling would do him any good. The farm was set well off the main road, and the wind, blowing in gusts, would swallow his voice along with the dogs' barking. No one would hear him.

More important, Ferguson now knew the men were armed. Why? What could they possibly want from him?

The gravel ended. He felt dirt beneath his feet, but the familiar soil did not bring comfort. Stored images re-created the layout of his farm, and the intruders' path. They were dragging him to the barn.

Panic brought another rush of adrenaline, and with it, strength. He dug in his left heel and jerked free his right shoulder, lunging at the spot on his left where he'd heard heavy breathing. The top of his head struck solid. A man groaned and swore.

Ferguson spun and kicked, missing, shuffling around the yard like a blind rooster. He hit another mark, draw-ing another grunt, then bull-rushed forward. The butt of the gun crashed into the small of his back. This time, it was no warning. The pain buckled his legs and he col-lapsed, rolling on the ground, fighting to get back to his feet. A kick drove the air from his lungs. Another caused him to bring his knees to his chest and curl into a fetal position.

"Enough." The voice was deep, authoritative. The beating stopped. "Get him up."

The men lifted him by his arms and carried him the remaining distance. His shoulders burned from the strain. His ribs felt like they were on fire. The barn door creaked open. After a few more steps the men dumped him on the ground.

Ferguson lay curled in a ball, coughing and wheezing, struggling to catch his breath while smelling the odor of damp straw, sawdust, and manure. His daughter's horse thumped about its stall, anxious. Overhead, pigeons disturbed from the rafters flapped and fluttered.

The intruders lifted him to his knees, but the searing pain in his side caused him to slump, head bowed. Despite the cool temperature inside the barn, perspiration dripped down his forehead, stinging his eyes. He envisioned the barn as he once could: the slatted light and shadows through the plank siding, wood support beams carved with initials, the leather saddles and blankets resting on sawhorses, reins and hackamores hanging from hooks alongside pitchforks and shovels, and the tractor parked in the back, its engine cold.

"Who are you?" Ferguson asked, his breathing still labored. "What do you want from me?"

The leader spoke again. "Why did you file a claim, Sergeant?"

The man's use of Ferguson's rank did not catch him completely off guard, though it further alarmed him. "I'm not a sergeant. I'm just a farmer."

"Why did you file a claim?"

From the sound of the man's voice, Ferguson sensed him circling, keeping a deliberate pace.

"I don't know what you're talking about."

The pacing stopped. The man now knelt directly in front of him, his breath a bitter, acrid odor. "The claim for your injuries, Sergeant. Why did you file it?"

"I told you I'm not . . ." Katherine had mentioned talking to an attorney, something about a claim to get money. "What do you care?" he asked. "What does that have to do with this?"

Something jammed under his jaw, forcing his body upright. Ferguson stiffened at the familiar shape. Two barrels, one positioned over the other, the distinct odor of the Hoppe's. His Ruger shotgun.

"Answer the question."

The pressure of the barrels made it difficult to move his jaw. His mouth was bone dry. "An attorney . . ." He sputtered, swallowing with difficulty. "An attorney told us to do it."

Wind whistled between the cracks in the wood slats, a high-pitched wail like the sound of a distant scream.

"Bad advice," the man said.

CHAPTER ONE

Theresa Gonzalez squeezed David Sloane's biceps as each juror responded to King County Superior Court Judge Anthony Wartnik's question.

"Is this your verdict?"

"Yes."

After the twelfth and final juror confirmed her decision, Wartnik adjusted his black-framed glasses, made a few notes, and thanked the members of the jury for their service before dismissing them. Turning, he spoke briefly to the attorneys, complimenting them on having tried a fine case, and for their professional demeanor in his courtroom. Then he, too, stood and left the bench.

Sloane walked to where his young adversary

remained slumped in his seat. Frank Martin was not gathering his documents or shoving binders into briefcases. He was not talking to his client, who sat looking just as forlorn in the chair beside him. Martin wasn't moving at all. Pale, he looked stunned.

Martin looked up at Sloane as if he were from Mars. His client, apparently in no mood to be collegial, shoved back his chair, and brushed past Sloane, already pulling his cell phone from his pocket. Pacific Northwest Paper had sent the portly plant manager, rather than a corporate officer, to sit through the trial, and the man now bore the unenviable task of telling PNP's officers exactly why they would have to pay Sloane's client $1.6 million in damages.

It had not had to come to this. The case should not have gone to trial.

The first day Theresa Gonzalez visited Sloane's office, she sat across his desk looking like a scared mouse. She told him she was terrified to go to court, that her English was poor and she feared not understanding the judicial system. Her husband, Cesar, had been electrocuted while operating a piece of equipment that had not been properly grounded at a PNP production plant. Cesar had been illegal at the time of his death, his green card long since expired. Theresa feared deportation, not for herself but for their three children. Sloane made sure that wouldn't happen. Then he gave PNP every opportunity to settle. They had refused.

"You tried a good case, Frank."

Regaining some color to his cheeks, Martin stood. "Apparently not," he said.

"Your closing was excellent," Sloane said. "I thought you had me."

"So did I." Martin continued to shake his head in disbelief.

Sloane felt no need to rub the young man's nose in the verdict, having once been in Martin's shoes. For thirteen years Sloane had represented similarly arrogant corporate clients in San Francisco before moving to Seattle two years earlier and changing his practice to nearly 100 percent plaintiff's work. "Juries are unpredictable. You never know what they'll do."

Martin eyed Sloane with a sharper focus. "You did." His eyebrows narrowed. "You said the verdict would be unanimous."

"I was just—"

"How could you have known that?"

Sloane had made the prediction after PNP's final refusal to settle at a mediation just before trial. He had hoped his certitude, and his reputation, would convince the company to reconsider. But PNP had remained recalcitrant.

"I was bluffing," Sloane said.

Martin scoffed. "Remind me not to play poker with you." He looked to the empty seats in the jury box. "It was as if they forgot all the evidence. You stood to give your closing and they just . . . forgot everything."

Martin turned to the doors at the back of the courtroom with a look of dread. PNP's officers were not the only ones who would be unhappy. Martin would have to explain to the law firm's partnership board how he had lost a certain victory for a signature client. He looked once more at Sloane, then, with nothing left to say, he gathered his things and packed his briefcases.

Gonzalez stood huddled with her family at the back of the room. As Sloane approached, she stepped forward, still trembling. Tears streaked her cheeks with mascara. No more than five feet, she had to reach up to hug him. "Thank you, David. Thank you for everything."

He let her cry for a moment. Then she stepped back, and one by one her relatives thanked him, her mother, white-haired and frail, last. The old woman stood on her toes as if to kiss Sloane's cheek, but when he bent she whispered softly in his ear.

"Usted tiene el regalo. Usted es un curandero."

She touched his cheek with a wrinkled hand, her brown eyes considering him as they had throughout the trial, not with curiosity, but with a knowing glint. A hint of a smile curled the left side of her mouth and she gave him the briefest of nods.

Sloane led the family to the courtroom doors, taking a moment to explain to Theresa what were likely to be the next steps in the legal process, including a defense motion for a judgment notwithstanding the verdict, and an attempt to settle the claim for less than the jury amount. Other attorneys had tried the same tactic. They had yet to succeed.

"Judges respect the jury system," he explained. "They don't like to overturn a verdict. But don't think about that now. Just go home and enjoy this," he said. "We'll talk further."

As the family filed out of the courtroom, the mother last, still smiling at him, Sloane let the courtroom door swing shut.

"You have the gift," she had whispered, using the Mexican term, *un curandero*, referring to a shaman.

Sloane strode back to counsel table to pack his brief-case and felt the fatigue from the long days in the muscles of his legs and lower back. He wanted to get home to Tina and Jake, to think of nothing but a week of lying on the beach in Cabo San Lucas, their first vacation together. He and Tina had honeymooned in Italy after their wedding the previous summer, but because of the move to Seattle—both of them settling into new jobs, Tina trying to get an architectural practice off the ground and Sloane trying to re-create himself as a plaintiff's lawyer—this would be the first time they took Jake with them for anything more than a day or weekend trip as a family.

The word made him pause. *Family*. The last time Sloane had considered that word was the day he left the fourth and final foster home in which he had been raised in Southern California. Sitting at the kitchen table, his foster father had turned to him in between bites of pot roast to advise that when Sloane turned eighteen he was on his own.

"The money from the state stops then. It'll be time for you to go figure things out on your own. This family tried to do right by you, but you got to stand on your own now."

That afternoon Sloane had walked to a hardware store to buy bolts to fix the Honda motorcycle he'd purchased, and instead found himself inside a marine recruitment center. He enlisted and went through boot camp thinking he'd found in the Corps the family he had never had, but after a while the empty feeling that something was missing returned, and the camaraderie and brotherhood that had initially filled that hole, no longer could.

Sloane heard the courtroom door swing open and turned, expecting Theresa Gonzalez. An African American woman entered instead. She held a manila file and spoke as she approached.

"Mr. Sloane?"

Sloane had noticed the woman in the courtroom during his closing argument. He estimated her to be late thirties to early forties, an attractive woman in a functional gray-and-black tweed skirt and jacket with her hair pulled back in a tight bun that accentuated high cheekbones and beautiful skin.

"My name is Beverly Ford," she said.

He detected a subtle hint of perfume. "What can I do for you, Ms. Ford?"

"Adelina Ramirez is a friend of mine," she said, referring to one of Sloane's recent clients. Sloane had obtained a jury verdict on behalf of Ramirez and her two daughters after her husband was killed in a construction accident. "She said I need a wrongful-death attorney. She says you're the best. She says you never lose."

Sloane deflected the last statement. "Every lawyer loses, Ms. Ford. Nobody wins every case."

"You do." Ford spoke with a conviction that indicated she had not just taken a friend at her word. The verdict in the Gonzalez case was his eighteenth jury verdict in a row.

Sloane gestured to the bench behind counsel table. "Tell me how I can help you."

Ford sat with her knees angled to face him. Her eyes, hazel with traces of yellow that reminded Sloane of sunflowers, regarded him steadily. "It's about my husband, James . . . about what happened to him."

"Tell me about it," he said.

She took a moment and spoke deliberately. "James was a schoolteacher. He was a schoolteacher . . . and they went and made him a soldier." Sloane sensed the story's direction. "Then they shipped him off to Iraq and he got shot." She pointed to a spot between her ribs. "He got shot in his side."

"I'm sorry," Sloane said, taking a moment to allow her to continue, but Ford sat stoically. "What is it you would like me to do?"

"I want to file a suit, a wrongful-death suit."

Perplexed, Sloane asked, "Who is it you want to sue?"

"The United States government," Ford said matter-of-factly. "And the military."

BEVERLY FORD OPENED the manila folder and handed Sloane an article clipped from the *New York Times* discussing a confidential report from the Office of the Armed Forces Medical Examiner on Marine fatalities in Iraq. The report concluded that a large percentage of those fatalities had been from torso wounds that might have been prevented had the soldiers been wearing new ceramic-plate body armor that the Pentagon had, for two years, largely declined to supply to all troops.

Ford sat twisting her wedding ring and staring into the distance. "The day after he got his letter calling him to active duty, James kept trying to console me. He kept saying, 'Don't worry, baby. They're not going to put me on the front lines—that's for the marines. Besides, I'm going to be riding around in a big old tank. There's nothing anybody can do to me inside a tank.'" She looked back at Sloane. "Then they put him in a Humvee and sent him to the front lines. Can someone explain that to me? He was sent to fight the war on terror in an SUV." Her voice softened. "He was a high school math teacher."

Sloane knew little about military law and what he did vaguely remember wasn't encouraging. He seemed to recall from his own service that it was exceedingly difficult for a soldier to sue the government.

"How did your husband get shot?" he asked. "Do you know the circumstances?"

Ford flipped through her file and handed him four multi-page documents. "The military gave me these. They didn't want to, but I made a Freedom of Information Act request."

A quick review indicated the documents to be witness statements, apparently from men who served with James Ford the night he died. Sloane thought it curious the military would give up witness statements, even to a surviving relative. In civil litigation, witness statements were rarely produced and normally protected as an attorney's work product. A FOIA request didn't change that.

"They awarded James the Purple Heart," Ford said. "They said he dragged a soldier from a building just before it exploded." She tapped her finger on the *Times* article. "No one told me about this. I found this out on my own."

Having been wounded in combat, a Cuban bullet to the shoulder fired from a Kalashnikov rifle during the invasion of Grenada, Sloane knew the military had a claims process for injuries and deaths, though he had not personally used it. "The military has a procedure—" he started, but Ford interrupted him.

"I filed a claim," she said. "The claims office said if I didn't get a response within six months I had the right to file a lawsuit in court. I want you to take my case."

Sloane sought more information. "Why do you think James died because he didn't have the new body armor?"

"It's all in there," she said, tapping the file. "The armor wasn't adequate, and the military knew it."

Though it was tragic, Sloane sensed this was a case he could not win, and he did not want to give Ford false hope that he could, his reputation aside. Regardless of what James Ford had been stateside, in Iraq he had been a soldier, and soldiers died in war—too many, always, but it was a sad fact of combat. The difficulty was how to explain that to a widow of one of those soldiers looking to him for help.

"Mrs. Ford, my instincts and experience tell me we'd have a very difficult time proving your husband died because he had inadequate body armor." He struggled to avoid the legalese while not sounding condescending. "What I mean by that is—"

"I know what you mean," Ford said. "You don't think we could prove that even if James had been wearing the new armor he would have lived."

Sloane nodded. "I'm afraid so."

Ford regarded him steadily. "James did what was asked of him. He did it without question or complaint. He did it despite having four children at home. He kept his end of the bargain, Mr. Sloane. All I want to know is if the military kept its end of that bargain."

SLOANE DROVE WEST on Highway 518 past the Seattle-Tacoma Airport. Normally after a trial his thoughts were about all that had gone right. Tonight he could think only of Beverly Ford, a widow with four children, and the steely resolve that had burned in her eyes.

He looked at her file on the passenger seat and wondered if fate, more than Adelina Ramirez, was responsible for bringing Ford to him. He took a hand from the wheel and felt the raised red scar beneath his shirt just above his right pectoral muscle. More than twenty years later, Sloane could still see the fear in the eyes of the marine standing beside him on Grenada; as their helicopter transport lifted off, the young father of two realized he didn't have his flak jacket. Just twenty, Ed Venditti carried a photograph of his family inside his helmet. Sloane had no photograph. He had no family. He had no one, no mother or father, no grandparents or aunts or uncles. No wife or child.

"Take mine," Sloane said, pulling him behind a rock cluster and slipping from his jacket.

Venditti resisted.

"Take it." Sloane thrust the jacket against Venditti's chest before Venditti could argue the matter further. After being shot, Sloane knew the truth would likely get Venditti court-martialed. He told the doctors and his commanding officer that he had taken off his jacket because it made him feel weighted. They thought he was nuts, which prompted a psychiatric exam, whereupon the doctor had concluded:

> His spontaneous decision to join the Corps is consistent with his spontaneous decision to remove his flak jacket. It is indicative of a man dissatisfied with his life and therefore prone to making rash decisions to change it. Such decisions could, in the future, endanger not only himself, but also those for whom he is responsible.

There were times when Sloane wondered whether the psychiatrist had been correct.

The freeway ended at First Avenue South, a thoroughfare of strip malls. Sloane considered pulling into the local Blockbuster and picking up a movie, then thought again of the file sitting on the passenger seat. Though dog-tired, he wanted to get through it before the weekend; he wanted to leave for vacation with a clear conscience and focus only on Tina and Jake. That meant reading it tonight.

He drove across the intersection through the town of Burien and descended Maplewild Road. The steep, winding access road led to Three Tree Point, a tiny beach community on the edge of the Puget Sound said to have been named for the three cedar trees at the tip of a spit of land that jutted into the slate-gray waters. Bald eagles nested in the limbs of one of the trees, and king salmon swam along the shores.

At the bottom of the hill, Sloane turned past the darkened windows of what had been a community store and parked perpendicular to a ten-foot-high laurel hedge separating his property from a public easement that led to the rock and shell beach at the edge of the Sound.

He stepped from his Jeep and pushed through a wooden gate he'd installed in the hedge to allow access to his back porch. The front door was around the other side, hard to access and rarely used by anyone. The three-story colonial with white clapboard siding had been built on a small bluff. Crabgrass sloped twenty yards to a cement break, buttressed by driftwood logs that had washed ashore, which separated the property from the beach. Sloane had rented a house for a year before his Realtor found the property. He wanted to live near the water, as he had in California, and he relished the chance to restore the 1930s home to its original grandeur. But as was normally the case, his legal practice had allowed him limited time to make the desired improvements.

He climbed the back stairs and removed his shoes, a house rule since he'd refinished the hardwood floors. Then he stepped inside the nook off the kitchen and hung his keys on a hook protruding from a life-size cardboard cutout of Larry Bird, the legendary Boston Celtics basketball player. The cutout had made the trip north from Pacifica when he moved. Tina had only mildly protested, knowing what the cutout meant to Sloane. It had once belonged to Joe Branick, the White House confidant of former president Robert Peak. Branick's sister, Aileen Blair, had sent it to Sloane as a gift. Blair had been a lot like Beverly Ford when Sloane first met her at Joe Branick's home in Virginia, resolved and determined. Sloane needed to know why Branick had sent him a package of documents just before he died, and Blair wanted to know who killed her brother and why. They struck a deal.

Aileen Blair had read the documents inside the package and looked up at Sloane in astonishment.

"But if the woman listed on these forms didn't give her child up for adoption, then these papers make no sense," she had said.

Sloane had come to the same conclusion. "No, they don't. Someone forged them to make it look like Edith and Ernest Sloane adopted that child and named him David."

"Who would have done that?"

"The only logical assumption is that it was your brother."

"Joe? Why would Joe have forged them?"

"I think it was to hide my identity."

"Why would you assume that?"

"Because Edith and Ernest Sloane did adopt a young boy, Aileen, but David Allen Sloane, seven years old, died in that car accident with them."

Bud jumped onto the counter and meowed. It wasn't love. He wanted to be fed. Sloane cradled the cat in his arm and walked into the kitchen, smelling garlic. He stopped at the stove to lift the lid on a pot. Tina's marinara sauce simmered inside. He lowered the lid and walked from the kitchen into the family room, sprinkling fish food in the tank, which had also survived the move north.

"Anyone home?"

"In here."

Tina sat in one of the two white wicker chairs on the enclosed porch. She lowered a paperback, set it on the navy-blue wool blanket covering her legs, and pushed her shoulder-length auburn hair behind her ear. "Isn't it beautiful?" she asked, looking out the plate-glass windows. Wisps of maroon from the setting sun streaked the gray sky above the jagged, snowcapped Olympic Mountains.

Sloane ignored the view, thinking her just as stunning, and wondering how he had not seen it for so many years. Married less than one year, they had known each other for more than ten. Tina had been his legal assistant at Foster & Bane, in San Francisco, where interoffice relationships were taboo. He had not even known that she was attending school at night to earn a degree in architecture until the day she told him she was quitting and moving to Seattle.

Tina turned back from the view and caught him staring. "What?" she asked, with a hint of a smile, her eyes widening.

Sloane kissed her, and let the kiss linger. When their lips parted, Tina smiled up at him. "What was that for?"

"Just to let you know how much I love you."

"Well, let me know some more," she said.

He kissed her again, put Bud on the floor, and picked up what he thought to be iced tea, but tasted something stronger. "Getting an early start on our vacation or hard day at the office?"

"Both."

He handed back her drink and sat in the other chair. "Still no word on that building retrofit in Des Moines?"

"They told me they liked our design, but they say the decision will be a while longer."

"You know how cities work. It takes forever to get them to approve anything."

"I know, but it would be nice to know before we leave."

"So you'll have a nice surprise when we get back," he said.

She shook her head as if to shake away the thought. "Saturday we'll be sipping margaritas on the beach in Cabo." They'd timed the trip with Jake's spring break from school.

"Amen to that."

"Will the defense fight the verdict?"

"They always do." He looked out the windows.

"You okay?"

"Hmm? Fine."

"You don't look like a guy who just won another big case."

He turned to her. "You remember Adelina Ramirez?"

"Sure."

Since leaving San Francisco, Sloane had devoted much of his current practice to helping Hispanic immigrants. Having not known who his biological parents were for many years, he had come to realize his own Hispanic heritage late in life. His dark hair and complexion came from his mother's Mexican descent, but he was also tall, six foot two, with light eyes, genes that likely came from northern Spanish blood.

"A friend of hers came to see me after court today. Adelina told her I'm the best wrongful-death attorney in the state."

"Smart lady."

"She said I never lose."

"You don't. What happened?"

"You remember the report in the *New York Times* article attributing the deaths of some soldiers to inadequate body armor?"

"He was one of those?"

"The report was about marines; her husband was in the National Guard. He got shot in the side. I don't know much about military law, but I remember after I'd been shot a JAG officer came to my room. The specifics are a bit fuzzy, but I recall something about a soldier not being able to sue the military, the possibility of injuries and fatalities being inherent in the job and benefits being the only remedy."

"Did you explain that to her?"

"I told her I didn't think she'd have much chance of success."

"But . . ." Tina said, drawing out the word.

He shook his head. "I don't know, maybe I just like a challenge."

Tina smiled. "Or maybe you think you can help everyone."

There was more truth in the comment than he wanted to admit. "She has four children."

"Tragic," Tina said. "So what's bothering you?"

He turned to face her. "I don't know. I also thought about Joe Branick today."

"We've had this discussion. He wasn't killed because of anything you did."

"It was a selfless act, sending me that information."

Tina put her paperback next to her drink, pulled back the blanket, and went to him. She leaned forward and looked him in the eye. Then she kissed him.

"And what was that for?" he asked.

"Just promise me you'll start giving yourself credit for all the people you do help." She struck a pose and changed the subject. "I bought a new bathing suit for Cabo. Interested in seeing it on?"

"On? Not really."

She grinned. "Saturday we'll be soaking up sun, and you'll have a week to unwind. Think about that."

"You'll be soaking up sun. I'll be puking off the side of a boat and getting sunburned while Jake fishes. Speaking of which, where is he?"

She rolled her eyes. "He won't give up until he catches a king. I figured I'd let you reel him in tonight."

"Thanks."

She laughed and walked toward the kitchen. "It'll be good practice for when you have to drag him off that boat."

SLOANE ZIPPED CLOSED his leather jacket and stepped over the tree trunks and debris the Sound had washed ashore. Jake stood twenty yards down the beach, a lone figure outlined in a ghostly silver glow. The wind off the Sound prevented Sloane from calling out to him, and the boy was too fixated on his line in the water for Sloane to draw his attention.

During certain months king salmon, and the smaller silvers, swam along Three Tree's shore, bringing out a parade of boats and anglers who fished from shore each dawn and sunset. Jake had caught the fishing bug after watching a neighbor boat a 31 pound king. Outfitted at the local Fred Meyer, he rushed to the water's edge each day before and after school, sometimes at the expense of his homework. Sloane was learning that being a parent was a lot like being a lawyer. Finding out what the child really wanted was the first step to negotiating a compromise. They agreed that Jake could fish, but only after completing his homework, and only if he maintained his grades. His study habits had actually improved.

As Sloane neared, Jake caught sight of him. "David. Hi."

"How're they biting, Hemingway?"

Jake shook his head. "Not too good tonight."

Now 11, the boy had lost much of his baby fat and was tall and lean like his mother. His sandy-blond hair and fine facial features bore a strong resemblance to his biological father, a man who continued to have little involvement in his son's life since the divorce when Jake was four. Frank Carter wasn't a bad guy. Sloane had met him a handful of times. He seemed decent, just too young to be a father. He didn't want the responsibility of a child. It was easier just to show up for the special events, like birthdays and holidays. Sloane hoped someday Jake might take to calling him "Dad," but he wasn't pushing it.

Despite the chill wind, Jake wore baggy shorts, a hooded sweatshirt, a worn San Francisco 49ers baseball cap, and the clownish rubber boots Tina mandated after he ruined multiple pairs of shoes in the salt water.

"Well, it's likely getting to be too late now. Your mother wants you to do some reading before bed."

Jake snapped back the catch on the reel, prepared to cast. The green buzz-bomb lure twisted at the end of the line. "One more cast?"

Sloane looked at the light shining in the kitchen window and turned his back slightly. "I don't think I saw you take your line out of the water."

Jake drew back the pole and snapped it forward.

SLOANE LIFTED HIS head from the papers spread across his desk and looked out the windows of his home office. The lights in the houses on Vashon Island, four miles across the Sound, sparkled back at him, and the faint sound of cellos and violins resonated from the portable CD player, a Christmas gift from Jake and Tina.

Beverly Ford had done considerable research. At the start of the war, the military had issued body armor only to what it thought would be dismounted soldiers fighting on the front line. Command had to ditch that plan when it became clear there was no front line. That meant it suddenly needed 80,000 more vests, a need that could not be met overnight. Eight months after the start of the war, nearly one-quarter of the troops still did not have the new ceramic armor and were being forced to take their chances with inferior vests, or to rotate what new armor they did have. At a congressional inquiry, General John Abizaid, then the commander of the forces in Iraq, admitted he did not have a good explanation for the shortage of vests, given that the invasion had been contemplated for more than a year.

The improved vests, called Interceptors, included removable ceramic plates fifteen times stronger than steel and capable of stopping bullets fired by the Kalashnikov rifles favored by the insurgents in Iraq and Afghanistan.

Sloane picked up the SF-95 form Beverly Ford had sent to the regional claims office. Stapled to it was a standard letter advising that her claim had been received and would be considered in due course. Not content to wait for the military's response, Ford made a Freedom of Information Act request seeking documents related to the investigation of her husband's death. Subsequent replies had more or less denied her request, citing national defense concerns. But Beverly Ford had been persistent, and, perhaps in an effort to appease her, the claims office eventually provided her the witness statements.

Sloane picked up the first of the four, a statement by a Sergeant Phillip Ferguson, and read.

HIGHWAY 10
OUTSIDE FALLUJAH, IRAQ

JAMES FORD LEANED forward, eyes straining to see through the dirt-and-grime-smeared windshield. The seven-ton trucks in front of him continued to kick up dust as the convoy rumbled along single-file, each vehicle maintaining a fifty-meter buffer with the vehicle in front. Proper spacing was a necessity in Iraq, where every paper bag, dead dog, and pile of garbage could be an insurgent's improvised explosive device, or IED. In Iraq the question wasn't if your convoy was going to get hit, but when.

Ford swerved to avoid a large pothole, but the Humvee's left-front tire caught the depression, causing the vehicle to rock violently.

"Jesus. Can you miss one?" Dwayne Thomas groaned from the backseat over the strain of the diesel engine.

Ford didn't like hearing the Lord's name used in vain. "Jesus isn't driving, DT. If he was, I'm sure he'd miss every one. You want to take a shot at it?"

"You're supposed to be the damn driver."

"At ease," Captain Robert Kessler said from the passenger seat.

The potholes were mostly nuisances, but the burned black craters, likely from exploded Soviet-era surplus mines buried beneath the road, served as a vivid reminder of the danger troops faced each time they left Camp Kalsu, their forward operating base near Fallujah.

The convoy, which the soldiers referred to as the "traveling road show," had nearly completed the hundred-mile round trip to the large PX near Baghdad International Airport to restock supplies like water, toilet paper, and cigarettes. Ford's Humvee was last, providing rear security, and the men were hot, tired, and uncomfortable.

Ford wiped a trickle of sweat from the side of his face. Normally they left Camp Kalsu either at night or very early in the morning, but today they had left mid-afternoon, with the June sun still a bright white orb that caused him to squint, even wearing sunglasses, and baked the top of his head beneath his Kevlar helmet. Still, they didn't even consider rolling down the windows. During their training in the Mojave Desert troops had driven through mock Iraqi cities with M16 and M4 rifles sticking out the windows in what they called "the porcupine." The tactic was meant to intimidate, but as the insurgents became more sophisticated and better shooters, it also turned into a good way to get killed. An order came down the chain of command to keep the windows closed, no matter how hot or piss-poor the air-conditioning.

Ford envied Phillip Ferguson, who stood in the center hatch, head out the roof, manning his M249. At least Fergie got a breeze and wasn't suffocating on the smell of sweat-soaked cammies. The pungent odor reminded Ford of the smell of unwashed gym clothes and sneakers in his sons' bedroom.

"Everyone hydrating?" Kessler asked.

Ford held up a half-empty bottle of water.

"Doesn't help to hold it, Ford."

"I just drank a full one, Captain."

"Drink another."

Ford unscrewed the cap and chugged the rest of the bottle. He had actually grown to dislike the taste of water. Seemed like all he did was drink water, sweat, and drink more water. About the only good thing that had come from it was he had shed thirty pounds from his six-foot-five frame. He wasn't svelte, but 220 pounds was better than 250.

He stretched his neck, popping vertebrae, which caused Michael Cassidy to lean forward from his seat directly behind him. "Dude. Don't fucking do that! It creeps me out."

Ford grimaced. "Sorry, Butch, back's killing me."

Cassidy wasn't much older than the high school kids Ford taught in Seattle. They had nicknamed him Butch, as in the movie Butch Cassidy and the Sundance Kid, but Cassidy wasn't anything like the calm, polished bandito Paul Newman had portrayed. He was a bundle of exposed nerve endings and tics from a liberal use of caffeine pills he washed down with cans of adrenaline like Red Bull or Ripped Fuel. Cassidy, too, had lost weight, but he hadn't had a lot to lose, and it had left him looking like a strung-out dope addict, gaunt through the face with sunken eyes and dark circles. His uniform hung from his shoulders and bunched at his waist.

Being off base midday made all of them tense, and when Ford got tense he thought about his family. He pulled an envelope from his ammo vest and slid out the photograph Beverly had given him the morning he'd left their home in Seattle. In the photo he stood behind his wife with his arms around her waist, nuzzling her neck and breathing in her beauty. It had been a split second of intimacy before the kids jumped into the fray, clinging to his arms and legs like ornaments on a Christmas tree. His mother-in-law had snapped the photo.

"That your family?" Cassidy asked, head still between the seats.

"No," Thomas said, "he's carrying a photo of someone else's family."

"Shut up, DT," Cassidy replied.

Kessler, who was also married and had kids, pointed to Ford's baby girl sitting atop his shoulders and beaming down at the camera. "Who's she?"

"That would be my Althea," Ford said.

"She has quite the smile."

"She's my angel. We were supposed to be done after the third. She was a surprise. I believe God sent her to me special."

"I got a little girl too," Kessler said. "They're special until they turn thirteen. Then the aliens snatch their brains and you can't do anything right. Enjoy it while it lasts."

Thomas muttered something from the backseat.

"How's that, DT?" Ford asked. Being another black man, Ford had thought he and Thomas might develop a friendship, but Thomas seemed perpetually angry, with a chip on his shoulder he never shook.

DT raised his voice. "I said, you just torturing yourselves, carrying around pictures and shit. Why you worrying about that stuff? This shit is hard enough to do without all that other crap."

"You married? Got kids?" Ford asked.

"Nope."

"Then you wouldn't know what it's like to be away from them, worrying about them."

Thomas leaned forward, defiant. "Don't want to know. What does it get you? Nothing." He sat back. "Me? I'm just here doing a job. Didn't join the Guard to go fight Muhammad in the desert, but here I am. So be it. I just stick to routine. Wake up, put on the same clothes, eat in the same place looking at your same sorry-ass faces, mount up for patrol, sleep, wake up and do it all over again. Only thing I'm going to die from over here is boredom, and that's just fine by me."

"Where's home?" Ford asked.

"Tacoma."

"The Aroma of Tacoma," Cassidy chirped. "Smells like shit driving through there."

Thomas scowled. "You smell like shit."

"At ease," the captain said again, trying to keep the peace.

"They cleaned that shit up long time ago," DT said. "The pulp mills caused it."

"What do you do there?" Ford asked.

"I used to work at a health club, but I got an application in with the city, and being in the Guard is going to put me top of the list. I get on with the city and I'll be set for life. Get me benefits and a pension."

"Bet you didn't think that deal would include an all-expense-paid trip to Iraq, though, did you?" Kessler said.

Cassidy laughed.

DT sat back, disgruntled.

"I like it here," Cassidy offered.

"That's because you're a dumb shit," Thomas muttered.

"I do. I like wearing the same clothes and eating in the same place. You don't even have to think about it. Einstein did that, you know, wore the same clothes so he didn't have to use his brain."

"You and Einstein have that in common all right," DT said, causing Ford to chuckle.

Cassidy said, "I look at this like a hunting trip."

DT scoffed. "That why you keep that dumb-ass Rambo knife strapped to your ankle?"

"You a hunter, Butch?" Ford wasn't buying Cassidy's bravado. He had a lot of experience with kids like Cassidy. They were usually loners from abusive homes. When they did get some attention, it usually wasn't for anything positive, but they relished it anyway because at least it acknowledged their existence. Columbine and other school shootings had proved that.

"Hell, yeah," Cassidy said. "Me and my dad hunted all over eastern Washington. Bird mostly."

DT mocked him. "Bird? That don't make you no hunter."

"And deer."

"Bambi? You shooting Bambi!"

"Not just deer neither," Cassidy persisted. "Boar."

"Boar?" Kessler gave Ford a look. Wild boar did not live in eastern Washington.

"You know," Cassidy said, "those big pigs with the tusks and hair all over them. Mean sons of bitches."

"You sure that wasn't your girlfriend?" DT said, bringing laughter.

"Laugh all you want. But I shot one with a compound bow once and chased it for miles. Slit its throat and gutted it *right there and brought the meat home." Cassidy looked out the window. "The way I figure it, killing Hajji ain't going to be no different. I'm looking forward to getting me some."*

"One big difference," Kessler said, turning to stare out the windshield. "Bird and deer don't shoot back. Hajji does."

WHEN HE HAD finished reading the statement, Sloane sat back, thinking. Something here, something. He thought of a sermon he'd recently heard by the pastor of the church he attended with Tina and Jake. Then, rising quickly, he made copies on the Xerox machine in his office and placed the duplicates side by side on his desk to reconsider them more closely. As he read, he picked up a yellow highlighter.

CHAPTER TWO

SEATTLE, WASHINGTON

The following morning, Sloane pushed open the door to his office and stepped into the entry. He leased a suite in the One Union Square Building in downtown Seattle, sharing a receptionist and two conference rooms with other businesses on the floor.

"Are we sleeping in now?" Sloane's secretary stood like a sentry at her cubicle. With her arms crossed and a bun of graying brown hair on the top of her head, Carolyn had the look of a school principal on hallway duty. She gave him the same arched-eyebrow, disapproving look that put the fear of God in grade school kids.

Sloane had stayed up late reading the witness statements and had awakened to an empty house. He lay in bed thinking about what he had read while listening to the waves rolling on the beach, likely from one of the huge cargo ships that passed between Three Tree Point and Vashon Island on the way to the Duwamish. Then he remembered that he hadn't exercised since the start of the Gonzalez trial and got up and ran six miles.

"I thought I'd take an extra hour this morning."

"I know *you* slept in," Carolyn countered. "I asked if *we* were sleeping in. I would have liked an extra hour myself. At my age every minute of beauty sleep helps."

Sloane wondered what Carolyn might look like without the pancake makeup and dark eye shadow she wore without fail. A strand of colored glass beads hung from her neck to accentuate her multicolored dress.

Sloane had a knack for hiring assistants who put him in his place. In San Francisco, Tina had not been bashful about keeping him humble, even when he was racking up fifteen jury verdicts in a row.

"Someone has to be here to open the office and answer the phones," he said, thumbing through a large stack of mail. "We're running a highly successful legal practice here."

"Are we?" Her eyebrow again arched. "That would be news to me."

And therein was the source of her annoyance. Sloane had forgotten to call and tell her the Gonzalez verdict. For legal offices, trials were like marathons; failing to tell the staff the verdict was like having them train you without telling them your time.

"I'm sorry," he said. "I got tied up after court and ended up working most of the night." She gave him her best blank stare, not about to make it easy. "The jury came back twelve zip; I couldn't have done it without you. Theresa Gonzalez asked that I send along her personal thanks."

That seemed to soften her a bit. At least she uncrossed her arms. "I know. She called this morning wondering when she'd get a check."

Sloane bit his tongue and walked to his office, still checking the mail.

Carolyn followed him. "Why were you working last night? Most lawyers I've worked for take vacations after trials."

"Cabo on Saturday," he said. "I had some reading to do." He opened an envelope with a multimillion-dollar check made payable to his trust account on behalf of Adelina Ramirez. It had cost the insurance company for the construction company a lot of money to call Sloane's bluff.

Carolyn plucked the check from his hand. "I'll deposit this before you decide to donate it to some worthy cause that doesn't have my name attached to it, and get a check cut to Ms. Ramirez." She started from the room but stopped at the door. "Congratulations. Twelve nothing? I'd have bet my virginity you were going to lose that case. You really are as good as advertised—that's unusual for a man."

"Wow. That was darn near a compliment."

She rolled her eyes. "Don't let your head explode."

"Do I have anything scheduled for today?"

"Not unless you forgot to tell me . . . again. You were

supposed to be in trial through the end of the week. As far as I know, your calendar is wide open. I vote we take the rest of the week off. All in favor?" She raised her hand.

"Sorry."

"I'll cancel my tee-time at the club."

"Before you do, call Charles Jenkins. Ask him to meet me at the Coco Cabana for lunch. Tell him I'm buying."

"Lunch with Big Foot? That doesn't sound like work to me."

"And see if you can find a lawyer who knows something about military law."

"Military law? Why would you need to know that?" She made it sound distasteful.

"Because I may very well be suing the government."

"Lord help you," she said. "I hope you haven't been skimming on your taxes."

THE PIKE PLACE MARKET bustled with the lunch crowd. People in the Northwest knew to get outside when good weather materialized, and the day had dawned cold and clear, though ominous dark clouds gathered to the north. Sloane took a seat at a wrought iron table on the deck of the Coco Cabana and sipped an Arnold Palmer, lemonade and iced tea, while looking down on the open-air market where fish vendors barked out orders and crowds gathered to watch them toss huge salmon.

Charles Jenkins had called on his cell phone to let Sloane know he was going to be late due to traffic from freeway construction. The big man had lived like a hermit in a four-room caretaker's shack on Camano Island for thirty years until, two years earlier, Joe Branick had also sent him a package. Inside had been a classified CIA file compiled largely by Jenkins, one that he had long thought had been destroyed. Jenkins had ultimately handed Sloane that same file when the two men met on a West Virginia bluff overlooking the darkened waters of Evitts Run, a tributary of the Shenandoah.

"Joe meant for you to have this," Jenkins had said. "Hopefully it will answer some of your questions."

"Can you tell me what happened?" Sloane had asked.

"You sure you're ready to hear this now?"

"I don't know if I'll ever be ready to hear it, Mr. Jenkins. But I don't have a choice. I have no idea who I am."

Jenkins told Sloane of a village in the mountains of southern Mexico where a young boy, Sloane, was giving speeches so moving the people were referring to them as "sermons." Southern revolutionaries were promoting the boy to be the one to lead them from poverty and oppression and restore a proud and independent Mexico. Unfortunately, the uprising coincided with the Middle Eastern oil embargoes, and the United States, in need of an alternative fuel source, could not allow the uprising to destabilize its relationship with the Mexican government. Jenkins had been the CIA field officer tasked to infiltrate the village and report on the boy.

"I filed a report after each visit," he had told Sloane as they watched the moon shimmer off the water's blackened surface. "I convinced them that the threat was real, that you were real."

What had resulted was an assault on the village by

a U.S. paramilitary force, and a massacre. Sloane had miraculously managed to survive, but not before witnessing horrible atrocities, including the rape and murder of his mother. When Joe Branick and Charles Jenkins entered the smoldering remains of the village the following morning, they found the boy hiding and decided to keep him hidden. They created a new identity, David Allen Sloane, a seven-year-old who had died in a car accident, forged adoption papers, and placed him in a foster home in Southern California. Then Jenkins, too, went into hiding, moving as far from Langley as he could, to the horse farm on Camano Island.

For nearly thirty years they had both lived in anonymity.

When the waitress returned, Charles Jenkins towered behind her. Jenkins was like the container ships that passed Sloane's home. Big enough to block out the sun, he caused waves wherever he went. When he removed his wraparound sunglasses, revealing sparkling green eyes—uncommon for a man of African American descent—women swooned.

"Can I get you anything to drink?" the waitress asked, beaming.

Jenkins pointed to the glass in Sloane's hand. "Bring me whatever he's drinking. What are you drinking?"

"An Arnold Palmer," Sloane said.

Jenkins gave it a disapproving frown. "As long as it doesn't come with an umbrella," he said, causing the waitress to giggle as she left. He sat rubbing his bare arms. "What do you have against sitting inside?"

"How long have you lived here and you don't wear a jacket?" Sloane was comfortable in the black leather jacket Tina had bought him on their honeymoon to Florence.

"I do wear a jacket, when I'm outside. Lady Frankenstein said you wanted to have lunch. I eat *inside*. I left my jacket in the car." He continued to rub his arms. "It's freezing."

"I thought you grew up in New Jersey?"

"Why do you think I left? I don't do snow or ice unless it's in a drink."

One of the fish vendors called out an order from below and the crowd screamed and scattered from a flying fish. It was a tourist gimmick, the fish made of fabric.

"How's Alex?" Sloane asked.

"Still using the 'M' word. Last night she tried to lure me into sex on a blanket in the garden."

"I hope you fell for it."

Jenkins smiled. "The things I do for love."

Sloane sipped his drink. "Why don't you get married? Guys would kill to have a woman like Alex swooning over them."

"Trust me, the swooning part is over."

"What, did she get glasses?"

"Ha-ha. You're a regular Henny Youngman this morning, aren't you?"

"Henny Youngman?" Sloane asked.

"You don't know Henny Youngman?" Jenkins shook his head, disgusted. "'A man goes to a psychiatrist. The psychiatrist says, 'You're crazy.' The man says, 'I want a second opinion!' So the doctor says, 'Okay, you're ugly too!'"

Sloane gave him a blank stare.

"I am old." Jenkins looked out over the roof of the market at the sun shining on Elliott Bay. "Maybe I should get married."

Though Jenkins had never confided in him, Sloane suspected that he was uncomfortable with the disparity between his and Alex's ages. Alex was just twenty-eight.

"It's not as scary as you make it sound."

"Alex wants kids."

"So?"

"So, I'll be fifty-four in May," Jenkins said.

The waitress returned with Jenkins's drink. Sloane ordered a salad and a bowl of black bean soup. Jenkins ordered the soup plus a chicken and rice entree. "I have to have something more than rabbit food," he said, bringing more giggles from the waitress.

Sloane handed him an envelope. "We received the check on the Ramirez matter."

"No appeal?"

It had been Alex's idea that Jenkins work for Sloane, though Jenkins didn't know it. She had pulled Sloane aside at a barbecue on the Camano farm when he and Tina moved to Seattle, and said she thought Jenkins was bored and looking for something to do after rebuilding their home. Sloane needed an investigator, but he had been reluctant to ask an ex-CIA field operative, thinking it would be an insult. Alex, who had also once worked as a field operative—the person Joe Branick chose to deliver the classified file to Jenkins—convinced Sloane otherwise, though he knew her true motivation was to get Jenkins out of the house. He was driving her crazy just sitting around. Jenkins had initially feigned disinterest, but he took the work and had since helped Sloane on several of his cases. Sloane had enjoyed his company.

"They always talk a good game. In the end they pay."

"What happened with Gonzalez?"

"Jury came back yesterday. One point six," Sloane said.

"No wonder you're buying lunch."

"Actually, I need your help on another matter."

"That was fast."

"A woman tracked me down after court yesterday. Her husband was a national guardsman killed in Iraq."

Jenkins shook his head. "The similarities to Vietnam frighten the hell out of me."

"Let's hope we don't have to lose fifty thousand before we get out."

"Amen to that. How did your guy die?"

"A bullet to the side," Sloane said.

"How does that translate into a lawsuit?"

"I'm not sure it does," Sloane agreed. "I told her I'd look into it. She was willing to accept his death until the *New York Times* published that report about soldiers dying because their body armor was insufficient."

Jenkins sat back and sipped his drink. "If she had anyone else as her lawyer, I'd say it's a dead-bang loser. And I'm not sure even you can pull the rabbit out of this hat."

Sloane pulled the witness statements from his brief-case and handed them across the table. "She got these through a FOIA request. Something caught my eye while reading them last night. Take a look."

Jenkins removed his sunglasses and stretched out his arms.

"Alex isn't the only one who needs glasses," Sloane said.

"Don't start."

By the time Jenkins had finished reading the four statements, they were halfway through lunch. "Are these your highlights?" he asked.

"Have you read the Bible, Charlie?"

"I was raised Baptist. I didn't have a choice. It was burned into my memory. I can recite chapter and verse."

"So you're familiar with the four Gospels."

"Intimately."

"Matthew, Mark, Luke, and John. Four men, all recording the same historical events, yet each Gospel is different. Why is that?"

"Different perspectives."

Sloane put down his fork. "I once heard a priest reason that an argument for the accuracy of the Gospels is the fact that they are *different*, that if someone had wanted to perpetrate a fraud, they would have made them identical, or nearly so. I can also tell you from experience that people don't inherently remember or see things the same way. Put two people on a street corner to witness a car accident and you'll get two different versions." Sloane tapped the witness statements. "These four men were involved in a harrowing ordeal, and yet they each remember it damn near identically: Caught in a sandstorm, they drive off course and are suddenly ambushed. The details are impressive."

Jenkins flipped through a statement. "You think these were coordinated, someone *made sure* they said the same thing?"

Sloane shrugged. "I don't know. The other options are the men got together to get the story straight, which also makes it interesting, or it's a coincidence."

"Which neither of us believe in." Jenkins put down the statements. "Still, seems thin for a lawsuit, Counselor. You sure you're only curious?"

Sloane watched a ferry crossing Elliott Bay. "I thought about Joe Branick yesterday."

"Listen, what Joe did he did as much out of guilt as he did out of altruism. Both of us felt responsible for what had happened to you. He was trying to right a wrong and he died doing it, but that doesn't mean you have to try to right every wrong to honor him."

"She needs help. I'm thinking maybe my reputation might, you know . . ."

"Get the government to pay her some money to get rid of her."

"It's better than nothing."

Jenkins picked up the statements. "You want me to find these guys?"

"They should be back stateside by now." Sloane's cell phone rang. He considered the caller ID window. "It's Carolyn."

"That woman scares me," Jenkins said. "Why doesn't she like me?"

Sloane flipped open the phone. "She loves you."

"Can you and the Jolly Green Giant take a break from checking out the eye candy for a minute to work?" Carolyn asked.

Sloane chuckled. "Charles says he loves you too."

Jenkins looked genuinely concerned.

"Right," Carolyn said. "I found you a military lawyer. Don't know anything about him, but you said pronto, so this is pronto. You get what you get."

Sloane took out a pen and turned over the napkin. "Thanks. Go ahead."

"He's a solo practitioner in Pioneer Square. Says he has to be in court at two-thirty for a DUI hearing—not sure if he's the defendant or the lawyer. Otherwise, he starts an assault and battery trial tomorrow and won't be available for the next four to five days. So it's today or two weeks, unless he's convicted and gets sent to jail."

"Carolyn, do you know Henny Youngman?"

"Who?"

"Never mind." Sloane considered his watch. "Call him back and tell him I'll meet him at his office at one-thirty. Anything else going on?"

"I'm getting my nails done at two."

"Good for you. Tell you what, bring me the bill. We'll call it a perk for the Gonzalez verdict."

"Big spender. I should have told you I was shopping for a big-screen TV."

SLOANE PARKED IN the triangular garage at
First Avenue and walked down Washington Street looking for building addresses. Pioneer Square was Seattle's
other downtown tourist attraction, with maple trees and
low-rise, red-brick buildings that harked back to a different era. The entrance to John Kannin's building was near
Occidental Square, a haven for the homeless and mentally ill. Shopping carts stuffed with plastic bags circled a
bronze monument to Seattle's firefighters that pigeons
had defaced a gray-white.

Sloane walked into a small lobby and considered a
display case identifying the building tenants. He ascended
an interior marble staircase and pushed through a smoked-
glass door stenciled "John Kannin Law Firm P.S." Legal
books, binders, and files cluttered a desk in a small reception area with shelving along three walls. Narrow windows
emitted slats of dull light in which danced floating dust
motes.

"Are you David Sloane?" The man who appeared in
the doorway to Sloane's left looked younger than Sloane
had, for some reason, expected. "I'm John Kannin." He
had a deep baritone voice, befitting a trial lawyer.

"Thanks for seeing me," Sloane said.

"You're interested in military law?"

"My secretary said you don't have much time."

Kannin gestured to the desk. "My secretary didn't
come in today. If she had, I would have known that my

two-thirty hearing has been kicked over a week. Come on in."

Kannin led Sloane into an interior office with the same dark wood shelving along one wall. The other walls were brick. A book wedged in the sash propped open a window behind a large desk, allowing in the sounds of passing cars, the trolley, and men arguing on the street below.

"Fresh air," Sloane said. "You don't find that inside buildings too often anymore."

Kannin looked to the window. "It helps clear my brain." He removed a file from one of two chairs. "Take a seat." There was a round table in the corner, covered with stacks of paper—obviously the overflow from the neat stacks on the floor lining the brick wall. Post-its atop the stacks served as to-do lists. Kannin looked to have a thriving practice. Diplomas hung from the picture molding by fishing line. He had graduated from the U.S. Air Force Academy and the Willamette University College of Law in Oregon. Both were good schools.

Sloane estimated Kannin to be six foot three and well built through the shoulders and chest. He had coal-black hair with traces of gray and eyes the same color. He wore a white dress shirt and a blue tie, though he'd lowered the knot and unbuttoned the top button. Slipping behind his desk, he said, "I'd offer you coffee, but the way I make it, you might as well lick the asphalt."

Sloane sat. "Then I'll pass, thank you." He pointed to the diplomas. "You graduated from the Air Force Academy."

"I played a little football there."

"Linebacker," Sloane guessed.

"Offensive line. Players weren't as big back when I was playing. What I really wanted to do was to fly jets, but I was too big for the cockpit." He laughed. "After that I lost interest. I graduated with a degree in engineering."

"How'd you make it to law school?"

"I decided I liked arguing with people better than math. How about you? What's your story?"

"Marines out of high school, saw some combat in Grenada, but lost interest too. I decided I better get an education and moved to San Francisco based on a picture I'd seen in a magazine."

"Pretty spontaneous."

"I've been known to do that," Sloane said, thinking of the military psychiatrist's assessment. "Eventually I graduated from Hastings and had a practice for about a dozen years in the city before moving here a couple years ago."

"What brought you to Seattle?"

"My wife took a job here as a partner in an architecture firm with a friend. If I wanted to marry her, I had to move."

Kannin nodded. "Ah. Love. How do you like Seattle?"

"The summers are easy. It's taken a bit to acclimate to the winters. Bought my Gore-Tex and waterproof shoes." Sloane pointed to one of the framed diplomas. "Are you in the reserves?"

This brought another laugh. "When I realized I wasn't going to fly jets, I pretty much decided the military wasn't my mug of beer. I did my four years and got out."

"So I take it you weren't a JAG," Sloane said, referring to a judge advocate general, a military lawyer.

"I'm a JAG's worst nightmare. I represent families trying to obtain their military benefits. As you might imagine, business has picked up with the war. The JAG lawyers think I'm a nuisance, but so do the prosecutors I try cases against, so at least I'm consistent. I like to shake things up—lets me know I'm doing my job."

Sloane laughed. He got a good feeling about Kannin. "Have you ever sued the military in a non-benefits case?"

"Once," Kannin said. He sat up. "Private Jasmine Evans was living in military housing on base. One Friday night there's a knock on her door. Three off-duty soldiers stand on her porch with a bottle of Jack Daniel's, a case of beer, and a deck of cards. She knows them. They're all friendly, so she lets them in. They start playing cards and drinking. Things are okay until one of the guys suggests they play strip poker. She declines, but the others think it's a good idea and start removing their clothes. Private Evans starts to feel uncomfortable and asks them to leave. They start calling her names: 'tease,' 'bitch,' 'whore.' She tells them to go fuck themselves. The soldiers beat and rape her."

"Horrible," Sloane said.

"I'm just getting started. She goes to the military hospital and shortly thereafter an officer pays her a visit. Ostensibly he's there to take a report. Only she notices he's more interested in her blood alcohol level than the rape. He tells her it would be best to drop the matter, that it will only make her an outcast among the troops."

"What did she do?" Sloane asked.

"She told him to *also* go fuck himself. Then she filed a grievance. The military court-martialed the three soldiers, but none were convicted of rape. They all stuck to the same story: Private Evans was a willing participant; the bruises and cuts were because she liked it rough. When her administrative action finished, she found me. I did some research, came to the conclusion she was shit out of luck, and filed a claim in federal district court against the government, the army, and the three soldiers."

The latter two sentences didn't make sense. "She was shit out of luck, but you filed the complaint?"

Kannin shrugged. "Like I said, I like to shake the trees and see what falls out. I'm not afraid to lose, but I hate rolling over. I learned playing football that things can turn around quick. I was hoping that would happen in Private Evans's case."

"Did it?" Sloane knew it was likely or they wouldn't be discussing the case.

Kannin nodded, still smiling. "During discovery I learned two of the soldiers had a propensity for violence against women, and one had earlier confided to the same investigating officer that, given the chance, he'd, quote, 'like to fuck the shit out of Private Evans,' end quote. But this officer is a wannabe, a weenie. You know the type? He's trying to be one of the boys. So he says nothing about it. Then they go and do it. Now his ass is on the line."

"Sounds like a pretty good case. Why would you be shit out of luck?"

Kannin put up one finger. "You're thinking like a civil lawyer. Remember this is military law. The assistant U.S. attorney brought a motion to dismiss, arguing that the Feres doctrine barred the claim."

"The Feres doctrine?"

Kannin's smile now had a bit of the Cheshire-cat grin. "And you were a marine. The first rule of military law is understanding the hurdles, and the Feres doctrine is about a ten-foot hurdle. This is where you might want to take notes."

Sloane took out a pad of paper and a pen from his briefcase. Kannin spoke in a rote tone, as if reciting a legal treatise from memory. "When an inductee takes the oath of enlistment, he swears to protect the Constitution of the United States against all enemies both foreign and domestic."

"I remember it well," Sloane said.

"But I'll bet you didn't know that at that very instant you also forfeited your right to sue the government, the military, and your superior officers for injuries incurred 'incident to service,' even if you could prove those superior officers acted negligently or deliberately to deprive you of your constitutional rights."

"Incident to service. What does that mean?"

Kannin shrugged. "Hell if I know. Hell if the courts know. But there's a case directly on point that says getting raped on base fits the definition."

"You're kidding?"

"There's also precedent that says having the wrong leg cut off by a military doctor, or having surgical tools left inside your stomach is 'incident to service.' So is being unwittingly exposed to nuclear radiation during atomic testing, or to chemical weapons, LSD, and electroshock treatment as part of a military test program. I could go on, but I think you get my point."

"This all developed from one case?"

"Three, actually. In 1950 the Supreme Court consolidated three cases with a common thread—families of soldiers suing the government and members of the military for their deaths. The family of Lieutenant Rudolph Feres claimed their son died because the government negligently quartered him in barracks it knew had a defective heating unit. The barracks burned to the ground."

"How have the courts rationalized the doctrine?"

"Not well. But you have to remember that 1950 was not long after the end of the Second World War, which meant the Supreme Court was faced with the potential of hundreds of thousands of civil claims by soldiers and their families. The justices opined that military benefits rather than lawsuits were the appropriate remedy."

"Makes sense in theory," Sloane agreed.

"It did. But obviously, the courts didn't anticipate that civil jury awards would eventually dwarf military benefits, or that lower courts would extend the doctrine as far as they have."

"I take it people have challenged it?"

"Some," Kannin said. He lifted a thick black binder

from his desk and handed it to Sloane. "I took the liberty of pulling this off the shelves when your secretary called. These are the highlights. I think my research pulled up around three thousand total cases."

"Three thousand? And nobody's punched a hole in the rationale?"

"The rationale changes, but the most frequent explanation is that claims by soldiers could subvert the chain of command and make officers hesitant during combat."

"That's ridiculous. No officer is going to be thinking of a lawsuit in the middle of a battle."

"I agree, and the Supreme Court was leaning that way too the last time it heard a Feres case. The justices split five to four. Justice Scalia wrote that Feres was wrongfully decided then and remained wrongfully decided."

"But they didn't overrule it."

"It was the wrong case for a reversal. You think you got a better one?"

"I don't know. Sounds like you didn't."

"We never got that far."

"What happened?"

"The morning of the hearing I'm standing in the hall with my ass in hand when I get a gift handed to me. My investigator calls to tell me that a certain army officer who visited my client in the hospital is the nephew of a prominent politician whose name I am not at liberty to divulge pursuant to a confidentiality order I would never deliberately violate—Jack T. Miller."

"The senator?"

Kannin put up both hands. "I can't say. But when I bring this up in the hallway with the assistant U.S. attorney, along with my intent to tell the media, she's suddenly willing to kick over the hearing. Two days later I have a settlement offer on my desk, which, of course, I rejected. Two offers later we're in the six-figure range and the first figure, which I am also forbidden to reveal, was not a one, or two, but comes before four." Kannin sat back. "Enough of my war stories. Tell me about your case."

Sloane explained what he knew about James Ford's death. As he did, Kannin shook his head. "You're right in the jaws of Feres, I'm afraid, and it's especially tough in your situation because the Federal Tort Claims Act prevents soldiers from recovering for injuries incurred serving during a war in a foreign country."

Sloane sighed. "Sounds like I'm at a dead end."

"What you need is something to bargain with," Kannin said. "The government is sensitive—the war hasn't exactly gone as the administration led us all to believe. You need to make someone important's ass pucker."

"And if I can't?"

"Based on what you've told me, you'll lose. Unless you can do what about three thousand other lawyers couldn't."

"What's that?"

"Find a loophole in the Feres doctrine."

CHARLES JENKINS STOOD waiting on the sidewalk outside John Kannin's building looking like a well-paid bodyguard in a black leather car coat, black jeans, and sunglasses.

"You can be arrested for loitering," Sloane said.

"Elvira gave me the address. My alternative was to wait for you in your office with her giving me the evil eye. I'd rather be arrested."

"Carolyn's harmless," Sloane said.

"That's what they say just before the vampire sinks her teeth into your neck. I recommend a garlic necklace."

Sloane slipped on sunglasses. A breeze rustled the leaves in the dwarf maple trees and kicked up pieces of litter, creating small tornadoes in Occidental Square. "So why are you waiting for me?"

"I found someone who was with James Ford the day he died."

"That was fast."

"It will be reflected in my bill." He handed Sloane a piece of paper with an address and phone number.

"Marysville?" Sloane checked his watch. It was getting late, and like the Bay Area, Seattle had too many cars and not enough means to escape the downtown. Traffic would be heavy on I-5 heading north, which was the opposite direction from Three Tree Point. "You sure this guy will talk to me?"

Jenkins shrugged.

"You haven't talked to him?"

"You just said to find them. I found him. Besides, you told me you like to talk to the witnesses yourself."

"But you're sure he served with Ford."

"Same platoon, same squad, injured the same day."

"What type of injuries?"

"Don't know. But he also received a Purple Heart. Five of them did."

"Must have been a hell of a battle," Sloane said.

"Must have been."

"How many died?"

"Just your boy Ford."

MARYSVILLE, WASHINGTON

SLOANE TOOK THE exit just past a salmon, rock, and waterfall sculpture in the front of the Tulalip Indian casino. Tribal money was abundant in the area. The forest along the freeway had been recently clear-cut, and according to a large construction sign, nature was to be replaced by both a Home Depot and a Wal-Mart. During the drive north, clouds had rolled in overhead and the weather had changed quickly—not unusual for the Northwest, as Sloane had learned. He should have become a weatherman. He only needed to be right fifty percent of the time and he'd still get a paycheck. Rain began to splatter the windshield and soon the wipers beat a steady hum.

Uncertain of the area, he took an exit and pulled into a gas station, parking for a moment to retrieve the map from the glove compartment. Being a guy, his first instinct was to drive around and hope he stumbled onto the address. Being a woman, Tina had purchased a set of maps for each car when they moved from San Francisco. Sloane found the street name on a map that included Marysville, neatly refolded it so Tina wouldn't know he'd actually used it, and replaced it in the glove compartment.

Marysville had at one time been rural farmland, but as with other areas of the Pacific Northwest, farmers had sold to developers. Fences now separated farm acreage from tract homes. Sloane turned off the paved road onto a dirt and gravel road and drove through a field of strawberries that led to a two-story yellow farmhouse. As he neared, the road became a circular drive around an area neatly gardened with shrubs and flowers, brightly colored tulips. Dogs lounging on a wraparound porch sat up and barked. He wouldn't sneak up on anyone.

He stepped from the car into a steady rain and walked a gravel path to the porch, the dogs continuing to bark, but remaining dry beneath the safety of the covered porch, and showing no real threat. One cocked his head and took a step back as Sloane reached the porch, as if he understood barking to be his job, though he wasn't particularly enthusiastic about it.

"Shush now," Sloane said, never having become comfortable around dogs and not sure how to act. It worked. The dogs lowered their heads and padded behind him. He drew back a screen to knock but the inner door pulled open, the dogs having announced his presence. An attractive woman in a red knit sweater and blue jeans greeted him. "Can I help you?"

"I'm sorry to bother you." Sloane handed her a business card, which she took with some hesitancy. "My name is David Sloane. I'm an attorney. I was hoping to speak with Phillip Ferguson."

The woman's brow furrowed and she looked down at the card. Rain beat on the shingles overhead. She lowered the card. "I'm afraid that's not possible."

"I won't take much of his time, just a few minutes."

"You won't take any of his time," she said. "My husband is dead."

SHE STOOD WITH one hand holding the edge of the door.

"I'm very sorry," Sloane said.

"What is it you wanted to talk to Phil about?" She looked down at the business card. "Mr. Sloane."

"I represent the wife and children of a soldier who served with your husband and died the night he was injured, James Ford."

"Phil said something about that. I guess you could say Phil died over there in Iraq too."

"I understood that he was injured," Sloane said. "That he received the Purple Heart."

Katherine Ferguson's bangs fluttered in a breeze. A tear escaped, but she wiped it halfway down her cheek. "My husband lost his eyesight that night. Shrapnel from an explosion damaged the optical nerves behind both his eyes."

"I'm sorry."

She gestured to the strawberry fields. "Phil was a farmer. This was his father's property. It was split between my husband and his brother." She shrugged as if to say, What are you going to do? "Phil couldn't farm blind and . . . well, farming was what he did."

Sloane sensed the conversation's direction. He'd heard and read of similar stories of Vietnam veterans.

Katherine Ferguson let the screen door slap closed and walked to a corner of the porch. She pointed to a rust-colored barn, a traditional structure with wide doors and a hayloft. "About six months ago Phil went to the barn and shot himself."

Sloane was at a loss for words. It struck him that Katherine Ferguson was a young woman, like Beverly Ford, both too young to be burying a husband. "I'm not going to pretend to understand your loss, but I am truly sorry."

"What are you doing for the family?"

"Mrs. Ford filed a claim—"

"Did they deny it?"

Sloane heard a bitterness he had not previously detected. It gave him pause. "Yes, they did. Did you file a claim, Mrs. Ferguson?"

"Katherine," she said. "I had an attorney file a claim for me." She rolled her eyes. "I have two children, Mr. Sloane. My husband was forty-three years old and in a hospital bed. I wasn't sure how we were going to get by. Someone told me you could file a claim and maybe get some money. I went and talked to an attorney about it and had a claim filed. Phil didn't want to, but . . ."

The clouds burst, unleashing a torrent of rain. Sheets of water overwhelmed the gutters and spilled from the overhang, splattering the porch steps. "I'm sorry," she said. "Please, come in out of the rain."

He followed her inside to a living room and sat on a

love seat, waiting for her to sit in an adjacent armchair. She sat on the edge of the cushion, looking anxious. "I don't want to take up too much of your time, Katherine."

"It's okay," she said. "The kids aren't home from school yet and I'm just doing the bills and stuff for the farm. Phil's brother is teaching me and I'm taking some classes at a community college. I'm thinking of maybe becoming a CPA."

"I know it's hard treading over difficult memories, but do you happen to know anything more about the night your husband was injured? Did he ever talk with you about it?"

Ferguson's gaze found a spot on the wood plank floor. "Not in any detail. I remember him saying they never should have been there."

"Did he say what he meant by that?"

She shook her head. "I assumed he meant Iraq."

"Had your husband ever made a statement like that before?"

"No. I mean, Phil wasn't necessarily in favor of the war, but he did believe in serving, in performing his duty."

"Did he ever mention James Ford?"

"Not by name. Like I said, he told me a guardsman was killed and another one paralyzed that same night. He said there were five of them when they got ambushed. I remember because he said they didn't have enough fire-power."

When Jenkins mentioned that five guardsmen had received the Purple Heart Sloane assumed that was five of many, not five men total. It seemed like a small number given the battle the witness statements described. "Just five?"

"That's what he said."

Sloane suspected Katherine Ferguson was, like most witnesses, trying to forget a painful memory. They professed not to remember it, but if you pressed, they usually remembered more than they realized. The key was not pressing too hard. "Did your husband say anything more about that—about how they got ambushed?"

She thought for a moment. Then she sat back. "A little bit."

HIGHWAY 10, IRAQ

"*I CAN'T SEE.*" *Ford leaned forward, his nose nearly pressed to the windshield. "I don't even know if I'm on the road anymore, Captain."*

Out the windows it looked as if the Humvee had driven off a cliff into a brown sea. Ten minutes earlier it had been sunny, not a cloud in the sky. Then the sandstorm blew in from the south, what the Iraqis called a "turab," and quickly turned the sky a reddish-orange before totally eclipsing the sun. The convoy had attempted to roll through it, but visibility had deteriorated to less than a foot.

Kessler picked up the headset to the radio mounted below the FBCB2 communication system on the dash. He used his call sign to try to reach the rest of the convoy. "Alfa one-two, this is Charlie Tango Three, over." The response was static. The storm could wreak havoc on their communication systems. Kes-

sler waited a beat before trying again. "Alfa one-two, acknowl-edge. Over." When he received no response, he set the headset back atop the radio.

Ford looked at him from the driver's seat while continuing to inch the truck forward. In the absence of specific orders, it was the vehicle commander's decision to stop.

"All right, shut it down," Kessler said. "We'll ride it out here."

Ford braked to a stop. Wind rocked the Humvee and whis-tled through every crack. Sand swept over them, sounding like brooms brushing metal.

Cassidy poked his head between the seats. "You think the others stopped, Captain?" His jaw worked a piece of chewing gum.

"Likely," Kessler said, though Ford didn't know how the captain could tell. He couldn't see six inches from the hood.

Kessler said, "Sit back and relax, Butch. And bring Fergie in."

Cassidy tapped Ferguson's leg. A moment later Fergie slid down the hatch from his position manning his M249. His upper torso looked like someone had rolled him in flour. When he pulled down his face guiter, sand shook free, drawing a com-plaint from DT, which only made Ferguson shake more vigor-ously. His goggles had imprinted raccoon eyes on his face.

"Could you see the rest of the convoy?" Kessler asked.

"Couldn't see anything, Captain." Ferguson blew his nose into a handkerchief.

Cassidy asked, "What if they continued on, Captain?"

"Not likely, Butch." Ford knew that Kessler was trying to sound like it was just another day at the beach, but none of them liked being stopped in the open. The best part of a convoy was getting back to the base. "We'll roll when the storm passes."

"I don't like being out here," Cassidy said, expressing what Ford knew they were all thinking.

"Thought you were the great white hunter?" DT smirked. "Sure your nickname ain't Bitch instead of Butch?"

"Enough, DT." Kessler turned sideways and addressed the men in the backseat. "If we can't see Hajji, then Hajji can't see us. Man your sectors and keep it buttoned up."

Cassidy looked out his window but continued to bite and spit out pieces of his fingernails. Ford suspected from the coffee-stained color of the kid's teeth and all his tics and jerks, that Cassidy had abused drugs at some point in his life. And despite the young's man's bravado, he doubted that Cassidy had ever shot anything in his life. The captain, who was on a second tour and had also served in Desert Storm, had expressed his concern to Ford about how Cassidy, and DT for that matter, would react when the shit hit the fan. He told Ford that you could train a soldier to fight, but nothing compared to having someone shooting at you. Some soldiers performed as they trained, others fed off the combat adrenaline and flat-out kicked ass, but a third group simply shut down, paralyzed by fear.

Hoping to keep them occupied, Ford asked, "Why don't you tell us again about that time you killed that wild boar, Butch?"

Cassidy gave him a blank stare in the rearview mirror, further confirming his story had been bull. People didn't easily forget real-life experiences. It was more difficult to remember the things you made up.

Ford further prompted him. "You know? How you shot that boar with a compound bow while hunting with your father?"

"Oh, that," Cassidy said. "I wasn't with my father that time. That time I was alone." He adjusted in his seat. "Okay. Let me think. So I seen this boar, big fucker, like five, six hundred pounds rooting in the dirt and leaves and stuff—"

The radio crackled and spit out a data burst of cryptographic information. Kessler raised a hand to quiet Cassidy and picked up the headset. "This is Charlie Tango Three. Say again. Over." He waited a beat. "This is Charlie Tango Three. Say again. Over."

"You think it's the convoy?" Cassidy asked.

The initial response was more static, but what followed, intermittent and unclear, was definitely not the convoy.

CHAPTER THREE

I remember him saying they got ambushed. He said they were lucky they weren't all killed," Katherine Ferguson said.

"And that's when your husband lost his eyesight?" Sloane asked.

"He said a building blew up and he got hit by the debris."

"Who blew up the building, the Iraqis?"

She shook her head. "I don't know for sure. I think Phil said we did."

Again, Sloane found it unlikely five men fighting through an ambush would have the firepower to blow up a building, but he could also see by the way Katherine Ferguson's shoulders had begun to slump that she was physically and emotionally shutting down. He looked about the room and spotted a photograph atop the piano.

"How old are your children?"

Ferguson smiled. "PJ, Phil junior, is eleven. Sophia is seven." She looked back to Sloane. "Phil was a good dad. The kids miss him terribly."

"I'm sure he was." Sloane had not meant to imply otherwise. "Was he depressed about his condition? It would be understandable given his circumstance."

"He was," she said, though not with conviction. "But never around the kids. Phil was strong that way. He didn't want the kids to be scared, so he made jokes, you know. He'd tell PJ, 'You better duck from now on when we're hunting.' Things like that." She smiled. "But when we were alone he worried about how we were going to get by. He wanted to be sure we were taken care of. I'm sure he thought our insurance would cover . . ." Her voice trailed.

"That's understandable."

"He leased his land to his brother. Joe lives on the other end of the farm. They signed the agreement just a couple days before . . ."

Her voice caught. She looked as though she might cry again.

"Has that helped?" Sloane asked, gently prodding.

She nodded. "We're okay. He also sold the land to the south, the field just as you drove in. We put the money in a trust to pay for the kids' college. Education was important to Phil."

"Your husband sounds like he was a sharp business-man."

She smiled. "I guess you'd assume he was just a dumb farm boy, but Phil graduated from the U-Dub with degrees in agriculture and business. He was no dummy." She looked at her watch.

"I won't keep you any longer."

"I have homework." She sighed at the irony.

Sloane stood. "Thank you again for talking with me. I'm sorry to have disturbed your day."

"Not at all." She walked him back to the front porch. When she opened the door the dogs rose quickly, as if caught napping on the job. One padded over, a collie mix. Sloane scratched her behind the ears as he contemplated his final area of questioning. "I'm sorry about your husband. I'm sure his death was very traumatic for all of you."

She nodded. "When I got the call that day, my whole world crashed."

That was his opening. "You weren't home?"

"I was at work. I worked for a local Realtor part-time, just helping in the office."

"That must have been horrible to come home to."

"Joe handled it. He found him. Phil's therapist had a flat tire that day and got here late. There were guns on the table and she couldn't find Phil anywhere, so she called Joe."

"Guns as in more than one?"

She nodded. "It looked like maybe he was cleaning them. That's what Joe said."

Sloane looked at the staircase behind her leading to

the second floor. It was steep. "How long had Phil been back from Iraq?" he asked, though he recalled her telling him it had been six months.

She looked past him into the yard. "About six months, but he'd only been home from the VA hospital a couple weeks."

"So being blind was still relatively new to him."

"It was, but therapy was helping. He was learning to use a cane and organize things so he knew where they were. But his balance was off because his eyes couldn't judge things for him. They said it was going to take time."

"How often did your husband have therapy?"

"Every day. They called it an immersion. His therapist was starting with the basics, organizing his closet and drawers, getting dressed—things like that." She shook her head, smiling. "But Phil was never one to take the easy way out. He was bugging her to teach him Braille so he could read again."

"I imagine your husband's condition was an adjustment for all of you."

"It was hard," she agreed. "We were like old dogs learning new tricks. Phil stayed mostly upstairs during the day when his therapist wasn't here. Then I helped him down when I got home so he could sit with us at dinner or watch television." She chuckled. "I guess that sounds strange, 'watch television.'"

"Not at all." Sloane waited a beat. "So your husband didn't go outside much?"

"Not too much. He'd occasionally sit on the porch to get some fresh air."

Sloane noticed a wicker porch seat with a floral pad. "Did he keep his guns in the barn?"

"Oh no, not with the kids around. He kept them locked in a cabinet in his office," she said, gesturing vaguely inside the house.

Sloane walked to the corner of the porch as if to look at the barn, but focused instead on the path leading to it. A good fifty yards, it was littered with farm equipment and scrap metal, and pocked with potholes filled with rain water.

AS HE DROVE from Katherine Ferguson's property, Sloane flipped open his cell phone and pressed the preprogrammed number. "You know what we always say about coincidences?"

"Don't believe in them," Jenkins replied.

"Phillip Ferguson is dead."

"My source said he made it home alive."

"He did, but blind. He took shrapnel in the head."

"I sense where this is going."

"He shot himself in a barn behind his house. I'm just leaving his wife. Another tragedy, two young kids. She says he shot himself because he thought the family could recover the insurance. Proceeds of a policy he took out before leaving for Iraq. Sounds like the perfect scenario, doesn't it?"

"What are you getting at?"

"Depressed soldier comes home injured in the war, can no longer do all the things he once did, so he decides his family is better off with him dead and makes the ultimate sacrifice. Unfortunately, he miscalculates and doesn't realize suicide is not a covered event under any insurance policy."

"You have reason to suspect otherwise?"

"His therapist normally arrived about an hour after his wife went to work. That day she had a flat tire and was late."

"It happens."

"Before he died, Ferguson worked out an arrangement to lease his portion of the land to his brother. His wife says it's enough to pay the bills with some left over at the end of each month. They also sold some land and put the proceeds in a trust for the kids' education and their retirement."

"He was getting his affairs in order, making sure his wife and kids would be all right. That your point?"

"My point is he doesn't sound like an idiot—like the kind of guy who wouldn't have known, or at least have checked to see if his life insurance policy included an exclusion for suicide."

Jenkins continued to play devil's advocate. "He was blind and depressed. Depressed people don't always act rationally and he couldn't read the policy."

"He had two college degrees," Sloane said.

"One more than I have."

"And I'll bet you know that most insurance policies exclude suicide for a period after purchase."

"I'd suspect as much."

"He wanted to learn Braille so he could start reading again."

"His mood swings could have been flip-flopping. Who knows what his mental state was?" Jenkins countered.

"His wife also said he'd taken out all his guns and was cleaning them."

"All of them?"

"That's what she said."

"Hmm."

"Do you know much about being blind?"

"I've read some things."

"I had a case in San Francisco once. A guy tried to heat a can of air-conditioning fluid on a stove to get it to flow easier. The can exploded like a rocket, took out one eye and damaged the other. An expert I hired to fight the damages said that being born blind is one thing—your body doesn't know any different. But to suddenly go blind creates a whole different set of problems, balance being one of them. Ferguson's wife said it was her husband's biggest adjustment. He generally stayed upstairs until she got home."

"So how did he get out to the barn?"

"Good question. I asked it myself. Here's the scenario. The wife is at work. The kids are in school. The brother is gone, and the therapist is late because she gets a flat tire. Just months after being blinded, and weeks after coming back to his own home, and still dealing with major balance issues, he navigates down a steep staircase, gets his shotgun from a locked cabinet in his office, finds his way out the front door, down the porch, around the side of the house, and walks fifty plus yards through what looks like a junkyard of scrap metal and potholes to blow his head off in a barn."

"Again, it could have happened that way."

"Could have, but in light of all the other things I just told you, is it plausible?"

"We'd be speculating. We don't really know."

"And if I'm wrong, it's no big deal. But if I'm right . . ."

"Okay, so how does this relate to James Ford?"

"I don't know, but my gut is bothering me. Have you found anyone else?"

"For a guy who didn't sound all that enthusiastic about taking this case this afternoon you're awfully pushy."

"Yeah, well, things have changed."

"I have a bead on a guy in Tacoma, but I haven't been able to reach him yet. His sister says he works nights."

TACOMA, WASHINGTON

THE WAY DWAYNE Thomas figured it, there was a predetermined day and time for everyone to die, and there was no getting around it. To his way of thinking, heaven was a warehouse filled with billions of timers, all ticking at once, and every second another bell rings to indicate someone has died. That's why people said things like "His time was up" and "The bell tolls for thee."

People did everything they could to avoid that bell. Thomas saw them every day at the health club, people damn near killing themselves trying to prolong their lives. They didn't get it. They didn't understand that they could work out for hours, take a long steam in the locker room, and walk out the door and get hit by a bus. That was how it happened to Brad Pitt in that movie *Meet Joe Black*. One minute, he's sitting in a restaurant meeting a girl. The next minute he walks out the door and his bell rings.

That was destiny. That was fate. And all the hours sweating on the damn StairMaster weren't going to change that.

Thomas knew about fate. He'd learned all he wanted to know about it waking up every morning in Iraq wondering if it was his day to die. He'd been sure his day had come in that ambush, but God had kept his clock ticking and stopped James Ford's instead. Shitty deal for sure, but nothing to be done about it. After that, he figured if it was his time, then it was his time, so there was no reason to get all worked up about it. That was fate.

When he got back to Tacoma, he learned a different lesson about fate, except they called it irony. The city rejected his employment application. So much for his grand plan to use the Guard to catch on as a city worker; he was no better off for humping his ass in 130-degree weather than if he'd never left Tacoma. Well, screw that. He was owed something for his trouble and not just some damn medal, either. Hell yeah, he was. So when the attorney called to tell him he was filing a claim for Fergie and wondering if DT was interested, he figured why the hell not? Why shouldn't he get *something* for serving? He'd nearly died in that ambush and the doctors had said he lost 30 percent of his hearing in one ear when that building blew up. That had to be worth something, didn't it?

He tossed dirty towels into the laundry basket and replaced them with clean ones. The muscled guy on the treadmill had given up and left, leaving the old fart on the StairMaster to push on alone, red-faced and sweating buckets. Thomas half-expected the guy to suddenly clutch his chest and fall off the machine. If he saw the guy alive again, it would be a miracle.

He wheeled the cart into the laundry room, left it, and retrieved his belongings from his employee locker. When he walked out the back of the building, the cold night air made his skin tingle like a slap across the cheek. God, it felt good to be cold again. If there was a hell, Iraq was the simulator for it. Thomas had never experienced that kind of heat before. Then the sand would start blowing and grains would stick to parts of your body you didn't even know you had. The best part of coming back home was coming back to weather that rarely got above 80 degrees, and the only sand to be found was if you went looking for it at the beach.

He pulled the knit Seahawks cap down low over his ears and started the walk down Market, crossing through the Republic parking lot as he did each night to cut the corner to his bus stop. The muscled guy who'd been running on the treadmill stood in the lot wearing a blue ball cap, his hands cupped to his mouth, flicking a lighter. It sparked three times without drawing a flame.

He looked up as Thomas approached. "Can I get a light?"

Thomas pulled his lighter from his pocket. Smoking was another bad habit he'd brought back from Iraq, two packs a day. Only cigarettes weren't cheap like they'd been over there. They were expensive as hell. He flicked his lighter and cupped the flame.

The man lit up and stepped back, blowing a patch of blue smoke into the night. "Thanks. You need one?"

Thomas had a few minutes to catch his bus. "Yeah, why not? Keep me warm against this cold," he said, making conversation.

"Don't I know it, brother."

The guy shook a butt from the pack. Thomas pulled the cigarette free and pressed it between his lips, about to flick his lighter when the man stepped forward and flicked his own—a gold-plated type with a flip-top that immediately produced a blue flame.

The man shrugged and snapped shut the top, making a metallic ting. It sounded like a bell.

THREE TREE POINT, WASHINGTON

EARLY THE FOLLOWING morning, Jenkins appeared at Sloane's home with two cups of coffee.

"I'd thank you," Sloane said, "except it's too early to talk."

"Tell me about it," Jenkins said. "I've been up for an hour and a half. Get dressed. We have an appointment."

"The guy in Tacoma?"

"Haven't heard back from him yet. This is better."

"It better be."

Fifteen minutes later, Sloane drove his Jeep south on I-5. He'd always considered the car roomy, but Jenkins looked like he'd been squeezed into the passenger seat. His head brushed the ceiling, his legs were uncomfortably bent, and despite the brisk morning temperature, he had the window down, elbow out.

"This guy was their captain?" Sloane asked.

Jenkins nodded. "Robert Kessler."

Sloane assumed that officers would tend to be more reticent about giving information that could be harmful to the military. "And he'll talk to me?"

"Said he'd thought a lot about what happened that night. Ford was apparently the only guy he failed to bring home. I got the impression it still eats at him."

"Did you tell him I'm thinking about filing a lawsuit on behalf of the family?"

"I told him you were Beverly Ford's attorney. Most people figure out the lawsuit part on their own. I don't imagine he thinks the family hired you to put together a scrapbook."

FORTY-FIVE MINUTES LATER, Sloane drove past Fort Lewis and exited the freeway. They descended a winding road into an area heavily wooded on both sides of the road. Rail spurs paralleled the pavement and eighteen-wheel trucks passed in the opposite direction.

"Who does this guy work for?" Sloane asked.

Jenkins handed him a scrap of paper from his coat pocket.

"Argus International?" Sloane asked, reading.

Jenkins wasn't impressed. "You know it?"

"Don't you watch the news?"

"Not if I can help it. It depresses me."

One of the largest chemical manufacturers in the world, Argus had recently been in the news for receiving a 1.2-billion-dollar reconstruction contract in Iraq. The contract sparked controversy because Argus had a long-standing penchant for hiring out-of-office, high-profile politicians and paying them large "retirement" packages when they found their way back into public service, usually in influential positions inside the administration's cabinet. One of those former employees, an Argus president in the 1990s, was Frederick Northrup, the current secretary of defense.

"The turn is coming up," Jenkins said. "Slow down."

Given its prominence, Sloane expected Argus's entrance to be grand, but the turnoff was marked by nothing more than a three-foot-high stucco wall bearing the company name in gold letters. Two hundred yards down a gravel road they came to a guard booth and a ten-foot-high chain-link fence with barbed wire strung across the top. A black-and-yellow gate also blocked the road. It looked like a border checkpoint to a Cold War–era Soviet country.

A guard in a starched white shirt and a blue polyester uniform stepped from the booth adjusting a police-style hat squarely on his head and tucking a clipboard under his arm. With reflector sunglasses he looked decidedly serious.

"Can I help you, gentlemen?" The guard directed the sunglasses across the seat at Jenkins, then to the backseat before redirecting to Sloane.

"We're here to see Robert Kessler," Sloane said.

"Do you have an appointment with the captain?"

"Yes, we do," Sloane said, noting the guard's reference to Kessler's military rank.

"I'll need picture ID from both of you."

They fished out their licenses and the guard put them on his clipboard as he walked to the back of the car. In the rearview mirror Sloane watched him log the license plate, then circle the car looking through the windows into the interior before returning to the booth and picking up a telephone.

Sloane looked to Jenkins. "What do they make here, enriched uranium?"

Jenkins put a finger to his lips, turned on the radio, and pointed through the windshield to a long black rod atop a light pole just beneath a surveillance camera. "Someone's watching, and listening—those rods are directional microphones." He pointed to a disc inside the gate. "And that's a satellite dish."

"Maybe they watch cable," Sloane joked.

Jenkins turned off the radio as the guard returned with their licenses and handed them white plastic cards dangling at the end of strings. "Wear these around your necks at all times while you're on the property." Straightening, he pointed down the road. "Take your first right and park in front of the third warehouse building on your left. Someone will meet you."

Jenkins leaned across the seat. "What number building is that?"

"It's the third building," the guard repeated without elaboration. Then he stepped back from the car, pressing a button on his belt. The arm rose automatically and the chain-link fence rolled to the right.

Dropping the transmission into drive, Sloane drove onto the property. "The guy has the demeanor of a concrete wall."

Jenkins turned the radio back on. "The buildings aren't numbered."

"Is that significant?"

"I don't know yet."

Around a bend in the road, Sloane saw a large industrial complex of corrugated metal buildings that looked like small airplane hangars. The railroad spurs ran behind the buildings, disappearing behind a large processing plant. Smokestacks emitted white steam.

Jenkins pointed to vans and eighteen-wheel trucks parked in multiple loading bays. "No advertising on the trucks or the buildings. Understated entrance. They keep a low profile." He flipped up his white card. "What do you want to bet these cards have sensors to track our location while on the property?"

Sloane looked down at the card, reading the word "Visitor" upside down. "Do you think you're being a little paranoid? Maybe it's just to show we're visitors. A lot of companies require this."

"Do those companies pick locations that butt up against a military base that limits access to designated checkpoints?" Jenkins asked.

Sloane looked over at him.

"This place abuts Fort Lewis," Jenkins said. "I doubt they picked it by chance."

True to the guard's word, as Sloane neared the third building, a woman stood waiting at the foot of two concrete steps. When they got out of the car, she approached Sloane with a rigidly outstretched arm.

"Mr. Sloane? I'm Anne, Captain Kessler's assistant."

Anne had the lean features and weathered skin of someone who ran long distances. It had aged her. Sloane guessed she was early thirties or younger but looked forty. Her handshake was rock solid. She looked at Jenkins as if uncertain about him. No wonder. With his sunglasses and black coat, he looked like Arnold Schwarzenegger in one of the *Terminator* movies.

"Mr. Jenkins arranged my meeting with Mr. Kessler," Sloane said, as if to explain Jenkins's presence.

Anne gave a pleasant smile. "I'll escort you to the captain."

They stepped through a heavy metal door into a nondescript interior of paneled walls and a drop-down tile ceiling with dull fluorescent lighting and protruding sprinkler heads. It looked more like the interior of a construction trailer than the offices of a billion-dollar conglomerate. Because of Jenkins's comment about the buildings not being numbered, Sloane looked for names and titles on the doors they passed, but found none. There were no name plates on the desk cubicles either.

"What kind of business is Argus?" Sloane asked, playing dumb.

Anne spoke over her shoulder. "We make agricultural chemicals."

"Pesticides?" Jenkins asked.

"Some."

Anne stopped outside a closed door and knocked twice before turning the knob and entering. Sloane followed her. The man behind the desk waved them further in and gestured to two seats across from him. He looked to be talking to himself until he turned his head and Sloane saw a wireless earpiece.

Captain Robert Kessler wore a cream-colored dress shirt pressed to perfection and looking like it should be emblazoned with medals. His tie was equally perfect, cinched tight, the knot flawless. As Kessler spoke, the muscles in his neck undulated, and a vein at his temple bulged. His close-cropped hair was more salt than pepper, a contrast to his youthful features and an indication that perhaps he hadn't left the military completely behind. Behind him, a map of the world, marked with several dozen red triangles, hung on the wall.

A beam of light drew Sloane's attention to a pitch-black, floor-to-ceiling, plate-glass window. With effort he detected movement on the other side of the glass.

"All right, that's enough for now," Kessler said.

A burst of light illuminated what appeared to be a village of flat-roof, stucco, and stone homes set behind exterior walls. Debris and the burned-out shells of cars and military vehicles littered potholed streets. It looked like the back lot of a Hollywood set.

Kessler gestured to the window. "Welcome to Iraq."

But for the metal beams and ductwork crisscrossing the ceiling, the skeletal framework of a huge warehouse, the village looked just like pictures Sloane had seen in magazines and on the front page of countless newspapers. Half a dozen men dressed in black camouflage, their makeup smudged by perspiration, filed out from behind a wall carrying automatic weapons and wearing helmets equipped with night-vision goggles. Following them were men and women dressed in nightshirts and headdresses. Though almost all were Caucasian, they were obviously playing the role of Iraqis. The men's arms had been bound behind their backs.

"Take a break. We'll run it again," Kessler said. "We want to be consistent. Mistakes cause confusion, and confusion is what gets somebody killed. Make sure everyone is well hydrated. I don't want anyone cramping."

Kessler removed the earpiece and clipped it to his shirt pocket as a motor hummed and a drape pulled closed across the glass. He pushed back from his desk and, to Sloane's surprise, rolled toward them in a wheelchair of a design similar to ones Sloane had seen used by paraplegics to play basketball, a seat cushion atop two wheels. Straps held Kessler's legs in place. Sloane recalled Katherine Ferguson's comment that another soldier had been paralyzed the night her husband was blinded and Ford died.

Sloane and Jenkins began to stand. Kessler raised a hand. "Please, sit. I am." He smiled. "It's a bad joke, I know." He motioned to the now-curtained window. "I'm sorry to have kept you waiting. We were just finishing a training exercise and it ran a few minutes longer than expected."

Sloane gestured to the window. "Looks like a military exercise."

"Did you serve?" Kessler asked.

"Marines." After hearing the guard and the assistant, Anne, refer to Kessler as "Captain," Sloane had wanted to impart his own military service early in the conversation, hoping it would give them common ground. He was glad for the opportunity.

Kessler looked to Jenkins.

"Vietnam," Jenkins said, without adding, Special Forces. He looked to the drape across the window. "Where in Iraq is that?"

"An exact replica of six square blocks in Mosul," Kessler said. "Would you like a closer look?"

Sloane nodded. "Sure."

Kessler turned the wheelchair and pulled open his office door. "You might want to leave your coats. It's a hundred and thirteen degrees in Iraq."

Sloane draped his leather jacket over the back of his chair. Jenkins kept his on.

Kessler wheeled to a metal door at the end of a hall and punched in a code on a sensor pad mounted on the wall. That activated a buzzer, followed by the sound of a deadbolt sliding. When Kessler pulled open the door, a blast of heat greeted them as if someone had stuck a huge hair dryer in their faces.

"We try to simulate the exact conditions," Kessler said, wheeling onto dirt streets and adeptly avoiding debris and potholes. "We can even kick up a realistic sandstorm."

"Is it always this oppressive?" Sloane felt his shirt already sticking to his skin.

"Actually, this is mild. It's night. Temperatures in Mosul during the day can exceed a hundred thirty degrees. The residents sleep on their roofs because the interiors are just too hot. That's important to what we do."

"Because people sleeping on roofs make sneaking up on a target more difficult," Jenkins said.

"The insurgents use cell phones," Kessler said. "If one sees us coming he starts phoning. Pretty soon everyone is awake."

"Why would Argus need to run military maneuvers?" Sloane asked.

Kessler stopped rolling. "Sorry, force of habit. Argus doesn't run military maneuvers. We're a civilian contractor. But we can't lose sight of the fact that there is still a war going on and we're in the middle of it. The military has its hands full with the insurgency. My job is to ensure our employees are safe and that shipments reach their designated end users."

"A private military force," Jenkins said.

Kessler wouldn't go that far. "Most of the men here served in various branches of the military," he acknowledged. "But they're civilians now. My job is to keep their skills sharp by simulating the environment in which they could find themselves working."

"So if an Argus employee is kidnapped, for instance, they might be called to try and rescue them," Sloane said.

"You saw the map on the wall in my office? Argus has offices, or subsidiaries, throughout the world. We have projects in twenty-three foreign countries, employing sixty-five thousand people."

"The other warehouses have similar setups?" Sloane asked.

"We have tunnels, rivers eight feet deep, a suburb outside Paris, and jungles so thick and hot you'd swear you were back in Southeast Asia." He looked to Jenkins. "Care to have a look?"

Jenkins shook his head. "Once was bad enough. I'll take Paris in the spring."

Kessler gave them another minute to look around. Perspiration dripped down their faces.

Kessler swung the wheelchair around. "Let's get out of this heat."

"Have you had to extract any employees?" Sloane asked as they walked back to the entrance.

Kessler repeated the process of entering a code on the sensor. "I can't answer that. I'm sure you can appreciate that what we do over there can be sensitive. It doesn't always make the news, and we try to keep it that way. Given the current climate, working there is sort of like living with a tiger. You don't want to be poking it with a stick, drawing its attention and making it angry if you don't have to."

. . .

BACK BEHIND HIS desk, Kessler looked as normal as the next guy, but Sloane knew appearances could be deceiving. Despite Kessler's upbeat demeanor and jokes, Sloane couldn't help but wonder what happened to a man's psyche when he lost so much so quickly, and how much of Kessler's demeanor was an act for their benefit, part of the unwritten "man's code" not to show weakness.

"You wanted to talk about James Ford?" Kessler asked.

"Mrs. Ford has asked me to look into James's death. They have a lot of questions about what happened to him, about how he died. You gave a statement in some detail," Sloane said. He pulled out Kessler's witness statement from his briefcase and handed it to him. "The family obtained a copy. I assume it's an accurate recollection of what occurred?"

"Yes," Kessler said, without giving the statement a glance. "And I'm aware that Mrs. Ford filed a claim."

"Who told you that?"

"The claims office."

"So you understand Mrs. Ford takes issue with Mr. Ford's body armor?"

The vein in Kessler's temple became more prominent, though his voice remained even. "I'm aware that Mrs. Ford is upset because in her mind James did not have sufficient body armor, yes."

"You don't agree."

Kessler paused, as if to measure his response. After

a moment he said, "I understand there were quite a few claims after that article that the new armor might have saved lives."

"You don't agree?" Sloane asked again.

"The article's implication was that the soldiers did not have to die—that better armor would have kept them alive. In my opinion that's just speculation."

Sloane decided to push him. "The report indicates the wounds were inflicted in areas left unprotected by the older armor. Why is that speculation?"

"Because we could reach the same conclusion about every soldier who has died in every war. Soldiers don't die unless they incur a wound in an unprotected area." Kessler paused. "The fact is, there never has been and there never will be body armor that will keep every soldier alive. If there were, we'd be in a constant state of war."

The latter comment surprised Sloane. "It seems the opposite would be true."

"Would it?" Kessler adjusted in his chair. "War is inevitable. I'm not a pessimist by nature, but you can't ignore history. Men have been fighting since we could stand on two legs and throw a spear. If no soldier died, there would be no casualties, and as we all know, wars usually end when the casualties become unacceptable to one side or both." Kessler looked at Jenkins. "You served in Vietnam; you're familiar with the vests we used over there."

"Couldn't stop a fart and weighed a ton," Jenkins said.

Kessler turned to Sloane. "They called them 'flak jackets' because that's all they were designed to protect against, flak from shrapnel and other low-speed projectiles."

"I'm familiar with the term, and the jacket, Captain."

"Then you know they were the best we had at that time. They saved lives. Not enough, for sure. What we wore in Desert Storm wasn't much better. The technology didn't change until production of the Interceptor in 1999. It was supposed to be part of a ten-year plan to replace the flak jackets. Unfortunately, nine-eleven occurred in the fifth year of that plan, and we hadn't produced enough to outfit every soldier before the invasion. You go to war with what you have."

It was an argument Sloane knew he could anticipate from an assistant U.S. attorney if he ever filed a complaint in federal court. He sensed that further argument would only make Kessler guarded, and what he really wanted was to better understand why the witness statements were so uniform.

"What can you tell me about the night James Ford died?"

Kessler shook his head. "Nothing, I'm afraid."

Sloane looked to Jenkins, but the big man appeared equally perplexed by Kessler's sudden reticence. "I don't understand. You knew we wanted to talk about James Ford."

"About his vest, yes, but I can't talk about what happened to him that night."

"I thought you indicated to Mr. Jenkins that you were willing to talk to me?"

Now it was Kessler who looked perplexed. "I did. But . . . I'm sorry, I thought you knew."

"Knew what?"

"That Mrs. Ford's claim has been reopened."

INSIDE THE JEEP, Sloane put on sunglasses and turned on the radio.

Jenkins smiled. "Are we getting paranoid, Counselor?"

"You told him we wanted to discuss the night Ford died."

"Yep."

"And he said he'd talk to us."

"Yep."

"And by the time we get here he tells us he can't say anything?"

"Yep."

Sloane backed the Jeep from the building and drove toward the entrance. "So what was the damn point of making us drive all this way?"

"Don't know. But isn't the real question why the claim has been reopened?"

The fence pulled apart. Jenkins turned down the radio as Sloane handed the two plastic cards back to the guard in the booth. The man never uttered a word.

As they drove off, Jenkins said, "I don't like that guy's attitude."

"He has no attitude. He's a robot."

"He's got attitude," Jenkins said.

"Why provide Beverly Ford the statements at all?" Sloane asked.

"What?"

"Why did they give her the statements? I've never come up with a good answer."

"You said she made a FOIA request."

"It's the government, Charlie—they invented stone-walling. They could have come up with a dozen legal reasons to not turn the statements over, not to mention playing the national security card. I've been focused on why the statements are so similar. Maybe I need to focus on why the government would give them up at all."

"You have a theory?"

"What's the best way to get rid of a squeaky wheel?"

"Oil it."

"Let her read about how her husband tragically died a hero. Let her believe there's nothing to hide and hope that will be the end of it," Sloane said. "But it isn't the end of it. She isn't pacified by a Purple Heart. She continues to press for information, and they go back to ignoring her."

"Enter you," Jenkins said, following Sloane's reasoning.

"Now she has a lawyer asking questions."

"So they reopen the claim and tell Kessler he can't talk about it."

Sloane shook his head. "That's where I'm having a problem. If the claim is as unviable as John Kannin believes, if the Feres doctrine is as impenetrable as he says, we have to assume the regional claims office knows that, right? I mean this is what they do on a daily basis."

"One would assume."

"And if that's the case, then the smart move would be to let me talk to the captain. Either that's the end of it, or, if I do file my complaint in federal court, the government brings a motion to have it dismissed, and they're done with the whole thing."

"So we have to assume that whoever ordered the claim reopened isn't comfortable with either scenario," Jenkins said.

Sloane nodded. "And the only reason they wouldn't be comfortable is because they don't want us talking to the other soldiers about what happened. Maybe the claim isn't as unviable as we think."

"If they were going to cover something up, they'd make sure everyone was saying the same thing."

"Kessler never even bothered to look at his statement. Did you notice that?" Sloane merged the car onto the freeway, heading north.

"A lot of soldiers want nothing to do with those memories, David. That's a tough place to return to."

"Maybe, but I keep thinking of two things Katherine Ferguson said to me."

"What was that?"

"She said her husband told her that they never should have been there."

"Iraq?"

"That's what I thought, but now I'm not so sure.

Where was their support? A single squad? Five guys? It doesn't make sense."

"Their statements say they drove off course during a sandstorm."

Sloane nodded. "But if we're assuming we can't trust those statements . . ."

"I follow. So what was the second thing she said?" Jenkins asked.

Sloane stared out the windshield. "She said her husband never took the easy way out."

CHAPTER FOUR

What can I do for you, David?" John Kannin's voice reverberated over the speaker on Sloane's cell phone so Jenkins could hear the conversation.

"I have a couple more questions," Sloane said.

"Shoot."

"If a soldier's claim is denied, how would the family receive notice?"

"It can be formally denied, in which case the regional claims office will send a letter to the service member or their spouse, or if it isn't formally denied within six months, it's deemed denied, in which case there might not be a letter."

"Have you ever heard of a claim being denied and then reopened?"

"Reopened? Why?"

"No idea at this point."

"I've never had that happen before."

"Any guesses why they might?"

"Off the top of my head?" There was a pause to indicate Kannin wasn't overwhelmed with possibilities. "The JAG attorneys rotate out of that office after a year; it's not unusual for me to deal with more than one on the same claim. I guess it's possible a new JAG could come in and assess a claim differently from his predecessor."

"How likely is that?"

"Not likely with the volume of claims they have, unless perhaps someone draws their attention to the particular claim."

Sloane had done just that. Could it be that simple? Could a new JAG have reopened the claim to take another look at it? "Any other reasons you can think of?"

"Claims can get passed up the chain if greater settlement authority is needed. It could be that a superior got a hold of it and wants to take a closer look."

Given the Feres doctrine, that did not seem likely. Then again, if someone had researched Sloane's reputation it was possible, as he'd hoped.

"Anything else come to mind?"

"Only other thing I can think of is maybe if the family provided additional information for the officer to consider."

"What about reopening the claim to impede a civilian investigation into the circumstances that led to the service member's death?"

"*Now* this is getting interesting." Sloane envisioned Kannin sitting up with his Cheshire-cat grin. "Tell me more."

Sloane explained what had happened when they tried to speak with Captain Robert Kessler.

Kannin interrupted. "Wait a minute. They *gave* her the witness statements?"

"I take it that's unusual."

"Highly. Ordinarily an investigation into a soldier's death includes the tactical methods employed. They want to determine whether what happened was an isolated incident or potentially endemic of a larger problem necessitating a change in field tactics. In my experience that part of the investigation is *always* classified."

"Assuming that to be the case, any reason you can think of to explain why they'd turn over the statements to his wife?"

"None. I mean maybe you get a JAG who understands the family is looking for answers and wants to do the right thing. The ones I've dealt with are decent people. And they're soldiers too, remember. But I would doubt it."

Sloane's phone indicated an incoming call. He'd called Carolyn requesting Beverly Ford's phone number. "I have another call. Thanks for the help, John."

"No problem. Keep me posted. I'd like to know how it turns out."

Sloane switched the call and Carolyn provided Ford's number. "Do me another favor," he asked. "Check Mrs. Ford's files for letters from the regional claims office. Find me a name and a phone number."

"Hang on."

He heard papers rustling and handed Jenkins a pen and piece of paper, repeating the name Carolyn provided. "Captain F. Lloyd Bitterman." He was about to hang up when he saw a freeway sign that provoked a thought. "What's the address for the claims office?"

"The address? Fort Lewis. Why?"

Sloane cut quickly across two lanes of traffic, eliciting a honk and a one-finger salute from the driver of a blue BMW.

Jenkins braced an arm on the dash. "What the hell?"

Just off the exit, Sloane turned into a parking lot outside the gated entrance to Fort Lewis. "Thanks, Carolyn. That's all I need for now."

"Are you coming in or did I blow another chance to get better looking?"

"I'll be in," he said. "Call me if anything comes up." He disconnected the call and dialed Beverly Ford's number. She answered after four rings and sounded as if she had a frog in her throat. He had awakened her, and apologized.

"Don't apologize. I'm glad you called. I worked an extra shift last night, but it's about time I got up. What can I do for you?"

"Has anyone informed you that they were reopening your claim?" Sloane asked.

"Reopening it? No. Why?"

"You haven't received a letter or a phone call telling you it was being reconsidered or re-evaluated, anything like that?"

"No. Nothing like that."

"Did you ever get a letter advising that your claim was denied?"

"Not a formal letter. I just assumed it because I read in the papers they gave me that if I didn't hear from them within six months, the claim was considered denied. Was I wrong?"

"No, you weren't wrong, Beverly. And you haven't recently sent the regional claims office additional information for them to consider?"

"I don't have anything else for them to consider. *They* have all the information. Why are you asking?"

"I just came from a meeting with the man who was James's captain the night he died. He told me your claim had been reopened."

"I haven't heard anything about that," Ford said. "But that's a good thing, right? It means someone is going to look into it."

Again Sloane wondered if maybe it was that simple. "I don't want to jump to any conclusions or get your hopes up unnecessarily."

"Don't worry about my hopes," Ford said. "I thought I'd lost all hope when James died, but God finds the way to build us back up."

Maybe, Sloane thought, but he remained concerned about giving Ford a false hope unnecessarily. "Let me

make some more calls and see what I can find out. I'll
keep you posted."

He disconnected and called the number Carolyn
provided for the regional claims office. If he was already
there, Sloane figured he might as well pay the claims officer a visit and find out what was going on. Three minutes
later he hung up, and he and Jenkins stepped from the
car and walked into the Fort Lewis processing center. A
soldier seated behind a desk asked to see their driver's
licenses. Upon considering Sloane's license, he said,
"Didn't I just speak to you?"

"I was in the area."

The processing center had connected Sloane to a
paralegal, Sergeant Bowie, who said Ford's claim had
been assigned to a Captain Thomas Pendergrass.

"I'm not familiar with that name from the file," Sloane
had said.

"Captain Pendergrass just recently rotated in,"
Bowie explained. He told Sloane that Pendergrass was at
a dental appointment, but expected back at any moment.
Sloane apologized for the late notice, and told the sergeant it was urgent he speak with the captain. The sergeant said he'd fit him in.

Jenkins and Sloane peeled the backing from visitor
passes and stuck them onto their jackets as the soldier
behind the desk provided directions to the judge advocate general's office. They got back into the car and
drove through the security checkpoint, which involved
another review of their driver's licenses, passes, and
car registration while another security officer walked

around the car using a mirror to look beneath it.

Entering the base, Sloane drove through what appeared to be Everytown U.S.A., with a Chevron gas station and an assortment of businesses, including a Starbucks. Moments later the scenery changed. They drove past three-story, red-brick buildings with white wood trim and dormer windows. Maple trees lined spotless sidewalks and well-manicured lawns. *

"Looks like an Ivy League campus," Sloane said, except that every man and woman wore the same green-and-beige camouflage combat uniforms, some with black berets.

Jenkins pointed out the two polished bronze cannons on the lawn in front of a building. The soldier in the processing center had given them the cannons as a landmark. Sloane turned into a parking lot just past the building.

"I think I'll take this alone, lawyer to lawyer," Sloane said.

Jenkins shrugged. "Have at it."

Sloane entered the building through oak doors, took half a flight of stairs, and found the judge advocate general's office. Sergeant Bowie turned out to be a burly man with a firm handshake and warm smile. He led Sloane to an office with a low tiled ceiling.

Captain Pendergrass stood behind an L-shaped desk, the word "Pendergrass" stitched on his uniform over the right breast, "U.S. Army" stitched over the left. The tops of several pens protruded from a pocket on his right-forearm sleeve. With the low ceiling, Pendergrass looked huge, but was actually perhaps five foot seven in his combat boots and military-fit. Irish or Scottish, he had a fair complexion, red hair, and boyish features. He looked to be fighting a headache.

Sloane thanked Pendergrass for seeing him. "I understand you just had dental work."

"A root canal. I thought I was just coming in to pick up some files," he said, implying that he had not appreciated Sergeant Bowie setting a meeting. Sloane didn't have a lot of time.

"I had one last year   they're a bitch. I promise not to take too much of your time."

Pendergrass gestured to one of two chairs. As the captain slid behind his desk Sloane glanced at his credentials hanging on the wall. A brown flag hung near the framed certificates indicating Pendergrass had been the Combat JAG for the 81st Brigade Combat Team in Operation Iraqi Freedom, which explained the well-worn desert combat boots propped on a box near his desk.

Sloane gestured to the boots. "You don't find those in every attorney's office."

Pendergrass smiled, though only the right side of his mouth rose. "I wore those out of Iraq. I hope I never have to put them on again. You told my sergeant this was urgent?"

Wanting to gauge Pendergrass's reaction before he could look up the status of Ford's claim, Sloane had been deliberately vague with Sergeant Bowie about the specifics for his visit. "I represent the family of a national guardsman killed in Iraq."

"My condolences." Pendergrass turned to his keyboard.

"I was hoping you could tell me the status of the claim."

"What was the soldier's name?"

"Ford. James Ford," Sloane said.

Pendergrass typed, then scrolled through a screen, his eyes shifting left to right, reading. "That claim was denied."

Sloane paused in case the captain was going to add, "and has recently been reopened." When he didn't, Sloane asked, "I assume that decision was made before you rotated in?"

Pendergrass nodded, eyes focused on the screen. "Yes."

"So you didn't conduct the investigation?"

"This office doesn't conduct investigations," Pendergrass corrected. "Command is responsible for investigating every U.S. fatality overseas. The Criminal Investigation Division also conducts its own investigation. We evaluate the claim from a legal basis only."

"So then you didn't conduct the witness interviews."

"*If* there were witness interviews, they also would have been conducted by command or CID, maybe both. The investigation is normally performed by an officer who was not a part of the operation."

"You mean an officer in Iraq?"

"Yes."

"How would I get a copy of any witness statements?"

Pendergrass shook his head. "You wouldn't. That

portion of the file is classified. I don't even get it."

Time to go for broke. "Then can you tell me who made the decision to reopen Beverly Ford's claim?"

Pendergrass had been militarily calm, despite his physical discomfort, up to that point. When you represent the proverbial 800-pound gorilla, there is no reason to be concerned. But now his eyes narrowed and he seemed genuinely caught off guard.

"Excuse me?"

"Can you tell me who made the decision to reopen Beverly Ford's claim?"

Pendergrass's eyes shifted to the monitor.

"You do know that the claim was reopened?" Sloane asked.

"As I said, I just rotated in." Pendergrass typed again and took longer to read the file. Sloane did not interrupt him. After a few minutes, Pendergrass picked up a pen. "I'll have to look into it. Who told you the claim was reopened?"

"Captain Robert Kessler."

Pendergrass shook his head, unfamiliar with the name.

"I just drove an hour to talk to Captain Kessler only to have him tell me he couldn't talk to me because the claim had been reopened. Wouldn't your office ordinarily make that decision?"

"Not always. Not if command or CID found out additional information warranting that the claim be reopened."

"How often does that happen?"

"I don't know."

"But you're not aware of it in this instance."

"I'm not aware of it, no."

Sloane tweaked him a bit. "Shouldn't you know?"

Pendergrass appeared to be contemplating his choice of words. "I can look into the matter and get back to you. The decision might still be coming down the chain of command."

"I'm not trying to be difficult, Captain, but I just got off the phone with Mrs. Ford, and she believed the claim had been summarily denied. This is all news to her. She's frustrated. She thinks the timing of the claim being reopened is suspicious."

"Suspicious?"

"Put yourself in her shoes. The claim lingered for months without a formal response, but when she finally hires an attorney and I try to talk to a witness, we're told the claim has been reopened and he won't talk to us. You indicated that doesn't happen often."

"I didn't say that," Pendergrass interjected.

"The family is anxious to move forward. They've authorized me to file a complaint in federal court."

Pendergrass smiled, smug. "Have you handled many military claims?"

"My first one."

"Mind if I give you a suggestion?"

"Not at all."

"You might want to consider doing some research on the Feres doctrine before you go to the expense of filing a complaint."

"The Feres doctrine?" Sloane said, playing dumb.

"It precludes a soldier or his family from filing a claim against the government or military for his injuries. I don't know the details of this case, but if Specialist Ford died in Iraq while in combat, I can tell you that Feres will apply."

"It sounds like a significant legal hurdle," Sloane said.

"Think the Great Wall of China."

Sloane already had.

SLOANE DROVE NORTH on I-5. "He didn't know the claim had been reopened. The computer still had it as closed."

"So the claims office didn't make that decision," Jenkins said.

"And whoever told Kessler either didn't tell them or didn't get to Pendergrass in time. Before I got there, he'd been sitting in a dentist's chair. He also said we'd never win in federal court, that we had no case under Feres."

"Which begs the question you asked earlier: Why reopen the claim? What are you going to do?"

Sloane smiled. "Continue poking a stick at the tiger and see if I can draw its attention. Captain Kessler won't tell me what happened over there. Maybe someone else will."

HIGHWAY 10, IRAQ

THE RADIO CRACKLED, *spitting a data burst of cryptographic information. Kessler raised a hand to quiet Cassidy's story of killing the wild boar. "Hold that thought,*

Butch." He spoke into the mouthpiece. "Alfa one-two, this is Charlie Tango Three. Say again. Over."

Ford asked, "You think it's the convoy?"

Kessler waited a beat before repeating his transmission. "Say again. Over."

More static, then a voice, the words intermittent and unclear.

"Bravo three-sixteen . . . Any . . . get . . . sage?"

Kessler waited for an "over."

"That isn't the convoy," Ford said.

Kessler agreed. "This is Alfa one-two, Bravo three-sixteen. Say again. Over."

"We're und . . . fire. Need reinf . . . Over."

Kessler looked to Ford. The three men in the backseat sat forward.

"Who is it?" Ferguson asked.

Kessler's voice remained calm. "Bravo three-sixteen, this is Alfa one-two. Say again. Over."

From the radio they heard the distinct clatter of AK-47s and the rapid three-round bursts of M16s and M4s. Then the voice shouted, causing Cassidy to flinch and jump back in his seat.

"Gun right. Gun right."

A series of explosions followed, what sounded like a hell of a firefight.

"Red on ammo . . . MASSCAL! MASSCAL . . . God-damn . . . need CASEVAC. Time: now."

Ford couldn't tell if the soldier was responding to Kessler's transmission or sending out a general transmission to anyone in the area.

Kessler responded calmly. "Bravo three-sixteen. Send your nine-line. Say again. Send your nine-line. Over."

A nine-line alerted the tactical operations center to a squad's location and advised that it needed immediate assistance.

"We're getting . . . every . . . all over."

"Bravo three-sixteen. Slow your transmission. What is your grid? Send your grid, over."

The soldier barked amidst the constant clatter of gunfire and intermittent explosions. "Grid . . . Echo. Hotel . . . five, one . . . zero, six."

Kessler pulled out his topographic map and handed it to Ford, who unfolded it in his lap. He traced the grid square, trying to map the coordinates.

"Say again, Bravo three-sixteen. Over."

The radio crackled. "Grid Echo . . . Hotel . . . zero , , , six . . zero . . . five . . . six."

Kessler repeated the coordinates to Ford. "Echo, Hotel, zero, six, zero, five, one, zero, six."

Ford scribbled them on a piece of paper, then went back to trying to map them. He knew that grids were usually eight- to ten-number sequences. "We're missing part of the grid."

Kessler was ahead of him. "Say again, Bravo three-sixteen. Say again."

The radio spit more static, followed by what sounded like a loud explosion. "Shit . . . stat report: Red. Red. Red."

Three reds meant soldiers injured or killed, weapons inoperable, and the squad seriously low on ammunition and fuel.

"Bravo three-sixteen. Send your nine-line," Kessler repeated. "Send your grids, over."

"Grid: Echo, Hotel, zero, six, zero, five, one, zero, zero, six."

Kessler removed the protractor from inside his helmet and handed it to Ford, who used the black thread tied to it to mark the distance between their location and the grid coordinates. As he did, Cassidy's arm protruded between the seats and pointed to a satellite image on the plugger mounted to the dash.

"Look."

A blue square with an X through it had suddenly appeared on the screen in damn near the exact spot Ford had traced on his topo.

"Captain?" Ford said.

"Command must know," Kessler said, confused.

"But we can get there," Ford said. "We can beat anyone else there."

But even as he spoke, Ford knew the radio was unsecured. Not only could they be driving into what sounded like a shitload of trouble, every insurgent listening had the same grid coordinates and could be rushing to kill the infidels. And visibility remained limited, perhaps twenty feet. Sand continued to blow across the road.

"Fergie, get up there and see if you can see anyone in front of us," Kessler said.

As Ferguson hurried to put back on his goggles and face gaiter, Kessler tried to raise the rest of the convoy. "Alfa one-two, this is Charlie Tango Three," he said, using his call sign. "Acknowledge, over. Alfa one-two, acknowledge, over."

No response. He transmitted again.

Fergie dropped back down the hatch. "Can't see anyone, Captain. I think they're gone already. Maybe they heard it too?"

"They're in trouble, Captain," Ford said. "We can get there."

"We have to try," Ferguson agreed.

Cassidy and Thomas remained silent.

Kessler pulled the keyboard from beneath the FBCB2, which stored communications spoken or typed with their tactical operations center. If a squad was in danger of imminent capture or otherwise had to abandon its vehicle, the commander was to hit a destruct button and burn the hard drive. Ford knew they remained a questionable distance from their FOB for their TOC to be able to contact them, especially in the storm, which was what had him puzzled about the sudden appearance of the blue X.

"Wolverine six, this is Alfa one-two. We have traffic from Bravo three-sixteen seeking immediate CASEVAC. Send guidance from higher, over."

They sat listening to the low howl of the wind.

"Captain?" Ford asked.

Kessler repeated the transmission. "Wolverine six, this is Alfa one-two. We have traffic from Bravo three-sixteen seeking immediate CASEVAC. Send guidance from higher, over."

No response.

The soldier's voice grew more urgent. The gunfire and explosions became more distinct. "We are . . . Need . . . Shit. MASS-CAL . . . Evac. Now."

Bravo was out of time. Kessler needed to make a decision.

He looked to his men. Then he shoved the keyboard back under the dash.

"Let's roll."

SEATTLE, WASHINGTON

LATE THAT AFTERNOON, Sloane stood staring out the windows of his office sipping a mug of tea and listening to Tina on the speakerphone.

"I'll let you go," she said. "You're starting to give me the 'uh-huh' routine. I should have asked for a summer house in the San Juans."

"Sorry," he said.

"Everything all right?"

"Just trying to tie up loose ends so I don't have to worry about them," he said, which was only partly true. He wanted to leave for Cabo with a clear conscience and not feel like the sword of Damocles was hanging over his head. But there was more on his mind, and while ordinarily he multitasked well, that afternoon he found himself distracted. His thoughts continued to drift to why the military had reopened Beverly Ford's claim. Maybe they were just taking another look at it, as Kannin had suggested. And if true, that was a good thing, as Beverly Ford had concluded. After all, nothing had changed to alter Sloane's opinion that this was a case he likely could not win, especially after learning that a Feres case was tried to a federal judge, and not a jury. In fact, after his meeting with Kannin, it seemed highly unlikely the military would even be interested in a settlement.

"How's Jake?"

"Excited. I just dragged him in off the beach to pack."

"Did he actually catch something?"

"No, but apparently he was using the wrong type of lure. A fisherman gave him a new one today and Jake is convinced he'll be landing fish by the dozens."

"Tell him I said good night. Don't wait up for me."

He told her he loved her and disconnected as Carolyn walked into the office.

"I've completed the proof of service." She placed a pleading down on his desk. When Sloane didn't immediately sign it, she cocked her head. "Whatever you decide to do, it better be this century or I'm stealing your Dictaphone. The stack of tapes out there is liable to fall and kill me."

"Look on the bright side," he said. "After tomorrow you'll be rid of me for a whole week."

"I've heard that before. You attorneys do more work on vacation than in the office."

"Not this attorney." He signed the pleading and handed it to her.

She turned to leave, speaking with her back to him. "And fair warning, if you come back with one of those gorgeous golden tans, I'm liable to pummel you."

He smiled and picked up the stack of mail that had accumulated while he was in trial, continuing to separate that which could wait from mail that required a more urgent response. He tossed magazines and legal newspapers in a third pile. Having maintained his California bar membership, he continued to receive California's periodicals in addition to the stack sent by the Washington bar. He was about to toss his copy of *California Lawyer* onto a toppling pile when the headline beside the face of a determined-looking attorney caught his attention. Intrigued, he flipped to the cover article, feeling his pulse quicken as he read. His eyes stopped reading when they came to an embedded box in the middle of the second page.

"Carolyn. Carolyn!"

She sauntered into his office with the bored expression of someone interrupted while doing her nails. "You bellowed?"

"I need a plane reservation," he said, continuing to read the article.

"When?"

"Tomorrow, as early as you can make it."

"You're flying to Mexico on Saturday."

He handed her the magazine. "Look this guy up. Get me an appointment to see him tomorrow, any time. Tell him I'm coming from Seattle and it's urgent. Do whatever you need to do to make it happen."

LOS ANGELES, CALIFORNIA

CAROLYN HAD DONE as instructed, getting Sloane on a 6:00 AM flight to Los Angeles. During the flight he reread the article three times, making notes on a yellow legal pad. The article profiled a Los Angeles attorney named Ken Mills. Mills had instituted a civil action on behalf of several thousand Gulf War veterans claiming a debilitating series of ailments that included chronic fatigue, skin rashes, muscle and joint pain, and memory loss. Pentagon officials conceded that some veterans had likely been exposed to chemical weapons while serving in Iraq. They had little choice. Czech chemical-detection equipment, the most sophisticated in the world, had registered mustard and sarin nerve gas near American troop bases as many as seven times during the first week of that war. Mills's suit went further, however, accusing foreign and domestic companies of supplying Iraqi president Saddam Hussein with the precursor chemicals used to create the Iraqi chemical warfare arsenal that ultimately injured the American soldiers.

The suit had progressed slowly, largely because Mills had been unable to prove which companies were responsible. Though Iraq had provided a weapons declaration to the United Nations in 1997, the UN Special Commission kept that declaration confidential, trading anonymity for the companies' voluntary cooperation. Iraq supplanted that declaration in December 2002 with an 11,800-page report to the UN Security Council, but the United States had insisted on examining that report before release, and promptly removed 8,000 pages. The four other permanent members of the council, Britain, Russia, France, and China, had also resisted revealing the extent of the foreign companies' involvement. Mills was at a dead end. Then a former UN weapons inspector traveled to Baghdad and managed to obtain an unedited copy of the declaration, a German newspaper published a list of the accused companies, and Mills was in business.

The lawsuit sought more than a billion dollars for medical expenses, lost wages, and pain and suffering, and the article indicated that figure could be just the tip of the proverbial iceberg. Of the 567,000 American troops in the Gulf War, more than 293,000 had filed claims with the Department of Veterans Affairs, and the Veterans Administration had already paid more than $1.8 billion in disability benefits. Mills argued that the American and foreign companies that had, for years, profited from Iraq's chemical and biological weapons program should share that financial burden, and their directors and officers should face criminal punishment.

As the plane taxied to the gate at LAX, Sloane called Carolyn. Mills had been out the prior afternoon and his secretary said he could not see Sloane until 11:00 AM.

"You told her it was urgent?"

"It wouldn't have mattered if I had said you were the King of England come to knight him to Arthur's Round Table," Carolyn told him. "It was eleven or nothing. His secretary was one of those perky types. If she said 'I'm sorry, those are Mr. Mills's rules' one more time I was going to fly down there and steal her peroxide."

SLOANE KILLED TIME drinking a cup of coffee at an outdoor table in Santa Monica's Third Street Promenade, a three-city-block mall, which was like sitting in the front row at a theater performance. Though raised in foster homes throughout the San Fernando Valley, Sloane had spent little time in Southern California since enlisting in the Marine Corps at seventeen. Coming back never felt like coming home. It felt like being a tourist at a theme park. Everyone, it seemed, had a healthy tan, toned body, and flashed the perfect smile for a chewing gum or toothpaste commercial.

Growing up, Sloane felt something of substance was missing from his surroundings, but soon realized what was missing had nothing to do with the scenery. As he got older, a hole began to develop inside of him that he could not fill. He had never been abused in any of the foster homes, but he also had never been loved. No one tucked him in at night or gave him a hug. When he brought home his report card, nobody patted him on the back for a job well done. Athletic, he played both basketball and baseball in high school, but no one sat in the stands watching with pride and joy. No one waited for him outside the locker room. He had friends, and an occasional girlfriend, but he wasn't often invited to homes and he sensed when he met parents that they were wary of him, like a stray dog. Not knowing his background, they had no way to judge his temperament, and he wasn't of much help.

"Where were you born, David?"

"I don't know, sir."

"Did you know your parents?"

"No, sir, I didn't."

"No relatives? What about grandparents or aunts and uncles?"

"No, sir, I've never met any."

"Rebecca says your parents died in a car crash."

"I really wasn't old enough to remember it."

"Well, Rebecca says you're a fine basketball player."

"I try, sir."

At that point the father would usually hand his daughter a quarter. "Call me if you need to. I'll be up waiting for you."

Sloane had contemplated trying to find his biological parents, but when he was young, he had no money to pursue the matter, and when he did have the money, he decided he didn't want to know. They had not wanted him and had made no effort to contact him. Sometimes it was best to let matters lie. At Foster & Bane he'd settled into a routine of work, taking comfort in his successes, and trying not to think too often about things he could not control. Then Joe Branick's package turned everything inside out and upside down. Sloane could no longer sit back, passive. He needed to know why Branick had sent him the information, including his true identity. But meeting his father, Miguel Ibarón, had only widened the hole.

"You used me, and your abuse killed my mother and all those people in the village that night. Because of me those men came and killed everyone, and they may just as well have killed me, because for the past thirty years I might as well have been dead."

"You had the power," his father had said.

"I was your son. You were supposed to be my father. You were supposed to protect me, to take care of me. But you used me to pursue your hatred and politics."

"God gave you a gift, a wonderful gift. You were the instrument to bring the people out of centuries of oppression and poverty. You were to deliver the Mexican people from so much misery, so much pain and suffering."

"And instead I've only caused them more."

AT QUARTER TO eleven, Sloane left a tip on the table under a saucer and walked through the Promenade to a black slate high-rise at the corner of Third Avenue and Wilshire Boulevard. He pulled open the glass doors and crossed the lobby. The guard standing behind a security console asked him for photo ID and slid a clipboard and pen at him. Then he picked up the phone.

"I have a David Sloane here to see Ken Mills."

Sloane considered the alphabetical list of businesses beneath the glass but did not see "The Law Offices of Ken Mills." The guard hung up, handed Sloane back his license, and came around the console to step to the elevator bank, inserting a key into a lock on the wall. The elevator doors pulled apart.

"Are the elevators always locked?" Sloane asked, thinking it unusual to lock down the elevators in a public building during regular business hours.

The guard held the door as Sloane stepped in. "Just the lobby."

"I don't know the floor or suite," Sloane said.

"Ninth floor. Take a left off the elevator and a right down the hall. It's the third door on your right."

Stepping from the elevator on the ninth floor, Sloane again noted no sign on the wall identifying the companies in the various suites. He followed the guard's directions to an unmarked door. When he stepped in, two men in jeans and tight-fitting polo shirts stood in the reception area.

"David Sloane?" The recessed lights reflected off the man's shaved head. "Do you have some identification, please?"

"I just showed my identification to the guard downstairs."

"We'll need to see it again."

Sloane tried to keep it light. "Do you think I changed identities in the elevator?"

Neither man smiled. Sloane flipped open his wallet and showed them his license.

"Are you carrying any weapons?" the bald man asked.

"Weapons? No. Should I be?" Again, his attempt at humor elicited no response.

The second man, whose hair looked to be the product of the bad peroxide job Carolyn spoke of, asked, "May we search your briefcase?" It didn't sound like a request.

Sloane handed the briefcase to him. "Is all this really necessary?"

"It is if you want to see Mr. Mills."

Sloane did, which was why he also tolerated a pat down. He retrieved his briefcase and followed the bald man past an empty reception desk to a closed door at the end of the hall. The man knocked twice and pushed open the door. For an instant Sloane wondered if Carolyn had screwed up: The man getting up from behind the futuristic glass and tube desk looked nothing like the ball-busting attorney on the cover of *California Lawyer* with the no-nonsense expression. He looked tired, haggard, like a slightly overweight actor in an indigestion commercial with a thinning hairline. Dark bags sagged beneath his eyes.

"You have an awful lot of security, Mr. Mills."

Mills's smile had the sad quality of someone greeting guests at a funeral. "I'm sorry about the inconvenience. I needed to be sure you were who your secretary said."

"Who else would I be?" Sloane asked.

"Someone trying to kill me."

CHAPTER
FIVE

CAMANO ISLAND, WASHINGTON

Charles Jenkins leaned on a garden hoe and contemplated the square patch of dirt where he had planted his vegetable garden every year for the past thirty-two years. Though it remained too early to plant, it was not too early to pull the weeds, turn over the soil, and cover it with black plastic to "cook." In years past he would have taken to the task with vigor. In years past he would have looked forward to it. In years past he didn't have a beautiful, twenty-eight-year-old woman living with him.

He looked across the field to the house he had rebuilt from the foundation up. After the fire that destroyed the four-room caretaker's shack that he had lived in for thirty years, Jenkins had debated whether to rebuild at all. The ten-acre parcel wasn't exactly the happy home of his youth. The property had largely been his escape from the world, and likely would have remained so had Joe Branick not sent Alex to deliver a file Jenkins long believed had been destroyed. Just seeing the package after so many years had taken his breath away.

"*Where did you get this?*"

"*I told you. Joe Branick gave it to me—*"

"*How did you know him?*"

"*How?*"

"*Tell me. How did you know him?*"

"*He was a friend of my father.*"

And that had triggered another recollection, one of a young girl with cascading dark curls riding her bike in the driveway of a family home in a wealthy suburb of Mexico City. Alex Hart's father had been an expert on Mexican politics, history, and revolutionary groups, and Jenkins and Joe Branick had consulted him often trying to determine the identity of el Profeta, the man believed to be behind much of the uprising in Mexico's southern states. Unfortunately, Jenkins and Alex didn't get the chance to reminisce for long. She had not only brought Jenkins the file, she had also, unwittingly, brought the men whose job it was to recover and destroy it. Jenkins and Alex had managed to escape, but not before the men had burned his home to the ground and killed his two Rhodesian ridgebacks, Lou and Arnold.

Inside the manila package were the reports Jenkins had generated each time he slipped into the village in the mountains of Oaxaca to hear the young boy speak. Speculation was that el Profeta was using the boy to stir the uprising, and that determining the boy's identity would eventually lead them to the man. They never got that far. The sermons had been mesmerizing; the crowds listened as if viewing a revered actor on a Broadway stage. Even Jenkins had found the boy's sermons intoxicating. And that had been the problem. His reports had been too believable, too convincing; the boy became more than just a boy. He became a threat. Jenkins never could shake the guilt that his reports had been responsible for the loss of so many lives in that village—men, women, and children, so many children. For thirty years he had been unable to forgive himself.

Sloane's forgiveness when the two men first met was the initial step to his healing.

"I was responsible," Jenkins had said that night. "My reports convinced them you were a threat. It was the reason they came to the village that night."

But Sloane had only shaken his head. "No. The man responsible was the man who sent me out to preach his hatred. You know who he is, don't you? He was my father, wasn't he?"

Still, forgiving himself and learning to love again were two different things. Jenkins had questioned whether it could ever really work between him and Alex. It wasn't just the discrepancy in their ages; it was whether he could ever truly live in the present and forget the past. The healing had not been immediate. After Alex came to live with him, they had some rocky moments, but in time she had given him hope that, at fifty-three, he could forget the sins he had committed, and replace them with new memories created with her.

Alex had convinced him that the property was too beautiful *not* to rebuild. Then she designed their new home, adding a second story with three bedrooms, an indication she wanted to expand more than just the square footage. She wanted a family. She had also reconfigured the downstairs. What had been Jenkins's bedroom became a library with built-in shelving to encourage him to rebuild his collection of classic books and movies lost in the fire. But as with his vegetable garden, Jenkins no longer had the same motivation; the books and movies had also kept him living in the past.

He was ready for the present.

After rebuilding, he'd started to feel a bit like Tom Hanks in the movie *Cast Away*, a man stranded on an island wanting to get back to civilization. David had provided him that opportunity.

When Sloane moved to Seattle to be with Tina, Jenkins invited them to a barbecue to celebrate the grand reopening of Chateau Jenkins, and the two men became reacquainted sitting outside on the deck smoking cigars.

"It must have been a lot of work," Sloane had said, considering the house.

Jenkins nodded. "It kept me busy."

"What are you going to do now?"

"What do you mean?"

"With your free time."

Jenkins shrugged. "Hadn't thought about it. Why?"

"Nothing. Forget it."

"Forget what?"

"You wouldn't be interested."

"Why don't you let me decide what I might be interested in?"

"I need to talk to a number of illegal immigrants who once worked at a Pacific Northwest Paper plant."

"You need someone to find them."

"Let's just drop it. These guys disappear. They travel through tiny communities in eastern Washington and move with the planting seasons. I'm told they rarely maintain an address long. You're busy."

"You don't think I could find them?"

"Maybe you could just find me someone—you know, like a private investigator."

"Three days."

"What?"

"If I don't find them in three days, all of them, you don't owe me a dime."

Jenkins had found all four men in two days. He also knew Sloane had offered him the job because Alex convinced him that Jenkins was bored and in need of something to do. He was, and just being off his island had helped Jenkins to further bury the sins of his past, perhaps in a shallow grave, but buried nonetheless.

A dog's bark aroused him from his thoughts. Sam bounded through the tall grass barking at the two recently purchased Appaloosas. Alex had expressed interest in a horseback trip that retraced Chief Joseph's failed flight from the U.S. Cavalry to Canada, and Appaloosas were a requirement to participate. Initially, Jenkins had leased them from an elderly woman who owned a ranch two hours east of Seattle in Ellensburg, a thousand-acre spread, complete with four houses and a private landing strip. Alex had enjoyed the ride so much they bought the horses for future years, and brought them back to Camano, which hadn't sat well with the two Arabians he'd boarded for ten years.

Jenkins considered his watch and dropped the hoe, uninterested in the garden. Halfway across the field to the house Sam appeared at his side, panting, tongue hanging from the side of her mouth. He walked up to the porch, removed his shoes, pulled open the door and glided across the freshly waxed hardwood. In the kitchen he filled Sam's bowl with breakfast and took it back outside onto the porch. She stuck her head in the dish before he'd even removed his hand, her jowls flapping furiously. Finished, she looked up with sad brown eyes as if to ask, Is that it?

Jenkins never recalled Lou or Arnold melting his heart with a look, but Sam could get him to do just about anything with her sad-eyed, droopy-eared face. Maybe it was a female thing.

"I can sympathize," he said. Alex had them all on diets. She'd cut Sam's meals in half.

Jenkins looked through the plate-glass window before reaching into his pocket for the bone-shaped doggy treat. He kept the biscuits hidden in his office drawer, but always carried a couple in his coat pocket. Sam hesitated.

"Don't tell," Jenkins whispered. "We'll both get in trouble."

She stretched out her neck and gently took the treat from his hand, then trotted off around the side of the house.

Jenkins checked the time on his cell phone, pulled the scrap of paper from his pocket, and punched in the number. It rang twice.

"Shirley? It's Charles Jenkins."

When Shirley didn't immediately respond in her chipper-as-a-bird tone, Jenkins sensed trouble. "I don't know who you are, Mr. Jenkins, but I know you don't work for the *Times*," she said curtly. "I called this morning and—"

"The *Times*? Shirley, I don't work for the *Times*."

"I thought that—"

"I work for the *Post-Intelligencer*," he said, indicating the second of Seattle's two daily newspapers. He could have used other means to find the National Guardsmen who had served with James Ford, but sometimes the best source was the easiest source. Shirley worked in the National Guard's public affairs office. Up to that point she had been willing and helpful.

"But I thought you said—"

"A lot of people make that mistake. Listen, I don't want to cause you any concern or get you in any trouble. Here's the number of my editor in the newsroom. Why don't you call?"

"Oh, I don't think—"

"I insist." Jenkins provided the number and the name of his editor. "Call and confirm. Then call me back, okay?"

He hung up and hurried inside the house, climbing the stairs. "Alex? Alex?" Halfway up, he heard Alex's cell phone ring. At the top of the stairs he heard the water for the shower. He grabbed her phone from the nightstand and pushed open the bathroom door, fanning the steam. "Alex?"

"Shut the door. You're letting all the hot air out."

Jenkins pulled back the curtain. She was massaging a head of shampoo. Suds dripped down her forearms and elbows. Ordinarily he wouldn't have even noticed the shampoo. "You're the news editor at the *P.I.* and I'm working on an assignment about national guardsmen injured in Iraq."

"What?"

"News editor. *P.I.* National Guard. Iraq." He flipped open her phone and held it up for her.

"I've got soap in my eye," she whispered.

Jenkins shook the phone at her.

She stuck her head out the curtain, one eye shut tight. "News Desk, Hart." She made circles with her hand indicating she wanted Shirley to get to the point. "Yes, he works here." She started to wiggle, the soap burning. She spoke quickly. "It's a feature piece about Washington national guardsmen injured or killed in Iraq. We're going to run it front page."

Jenkins covered the receiver. "Don't oversell it."

She gave him a one-eyed "If looks could kill you'd be dead" stare. He put the phone back to her ear.

"Yes, we're very excited about the project. What? Oh, yes, it is raining here. It's not? Well, it must be coming your way. There's my other line. If you have any questions please feel free to call back."

Jenkins flipped closed the phone just before Alex screamed and buried her face in the streams of water. By the time he reached the bottom of the staircase his cell phone rang.

SANTA MONICA, CALIFORNIA

BEING IN LOS Angeles, it would have been easy for Sloane to conclude that Ken Mills received some perverse pleasure from making himself appear important enough that someone would want to kill him, but Mills had spoken the words without melodrama or theatrics.

"Who would want to kill you?" Sloane asked.

Mills gestured to one of two black mesh chairs shaped like pears, and returned to his desk. The office was spacious, a small conference table in one corner, a black leather couch along the wall. Despite the office's being on the west end of the building, presumably with a million-dollar view of the Santa Monica Pier and the Pacific Ocean, the blinds were down.

Mills sat. "After the news articles and television reports about the lawsuit, I started to receive hate mail and telephone calls—people calling me an unpatriotic terrorist sympathizer. I'll spare you the four-letter words. Those we pretty much dismissed as the crazies. When I began receiving death threats at home, the FBI told me to get an unlisted number. It got so bad I had to pull my two daughters from school and send them and my wife out of the area."

"And you hired private security," Sloane said.

"I don't go to the bathroom now without an escort. When they inspected my house they found bugs everywhere, my bedroom, the bathrooms, the phones, my car." He opened his desk drawer and pulled out a black spherical object about the size of a quarter. "This one we found above a ceiling tile in the men's room down the hall. They sweep the office every morning and use a device to scramble my conversations in case anyone is pointing a directional microphone at the windows."

Sloane looked at the closed blinds and realized that the same people who could point a directional microphone could point something far more lethal. No wonder the guy looked uncomfortable. "And you believe it's because of the lawsuit on behalf of the veterans?"

Mills shook his head. "I filed that lawsuit nearly two years ago. The threats didn't start until I named the corporations that did business with Saddam. How much do you know about our history in Iraq, Mr. Sloane?"

"A fair bit."

"Then you know more than most Americans." Mills paused, as if considering where to begin. His voice took on a professorial tone, comfortable with the subject matter. "Iraq started batch production of chemical agents in the 1980s, relying heavily on precursor chemicals from foreign suppliers. Any guesses which countries supplied those chemicals?"

"The ones that made up the UN Security Council. I read the article."

Mills drummed his fingers on his desk. "I know it's hard to imagine now, but back then it was politically and militarily advantageous to use Iraq as an ally against a mutual enemy."

"The Ayatollah Khomeini," Sloane said. "'The enemy of my enemy is my friend.'"

Mills nodded. "We chose Saddam's despotism over the Islamic fundamentalists who had overthrown the Pahlavi monarchy. Our defense intelligence feared that if Iraq fell, it would have a catastrophic effect on the entire region, including Saudi Arabia. So President Reagan sent an envoy to Baghdad. You might recall seeing pictures of that person shaking hands with Saddam."

Not at the time, but Sloane had seen the picture in the article profiling Mills. "Donald Rumsfeld."

"Ironic, isn't it?"

"We chose the lesser of two evils," Sloane said.

"We really had no choice. We didn't have anything to interest the Islamic extremists—they hate us just to hate us. But when Iraq invaded Iran we had something Iraq needed."

"Weapons," Sloane said.

"Reagan directed the State Department to remove Iraq from its list of state sponsors of terrorism and was committed to doing whatever was necessary for Iraq to win that war. The Centers for Disease Control sent samples of every germ strain we had. And between 1985 and 1989, the Commerce Department licensed seventy biological exports, including at least twenty-one batches of the lethal strains of anthrax. American and other foreign companies were also allowed to sell weapons directly to Iraq or through intermediaries, and to funnel unreported loans used to buy the chemicals. Daily intelligence reports confirmed the weapons and chemical shipments, and there is evidence the CIA helped coordinate attacks on Iranian troops."

"Chemical attacks?"

"The Pentagon viewed the use of chemicals as just another way for Iraq to achieve its military objectives. They didn't envision those chemicals someday injuring American soldiers."

"What can you tell me about the companies that supplied the chemicals?" Sloane asked.

Mills shrugged. "More than one hundred and fifty total, with about half being American, are suspected to have supplied the basic building components and technical knowledge Iraq needed to develop nuclear, chemical, and biological weapons. UN weapons inspectors confirmed the chemicals to be part of Iraq's biological weapons program."

Mills handed Sloane a 1994 document bearing the imprint of the U.S. Senate Committee on Banking, Housing, and Urban Affairs. "Another Senate inquiry concluded that the precursor chemicals provided by U.S. manufacturers were likely the same chemicals used against U.S. troops and largely responsible for the illness known as Gulf War syndrome." Mills opened his palms toward the ceiling and shrugged. "What more do I need?"

"The magazine article indicates there's evidence some companies continued to illegally supply chemicals after the Gulf War."

Mills nodded. "Iraq was forbidden to develop chemical weapons. Yet between 1991 and 1996 the UN Special Commission uncovered a massive biological and nuclear weapons program. Documents have since revealed that the Iraqi government continued to purchase very large quantities of precursor chemicals and cultures from foreign companies."

"How could those companies get away with it?"

Mills explained a complicated system in which the chemicals were sold through intermediaries in Syria and Jordan with the money to pay for the chemicals coming from Iraqi oil sales. When he had finished he said, "Your secretary said you represent the family of a national guardsman killed over there. Why would you be interested in Gulf War syndrome?"

Sloane removed the magazine from his briefcase, flipped it to the dog-eared page with the embedded box, and handed it to Mills. "I'm not. I'm interested in one of the companies on your list."

KEN MILLS SIFTED through the alphabetically organized folders. The folder for Argus International was near the front of the box, three inches thick, not including public documents from the SEC and other government permitting agencies.

"They're in your neck of the woods," Mills said.

"I've been there."

Despite becoming one of the world's largest chemical manufacturers, Argus had maintained its headquarters in Old Nisqually, Washington, where Houghton Park Sr. had established the company fifty years earlier. Sloane thought it made sense. The property taxes were probably minimal, and as Jenkins had said, it certainly helped security when your business buttressed a huge military base.

Mills stood at Sloane's side as he flipped through the file. "Of all the companies, they appear the most discreet."

"Any thoughts why?" Sloane asked.

"The American public isn't exactly enamored with this war. That makes Northrup a natural target; every watchdog organization out there wants a crack at him. If Argus illegally shipped chemicals while he was president of the company, the ramifications would be a public relations nightmare for both the administration and Argus, not to mention financially catastrophic. We're talking about the potential loss of billions of dollars in existing contracts, and Argus would bear the brunt of any legal judgment because so many of the other companies listed in the report are either bankrupt or no longer in business."

Further documents in the file indicated that between 1988 and 2002, Argus received more than $10 billion in government contracts. "Looks like they can afford it," Sloane said.

"Maybe," Mills said. "But let me tell you, nothing makes a Harvard-educated businessman's ass pucker quite like the thought that he could go to jail. These aren't Enron-type crimes. We're not talking about the loss of retiree nest eggs. If Argus is implicated, they're potentially responsible for the loss of American lives. Think about it. Whose chemicals were we looking for?"

Sloane focused his attention on a list of current and former Argus executives. It read like a who's who of the president's current administration as well as of former administrations. Argus did not discriminate between Republicans and Democrats.

"So what's your connection to Argus?" Mills asked.

Sloane looked up from the documents. "The current head of its security forces in Iraq is the captain who led the mission the night my client's husband was shot. It may be nothing, but there have been a series of odd coincidences, and I'm not a big believer in coincidences."

Mills frowned. "Neither am I. Not anymore. I don't want to alarm you, but the security company I'm working with said Argus is known to hire Special Forces types, soldiers highly trained and skilled in covert activities."

"I know," Sloane said. "I've seen their operation."

"Then let me impress this upon you. If things continue to seem out of the ordinary, don't be a hero, and don't downplay it. Call the FBI."

"What did they say, other than to hire security?"

"The first thing they said was to protect the people I love."

SLOANE STEPPED FROM the elevator and walked across the building lobby with his cell phone pressed to his ear. Outside the building he struggled to hear over the traffic on Wilshire Boulevard.

Tina's cell phone rang through to her voice mail. Frustrated, he hung up without leaving a message. There was no point. She never listened to her messages. She only checked the call log. Sloane paced the sidewalk, waiting for his cab. Maybe it was better she hadn't answered. What would he have said? "How are things going? Notice anything unusual?"

He flipped open the phone and tried again. No answer. "Damn."

Speculating would only cause her alarm, and after what she had been through just two years earlier, abducted from a San Francisco street and held at knifepoint as ransom until Sloane returned the package Joe Branick had sent to him, she was liable to take Jake and leave.

He spotted his cab, hailed it to the curb, and climbed in. "LAX." Inside, he called his office. Carolyn had him booked on a three-o'clock flight.

"Can you make it?" she asked

It would be close, but a three-o'clock flight, barring any delays, would put him at Sea-Tac by 5:30. With luck he could be home by six. Tina and Jake would get home around four. That left them alone for two hours. "I'll make it," he told Carolyn. "Thanks. See you in a week."
Sloane disconnected and dialed a second number.

Charles Jenkins answered his phone on the second ring. "What did you find out?"

"Too much to explain over the phone. I'm on my way to the airport. How quickly can you get to my house?"

"Half an hour, why?"

"I don't want Tina and Jake alone. Make up an excuse to be there."

"What am I looking for?"

"Anything out of the ordinary," he said. "Sweep the house for bugs."

"Sweep it with what?"

"I don't know. Look for things."

"Argus?" Jenkins asked.

"I think so."

Sloane hung up the phone and asked the cabdriver to hurry. He sat back envisioning himself poking a stick at a tiger through the bars of a cage. Then the tiger grew angry, lunged, and snapped the stick off in his hand.

SLOANE DEPLANED AT Sea-Tac Airport, phone in hand. The flight had felt like the longest of his life.

"All's quiet," Jenkins said. "Jake's fishing and Alex took Tina for a walk along the beach to give me a chance to go over the house. It's clean from what I can tell. You want to tell me what has you so freaked?"

Sloane let out a sigh. "I'll be home in fifteen minutes. We can talk then."

THREE TREE POINT, WASHINGTON

CARS FILLED THE public easement—fisher-men who'd come to fish off the beach at sunset. Sloane double-parked behind a van he recognized as belonging to a company that brought scuba divers to the Point. He hurried up the porch steps, calling out as he entered the kitchen.

"Anybody home?"

"We're out here," Tina replied.

Tina and Alex sat in the wicker chairs on the sunporch, two glasses of white wine on the table. Sloane tossed his coat on the couch in the living room and walked onto the porch, greeting Alex first.

"This is a nice surprise. What brings you here?" He hoped he sounded genuine.

Alex flipped the dark curls from her shoulder. "You know me. I'm always up for coming to civilization to do a little shopping."

"Did you find anything?" he asked.

She shook her head. "No. Not a thing."

"Where's Charlie?"

"Just went to get another tank of propane," Tina said. "We want to barbecue."

He kissed her. "Where have you been? I called earlier."

Her face brightened. "I have good news. I wanted to tell you in person."

He wrapped his arms around her waist. "So tell me. I could use some good news."

Alex stood. "I think that's my cue to check on the coals."

"It's propane," Sloane said.

"Whatever." She picked up her glass and walked out, letting the screen door slap closed behind her.

"So tell me," Sloane said.

Tina pressed closer. He felt the curves of her body. She laughed. "I can feel your heart pounding. Relax. I'm not pregnant."

He took an exaggerated breath. "Whew!"

She punched his chest. "Stop."

"Okay," he said. "Start over. What's the good news?"

"You remember that design I was doing for the building retrofit in Des Moines?"

"You got it?"

She punched him again. "Don't spoil it."

"Sorry." He cleared his throat for a dramatic pause. "Yes, I remember the design for the building retrofit in Des Moines."

"Well, I got it."

"That's great—that's your first big job. You're right, we need to celebrate. How about a trip to Cabo? We'll leave tomorrow."

She punched him again and pulled away. "Fine. Be that way."

"I'm kidding. You know I'm happy for you. Tell me about it."

"They loved my use of the existing space and my idea for a glass entry to take advantage of the southern exposure."

"I knew you'd get it. You worked hard on that building."

"And that's not the only thing we'll be celebrating," she said. She laughed. "You deserved that. From the look on your face you'd think I told you I'm expecting triplets."

"Hey, a man can only take so much good news in one day."

"Uh-huh, sure." She picked up her wineglass.

"So what else are we celebrating?"

"I promised I wouldn't say, but Jake has something to show you."

"He caught a fish!"

Her eyes widened and she made another fist, causing him to flinch. "Don't spoil it. Act surprised."

"He really caught one?"

"A king. And it's *big*, so make a big deal about it. We're having fresh salmon for dinner. You're grilling it."

"So the new lure actually worked?"

"Looks that way." She headed for the kitchen. "I'm going to make a salad. Bring him and the fish up. He's dying to see the guts."

Sloane stepped outside. Alex stood with her back to the house as if enjoying the view. The cloud layer had calmed the wind; the gray waters of the Sound lapped lazily onto the beach and a seagull mewed from its perch on a neighbor's roof.

"Thanks for coming down," he said.

"No problem."

"Everything okay?"

She took a sip of wine and pointed out at the parade of boats on the water. "Charlie says everything is clean as far as a visual will tell us. When he comes back with the propane, he'll check your car. I haven't noticed anything out of the ordinary."

Sloane let out a breath. "I guess I got a bit paranoid."

"Better safe than sorry."

"I'll explain more later; right now I need to go act surprised at a fish."

"It really is *big*," Alex said.

Jake stood at the water's edge twenty yards down the beach, but this time his head swiveled as Sloane approached, which meant he'd been watching for him.

"David!" The boy nearly dropped his pole, realized he still had a line in the water, and jammed the rod into the rocks, using a bigger stone to keep it upright.

"How're they biting, Hemingway?"

Jake shrugged, hiding a grin. "Oh, you know, a nibble here and there."

Sloane played along. "Well, like I said, you have to have patience. Only the really experienced fishermen land the big fish."

Jake nodded. Then he burst. "Then that would be me!" He dropped to his knees in the rocks and pulled off the top of the cooler. He'd packed the salmon in ice. Its tail bent up the side. "Can you believe it?"

Sloane squatted. "My God, it's huge!"

"I felt it hit, and when I pulled back, I knew I had him. My pole was bending so far I thought it was going to break in half. But I didn't panic. I just let him take the line. Then I started reeling him in, but not too fast. I played with him and let him have his runs to tire him out."

The boy's knowledge amazed Sloane. "How long did it take to land him?"

"About twenty minutes. Mr. Williams used his net when I got him close, but only after I got him in." Jake pointed to the man fishing just down the beach, who acknowledged Sloane with a wave. "He said we've been using the wrong spinners."

"Your mother told me."

"The kings like the pink ones, not the green ones. And you have to put a piece of herring on the hook. He hit on my third cast. Can you believe it? Mr. Williams coached me on how to bring him in." Jake rushed to add, "But I did it all by myself. He didn't reel at all."

"I'm really proud of you."

"There must be a run going on," Jake said. "I'm going to get up early and fish."

"We leave for Cabo tomorrow morning."

The boy's face brightened. "We're going to catch so many fish," he said.

"Hey, you two!" Tina shouted to them from the lawn and waved her arms. "Are we eating salmon tonight or not?"

"I have to bring the fish up to Mom." Jake stood and hefted the cooler. "She's going to let me clean it. You want to watch?"

Sloane nodded. "What self-respecting guy wouldn't want to see fish guts?"

Jake started up the beach, stopped. "My pole."

"You go ahead. I'll reel it in and bring it up."

"Thanks, David." The boy did a duck walk carrying the heavy cooler between his legs. He set the cooler on the driftwood logs and yelled back down the beach. "Bye, Mr. Williams. Thank you."

The man smiled and waved. "Maybe I'll see you tomorrow, Jake."

"That would be great," Jake said, his joy apparently making him forget that he'd be on a plane to Cabo.

Sloane picked up the pole and reeled in the line until he felt it snag.

"Jerk it straight back." The fisherman approached. "Just give it a quick tug toward you." Sloane jerked the line, felt the lure pop free, and continued reeling. "It settles to the bottom when you stop reeling. Most people make the mistake of pulling to the side, but with multiple hooks it just sets the snag."

"He's sure excited." Sloane looked up the beach as Jake disappeared behind the hedge. "That's his first big fish."

The man focused on the water, deliberately reeling. He wore a green fly-fishing vest with multiple pockets and a floppy hat. "He's a nice kid. I enjoy his company. Most kids that age just grunt at an adult."

"I'll let his mother know. She's the guiding force."

Mr. Williams pulled in his line, cleaned seaweed from the pink buzz bomb, and checked the piece of herring hanging from the three-pronged hook. "He was using the wrong color. The kings like pink this time of year. Don't ask me why, though."

"Can I pay you for it?" Sloane offered.

The man flicked the pole back over his shoulder and snapped it forward. The reel hummed as the spinner shot through the air, ending with a plunk thirty yards offshore. He let it sink a moment before reeling in. "Forget about it. It was worth it just to see the look on his face. Reminded me of when I caught my first fish."

"Are you from around here?"

"Me? I grew up in Minnesota. We used to have to cut holes in the ice to fish."

"Well, I better get up and learn how to clean one. Looks like he might be catching more. Thanks again." He turned and started up the beach.

"Not a problem. You have a nice family, Mr. Sloane."

Sloane stopped, turned. Tina had taken his last name, but Jake had kept his biological father's name. "How did you know my name?"

The man continued to reel.

"How do you know my name?"

"I know a lot of things, Mr. Sloane: How to fish. Your name. Jake's name. Tina's name."

"Who are you?"

The man glanced up the beach in the direction that Jake had departed. "Me? You heard Jake. I'm Mr. Williams."

"Who the hell are you?"

The spinner came out of the water twirling and swaying like a pendulum.

"Who the hell—"

Mr. Williams calmly pulled a knife from his vest, snapping the blade open with a flick of his wrist. Sloane stopped. The man grabbed the lure, cut free the seaweed and piece of herring, and threw both into the water. Two seagulls descended quickly to fight for the scrap of fish.

"No luck today. Not for fish anyway." He snapped closed the knife and calmly fastened the hook on one of the pole's eyeholes, bending the tip slightly. Then he looked at Sloane. "Guess I'll have to come back."

"Don't even think about it."

Mr. Williams smiled. "That's not very neighborly, Mr. Sloane." He looked up and down the beach. "Public beach. Public access. Public water. Nothing private about it as far as I can tell. No way to keep me—or anyone else—out." He redirected his focus to Sloane. "You think about that. And you remember that it's just as easy for someone to find out information about you, and your family, as it is for you to find out information about them."

He stepped past Sloane, his boots making a crunching sound in the rocks. The sound stopped. Sloane turned. Mr. Williams stood atop the cement wall at the entrance to the easement, looking down at him.

"Enjoy the fish." He touched the brim of his floppy hat and walked off.

Sloane bent and put his hands on his knees fighting a sudden gag reflex, taking measured breaths. When he stood he felt the cool breeze off the water on his forehead and wiped at beads of perspiration.

Your name. Jake's name. Tina's name.

He hurried up the beach, stepped over the logs, crossed the lawn, and pushed through the screen door into the kitchen.

Tina stood at the counter holding a large meat cleaver, about to cut off the fish's head. She looked up at him. "What's the matter? You're pale as a ghost."

He couldn't answer. Ken Mills's voice echoed inside his head.

The first thing they said was to protect the people I love.

TINA QUIETLY CLOSED the door to Jake's bedroom and walked past Sloane, who stood at the top of the stairs.

"How is he?"

Sloane followed her into their bedroom and closed the door behind him. The soft light from the wall sconce spilled across the down comforter where Bud lay curled in a black ball, sleeping. Tina stood at the edge of the bed, folding clothes for their trip. Given the way she was throwing them into her suitcase, they'd have to be refolded.

"Tina, I didn't—"

"You lied to me." She tossed a T-shirt onto the bed.

"I didn't lie."

He walked to the armoire, opened it, turned on the stereo.

She looked up at him. "We can't even talk in our own home now?" She shook her head. "Don't play semantics with me. Withholding information is the same as not telling me the truth. You embarrassed me in front of Alex and Charlie. I feel like an idiot."

"I'm sorry. I didn't want to—"

She stopped folding a pair of shorts. "What? Didn't want to *what*? Upset me? And this is better?"

Sloane rubbed the back of his neck. "I didn't know what I was dealing with. I still don't."

"Then why did you ask Alex and Charlie to come here? Why does Alex have one gun strapped to her ankle and another one inside her jacket?" She threw a pair of

Jake's pants on the floor, hands on her hips. "What do you know? How bad is it?"

He realized now that he'd been wrong to keep the information from her, but this was all new to him. He had never had to worry about anyone else before. All his life the only person he'd had to take care of was himself. Then, in Ken Mills's office, he'd realized that was no longer the case. Standing on the beach, hearing Mr. Williams threaten Tina and Jake, knowing that the man had been to the beach on several occasions, had left Sloane horrified. He felt helpless and frustrated. The man was right. Sloane couldn't protect them, not forever.

"Tell me what you do know," Tina repeated.

Sloane started with his meeting with Robert Kessler and continued through his trip to Los Angeles to meet with Ken Mills. "Once he went public with the names of the companies, he began to receive threats. He had to send his family away. I knew I couldn't get home before you, so I asked Charlie to come down. I thought it would be less . . . What's wrong?"

Tina had paled and slumped to the bed, a hand to her throat.

"What's the matter?"

"The man on the beach . . ." She covered her mouth as if she might throw up. "He could have just taken him. He could have just taken Jake."

Sloane went to her. "I'm not going to let that happen, not ever again."

She pushed past him. "But you weren't here. You weren't there," she said, and he didn't know if she meant today, or two years ago in San Francisco when she had been home alone in her flat, packing to prepare for the move to the Northwest, and the men broke into her house. She had managed to escape outside, even to run to what she thought was a police car, only to find out it was not. The men had drugged her and flown her back to West Virginia. There, Colonel Parker Madsen, the former White House chief of staff and leader of a black-ops force, had held her for ransom until Sloane agreed to meet to return the file Joe Branick sent to him.

On the same West Virginia bluff where Sloane had met Charles Jenkins, Tina had endured the trauma of seemingly watching Sloane die, shot in the chest. But unlike in Grenada, Sloane had worn a protective vest that night, and it had allowed him to do what he could not do for his mother, to save Tina.

"Why didn't you tell me?" Tina asked.

He struggled to find the words. "I don't know."

"That's not good enough, David. I'm your wife."

"I'm sorry," he said. "I just don't know."

CHAPTER SIX

James Ford stepped lightly, a difficult task wearing combat boots. The paper star hung in the corner of the bedroom emitting a soft pink light to ward off monsters. He picked up the tiny articles of clothing from the floor, placed them on the end of the yellow bedspread, and bent to tuck in his daughter.

Althea's eyes popped open. "Hello, Daddy." She giggled, delighted to have fooled him.

"What are you doing awake so early, angel?" He had wanted to kiss her forehead and leave quickly, without waking her. He had wanted to avoid this.

"If I'm awake, then you can't leave."

"Who told you that?"

"You did. You said last night that when I woke up, you'd be gone. So I never went to sleep. Now you can't leave."

Ford felt a lump in his throat. "I wish that were true, angel."

Althea scrunched her face and grabbed hold of his beige uniform. "I don't want you to go."

"It's my job, honey."

"You're a schoolteacher."

"It's my duty. I signed up."

"Unsign."

"I made a commitment," he said. "And you know what we say. We Fords honor our commitments."

"It's a matter of the principal," she said.

"That's right. It's a matter of principle."

"Will there be bad people in Iraq, Daddy?"

"Some," he said, "but not too many."

"Do you want to take my night light?"

He smiled, fighting tears. "No, I bought that for you."

"But what will you do if the bad people come?"

"Well," he said. "I'll make a scary face, like this." He furrowed his brow, bugged his eyes, and growled. Althea laughed. "Not scary?"

"You better come up with a scarier one."

"You think of one for me and when I call, you can tell me what face to make."

"How far is Iraq? Will you come home to visit?"

"It's pretty far, honey, but I'll write and call you all the time."

"And Mom?"

"Of course Mom. You know she's my number one partner." He took a breath. "Now you go back to sleep."

Althea shook her head. Tears pooled in her eyes. Ford

pressed his cheek to hers and she wrapped her arms around his neck, squeezing. "Who loves you, angel?"

"Daddy," she sobbed.

"And I always will. Now you have to let me go, because the sooner I get over there, the sooner I can get back home."

"No."

"You want me to come home, don't you?"

Althea loosened her grip.

He stood. "Now close your eyes so Daddy can go."

Althea closed her eyes. He tucked the covers under her chin and kissed her forehead. At the doorway he picked up his duffel bag and fought the urge to turn back, walking quickly to the stairs, wiping tears. At the bottom of the staircase Lucas, Alicia, and James junior stood in their pajamas crying. Ford descended and hugged the rest of his children to his chest.

"Come on, now. This isn't so bad. I know it sounds like a long time, but I'll be home before you know it." He looked down at his oldest. "Lucas, you're the man of the house until I get back. I expect you to respect your mother and look after your brother and sisters."

Lucas nodded.

"And JJ and Alicia, your mother will be sending me your report cards."

"We know. You expect A's in math," JJ said.

"What would it say about me as a teacher if my own children didn't do well in math?"

He kissed them all.

Beverly stepped out from the living room. "Back upstairs now," she directed and the kids trudged up the stairs.

James hugged his wife and buried his face in her neck,

breathing as if each breath was his last. "This, I'm taking with me," he whispered.

She pulled back to look at him. "What?"

"This smell, you, I'm taking with me."

She grabbed him, clutching her to him. "And you let it bring you home," she whispered. "Don't you go being a hero, James Ford, not with four children at home."

He kissed her again, broke their embrace, and stepped to the door. They had agreed it best that she not drive him to Fort Lewis. A friend waited in a car out front.

She handed him an envelope. "Open it."

He pulled out a photograph, the one of him in front of the Christmas tree hugging Beverly, the children clinging to him like ornaments. "You take us all with you," she said. "And you let us bring you back home."

MONTLAKE DISTRICT
SEATTLE, WASHINGTON

RUBY-RED FLOWERING PLUM trees lined the street and soft light spilled from the windows of modest Craftsman homes with shingled or clapboard siding, pitched roofs, and covered porches. Darkness and a steady drizzle made it difficult to read the addresses. Sloane drove to the end of the block, circled back, and found the address on the second pass, an A-frame, two-story structure with brown shake siding and a dormer window. The driveway ran along the right side. He parked behind an older-model Honda and walked up a cement walk to three worn and paint-chipped wooden steps. A yellowed glass fixture lit the wraparound porch.

Sloane pressed the doorbell, producing a series of chimes. A moment later he heard a chain rattle, followed by the click of a deadbolt, but the door did not immediately open. The person on the other side seemed to be having difficulty pulling the door free of the jamb, the wood perhaps swollen from the moisture.

When the door finally shuddered open, a little girl stood behind a black mesh security gate, her hair in two braids, a gap in her smile where her two front teeth used to be.

"Hello," Sloane said. "Is your mother home?" The girl nodded but did not otherwise move. "Could you get her for me?" he asked. Another nod. Still no movement. Sloane heard a television from inside and could feel heat escaping the front door. "Tell her Mr. Sloane is here to see her," he said, trying to coax her feet.

The door swung open suddenly. "Althea, don't be opening the door by yourself." A muscular young man in a white T-shirt glared at Sloane. "Who are you?"

"My name is David Sloane. Is your mother home?"

"What for?"

"Your mother came to see me at the courthouse the other day." The little girl continued to beam up at Sloane like he was the ice cream man holding Popsicles. Sloane winked at her. "Tell your brother I'm okay," he said.

The boy, physically mature for his age, which Sloane guessed to be fourteen or fifteen, pulled his sister back by her shirtsleeve and closed the door. Sloane heard him shouting. "Mom, there's a white dude here to see you! Mom!"

Beverly sounded annoyed. "Lucas, do not yell at me. If you want me, come upstairs and talk to me like a civilized human being."

Lucas yelled louder. "White dude at the door for you."

Footsteps descended stairs. Beverly Ford pulled open the door, hesitated. "Mr. Sloane?" She reached to unlock the security gate and pushed it open. "I'm sorry. I was upstairs." Ford wore a powder-blue nurse's uniform and white tennis shoes. She ducked her head behind the door to admonish her son. "Lucas, where are your manners?"

"Yeah, like I'm going to let some white dude I don't know just walk in."

Ford made a face as if she might let the comment go, then put up a finger and stepped behind the door. Though she lowered her voice, she remained clearly audible. "Watch your mouth, young man. Do not get smart with me." She reappeared, looking chagrined. "I'm sorry, this must sound horrible to you. Excuse my son's lack of manners. Please come in."

Sloane stepped into a small entry. A staircase led to the second story. A hallway to the right of the stairs continued to a swinging door at the back of the house, presumably to the kitchen. Sloane smelled the aroma of baked chicken and spices. To his left, books and papers cluttered a dining room table, homework in progress.

"I'm sorry about the time," he said. "I should have called."

"I worked late," she said. "I had an opportunity to pick up overtime. Are you hungry? Can I fix you something to eat?"

"No, thank you. I won't be long."

Disappointment registered on her face. "Please." She led him into the room to the right of the door. Lucas sat slumped in a chair with a bored expression, his leg slung over the arm, a remote control pointed at the television. The little girl moved behind her mother's leg, staring up at Sloane.

"Lucas, get up." Beverly Ford snatched the remote from her son's hand and turned off the television. "We have a visitor. Introduce yourself like a man."

Lucas stood with what appeared to be great physical effort. "Hey," he said, and turned to leave.

His mother grabbed him by the arm and spun him toward Sloane. "Look him in the eye and shake his hand." The young man rolled his eyes. "And if you're going to roll your eyes to heaven, young man, get down on your knees and pray."

Lucas gripped Sloane's hand. "Nice to meet you," he said.

"Nice to meet you," Sloane said.

"Now please go get your brother and sister." Ford turned to Sloane as Lucas trudged up the staircase. She glanced at her file, which Sloane had removed from his briefcase, then ignored it, straightening pillows on a floral couch and gathering the newspaper, putting it along the side.

The furniture was serviceable. A plastic runner

led out the other side of the room where the carpet had worn threadbare. A painting of a serene lake and a meadow of wildflowers hung above the fireplace mantel, which was filled with framed family photographs. Sloane considered one frame containing a painting of a dove, and what appeared to be a prayer about building houses not of brick and wood, but of love.

"James loved that poem. He said it was a prayer," Beverly said, noticing Sloane's interest. "He loved the thought of it."

Sloane turned to her, struck by the words. "It's beautiful."

"The artist was a friend, George Collopy."

Sloane had never felt that love in any of the foster homes in which he had been raised. They had all been just brick, mortar, and wood. He had never felt "home," not until he and Tina and Jake made one together at Three Tree Point. Now someone was threatening that. Standing in James Ford's house with his wife and his children, Sloane realized what had drawn him to a case he knew intuitively he could not win. It wasn't the scar on his chest that bonded him to James Ford. It wasn't the body armor that Sloane had once sacrificed to another soldier. James Ford represented everything in life Sloane had never had. Ford had not just been a soldier. He had been a husband and a father. He had been the man Beverly Ford expected to grow old with, the man to teach his sons how to be men, the man to walk his daughters down the aisle on their wedding days, the man to be a grandfather to their children.

He was a mentor and a teacher. It made his death that much more tragic.

"Are you a religious man?" Beverly asked.

"I don't really know," he said, answering honestly. No one had ever taught him religion. He believed in God—that much he had decided. But mostly he believed in a more basic principle: In life you reap what you sow.

Sloane took a seat on the couch. "You're a nurse. I don't think I knew that."

Ford nodded. "I put James through school. I stopped when the children were born. James and I agreed it was better to sacrifice financially than to have them come home to an empty house after school. It was difficult, but we managed. I went back to work when James was called to active service to help make ends meet. Normally I work the swing shift, but I had the chance to pick up some overtime."

She looked again at her file in Sloane's lap.

Footsteps thudded down the staircase, drawing their attention. Lucas walked into the room with the same disgruntled expression, followed by a younger boy, perhaps twelve, and a girl who looked to be about the same age. Both bore a strong resemblance to their mother. Sloane stood as Beverly Ford made the introductions.

"You met my oldest," she said, but Lucas had already departed the room. "And this is my daughter, Alicia, and my son JJ—James junior."

Each shook Sloane's hand. Sloane squatted to eye-level with the youngest. "And who is this angel?"

The little girl's smile brightened.

"This is Althea," Beverly said.

"Althea. That is a beautiful name. How old are you, Althea?" She did not answer. "I'm guessing you're . . . twenty-two or twenty-three." The girl shook her head. "No? You can't be twenty-four."

"She don't talk."

Beverly's voice cracked like a whip. "Lucas, watch your tone."

Lucas leaned against the doorframe, head cocked, arms folded across his chest. "Not since Dad died," he continued, clearly testing his mother's patience. "Not since his funeral. So don't bother. She doesn't say a word. Not to *anyone*."

"That's enough, Lucas. Go finish your homework, all of you. Alicia, take Althea and get her ready for bed." The little girl departed the room holding her sister's hand, looking back at Sloane, still smiling.

"I'm sorry about Lucas," Ford said after the children had left. "He's developed an attitude—thinks he's the man of the house—but more times than not, he still acts like a boy."

"I'm sure this has been hard on all of you. Is it true what he said?"

Ford nodded. "The doctors say it's a post-traumatic stress disorder associated with her father's death. They were very close. In Althea's case her unwillingness to speak is a regressive symptom."

"Unwillingness? She's choosing not to talk?"

"The doctors call it elective mutism. She can talk—

physically there's nothing wrong with her. She just won't."

"How long will it last?"

Ford shrugged. "The doctors don't know. They said one day she might just decide to speak again, but I think it could be a while."

"Why is that?" Sloane asked.

"Sometimes the child chooses not to speak until something happens or someone returns. In Althea's case they think she's saving her first words for when her daddy comes home, or at least when she can accept that he is not." She turned her head and cleared her throat.

The hollow feeling in Sloane's gut felt like a chasm.

Ford picked up a framed photograph from a side table and handed it to Sloane. "That's James," she said.

The man in the picture towered over Beverly Ford a good eight inches. He was bald, with a goatee and the same bright smile and big eyes as Althea. James had his arms wrapped around Beverly Ford's waist; the three oldest children hung from him. Althea sat on his shoulders.

Ford put the picture back and nodded to the file in Sloane's lap. "You're here to return my file, aren't you?" Sloane handed it to her. "I'm grateful that you took the time to consider it—" Beverly started.

Sloane interrupted her. "I had my secretary make a copy." He opened the file and pulled out a retainer agreement authorizing him to represent Ford and her children. She looked up at him. Then she hugged him.

"We're going to find out if everybody kept their end of the bargain, Beverly."

THREE TREE POINT, WASHINGTON

DESPITE THE LATE hour, when Sloane parked in the easement, light glowed through the blinds covering his second-story bedroom window. Another burned downstairs as he entered the house through the kitchen. Charles Jenkins sat in the living room. The butt of a handgun protruded between his thigh and the seat cushion.

"You all right?" Jenkins asked as Sloane walked in.

He'd pulled the blinds to cover every window in the house, even the large panes of glass facing Puget Sound, which were never drawn.

Sloane looked up the staircase.

"She hasn't been down," Jenkins said.

Sloane handed Jenkins back the Glock he had borrowed, walked up the stairs, and opened the door to their bedroom. Tina lay on top of the comforter. The television and stereo were off. She had no book in her lap. "You took the case, didn't you?"

"It's not personal. It's not about what happened earlier tonight, on the beach."

"Then what is it? You said you can't win."

He went to her side of the bed, sitting on the edge. "It isn't about winning. It's about what someone took from this man and from his family, from all the lives he might have touched."

She waited in silence.

"Someone needs to be held accountable—to his wife and children, and all the students whose lives he could have changed. Someone has to stand up for this man, for all of them."

A tear rolled down her cheek. "Is it always going to have to be you?"

"He gave up so much to go over there. He had so much to lose, but he did his duty. He did his job. This is my job. What would it say about me if I walked away? I need to stand up for this man. I need to find out who is responsible for his death. I need to find justice for his family."

"Can you?"

It was a legitimate question. "I have to try. I'd like to know you support me."

Tina lowered her gaze. "Don't ask me to do that." She got off the bed and walked past him, speaking with her back to him. "I'm afraid of losing *you*. I'm afraid of Jake's losing you."

He walked to her. "I'm not going anywhere, Tina. You're not going to lose me."

She turned and looked at him. "Can you promise me that? Can you promise that to an eleven-year-old boy who's already had one father abandon him?"

CHAPTER
SEVEN

The drive to Tacoma Saturday morning would take less than forty-five minutes. Sloane sat in the passenger seat of Jenkins's Buick. Jenkins had found a combination GPS and listening device attached to the ignition switch of Sloane's Jeep. Every time he started the engine, the device turned on, allowing whoever was listening to hear every conversation in the car, and to track their location. They chose not to remove it, deciding it was better to let Argus think they were unaware of the surveillance.

"Anybody?" Sloane asked.

Jenkins glanced at the rearview mirror. "With traffic this light, I'd know. You all right with this?"

Sloane nodded.

"It's the right decision," Jenkins said. "Better to have them out of harm's way. Alex will take care of them."

Sloane didn't doubt it, but he remained unable to forget the look on Jake's face that morning when they explained that Sloane would not be going to Cabo. He knew the boy had heard similar excuses and broken promises from his biological father. Though obviously disappointed, Jake tried to remain upbeat, telling Sloane he'd bring him a fish so big it would dwarf the salmon. It only made Sloane feel more guilty.

Tina had not tried to be upbeat about the decision, and he hated having the issue unresolved between them. Sloane didn't want to dwell on it and changed the subject.

"You think I'm giving this woman false hope?"

"What's that?" Jenkins asked.

He explained how Beverly Ford had hugged him when he told her that he intended to take her case.

"By taking her case, do you think I'm giving her false hope?"

Jenkins thought for a moment. "You ever see *Cool Hand Luke* with Paul Newman?"

Sloane knew that Jenkins often equated life to classic movies.

"Newman plays a convict named Lucas Jackson. He's not a bad guy; he just doesn't know his purpose in life. One night he gets drunk, commits a petty crime, and finds himself on a chain gang in the South. Every chance Luke gets he runs. And each time the warden catches him, brings him back, and tries to break Luke's spirit. He doesn't understand that Luke never really expects to get away."

"Then why does he run?"

"Initially, he just likes the challenge. Sound like anyone you know?"

Sloane couldn't argue.

"But then Luke starts to realize that each time he runs, the entire chain gang is running with him, rooting for him to actually get away. Do you know why?"

Sloane looked over.

"Because he's their only hope of getting out. And it scares him because he knows it's a false hope. He knows he can't actually escape."

"What happens?"

"He runs again, but this time he finds himself cornered in a church. So he gets down on his knees and he asks God, 'What's my purpose?'"

"Does God answer him?"

"Big George Kennedy, another convict who ran with him, comes into the church and tells Luke that if he just gives up 'peaceful-like,' the warden has promised everything will be okay. Only Luke knows he's embarrassed the warden one time too many."

"So what does he do?" Sloane asked.

"Luke steps to the window, mocks the warden, and the boss man shoots him dead."

Sloane waited for Jenkins to continue. When he didn't, he said, "Hey, thanks for that. I feel better already."

Jenkins put up a finger. "That's not the end."

"Sounds like the end to me."

"No. First Big George rushes the boss man and knocks off his glasses and they're crushed by a car tire."

"A symbol of injustice destroyed."

"Exactly. Then, at the end, the chain gang is sitting around Big George, and one of the men asks how Luke looked when he died. And George says, 'He was smiling. He was smiling that Cool Hand Luke smile.' And all the men smile too." Jenkins looked over at Sloane. "That was Luke's answer. His purpose was to make those men smile, even after he was dead. Luke didn't realize that it never was about him actually getting away for them either. It was about having hope, because sometimes even false hope is better than no hope."

Sloane turned and looked out the windshield. "One big difference."

"Yeah? What's that?"

"I don't plan on getting killed."

SEA-TAC AIRPORT
WASHINGTON

ALEX LED TINA and Jake through the Seattle-Tacoma Airport. The wheels of their suitcases hummed behind them. She and Charlie had been up late trying to persuade David, and then Tina, that Tina and Jake should go with Alex to Cabo, that it would be safer for them. Alex had dual citizenship and was fluent in the language and the customs of Mexico. Her training would also help her to leave behind no leads. Once David and Tina agreed, Alex called a former colleague in the documents section at Langley. Getting herself on a plane without any record of the transaction would not be difficult. During her four years working counterterrorism in Mexico and South America, she had accumulated multiple identifications. Tina and Jake were more problematic, especially on short notice. Her friend had put her in touch with a local FBI agent who had run a task force to catch "coyotes," men who smuggle Mexican aliens across the border. He in turn advised her of a contact who trafficked in false identity documents. Expediting the new IDs had cost a premium.

Alex passed the ticket counter.

"Where are we going?" Tina asked.

"I need to get some money changed," Alex said, pointing to a currency exchange booth beside a coffee stand outside the security entrance.

"Everything in Mexico takes American dollars," Tina said, bewildered.

"Why don't you take Jake and get something to eat for the plane ride. I don't think a bag of peanuts will pacify him. I'll meet you by that display."

At the currency exchange Alex handed the woman behind the counter a hundred-dollar bill. The woman scanned the bill beneath an anti-counterfeit machine and counted out colorful Mexican bank notes. All the while, Alex subtly watched Tina and Jake, first in line at the coffee stand, then sitting at a table. She collected the money and took a seat at a table. When they stood and walked to the display of South American pottery and jewelry, she could detect no one following them, or looking overly interested. She got up and approached, though she continued to use the reflection of the glass to watch the people behind her.

"All set?" she asked.

Jake held up a bag of food.

In line for the ticket counter, Alex handed Tina a Canadian passport and driver's license, and a separate Canadian passport for Jake. "Just hand it over like always," she said as they neared the front of the line.

At the counter Tina did as instructed.

"Cabo San Lucas," the ticket agent said. "Can I fit in your suitcase?"

Tina smiled. "Not with all the clothes I packed."

The agent looked out from behind the counter. "Two bags, Ms. Simonetti?"

"Just two," Tina responded.

Jake looked like he was about to open his mouth, but Alex jumped in. "Help your mother with the suitcases, Jake."

The boy hefted the suitcases onto the weight scale beside the ticket counter.

They had all discussed that this would be a delicate balancing act with Jake. Tina and David didn't want to alarm him, but the precautions Alex would need to take to ensure their safety would alert Jake that things were not normal. She couldn't have him asking questions at inopportune moments.

"And for the boy?" the agent asked.

Tina handed the agent a ticket and passport for Jake Duprey. Alex wanted as many different last names as possible. The further she could distance them from two women traveling with a boy, the better.

"His father and I are divorced," Tina said.

Alex caught Tina's eye and slightly shook her head. Less information was better.

Nonplussed, the ticket agent sighed, "I know that routine."

CABO SAN LUCAS, MEXICO

WITH THE LAYOVER in Los Angeles and the time change between Seattle and Cabo San Lucas, their flight landed late that afternoon. Alex had sat a dozen rows behind them on the plane, and spent much of the flight considering the other passengers. No one gave her reason to be suspicious.

After deplaning, she told Tina and Jake to retrieve their luggage while she went to rent a car. It gave her another opportunity to watch them. Again she did not detect anyone following them. She used a different name to rent the car, and minutes later they had loaded their bags and were driving southeast, away from Cabo. Alex then proceeded north along the Sea of Cortez until she saw what she was looking for—a nondescript motel. She made a sudden, sharp U-turn, and doubled back.

"Whoa, that was cool," Jake said, lifting his head from his video game.

Alex passed the motel again, made a second U-turn, and pulled into the parking lot.

By now Jake was leaning forward. "Where are we?

This isn't the hotel you showed me on the Internet. Where's the pool and waterslide?"

"Remember how David and I said that you'd have to be flexible on this vacation?" Tina asked.

"Yeah," he said, reluctant.

"Well, this is one of those moments."

Alex paid cash for a room and signed the register using a third different name. They settled into a room with two beds and little extra space. Then she and Tina stepped outside, leaving Jake disappointed and shell-shocked inside.

"Keep the door locked and stay inside. Call me if you see anything suspicious, or anyone comes to the room, anything at all," Alex said. Tina appeared anxious, so Alex added, "I haven't noticed anyone following us. I just want to be sure."

After leaving the motel, Alex drove back toward Cabo with the windows down, letting the warm ocean air blow through the car. After contacting her former colleague at Langley, she had called a field officer with whom she had worked at the Counterterrorism Center. He had been promoted to the Mexico City office as the second-in-command and deputy to the station chief. At one time they had dated. Alex hoped he didn't hold a grudge. She needed a weapon.

She exited Highway 1 and followed the directions to the Puerto Paraiso Mall, circling until she saw the outdoor grill with the colorful red-and-yellow umbrella. The Mexican man stood hard at work cooking pork, chicken, and steak on a grill.

"*Me dijeron que usted hace los mejores burritos en todo*

Cabo," she said, flattering the man as having the best bur-ritos in Cabo.

The man smiled. *"Los burritos estan buenos, señorita, pero los chiles estan de chuparse los dedos,"* he replied, telling her that while the burritos were good, the chiles were to die for.

"I'll take three of each," she replied, and handed him the money.

Back inside the car, she put the two brown bags on the passenger seat and pulled out the foil-wrapped food. At the bottom of each bag she found two other foil-wrapped purchases, a .40-caliber Glock and an extra magazine. Apparently the field officer had gotten over her after all.

TACOMA, WASHINGTON

SLOANE AND JENKINS drove past the Tacoma Dome, which looked like the top half of a golf ball stick-ing out of the ground. Jenkins took the City Center exit. Paper manufacturing and pulp mills on the industrial flats had at one time emitted a distinctive acrid odor peo-ple in the Northwest dubbed the "Aroma of Tacoma," though much of that odor had been eliminated by air-quality controls implemented in the 1990s.

Sloane asked, "Do we know how he died?"

"Article in the paper said he was shot, but gave few details, which means the killing remains unsolved and the detectives are playing everything close to the vest. Like I said, we'll talk to them after we talk to the sister. I doubt they'll say much, but we might get someone interested in the fact that three of the five men in Ford's squad are now dead."

"What did his sister say?"

"Don't know. People can hang up the phone easier than they can close a door."

On Martin Luther King Jr. Avenue, Sloane noted cameras on the telephone poles and the conspicuous construction of a police precinct amidst the one-story businesses and residences. The Hilltop was mostly concrete, with little foliage. The houses, like the cars in the driveways, were a mix from decent to run-down, with bleak, postage-stamp-size yards. At eleven in the morning, the sidewalks remained deserted. Jenkins explained that meant most of the residents worked evenings. He slowed and parked across the street from a rambler the color of key lime pie with a yard of dandelions enclosed by a chain-link fence.

The edge of Sloane's door scraped the curb when he opened it; otherwise the area was eerily quiet. When he stepped from the car, he noticed two men sitting on a porch drinking beer from cans and watching Sloane and Jenkins as if they were the new movie in town. Jenkins nodded to them. One of the men responded with an equally subtle gesture, a silent understanding of some sort.

As they met at the front of the car Sloane said, "You look like Shaft," referring to the movie with the black police detective who always wore a long black coat.

"Exactly."

Though the sun was out, Sloane felt a chill as they crossed the street toward the rambler. Crossing the sidewalk, he reached for the latch to the gate of the chain-link fence.

"Don't," Jenkins said.

No sooner had he spoken than a very big and very loud Rottweiler sprinted around the corner of the house barking and growling. The dog left its feet as it approached the fence, and for one terrifying moment Sloane thought the animal would clear it. He stumbled backward, tripped over a raised crack in the sidewalk, and landed on his ass in the street. The dog's front paws, the size of baseball mitts, rested atop the fence, its snout lunging at them, snarling and barking, its pinch-collar rattling against the metal.

The two men on the porch cackled so hard one had doubled over and looked like he might roll down the steps. Apparently Sloane and Jenkins *were* the show for the day.

Sloane brushed off his pants as he stood. "Terrific. The demon from hell. I told you we should have called ahead."

"If we had, she might have left the gate open."

"How'd you know?" Sloane asked.

Jenkins pointed to the yard. "Big dog shit. Big dog."

"Brilliant."

Jenkins talked to the dog. "Easy now. Good dog."

"Good dog?" Sloane asked. "And you're afraid of Carolyn?"

"He's just doing his job." He continued to soothe the

beast. "Big dogs get a bad reputation because they're big and their owners abuse them. You've heard the saying about there being no bad dogs, just bad owners."

"I'll worry about the owners when they start biting."

As the dog calmed, Jenkins reached into his pocket and pulled out a bone-shaped biscuit. "Look what I got for you. I don't think Sam will mind. Can we be friends?" He held out the biscuit.

"Count your fingers," Sloane said, but the dog took the biscuit gently in its jaws and got down from the fence, chomping on it. As it did, Jenkins eased the latch and slowly opened the gate.

"I'll wait out here," Sloane said.

"Just walk in behind me. You'll be fine."

Sloane gestured to the dog. "Did he agree to that?"

The dog finished chewing the first bone and looked at them like they were the next meal. Jenkins let the dog sniff the back of his hand, then gently reached around and began to rub its bony head. "You're a good boy, aren't you? Sure you are."

The two men on the stoop watched slack-jawed.

"Should I do that?" Sloane asked.

"I wouldn't. I don't think he likes white people."

"The dog's racist?"

"In this neighborhood white people usually mean trouble. Dogs react the way their owners react."

"Terrific, you wait to tell me that when I'm on this side of the fence."

Jenkins gave the dog a second biscuit and tossed a third on the ground, then made his way to the front door.

Sloane followed him like a kid keeping his big brother between him and the bully. Jenkins knocked hard enough to shake the plate-glass window facing the street.

"You trying to knock it down?" Sloane asked.

"If she didn't come to the door with the dog barking . . ." Jenkins removed his sunglasses as an African American woman pulled back the curtain and scowled at them. She looked meaner than the Rottweiler. Sloane doubted a doggie treat would appease her.

"Ms. Thomas?" Jenkins asked through the window.

"Who are you?" It sounded like, What the hell do you want?

"I'm Charles Jenkins." Jenkins held his private investigator's license to the glass.

The woman gave it a cursory glance. "You a cop?"

"I'm a private investigator."

She pulled open the door. "A private investigator for who?"

"For him." Jenkins nodded to Sloane.

The woman shifted her glare and venom to Sloane. "Who are you?"

"David Sloane," he said. "I'm an attorney from Seattle."

The woman put up a hand and made a face like someone had just left yesterday's trash on her doorstep. "An attorney? That's worse than the police." She started to close the door.

"I tell him the same thing," Jenkins said. "You're stuck in an elevator with a tiger, a lion, and a lawyer. You have a gun with just two bullets. What do you do?"

The woman waited. "I don't know. What do you do?"

"Shoot the lawyer twice to make sure he's dead."

The woman looked to Sloane. This was the moment when Sloane expected her to yell, "Sic 'em, Fido," sending them running for their lives. But like the dog, she surprised him. She grinned, small at first, as if trying to hide her teeth. Then she started to wheeze, laughing.

Jenkins nodded to Sloane. "Actually, this guy's not too bad. That's why I let him work with me."

The woman frowned. "What is it you want, Mr. Attorney?"

"Could we step inside?" Jenkins asked.

The woman shrugged as if to say, Whatever, and stepped back, leaving the door open. The interior looked like the exterior—worn and tired, a mismatch of furniture cobbled around an enormous stand-alone projector TV. The screen had a hole in the corner where it looked as if someone had kicked it. The house held a pungent odor that reminded Sloane of rotting fruit.

"Are you Mrs. Thomas?" Sloane asked.

"Ms. Thomas."

"Dwayne was your brother?"

"Why you want to know? What you want with Dwayne?"

"I represent the family of a national guardsman named James Ford. Does that name mean anything to you?"

She shook her head like a defiant brat. "Nope."

"He served in Iraq with your brother. Your brother did serve in Iraq, didn't he?"

She nodded. "He was there. Damn fool. I told him not to sign up for no National Guard, but he said it was just a couple weekends doing nothing. Said it would help him hook on getting a job with the city. Then they shipped his ass off to Iraq. Didn't help him get no job with the city, neither. He had to take back his same old job."

"Where was that?" Sloane asked.

"YMCA downtown. And they put his ass on the graveyard."

"Did Dwayne ever talk to you about his time in Iraq?" Sloane asked.

She shook her head. "Nope. He didn't like talking about it, 'cept he said it wasn't as bad as everyone is making it out to be."

"So he never mentioned a guardsman getting shot over there and dying?" Sloane asked.

That seemed to catch her attention. "He might have said something about that. Is that who you here for?"

Sloane nodded. "His name was James Ford. I represent his wife and four children."

"I don't remember no names, just that Dwayne said someone got hisself shot and killed. Said he thought he was going to die too, but he didn't. Said it was destiny."

"Destiny?"

Her face scrunched like she'd smelled the foul odor in the house. "Dwayne came back talkin' 'bout 'destiny this' and 'destiny that.' Fool never shut up about it, saying shit like heaven being a big place with clocks and when yours stopped ticking, you was dead." She shook her head. "Fool."

"Did he tell you anything more about what happened that night?"

"What night?"

"The night the guardsman was shot."

"Just what I just told you. Is his wife trying to get some money or something?"

"She filed a claim, but the military denied it."

"Denied Dwayne too."

"Your brother filed a claim?"

"Attorney filed it. Said Dwayne was going to get some money but he didn't get nothing. If they denied it why you still asking about it?"

"I'm trying to find out if she has a civil action against the army."

"Does she?"

"I don't know yet."

"Could I file one of them too?"

"No, Ms. Thomas, you can't."

The woman picked up a can of Diet Pepsi from a Formica counter and drank from it. Then she said, "I heard that the military pays for the funeral. That right?"

"Yes," Sloane said.

"Then Dwayne would have been better off getting hisself killed over there. At least someone would have paid for his funeral."

"How did your brother die, Ms. Thomas?" Sloane asked.

"How? They shot him in the back of his head."

"Who shot him?"

"Don't know."

"Do the police have any suspects?" Sloane asked.

She made a face like it was the stupidest question she'd ever heard. "Hell, no. Police don't know and don't care—just another nigger getting killed to them. They saying Dwayne was dealing drugs."

"Did your brother sell drugs?" Sloane asked.

She looked indignant. "No. He did not sell drugs."

"Then why would the police say he was?"

"Probably so they don't have to work too hard to find out who killed him is why."

"Where was your brother shot?" Jenkins asked.

"I told you, in the head."

"No, I mean where did they find his body?"

"Down the street." She pointed vaguely. "Empty lot. They park delivery trucks there at night. Police have cameras up all over this place, but they said you can't see behind the trucks. So the tape don't show nothing."

"Why do the police think your brother was dealing drugs?" Sloane asked.

" 'Cause he was black and it was night is why. Don't need no more reason than that." She sipped from the can. "They said they found rocks on him, but I'm here to tell you that Dwayne stayed away from that shit. He didn't do crack, and he wasn't in no gang neither."

"Did he sell it?" Sloane asked.

"What did I just say?" She scowled. "Didn't I just say Dwayne didn't do *no* drugs? Didn't take 'em and didn't sell 'em. He was *trying* to hook on with the city." She raised her eyebrows. "What does that tell you?"

"Drug tests," Sloane said.

"Dwayne had to pee in a cup when he did his application. You think they'd be processing his paperwork if he had drugs in his pee?"

"Did he ever write to you? Send you any e-mails while he was in Iraq?"

"You see a computer around here?"

Sloane grew weary of the woman's attitude. "It could be important, Ms. Thomas."

"Why? What's this got to do with Dwayne?"

"Maybe nothing," Sloane said. "But we're trying to find out why James Ford was killed."

"Don't the military know?"

It was a good question, but someone was making sure the men who served with Ford that night wouldn't provide Sloane any answers.

CHAPTER
EIGHT

Tuesday morning, Tom Pendergrass stepped into what would be his temporary office. The freshly painted walls had no nail holes; the desk was free of dust. No papers filled the "In" or "Out" boxes, and no personal effects or photographs of Spot, the kids, or the lovely wife cluttered the desk.

Monday afternoon a process server had delivered a copy of a federal district court complaint filed by David Sloane on behalf of Beverly Ford and her four children. Any attorney with an ounce of common sense, after researching the Feres doctrine, would have known that the chances of such a claim succeeding were zero. The complaint bordered on frivolous, and federal court judges weren't bashful about imposing sanctions on attorneys who tied up their courtrooms with a frivolous complaint. Pendergrass didn't get it. Sloane certainly didn't appear dumb when they spoke in the regional claims office. It made him curious. He researched Sloane on the Internet, expecting to find out he was an attorney desperate to make a buck and willing to take any file that came in the door. To the contrary, he couldn't even find a Web site for "The Law Offices of David Sloane." What Pendergrass did learn, from articles and other information posted on various Web sites, was that Sloane didn't need the money or the work. He'd recently won several multimillion-dollar jury awards, and a two-year-old article from a legal periodical in San Francisco touted him to have been the best wrongful-death attorney in the state, one who apparently never lost. He'd won fifteen verdicts in a row in California, and from what Pendergrass could glean, Sloane had picked up where he left off when he got to Seattle.

"If you need anything, just call." The young woman who would be Pendergrass's assistant smiled politely before stepping from the office and disappearing down the hall.

Pendergrass knew the woman was treating her assignment as a temporary gig. He wasn't. This was an audition. And he intended to ace it. The U.S. Attorney's Office was the job to which he ultimately aspired once his military commitment expired. The chance to serve as a SAUSA, or special assistant United States attorney, was one more step in the right direction. Ordinarily the military officer who handled the claim at the regional office did not handle the subsequent civil matter. It was rare, though in theory it made perfect sense. Pendergrass argued to his superiors that he was familiar with Beverly Ford's claim, military law in general, and the Feres doctrine in particular. But his real reason for lobbying for the case was that he saw the chance to defeat an attorney who apparently never lost. Succeed, and he would be one step closer to making his temporary office permanent.

Pendergrass's lobbying led to a conference call with Western Washington U.S. Attorney Rachel Keane. Keane acknowledged that the claim could be politically sensitive and wanted to minimize publicity. Pendergrass suggested the best way to do that was to take an aggressive approach and immediately move to dismiss the complaint. Keane had said that she liked Pendergrass's initiative, which was all the JAG office needed to hear to temporarily assign him.

Pendergrass had his foot in the door.

He set his briefcase alongside the desk, turned on the computer, and entered the password he had been given that allowed him to reach the Justice Department network.

"You must be Captain Pendergrass." Rachel Keane walked into the office introducing herself as if Pendergrass didn't already know who she was.

He did. Most of Seattle knew Keane. Though approaching fifty, she remained physically attractive, with shoulder-length blond hair she had never styled, as so many women did, to fit the corporate or political image. She wore it down, or pulled back in a ponytail, giving her a youthful and vibrant appearance. A dynamic presence, she was frequently featured in the newspapers and on television and had recently been profiled in *Seattle* magazine as the most eligible woman in Seattle.

"I like to personally greet each attorney who comes to work for me," she said, extending her hand.

Pendergrass untied his tongue long enough to utter four words and immediately regret them. "I appreciate the opportunity."

He sounded like a contestant on a game show, just happy to be there.

Keane waved him off. "You're being modest, Captain. Magna cum laude from Montana, Order of the Coif from the University of Washington. We appreciate the opportunity to have *you*."

Pendergrass sat behind his desk, stunned that Keane knew *his* background. He felt disjointed and didn't know what to do with his hands. He folded them on the desk, crossed his arms across his chest, and finally laid his hands palms down on the desktop.

Keane, on the other hand, was as fluid as water poured from a pitcher. She lowered herself into a chair, effortlessly crossing her legs. When the president appointed Keane the U.S. attorney for the Western District of Washington, it was not without controversy. A divorce from an Internet entrepreneur had left Keane financially well off. Local and national magazines had linked her romantically to several prominent Seattle businessmen, Hollywood actors, and national politicians. Some felt that Keane had been chosen over other more qualified candidates, and rumor had it that the Republican Party had bigger plans for her, possibly a seat on a federal appellate court bench, or in the president's cabinet. While the president was ostensibly coming to town to stump for incumbent Republican senator Johnson Marshall, some speculated Keane was higher on the party's agenda.

"You're single, Captain?"

The question surprised him. Pendergrass felt himself blushing, the curse of fair-skinned redheads. When he lifted his palms from the desk, he'd left two sweaty imprints on the glass. He leaned forward to cover them with the sleeve of his jacket and cleared his throat. "I was seeing someone but—"

"This job can have long hours."

"Right. I'm used to long hours."

"Good." She uncrossed her legs. "So where are we?"

"Excuse me?"

"On this Ford matter, where are we?"

"Oh. I'll finish the motion to dismiss and file it today."

"I'd like to hear your arguments."

"Okay." Pendergrass gathered himself. He felt more comfortable in the law. "Sloane has alleged that because Ford's claim had not been officially reopened at the time he filed his complaint, she had a legal right to do so in federal court. I disagree, but I don't recommend we fight that argument too much, since it would leave the window open for Sloane to re-file when Ford's claim is officially denied. I'd rather the judge rule on the merits."

"So would I."

"Under Feres, Sloane will be hard-pressed to argue that James Ford was not acting incident to his service at the time he was killed. When he can't, the judge will be duty bound to dismiss the complaint with prejudice."

"Excellent."

"I also intend to ask for our attorney fees. The claim is frivolous and unsupported by federal law."

"Who's our judge?"

"Jo Natale."

Keane smiled. "Jo and I worked together for seventeen years. If Sloane was counting on sympathy for his client, he can forget it. What do you know about him?"

This was where Pendergrass could really make some points. "We've met. He's impressive. He's won eighteen jury trials in a row, fifteen in the Bay Area and three since he moved here, from what I've been able to determine. He was profiled as the best wrongful-death attorney in California."

"He sounds formidable," Keane said.

"Even the best have to lose sometime," Pendergrass said.

Keane smiled. "Confidence, Captain, I like that in the people who work for me."

Pendergrass felt himself starting to blush again.

Keane sat forward, a hand on the edge of the desk. "Call Sloane and invite him to a meeting, this afternoon if possible, or tomorrow morning, as soon as he is available."

"A meeting?"

Keane stood. "One thing about this job, Tom, you have to remain flexible to change."

CAMANO ISLAND, WASHINGTON

JENKINS REFOCUSED HIS attention on the computer screen in his home office. He felt like he was searching for a towel at a nudist colony. Shirley in the National Guard's public affairs office had been of no help. The National Guard's last known address for Michael Cassidy, the only surviving guardsman to have served with James Ford the night he died, was Maple Valley, Washington. Though just half an hour from Seattle, it might as well have been on the other side of the world. The house had been a rental, the phone number associated with it long since disconnected. A property records search revealed Cassidy did not own any real estate, not surprising given that he had been just twenty when he shipped off for Iraq, and the military had no forwarding address.

Posing as an administrator from the office of Veterans Affairs, Jenkins called the owner of the property and said he was trying to forward Cassidy a military benefits check. The owner confirmed Cassidy had rented the property but only until his deployment, which meant his last known address was Baghdad, Iraq. Cassidy had paid his rent in cash. The man had no record of a bank account.

"What about a security deposit?" Jenkins asked. "Did he leave a forwarding address?"

"He told me to keep it as his last month's rent."

"Credit check or references?"

"Lease was month-to-month. Like I said, he put down first and last. I didn't ask for any references—they just lie anyway."

"Did he give you a place of employment?"

"Said he was a painter and a handyman. I had no reason to doubt him."

"No employer?"

"Called himself an independent contractor. Like I said, paid on time."

Jenkins suspected the landlord never pressed the issue because Cassidy had paid in cash, and cash didn't need to be reported to the IRS.

A credit check revealed Cassidy had once owned a credit card with an address in Yakima, Washington, three hours to the east. Jenkins called a friend at the IRS, but that only revealed that Cassidy had not paid income taxes. A tax account for a Jennifer and Richard Cassidy listed a Michael Cassidy as a dependent on past income taxes. The address was in Yakima, the same as on the expired credit card. It was a start.

Jenkins used an online directory to obtain a telephone number and called.

"Hello?"

"Richard Cassidy?" Jenkins asked.

"Are you a solicitor?"

"No, Mr. Cassidy, this is Corporal Charles Jennings with the Washington National Guard."

"Christ, what's the boy done this time?" His voice

sounded rough and irritated from too many cigarettes and too much alcohol.

"Actually, sir, we're trying to locate an address for Michael to forward his military benefits check."

"Benefits? Hell, he didn't serve long enough for any damn benefits."

"It's a onetime benefit, sir—a modest amount for his service in Iraq. We don't have a forwarding address—"

"How much?"

"Excuse me?"

"How much is the check? That boy owes me close to five hundred dollars and hasn't paid back a penny. And that's not including interest."

Jenkins surmised this wasn't the feel-good, father-son relationship depicted on the television shows of the 1950s. "Well, sir, I'm afraid I have to forward the check to Michael to have it endorsed. You'll have to take that up with him."

"Sure, and I'll go out and get water from a damn stone while I'm at it."

"Do you have a current address for your son?" Jenkins persisted.

"Nope. Don't know where he is or what he's doing, and don't want to. He brings trouble whenever he shows up around here. We had hoped the military would shape him up. I wanted to put his ass in the marines and let them make a man out of him, but his mother begged me not to. She's always been soft on him. We compromised on the Guard. Best news I got was when he called to say they were shipping his butt to Iraq."

Ward Cleaver this guy was not.

"How about a past employer, Mr. Cassidy, or a close friend? Is there someone who might know where I can forward this check?"

The man chuckled. "Past employer? That's a good one. That boy couldn't hold down a job to save his life."

"I understood he was a handyman of sorts, maybe did some odd painting jobs."

"Yeah, he said that once. Came by wearing one of those white hats, you know the kind, keeps the paint out of your hair. He wanted another loan, which is a joke since he ain't never paid back a penny in his life. I told him, 'It ain't a loan if you don't pay it back. It's just stealing.' He took off the hat and showed it to me like he was working at Microsoft or something. Said he was making good money. So I asked him why he needed the damn loan, then. He didn't have an answer for that one."

Jenkins tired of the conversation. "Do you remember the name of the company?"

"Wasn't a company, just some guy far as I know."

"What about a name? Do you remember a name?"

"Nah. I didn't pay no attention. Likely a bullshit story anyway. Probably found the hat and was just using it to try to get me to part with a few more bills from my wallet."

U.S. FEDERAL BUILDING
SEATTLE, WASHINGTON

WEDNESDAY MORNING, SLOANE stood in a concrete plaza gazing up at the twenty-three-story

Federal District Court Building at Seventh Avenue and Stewart Street in downtown Seattle. The glass-facade structure with green copper trim and copper roof was quite a contrast to the squat concrete blocks he traditionally associated with government buildings. So, too, was the plaza. One hundred birch trees surrounded a sixty-foot-diameter grassy area, in the center of which stood a cast aluminum sculpture that resembled a raised fist. To the left a black wall sloped to the street, the Declaration of Independence carved in the granite. To the right, water gently cascaded over three shallow lily ponds.

Sloane was not surprised to receive a call from the U.S. Attorney's Office. He had anticipated they'd want to meet. What did surprise him was the caller had been Tom Pendergrass, the regional claims officer. Pendergrass said he was working on temporary assignment, handling Ford's claim. He wouldn't elaborate over the phone, but Sloane could guess the agenda of their meeting. Pendergrass would try to persuade Sloane to voluntarily dismiss the complaint as premature. Sloane would decline. Pendergrass would then tell Sloane why Ford had no chance of success under Feres, and that the government would seek attorney fees and costs. Sloane would make a vague reference to interpreting the case law differently. He suspected the real reason for the meeting was that Pendergrass wanted to ascertain what evidence Sloane possessed to substantiate his allegation that Ford had not been acting incident to his service.

At the moment, Sloane had no such evidence, other than his gut, but he wasn't about to tell Pendergrass that.

Sloane could have delayed filing the complaint—it would have allowed him and Jenkins more time to find Michael Cassidy, and maybe some evidence to actually support the allegation, but there was no guarantee of that happening and Sloane wanted the complaint filed before Beverly received a formal notice that the claim had been reopened. Besides, filing a complaint was the best way to get people's attention, and to let them know that Sloane was not going away. It might also make them nervous, perhaps make them suspect Sloane knew more than he did about the man who came to his house to issue the threat. Nervous people tended to react, and the more someone reacted, the more chances they might make a mistake. The downside to filing the claim was that the clock would start ticking as soon as the government filed its inevitable motion to dismiss, and Sloane would have very little time to find evidence to corroborate his gut belief that there was more to Ford's death than the military was saying. Federal judges weren't partial to "feelings" and wouldn't hesitate to toss him out of the courtroom on his butt, with his wallet a little less thick to cushion the blow.

Sloane walked up the wide concrete steps and pushed through the glass doors. Metal detectors and a healthy number of federal marshals waited inside. He put his briefcase on the conveyor belt to be x-rayed and stepped to the gate. The gray-haired federal marshal waiting for him on the other side told him to empty all his pockets.

"Even a penny will set it off," he said.

Sloane wondered if that was the reason for all of the copper and silver coins reflecting off the black bottom of the lobby's shallow pool to his left.

He complied with the instruction and stepped through the arch.

The detector beeped.

"Probably your belt." The marshal pointed to the silver clasp. Sloane walked back through to the other side and removed his belt. "Put your coat through as well," the marshal instructed. "Do you have a cell phone?"

Sloane slipped from his coat and put it on the conveyor. He stepped through without a beep. As the coat and belt went into the machine, the marshal standing on the other side watching the monitor stopped the conveyor and studied the grainy images. Then he motioned to his partner to view something. They stood together considering the monitor before starting the belt again. When Sloane's jacket came through, the marshal picked it up.

"You have anything in the pockets?"

Sloane reached for the jacket. "I don't think so."

The marshal kept it. "We're going to rerun it." He walked to the other end and put the jacket back on the belt. By this time there were two other suit-clad men waiting to get through. Again the belt stopped. Again the marshals considered the jacket. When it came through, the gray-haired marshal picked it up and squeezed the pockets.

"Where did you get this jacket?" he asked.

"Florence. Why?"

"It's got something in the lining that's tipping off the detector."

"Really?"

"It's round. Could be a quarter that got through the pocket lining." The marshal put his hands in both pockets. "I don't feel a hole." He held out the jacket for Sloane to feel. "Right there," he said, and Sloane felt the quarter-size spherical object in the coat lining.

CHAPTER NINE

Jake grimaced, his face a beet red from the sun and exertion. Tina wanted to tell him to let the deck-hand take over, that he'd done more than anyone expected of an eleven-year-old boy, but she knew Jake would never give in. He was mentally that strong, and though she hated to admit it, he had her stubborn streak. This was his fish. He wanted to land it himself, even if it meant his arms falling off.

It didn't help that they were sharing the boat with three fraternity brothers from California. Jake would not want to quit in front of them.

"Keep ahold of him, little man," one yelled.

"You can do it, Jake," another encouraged. "That's it. Keep its head up."

Miguel, the bronze-skinned deckhand with a face like cracked leather, said the fish was a yellowfin and estimated it to weigh between thirty-five and forty-five pounds. He had been coaching Jake through the thirty-minute battle.

"*Tranquillo, tranquillo,*" Miguel shouted. "Let him run, *muchacho.*"

Jake relaxed and looked over his shoulder at Tina. Trickles of sweat rolled down his face. He smiled, but his relief was brief.

"*Enrollo, amigo.* Reel." Jake lurched forward, reeling down as Miguel had taught, keeping his left arm straight and using his legs to pull. He used the tension on the line and a slight bend in the tip of the pole to ease the fish toward him.

Tina was happy Jake was having a good time. She couldn't say the same for herself. She missed David terribly and felt sick with worry, unable to eat much and too preoccupied to enjoy their surroundings. They had not parted on good terms, and she now felt bad about how she had behaved. Making matters worse, Alex had forbidden any phone calls. The past three days in Baja had felt like a month.

"*Enrollo, amigo,*" Miguel continued to shout. "*Muy bien, muchacho.* You are tiring him out."

Jake was determined to bring David back a fish bigger than the salmon, which was the only reason Alex had relented about the fishing excursion. Up to that point she had avoided anyplace that would put two women and an eleven-year-old boy in a confined space. When they checked

into their new hotel in Cabo, Alex had taken a room by herself and let Tina book a room separately, though they all
shared Alex's room. They had driven to the dock at dawn,
and Tina and Jake waited while Alex spoke to half a dozen
different charters. Though they all understood English,
Alex had spoken only Spanish. Tina had been able to pick
up bits and pieces of the conversations. The debate had not
been about price, but about the other guests. Alex wanted
other people on the boat, but only if they had made a prior
reservation. She settled on the three fraternity brothers.
Tina had feared a long day, but the young men were not the
typical beer-swilling pigs she associated with most frater-
nities. That had not, however, stopped them from hitting
on Alex. Dressed in white shorts, a tank top, and sneakers,
Alex was a more prized catch than a marlin.

Tina applied a liberal dose of sunblock to her arms
and legs and felt the salt from the splash of the waves on
her skin. Despite her Italian heritage, number 45 sunblock,
and the wide-brimmed sun hat covering much of her face,
she felt as though she was baking.

"Reel, *niño*, reel," Miguel shouted.

Tina offered the sunblock to Alex, but she declined.
Alex remained quiet, and seemed to be constantly scanning the horizon, considering other charters that passed.
The fraternity brother named Vincent had been unsuc-
cessfully working to get her attention.

"*Ya parele, ya parele,*" Miguel yelled. "Stop. Stop."

He picked up a long pole with a hook on the end and
jabbed it into the water. On the second try his muscles
strained and he lifted a huge fish onto the deck to loud

cheers. The fish looked prehistoric, silver green with yellow fins along the tail. It thrashed on the deck, but Miguel held its head down with the pole and pinned its tail between his ankles, the fish's blood pooling on the deck. Jake looked exhausted, but had a grin from ear to ear.

Tina smiled back and congratulated him, then looked to Alex, but she was now focused on the captain, who stood on the deck above them behind the wheel talking on a cell phone.

"David would have loved this," Jake said. "Can I have it stuffed, Mom? We could hang it over the fireplace in the living room."

"You did great, Jake." She hugged him. "Really great. David will be so proud."

The captain yelled down in Spanish, and Miguel gave him a puzzled look before beginning to organize the poles as the diesel engines powered up, smoke sputtering for a brief second before the blades churned the water.

Alex approached Tina. "Do you have that sunblock?" Tina handed her the tube. As Alex rubbed the lotion into her copper-brown skin, she continued to look out at the water. Then she turned to hand back the tube. "When we get back to the dock, follow my lead and do exactly as I say."

U.S. FEDERAL BUILDING
SEATTLE, WASHINGTON

IT FELT LIKE the marshals' eyes were boring holes in the back of Sloane's head as he walked across the lobby to the elevators. Sloane told them that the black spot was likely a security device to keep someone from stealing the jacket from a store. He acted relieved, saying he'd had similar problems traveling through airports but had been unable to determine why the jacket kept tripping the sensor. The explanation seemed to pacify the marshals, if not completely convince them.

Sloane knew the hardened object was not a security device. There had been no security detector in Florence. There had been no store. Tina had purchased the jacket at an outdoor market not far from the Duomo. Sloane knew what the quarter-size object was. Ken Mills had pulled one like it from his desk drawer, and said it was a listening device.

And Sloane also knew exactly when the device had been inserted into the lining of his jacket.

It's a hundred and thirteen degrees in Iraq.

Captain Robert Kessler had encouraged Sloane and Jenkins to leave their jackets when they went to tour the Argus warehouse with the replica of the neighborhood in Mosul. Someone had slipped the bug in the lining then.

As the elevator ascended, Sloane struggled to recall what conversations he had engaged in while wearing the jacket. Had he discussed Cabo? If Argus had been listening to everything Sloane had said since leaving Kessler's office, they very well could know Tina and Jake were with Alex and where they were. He fought to recall where he'd put the jacket the night he sat with Alex and Charlie in the living room discussing the trip.

On the fifth floor he exited the elevator and pulled

open glass doors to the lobby of the U.S. Attorney's Office. A wood carving of the Great Seal of the United States hung on gray walls beside a picture of Western District of Washington U.S. Attorney Rachel Keane. Sloane slid his driver's license through a slot and advised the woman on the other side of the glass that Tom Pendergrass expected him.

"Who?"

"Tom Pendergrass."

The woman picked up a phone and had a brief conversation. Then she studied Sloane's driver's license as she typed out a visitor's pass and eventually handed both back through the slot. Sloane peeled off the backing of the pass and stuck it on his jacket.

"Could you direct me to the bathroom?"

"Down the hall to your left," the woman said.

He left his jacket, with his briefcase on a chair, and stepped into the hall, pulling out his cell phone and hitting the preprogrammed number. "Charlie?"

"No luck," Jenkins said.

"You need to call Alex. Tell her to change their plans. I don't care where they go in Mexico, but tell her to change everything."

"Whoa. What's the matter?"

"They put a transmitter in my coat."

"What?"

"Remember when Kessler gave us the tour—"

"You took your coat off."

"There's a transmitter in the lining. It just set off the metal detector at the U.S. Attorney's Office."

"I'm on it."

Sloane hung up and stared out the floor-to-ceiling windows. He pushed his thoughts aside and tried to focus. Alex and Charlie had been right. It had been the right decision to send them out of the country. They had Alex and all of her training to stay hidden. He couldn't help them. Besides, the best way to protect all of them, as John Kannin had said, was to find enough information to make someone important's ass pucker. Sloane needed leverage.

DARSENA MARINA
CABO SAN LUCAS, MEXICO

AS THEIR THIRTY-TWO-FOOT charter neared the marina, Tina fought the urge to look around. She envisioned another boat intercepting them and men with guns boarding, but the only boats she saw were other fishing charters returning to the marina to have their fish weighed and filleted into steak-size chunks. Still, her stomach felt as if it were in her throat.

Alex, by contrast, looked completely relaxed. She had struck up a conversation with the fraternity brother Vincent, whom she had previously ignored, telling him her name was Maria, and was smiling and laughing easily. Vincent looked about as excited as Jake when he landed the fish.

When the boat docked, Tina gathered her towel and belongings, shoved them into her beach bag, and accepted Miguel's hand onto the dock. Alex took at least a dozen pictures of Jake holding the fish, and Tina noticed that on several shots Alex had the telephoto lens extended and appeared to be using it to consider others.

"Te haz convertido en un pescador hecho y derecho, Jake," Miguel said, telling Jake that now he had become a real fisherman. "You come back next year and we'll catch a marlin together."

He pointed to the end of the pier where a flurry of Mexicans had gathered, negotiating the cost of stuffing or cutting up the marlins, tuna, and other fish that had been caught. Tina followed Jake and made arrangements to have the fish photographed so that its dimensions could be replicated and the copy shipped back to the States, despite a pricey cost. As she and Jake rejoined Alex, she was surprised that Vincent and his two fraternity brothers were also waiting for them.

"Our hotels are just down the street from one another," Alex said. "Vincent has invited us to have a drink and celebrate Jake's fish."

Tina forced a smile. "Why don't we go back to the hotel and shower? We can meet there."

"We don't need to shower," Alex said. "Let's all stay together."

Sensing Alex did not want to separate from the men, Tina agreed. At the end of the dock, as they approached a line of taxis, Alex turned to Tina and Jake and the other two men: "Why don't you four grab a taxi together and we'll meet you at the restaurant."

Tina felt a lump in her throat but continued to follow Alex's lead. "Okay. We'll see you there," she said, hearing her voice flutter.

U.S. ATTORNEY'S OFFICE

SEATTLE, WASHINGTON

WHEN SLOANE PUSHED back through the glass doors into the lobby of the U.S. Attorney's Office, Tom Pendergrass stood waiting.

"Sorry about that," Sloane said. "I had to take a call."

"Thanks for coming." Pendergrass made it sound like a social visit.

"I haven't been inside this building before. They did a nice job on the exterior."

"I'll give you the five-minute tour," Pendergrass offered. "There's a place with a great view."

"Just let me grab my coat and briefcase."

Sloane slipped his coat back on and followed Pendergrass onto an elevator. On the nineteenth floor Pendergrass stepped through glass doors out onto an observation deck with half a dozen unoccupied white tables and chairs. They stood at the railing looking at a view of downtown Seattle. Though the sun shone, the temperature was brisk. A breeze blew in their faces.

After admiring the view for a moment, Pendergrass spoke. "It's tragic when a soldier dies."

Sloane agreed. "I'm a marine, Tom. Ironically, I was wounded in Grenada *because* I gave up my flak jacket." Pendergrass turned from the view to look at him. Sloane shrugged, and told Pendergrass the same story that he had told to the military doctor who had questioned him after the incident. "Damn things were heavy back then. I felt like it was weighing me down." He looked back toward the buildings. "I watched two soldiers die, and as tragic as their deaths were, they didn't leave behind a wife and four children."

Pendergrass nodded. "Bullets don't discriminate. We're losing good men over there. I wish I could compensate the families of every one of them. I really do. I'm on their side. I'm one of them. But I can't. My job is to determine whether the death is compensable. It's difficult at times, as I'm sure you can appreciate, but it has to be done."

"We all have jobs to do."

"I'm surprised you filed the complaint."

"I'm surprised you're handling it," Sloane countered.

"I think we both know that Mrs. Ford's claim is not compensable."

Sloane shrugged. "The administrative claims office had Mrs. Ford's claim for over a year. They had ample opportunity to act on it. They didn't. There's no authority for it to be reopened."

"We can debate the court's jurisdiction, but we can't debate the merits," Pendergrass said, as Sloane had predicted. "Specialist Ford was killed while serving his country during a war in a foreign country. I've handled a dozen of these claims. It will never get past a motion to dismiss."

"Then tell me what caused the military to reopen it?"

Surprisingly, the question seemed to catch Pendergrass off guard. He fumbled for an answer. "A claim can be reopened for any number of reasons. I could ask you the same question. What evidence do you have to support an allegation that James Ford was not killed incident to his service? If it exists, let me have it so that I can evaluate it and recommend that his family be compensated."

That was, of course, the sixty-four-thousand-dollar question. "I can't give you that now."

"Can't or won't?"

"We're just getting started investigating," Sloane said. "You have the file."

"The witness statements explain what happened, and I know you have them. They're conclusive that James Ford was acting incident to his service."

"Maybe, but the court won't have those statements if you bring a motion to dismiss, and it has to accept any reasonable hypothetical set of facts I offer. The motion will be denied."

"Anything in that hypothetical that would convince a court to conclude James Ford was not acting incident to his service?"

"That's not my burden at this point in the proceeding." Sloane reached into his briefcase and pulled out several documents. "I've brought subpoenas with me for the investigative file and to speak to whoever conducted the witness interviews, under oath."

"We'll fight both, and you won't get either."

"I guess that's why the horses actually run the race. You never can be certain who'll win. I believe Judge Natale will grant us the right to conduct discovery before entertaining a motion to dismiss."

"I don't. You need to have some evidence to back up your complaint."

Sloane ignored the comment. "As I said, Judge Natale won't have the witness statements and she's duty-bound to consider the facts liberally in our favor."

Pendergrass raised a hand. "Enough saber rattling." He reached into his suit jacket, pulled out several folded pages of his own, and handed them to Sloane. "You might find this to be of interest."

Sloane unfolded the document, a copy of a federal court case. "What is it?"

"A way to resolve this that could be a win-win for everyone," Pendergrass said.

MONTLAKE DISTRICT
SEATTLE, WASHINGTON

BEVERLY FORD ANSWERED the door dressed in her nurse's uniform. Sloane had caught her in between getting the kids off to school, following a graveyard shift at the hospital, and much needed sleep. On the drive to her house he had called Charles Jenkins, but Jenkins had heard nothing back from Alex. Sloane was trying to take that as a positive sign, and not an indication that something was wrong.

"Can I get you something to drink?" Ford asked. Sloane declined. She invited him to the couch in the living room. Sloane had left his leather coat in his car.

"Well," she said, dispensing with the pleasantries. "You said you had news."

"You remember I told you that the administrative office had reopened your claim? They want to settle it, Beverly. They reopened it to make you an offer."

"An offer?"

One of the documents Pendergrass had provided was a legal case detailing an incident during the First Gulf War when two American F-15 fighter planes shot down two Black Hawk helicopters. The pilots mistook the helicopters for Iraqi, killing fifteen Americans and eleven Kurds on board. The secretary of defense exercised his discretion and paid the Kurd families $100,000 each, but concluded Feres barred compensation to the families of the American soldiers. That didn't sit well with the American families, Congress got involved, and eventually the secretary exercised the same discretion. Pendergrass intimated that same discretion could be exercised as to Ford's claim, though he didn't say why and Sloane wasn't flush with possible answers.

Maybe the government didn't like the potential public relations dust that Sloane could kick up about the lack of body armor, but the body armor issue had come and gone and the public seemed to be growing more and more numb to news of soldiers dying as the months, and the war, pressed on. Kannin had been given a different kind of trump card, the potential embarrassment to a powerful U.S. senator whose nephew tried to cover up a serious crime. Sloane held no such card.

"I was called to a meeting at the U.S. Attorney's

Office this morning. The government is prepared to pay you one hundred thousand dollars, though I think they will go higher. I know it's not a fortune, but it's a tax-free payment, and I would waive my fee. Invested wisely, it will allow you to stay in your home and keep your children in Catholic school. You'd be able to keep your promise to James and get some help for Althea."

At one point Sloane had considered a settlement to be the best that he could hope for to help Beverly Ford. But that was before Mr. Williams showed up at his door and he learned of Phillip Ferguson's and Dwayne Thomas's deaths. A settlement now looked like the best way to get rid of him, and Ford's claim. Still, Sloane was duty bound to notify Ford of the offer. The ultimate decision was hers alone.

Ford stood and walked to the mantelpiece, her back to Sloane. "Why?" She turned to him. "They denied my claim. What changed their minds?"

Sloane shook his head. That was the question gnawing at him. "I don't know."

"But it strikes you as odd, doesn't it? I can hear it in your voice. Something is bothering you too."

"It strikes me as odd, but this is your decision, and you have the right to do what's best for you and your family."

"What are they afraid of?" she asked.

Again he shook his head. "Maybe public sentiment—"

Her voice rose. "Public sentiment? How much worse can it get?"

"There could be other reasons we're not privy to,

Beverly, information the government does not want to come out."

"Such as?"

"I don't know."

"How would we find out?"

"We won't—not if we accept their offer."

"And if we don't?"

"The government's offer is contingent on you dropping your claim before the hearing on their motion to dismiss. If you don't, the government will withdraw the offer."

"Then we'll go to court."

"We could, but there are obstacles in our path that still might prevent us from getting answers. As I told you, it isn't likely we can get around the Feres doctrine unless we find someone who was with James the night he died and that person tells us James died while doing something not traditionally associated with being a soldier. At the moment, I haven't found anyone to tell us that and I have no evidence that's the case."

"But you filed the complaint."

"To let the government know we weren't going away, and to use the court to try to get more information."

"That's what I want, more information."

"I can't guarantee we'll get it, Beverly."

"James was a good man, David. The men would have genuinely liked him. If there is something, one of them will tell us. I'm certain of it."

"I don't doubt that."

"What is it, then?"

Sloane debated what more to tell her. "Two of the

three men who were with James that night are dead. We haven't been able to find the third."

"They died in the war?"

"No," he said. "They died after coming home."

She gave him an inquisitive look. "What are you not telling me?"

She had a right to know, Sloane thought. She'd earned that right when her husband put on a uniform and died for his country. For the next ten minutes he told her everything that had transpired since his meeting with Captain Robert Kessler to his finding the bug in the lining of his coat.

"The problem is we don't have any concrete evidence those two men died other than how it was reported."

"But you think it's possible they didn't."

"I think it is."

"My God," she said, hand covering her mouth.

"A hundred thousand dollars is not a small sum of money. You would have every right to accept it—"

She snapped. "I told you, this isn't about the money. This is about James." She caught herself. "What about those other men? If you're right, who will find justice for them? My husband did what he was told." She pointed to the front door. "He had four children and the hardest thing we've ever done was watch him walk out that door. But we made that sacrifice. If what you're telling me has even an ounce of truth, it means somebody didn't do right by him or this family. Somebody needs to acknowledge that. Somebody needs to accept responsibility for what happened to my James."

"I don't want to give you false hope, Beverly."

"My husband is dead. This isn't about hope."

"If you don't accept this offer, the government will move forward with the motion to dismiss your case, and as hard as it is for me to say this, at this point the judge would be duty bound to grant it."

Ford closed her eyes and inhaled deeply. She was about to speak when a voice interrupted her.

"Tell them no." Lucas walked in wearing a collared shirt and baggy blue jeans. He dropped his backpack with a thud.

"Lucas?" she said. "What are you doing home?"

"They're paying us to keep quiet. They want us to go away. Dad would have said, 'No.' He would have said we can't be bought. It's a matter of principle." He stepped further into the room, addressing Sloane. "We don't need their money— we'll be fine. We'll get by. I can work. But Dad always told us to never compromise our principles. I'd rather lose."

Sloane spoke to Beverly. "You don't have to make your decision now. Sleep on it."

Ford looked at her son, smiling. "I don't have to, David. My James just spoke to me." She hugged her eldest son. "He just made a man out of his boy."

DARSENA MARINA
CABO SAN LUCAS, MEXICO

ALEX WATCHED THE taxi depart the marina, then turned to Vincent. "On second thought, a shower would feel good. Do you have any extra towels in your room?"

Vincent smiled. "No, but I'm willing to share."

She laughed and slid inside the taxi, Vincent sidling up close beside her. The cabbie drove down Marina Boulevard through the shopping district and bars. "How many years did you say you and your friends have been taking trips like this?" Alex asked.

"Five," Vincent said. "We usually go to Lake Tahoe, but this being a milestone, we thought we'd go international."

"And how many came?"

"Twelve. Usually there's more. Some couldn't get permission from their wives."

"How did you swing a weekend pass?"

"I'm not married," he said, smiling.

"And do you get this lucky every year?"

He laughed. "You mean fishing, right?"

She grinned. "I didn't see you catch anything."

"Not yet," he said.

The taxi stopped at the hotel. Vincent stepped out and held the door open, insisting that he pay the fare. Alex let him. As they walked toward the arched entry to the hotel, Alex stopped suddenly.

"What is it? What's the matter?" Vincent asked.

"I don't think I'm exactly prepared for this." Vincent looked like the line on his fishing pole had just snapped. "Relax," she assured him. "I just need to go to my room for a second. I don't have my diaphragm."

"I'll go with you," he said, not wanting to let his catch out of sight.

She put a hand on his chest. "It'll only take a minute. I'll meet you in the bar. Order me a strawberry margarita and a shot of Cuervo Gold. I drink fast, and I'm a lot more fun after a couple of cocktails." She brushed a hand across his forearm as she turned and walked off.

Halfway down the block, she slipped into the pink sandstone entrance to another resort. Her sandals slapped against the red tile floor of an open-air foyer filled with leafy plants blowing in a light breeze created by multiple ceiling fans. Water trickled from a tile sculpture into a pond of lily pads and fish.

Alex approached the concierge, mindful of the man in the blue ball cap entering the hotel lobby seconds behind her. She had first spotted him on the pier. Her senses were heightened after the captain took the phone call on the boat and immediately looked down at her, Jake, and Tina. Alex wasn't as proficient at reading lips as she had once been, but from what she could decipher, the captain confirmed that he had two women and a young boy on his charter.

When they returned to the pier, Alex had spotted the man discussing a charter with a deckhand. When the man touched his ear unnaturally she noticed the tiny ear-piece. The man was likely letting his partners know that the boat had returned. Alex spotted a second man over by the taxis. He wore sandals, a yellow Tommy Bahama shirt, shorts, and sunglasses, just another tourist, except he, too, had an earpiece. She had Tina and Jake take a separate cab to force the men to split up. She had to be certain of the number following them, and now knew there were two, what Argus believed would be sufficient to handle two women and a young boy.

Alex also knew that she had been too careful for Argus to have randomly found her. They had to have known about the Cabo trip, and that meant either they had planted a bug somewhere other than in David's house and car, or they had learned about Cabo when Jake talked to the man on the beach. She chastised herself for not sticking with her instincts. The fishing excursion had been a mistake. Mr. Williams, or whoever the man on the beach was, would have known that Jake loved to fish, and even with the multitude of available charters, two men splitting the chore could easily call to find out if any had taken out two women and a young boy.

Alex spoke Spanish to the woman at the concierge desk, asking if the resort had an affiliated hotel in La Paz that could accommodate them for two nights. *"Me gustaria hacer una reservacion por dos noches. Me puede alojar?"*

The woman at the counter checked her computer and a minute later confirmed that she could.

"And I'd like to wire cash to a friend staying there," Alex continued. "He'll pick it up later tonight."

"No hay problema," the woman replied.

When she had completed the transaction, Alex asked for the restroom. The woman directed her across the tiled lobby past the fountain. *"Gracias.* And if my husband is looking for me, will you tell him I'll be right back?"

The woman said she would. Alex left the counter and walked to where the man in the blue ball cap had taken a seat in a wicker chair. "Excuse me." The man looked up from his paper, nonplussed, well trained. "Would you happen to have the time?"

The man smiled. "It's about cocktail hour. I was just about to head into the bar. Care to join me for a drink?"

She shook her head. "Sorry. I'm meeting someone."

"Too bad."

She stepped across the lobby to the bathroom and pushed open the door. A middle-aged attendant in a blue uniform who handed out towels and lotions for a small tip greeted her.

"Buenas tardes, señorita," the woman said. Then, *"Qué le pasa? Por qué está llorando tanto?"*

Alex lowered her hands. Tears flowed freely down her cheeks.

U.S. ATTORNEY'S OFFICE
SEATTLE, WASHINGTON

TOM PENDERGRASS HUNG up the phone and exhaled. He had been both disappointed and confused when Rachel Keane told him to make the settlement offer. There was no reason to settle. Sloane had no case.

"Government attorneys can never get too personally attached to a case," she had said. But Pendergrass still felt like Charlie Brown about to kick a field goal when Lucy pulled away the ball. Pendergrass had seen his chance to impress slipping away and felt powerless to stop it.

But now Sloane's client had teed up the ball again, rejecting the settlement, and Pendergrass was not about to miss a second chance to boot her complaint through the uprights, along with Sloane's reputation. Contrary to Sloane's smug opinion, Pendergrass would get the witness statements into evidence during the hearing on the motion to dismiss, and they would conclusively establish that Ford had died a soldier. Judge Natale would have no choice but to grant the motion.

Pendergrass reached for the phone to call Keane, but it rang before he could lift the receiver.

"Captain Pendergrass?" Pendergrass did not recognize the voice. Few had his number at the U.S. Attorney's Office. "This is Colonel Bo Griffin."

ONE UNION SQUARE BUILDING
SEATTLE, WASHINGTON

SLOANE HUNG UP the telephone as Charles Jenkins walked into his office and sat in the chair across from his desk. Sloane remained standing.

"Godzilla looks ready to eat New York," Jenkins said, referring to Carolyn.

"She was expecting a week off. Any word from Alex?"

Jenkins shook his head.

Sloane paced. "I'd feel better knowing they were okay."

"Alex isn't your typical girl next door; she can take care of them. We made this decision so you wouldn't have to worry, so you could concentrate on what needs to be done."

"It isn't working."

"We have no evidence you ever discussed Cabo wearing your jacket."

"I don't know that I didn't."

Jenkins nodded to the phone. "How did Pendergrass take the news?"

"As you would expect. He said the offer was a gift. The government will leave it on the table until the morning of the hearing. Then they'll pull it."

"When's the hearing?"

"Tuesday."

"That doesn't leave much time."

Sloane nodded. "Does that answer my next question?"

"I don't know. What's your next question?"

"You don't have a lead."

"That's not a question."

"Maybe I don't want an answer."

"I have a lead," Jenkins said, defensive.

"Really?"

"No, but since you're paying me, I thought it best to keep my employer happy."

"You're not making me happy."

"Okay, try this. Cassidy was a part-time painter, probably somewhere in Maple Valley. Unfortunately, I've called every painter in the phone book. No one has any idea who the kid is."

"That doesn't sound like a lead."

"A lead means a place to start. It's a start. I asked a friend at the DMV to run him through the system.

This guy sounds like a real prince. His license has been suspended twice for driving under the influence. I won't bore you with the details. The pertinent information is the police pulled him over three weeks ago for running a red light, which led to driving with a suspended license."

"So we know he was in the area as of three weeks ago."

"And driving a 1986 white Chevy pickup."

"What about a home address?"

"Not unless he's living in a P.O. box."

"So how do we find him?" Sloane asked.

"We drive out to Maple Valley and talk to the local police and businesses, and see if there's a painting outfit that knows him."

"If the locals know him, we could spook him."

"You got any better ideas?"

"Not at the moment," Sloane conceded.

"Then quit raining on my parade. Besides, I have a cover that never fails."

"Yeah, what's that?"

"I'm looking to give the kid money."

Sloane stared out the window. Black clouds had amassed on the horizon. They'd bring rainfall by early afternoon. His interior office line rang—Carolyn.

"There's a Colonel Bo Griffin on the phone. You have time for this bird?"

PUEBLO BONITO ROSE HOTEL
CABO SAN LUCAS, MEXICO

HE WATCHED HER cross the lobby, then walked in the direction of the bar. When she stepped through the door into the bathroom, he veered his course to the concierge.

"*Hola,*" he said. "I'm looking for my wife. She said to meet her here—tall with long, dark hair and dark skin."

"*Sí.* She was just here," the woman said. "She's in the bathroom."

"Story of my life. Did she get everything taken care of, or do I need to give you my credit card?" He pulled out his wallet.

"No, señor. It's all taken care of. You have reservations confirmed for two nights at the Grand Plaza in La Paz."

"Terrific," he said, knocking on the counter. "Thanks for your help."

As he turned from the counter, he caught a glimpse of the bathroom attendant stepping into a door marked "Employees Only," took out his phone, and contacted his partner.

"It's like a fraternity party," his partner said, confirming that Sloane's wife and boy remained in the restaurant, although mingling at a table with eleven young men.

The man's orders were to detain Sloane's wife and son without incident. That meant waiting until they were free of the fraternity. Their companion was not a target, but he had to be certain she had not somehow determined their presence at the pier and separated in order to call for help. Not that he had any real concern that was the case.

"They're heading to the Grand Plaza in La Paz tonight," he said. "We can intercept them there. Stay where you are. Alex Hart should be joining them shortly."

He hung up and went to wait near the pond. Five minutes passed. Hart had not emerged from the bathroom. Sensing it had been too long, he took off his blue cap and sunglasses, picked up the newspaper, and strode toward the bathroom door as if engrossed in reading. When he pushed open the door to the ladies room, an attendant looked up at him.

"I'm sorry—" he started, trying to sound embarrassed. But rather than appear startled by his intrusion, the attendant's eyes flickered as if she had expected, even feared him.

She wore white shorts and a tank top.

CHAPTER
TEN

MAPLE VALLEY, WASHINGTON

Charles Jenkins parked the Buick on the shoulder of the road and used binoculars to observe the one-story cinder-block building with the corrugated metal roof. He'd spent the better part of the afternoon driving around Maple Valley and the nearby towns talking to painting contractors. None knew a Michael Cassidy, and Jenkins was beginning to think Cassidy's father was correct, that the painting job was a ruse. He'd been looking for a freeway on-ramp when he spotted the building, partially hidden behind a gas station. A hand-painted plywood sign hung over a double-wide entry large enough to fit a commercial truck. The paint on the sign had faded and peeled, reminding Jenkins of an aging basketball hoop mounted on a barn in the Midwest. What the sign had in character it lacked in creativity:

VALLEY PAINTING

He strained to read the equally faded phone number, but couldn't decipher enough numbers, even using the binoculars. Information had no listing for a Valley Painting. Jenkins shoved the binoculars back under the passenger seat, drove down the block, and parked next to a brown truck splattered with paint. As he stepped from the car, a stiff breeze blew the branches of the alder and birch trees on the hillside behind the building. The humidity indicated an impending downpour. He removed his sunglasses as he walked inside.

"Anybody here?"

The dog burst from the shadows as if shot from a cannon and leapt. Instinctively, Jenkins spun to his right and swung hard, his left fist impacting the animal's rib cage. A radiating pain shivered up Jenkins's arm to his shoulder, but the blow knocked the dog off balance, causing it to land awkwardly, legs splaying. Undeterred, it scrambled to its feet, spun, and attacked again. In the split-second reprieve, Jenkins grabbed a gallon of paint off a plywood counter and swung the can by the wire handle, striking the dog across the jaw. This time the animal rolled several times. When it got to its feet, it shook its head, dazed, confused, or perhaps just reconsidering its attack.

Jenkins felt horrible. He didn't want to hurt the dog,

a mottled pit bull that, like the Rottweiler he and Sloan encountered in Tacoma, was just doing its job. He'd prefer to beat the crap out of the owner who had turned an animal that instinctively gave unconditional love into an untrusting, abused creature.

"Hey! Hey!"

The man emerging from the back of the building stumbled forward like a woman eight months pregnant. His paint-stained T-shirt rode halfway up a hairless belly of hardened flesh. The waist of his blue jeans rode below the gut, the seat hanging halfway to the ground, making the man's legs appear short and stubby. He held a half-eaten sandwich in one hand. Jenkins expected a confrontation for abusing the dog. Instead, he watched in horror as the man pulled back his leg and kicked the animal. The heavy work boot landed with a sickening thud under the dog's rib cage.

"Get out of here, you piece of shit."

The dog cowered and whimpered in pain.

When the man drew back his leg again, it was all Jenkins could do to keep from swinging the paint can across the back of the man's head. The dog, apparently well versed in this sadistic ritual, scampered, tail between its legs, out of the man's range, darting behind a pile of garbage at the back of the building.

Breathing heavily, the man tugged at his T-shirt and hitched up his pants. "Sorry about that. I told my dumbass kid to tie the bitch up before he left. What can I do for you?"

Jenkins struggled to control his anger. "I spotted your sign. You're not in the yellow pages."

The man shook his head. "Yellow pages are worthless." He put the sandwich down on the plywood counter next to an ashtray overflowing with cigarette butts. The counter bore the blackened marks of cigarettes left to burn. "By the time anyone gets to the V's the job is already done. I should have named the business 'Asshole Painting.' I would have got more calls."

He would get no argument from Jenkins.

"I take jobs word of mouth." The man stuck out a hand. "Chuck Kroeger."

Bingo. "Lansford Johnson," Jenkins said. "Then it's a good thing I saw your sign. I need a house painted."

"Where at?"

"Just down the road," Jenkins said. "Hundred and eightieth off Cedar Grove."

"I don't recognize you from around here," Kroeger said.

"It's a rental. I manage the property for the owner."

"Got it. Well, I can take a drive by tomorrow and give you a bid. Is this for the inside or the outside?"

"Both," Jenkins said. "But I'm in a bit of a bind. It rented faster than I expected, and the renter wants to move in day after tomorrow. The person who moved out really left the walls in bad shape. The exterior can wait, but the renter wants it painted before he moves his stuff in. I was hoping to get someone out there today."

Kroeger adjusted a black nylon baseball cap embroidered with the words "Beaver Liquors" onto the back of his head, struggling to solve the dilemma Jenkins had hoped to create. "I'm in the middle of a job now. Can't get to it today or tomorrow."

"Perhaps someone from your crew?"

Kroeger laughed, a single bark. "Hah! You're looking at the crew. Me and my kid, and only when I can get his lazy ass to work."

Jenkins removed a wad of bills from his pocket. Most were ones, but the two bills on top were hundreds. "I'm willing to pay extra to get it done quickly—cash under the table if that helps. Perhaps if you could get someone to do the interior, I could hold off on the exterior."

Kroeger scratched the top of his head, thinking. "There's a guy I use once in a while when I need the help. My kid knows him. He just got back from Iraq and needs the work."

Bingo again, Jenkins thought.

"Not a bad worker. He can do the basics all right. I could give him a call and see if he's interested."

"I'll add something on top for you, sort of a finder's fee?"

Kroeger nodded as if that happened on every job. He was seeing dollar signs for doing nothing, and not about to pass up that opportunity. He shuffled around the makeshift counter. Posters of women riding, straddling, and lying across the hoods of expensive cars and motorcycles covered much of the unfinished drywall along with graffiti symbols, phone numbers, and crude pornographic sketches. It was pretty clear what Kroeger's kid did during the down hours in the office.

"So much shit on the wall I can't find the number." Kroeger traced a stubby finger over a number on the wall. "Here it is. When do you want him out there?"

"How about this afternoon?" Jenkins said.

Kroeger picked up the telephone, keeping his finger on the wall to mark his spot and looking back twice to remember the seven digits. "I can't make any promises. He can be tough to get ahold of."

"What did you say the kid's name was?" Jenkins moved to memorize the number on the wall.

"Cassidy," Kroeger said, still looking at the wall. "Butch Cassidy."

THE TIN ROOM
BURIEN, WASHINGTON

IT WAS LATE for lunch and too early for happy hour, but a boisterous crowd had gathered at the Tin Room, a popular bar and restaurant in Burien. The establishment's popularity was one of the reasons Sloane picked it for his meeting with Colonel Bo Griffin. That, and Sloane knew some of the people who frequented the establishment, including the owner, Dan Hause, a local entrepreneur who had renovated a sheet metal and tin shop to create the restaurant, keeping an eclectic décor. The sign that had hung for decades on the exterior of the building now hung over the bar. Workbenches from the tool shop had been cut and turned into tables. Tools hung on the walls near a painting of Rolling Stones legend Mick Jagger. Near the entrance to the kitchen dangled a firefighter's bell. Ring it, and you bought everyone in the house a drink.

A man sitting on a bar stool stood as Sloane walked in the door. Though dressed in civilian clothes—khaki pants, a polo-style green shirt, and a windbreaker—Colonel Bo Griffin looked decidedly military, with short hair and the chiseled features of someone lean on body fat. This was the guy in the "break glass in case of war" box.

"Mr. Sloane?" Griffin had a firm grip. He eyed the orange-colored walls. "Interesting place."

"It's got good food," Sloane said, smelling what he decided was meat loaf and brown gravy, though that could have been because he had ordered it the last time he ate at the restaurant.

He led Griffin to a table beneath a large black-and-white photograph of tin snips and sheet metal tools lining a workbench. A waitress greeted Sloane by name and handed them each a menu. The colonel asked for a Diet Coke. Sloane requested an iced tea. Neither ordered food and they handed back the menus.

"You come here often?" Griffin asked, making a poor attempt at small talk.

"I've watched a few ball games," Sloane said, motioning to one of the flat screens to the right of the bar. He let the silence drag.

The waitress returned with their drinks. Sloane waited until she had left.

"You wanted to talk about James Ford?"

Griffin removed the straw and drank from the glass. Then he got down to business. "Every soldier's death overseas is investigated by his company and by CID. Regulations require that it be an officer not involved in the operation, but those were my men, and I believed it important to hear what they had to say, to understand what went wrong that night."

"You conducted the witness interviews?"

Griffin nodded. "One of my men died. It was my responsibility to make sure we minimized the possibility of reoccurrence."

"What did you find out?"

Griffin fixed Sloane with a cold stare. "You were a marine." It was not a question. "You saw combat in Grenada and suffered a shoulder wound when you removed your flak jacket in the middle of a military operation. Your psych evaluation said it was because you felt it weighed you down, that you wanted to move faster."

Sloane sat back. "Is this about me or James Ford, Colonel?"

"I like to know who I'm meeting, Mr. Sloane. It's an old habit. Don't take it personally. Besides, if I had really researched your background I'm sure I'd know the real reason you removed your flak jacket instead of the story you told that doctor who signed the official report." Griffin folded his hands on the table. "Am I right?"

Sloane kept a poker face. "So tell me, Colonel, since you conducted the witness interviews, did you find anything about them interesting?"

"You mean the fact that the four men told virtually identical stories?"

Sloane was surprised at the colonel's candor. "My

experience interviewing witnesses is that is not ordinarily the case. I find it even more implausible for four men engaged in battle. We've both been there. It's chaos. You react. You don't remember much of what you did."

The colonel nodded. "And my experience is that sometimes what gets put in reports is what the witness wants other people to believe happened, not what actually did happen." He stared across the table at Sloane, obviously implying that the report filed by Sloane regarding what had happened in Grenada was not the truth.

Sloane wasn't interested in revisiting his past. "You think those men with James Ford the night he died rehearsed their stories before you interviewed them?" he asked.

"Did you, when you told that doctor why you took off your flak jacket?"

"Water under the bridge, Colonel."

Griffin smiled. "I questioned the uniformity of what I was being told, yes."

"And the soldiers' responses?"

Griffin shrugged. "You read their statements."

"But you have reason to believe something else happened, something other than what those men told you?"

"I do." Griffin sat back.

"But not something that will turn up in any report I subpoena or get from any witness," Sloane inferred.

"Captain Kessler was well liked and well respected by his men, and for good reason. He was an excellent soldier. The men he commanded were fiercely loyal to him. The fact that he only lost one man in that ambush is a testament to his capabilities."

Sloane did not respond.

"I spoke to Captain Pendergrass," Griffin continued. "You will not find anything untoward, anything that will allow you to successfully argue that Specialist Ford was not killed incident to his service. I didn't."

"You're advising me to tell my client to take the money."

"I'm giving you the facts."

"Then I assume you are aware that Phillip Ferguson, one of the men in Captain Kessler's squad, is dead?"

Griffin nodded. "I know about it, yes. Captain Kessler attended the funeral."

"And are you aware that Dwayne Thomas, another man who served with James Ford that night, was found shot in the head in a vacant lot in Tacoma?"

Again Griffin nodded. "Someone showed me the article in the *Tribune*."

"And are you equally aware that a couple of days ago a man paid a visit to my house and threatened my family?"

For the first time since they sat, Griffin did not have an immediate answer.

PUEBLO BONITO LOS CABOS
CABO SAN LUCAS, MEXICO

THE MAN HAD put on a straw hat and removed his sunglasses, but Alex had no trouble spotting him in the yellow shirt. He sat on a stool at the hotel bar periodically letting his gaze slip from the television mounted on the wall to the mirror behind the bar. He watched the table on the outdoor patio where Tina and Jake sat with a horde of young men. Alex borrowed a pen from the hostess, wrote a note on a napkin, and intercepted a young woman selling red roses. She handed her $5 and the note. Then she stepped back out of view and watched the woman approach the table.

Tina accepted the rose without question and deftly slipped the note into her palm.

Alex looked over her shoulder to the entrance. She estimated she had no more than five to seven minutes before the man who had followed her realized something was wrong. When she looked back, the man at the bar was talking on his cell phone.

"Come on," she said. "Now, Tina."

Tina casually glanced down and opened the note. After a moment she stood as the note instructed, walked to one of the men from the boat, and kissed him on the cheek as if to thank him for the rose. Alex removed the blue bandana, part of the restroom attendant's uniform that had held her curls in place, and moved quickly across the restaurant, keeping her back to the man at the bar. Vincent eagerly stepped forward, looking relieved. He held a margarita and a shot of tequila. As she approached the table she let the tears flow.

"What's the matter?" he asked, not even noticing the blue uniform.

She shook her head.

"Maria, what's the matter? What happened?"

"That man at the bar, the one in the yellow Tommy Bahama shirt, has been following me," she said. "He said some horrible things to me. He called me a Mexican whore."

Vincent's head snapped in the direction of the bar. "He said what?"

Tina took Jake by the hand and walked casually toward the back exit. The man at the bar stood, grabbed his hat, and moved to follow them. That was apparently all the provocation Vincent needed. He stepped into the man's path.

"Hey, asshole, who are you calling a whore?"

Three of his friends, sensing a confrontation, quickly joined him. The man's gaze shifted to Alex. He raised his hands, palms out. "I'm afraid there's been a misunderstanding," he said.

"You got that right," Vincent said. "A big misunderstanding."

Alex stepped onto the patio, hurried around the tables with the colorful umbrellas, and darted around the corner of the building to the front of the hotel.

Tina had already hailed the cab, Jake was sitting inside, and they were waiting for her.

MAPLE VALLEY, WASHINGTON

THE "FOR RENT" sign listed to the side, pushed by the increasing wind. As Jenkins sat waiting, the skies opened. Raindrops danced off the roof of his Buick and sheeted down the windshield. It was like looking through a waterfall. Still, he liked the location because the street dead-ended at horse pastures, and the deciduous trees and thick foliage surrounding the property meant he didn't have to worry about attracting the attention of any neighbors.

Sitting with nothing to do, however, gave him time to think about Alex. He had been unable to reach her, and though he had tried to remain upbeat around Sloane, he, too, had begun to worry.

A white Chevy pickup turned the corner and inched down the street. For a minute Jenkins thought the idiot would roll right past the house, but the truck jerked to a stop, backed up, and sat idling. Three minutes passed, Cassidy likely waiting for another car to arrive before braving the rain, then the driver's door swung open and the blurred image of a thin man in blue jeans and a T-shirt dashed across the lawn holding a newspaper over his head. Cassidy quickly knocked, then tried the door handle. The one-story house had no eaves. He continued to get rained on as he cupped his hand to the plate-glass window. Earlier in the day, Jenkins had looked through the same window to ensure the house was empty. Cassidy knocked again before retreating back across the lawn to the safety of his truck.

Jenkins gave Cassidy five minutes. He lasted three before the windshield wipers started, Cassidy backed the truck into the gravel driveway, and drove down the road in the direction he had come. Jenkins started the car and followed. He could have confronted Cassidy at the house, but based on Cassidy's criminal record, Jenkins suspected that handing him a subpoena to appear in court would likely have about as much impact as handing him a roll of toilet paper. He needed to find out where Cassidy lived and sit on him until Sloane had a chance to talk to him.

Cassidy's truck turned into the gravel lot in front of Valley Painting and parked alongside a late 1980s Toyota Corolla. The brown truck was gone, Kroeger likely having returned to his current job. Jenkins pulled off the road and watched Cassidy hurry inside the building. Ten minutes later his phone rang.

"Mr. Johnson?" Chuck Kroeger sounded more anxious than annoyed.

"Mr. Kroeger, I'm glad you called. I was looking for your number. I'm afraid I lost the piece of paper on which I had it written."

"My guy was just out there. He said no one showed up."

"I'm afraid I've run into a snafu. My renter flaked out on me. Didn't show up this morning to sign the lease and make the first and last month's payment. Left me a message he and his wife found a place to buy."

"Don't you still need it painted?"

Kroeger was no dummy when it came to possibly making a buck. "I do, but given that I'm no longer under a time crunch, I'd prefer to wait. You indicated the kid wasn't too good. No offense, but if I'm paying top dollar—and I still will—I'd prefer the best. Why don't you give me a bid in the next couple days when it's convenient?"

Jenkins suspected Kroeger would be disappointed to not be making money for doing nothing, but his hard feelings would be tempered by the prospect of keeping the cash.

"All right," Kroeger said. "I'll let Butch know."

"Thanks again," Jenkins said. "I'll be in touch." He flipped closed the phone. No sooner had he done so than Cassidy exited the building followed by an overweight young man with shoulder-length blond hair and a goatee. He wore a black T-shirt with a skull and crossbones, and hitched up his pants as he walked.

"Like father, like son," Jenkins said.

The mottled dog skipped along at his heels, tail whipping from side to side as Kroeger's son shut the metal doors to the building and padlocked them. He lowered the tailgate of Cassidy's truck and coaxed the dog into the bed, clipping its collar to a short leash hooked to the side of the truck not long enough for the dog to even sit. He got into the truck next to Cassidy.

Cassidy backed from the lot, proceeded down the street, and jumped on 18 East toward Kent. Minutes later he exited to city streets. Staying close enough not to lose him to a traffic light without being detected would be tricky. Cassidy turned into a strip mall and parked. Jenkins did likewise, several rows behind. Kroeger's son exited the cab and entered a Bartell pharmacy.

"Great," Jenkins said. "Errands."

Ten minutes later Kroeger's son returned, holding a small white prescription package.

"Time to go home, Butch," Jenkins said.

But after another couple of miles Cassidy pulled into another parking lot and Kroeger again entered a drugstore, returning with another package.

"Interesting."

The pattern became quickly apparent. In between each excursion Cassidy made calls on his cell phone. After their fourth stop Jenkins realized he could be in for the long haul, checked his gas tank, turned on the radio, and decided he'd just have to wait it out.

THE TIN ROOM
BURIEN, WASHINGTON

"TELL ME EVERYTHING that happened," Griffin said.

"Not much more to tell, Colonel. A man came to my house and gave my son a fishing lesson—helped him catch the biggest fish of his life. When I went to thank him, he knew my name, my wife's name, and my son's name."

"Could he have obtained that information from your son?"

It was a legitimate question, and it made Sloane wonder if Jake could have talked to Mr. Williams about Cabo as well. "It was a threat, Colonel. He was letting me know I couldn't protect them. He wasn't subtle."

Griffin sat forward. "No one was hurt?"

Sloane shook his head. "Not physically, no."

"And your wife and child—they're somewhere safe?"

"They're safe," he said, wishing he knew for certain.

Griffin ran a hand over his face. "Could it have been someone else, someone with a different axe to grind?" He didn't sound like he believed it could.

"Doubtful. Too many coincidences," Sloane said.

Griffin looked to the window. The rain trickled off a

maroon awning, spilling into the gutter. "You wonder what it does to a man."

"What's that?" Sloane asked.

"To suddenly find himself confined to a wheelchair for the rest of his life. You wonder what it does to him psychologically."

Sloane had indeed wondered the same thing about Captain Robert Kessler.

"We have psych evaluations when the men are discharged." Griffin looked up at Sloane. "But if what you're telling me is true—"

"It's true. What do you think happened over there, Colonel? What is it Kessler doesn't want anyone to know?"

SHIMRAN AL MUSLO, IRAQ

"*I DON'T LIKE this, Captain," Ford said, and he knew Kessler didn't like their current situation either.*

The town, two- and three-story mud and brick buildings, looked to have been standing since biblical times. Some had been reduced to burned and bombed-out husks. Metal shutters and doors covered abandoned storefronts, and thousands of rounds pockmarked what remained of the walls.

"I don't hear anything," Ford said. "Why is it so quiet?"

He crept the Humvee farther down a street barely the width of the vehicle. Kessler scanned the alleys to the left and right, a maze of deserted dead ends. Ford saw no one, and couldn't imagine anyone still lived here. His instincts told him this had been a mistake, that he should hit the gas and drive them the hell out of there, but that had its own disadvantages, like failing to spot IEDs.

What the hell had they got themselves into?

Cassidy leaned forward and said what was on everyone's mind. "Let's get the fuck out of here. Let's get back on the main road and head back to base. This was wrong."

"At ease, Butch. Man your sector." Kessler scanned the buildings, searching every doorway and ragged wall opening.

"Dismount right," Thomas shouted.

"I own him," Ferguson replied through the headset, confirming that he had his M240 machine gun locked on the target.

"Burka!" Kessler shouted, quickly identifying the traditional head-to-toe black garment still worn by many Iraqi women.

Ford tried to swallow but it stuck in his throat. The fact that it was a woman both relaxed and unnerved him. It was another advantage for the insurgents—they could blend into the populace, with no way to distinguish between hostile and friendly.

"Dismounts alley left," Ferguson said.

This time Ford saw the muzzle flash of Kalashnikovs before he heard the retort of gunfire.

"Gun left! Gun left!" Kessler shouted.

As Fergie returned fire, Ford turned his attention to the road, searching for their escape, and saw what would have been just a pile of leftover scrap lumber in any other country in the world. Not in Iraq. With that realization came another: The person in the burka was not a woman.

Ford threw the transmission into reverse as the woodpile exploded. The inside of the Humvee flashed a brilliant white.

A deep, penetrating boom followed, and with it came a wave of energy. It lifted the front of the vehicle off the ground, causing it to bounce on its front wheels. The side-view mirror evaporated, and a shard of wood embedded in the bulletproof windshield, shattering the glass.

Kessler shouted through thick smoke. "Drive! Go! Go! Go!"

But another stake had pierced the Humvee's front block, causing the engine to emit a horrific roar and belch smoke. Ford stepped on and off the pedal.

"We're disabled," he yelled.

A string of three blasts erupted in succession. Large blocks of stone and concrete crashed down around them, a watermelon-size chunk crushing the hood.

And the gates of hell opened.

Insurgents wearing red-and-white-checked scarves poured from their hiding places like ants from a hole. Bullets pinged and thumped against the Humvee's armor. Another volley tore into the dashboard, the FBCB2, and the radio. Ford heard the supersonic, high-pitched whistle of rocket-propelled grenades and explosions all around them.

It was a textbook ambush. And they were caught in the kill zone.

Above them Ferguson unleashed a firestorm from his M240. Hot brass links dropped into the passenger compartment as quickly as the big gun could spit them out, the noise deafening, the acrid molten smell of heated lead and gunpowder suffocating.

Then the noise stopped and Ferguson dropped down the hatch shouting and coughing. "Two-forty down. I can't clear it."

Two thunderous roars followed two fireballs that again

lifted the Humvee. This time it did not drop back down. Ford felt himself being tossed about like a pinball. The next thing he knew, he was lying on the dirt ground, the Humvee on its side, the back end completely blown off. Sandbags and splintered pieces of plywood littered the street. He sat up and watched Fergie pop his head out the hatch and hand Kessler the M249 machine gun. Using the Humvee for cover, Kessler sprayed bullets as Fergie helped Thomas and Cassidy to crawl out the turret opening. Rounds pinged off the carriage.

Kessler handed the 249 to Ford, who continued to return fire. Fergie grabbed the M203 and launched a 40-mm grenade at a building from which they were drawing the most muzzle flashes.

Poomp! Pause. BOOM!

Kessler shouted, "Cover me."

He dropped back down through the hatch and crawled out with the radio. Pressing his back against the Humvee, he spoke calmly into the mouthpiece.

"Wolverine six, this is Alfa one-two." A bullet skimmed past his helmet. He slid lower on the ground. "Sending nine-line. Over. Wolverine six, this is Alfa one-two," he repeated. "Status report. Green. Red. Red. Over."

Bullets sprayed the ground near his boots. He tapped Ford on the shoulder and pointed. Ford saw two insurgents standing in the open, spraying and praying, and rattled off a burst, knocking both men down.

Kessler continued his transmission. "Need immediate CASEVAC. Time now. Sending nine-line. Over."

The voice came back clear and calm. "Alfa one-two, send your traffic. Over."

Ford continued to spray the buildings while Ferguson launched another grenade over their heads.

"Wolverine six, this is Alfa one-two. Our grid is—"

An RPG exploded behind them. Cassidy, who was in a fetal position, screamed. Then he vomited.

Kessler shouted, "Echo, Hotel, zero, six, zero, five, one, zero, zero, six. Over."

"Alfa one-two. Say again. Over."

Kessler repeated the grid.

"Alfa one-two, this is Wolverine six. We have your grid. Directing you to I.7 Proceed three blocks south. Left two blocks. Right two blocks. Rendezvous at traffic circle. Locate and secure granary. Pop smoke when you arrive. Over."

"Roger that," Kessler said. "Alfa one-two moving out. Over."

He dropped the handset and cradled the radio. Without missing a beat, he pulled a grenade off his ammo vest, cut the electrical tape holding down the spoon, and tossed it through an opening in a wall. It belched dust and debris. Then he pulled off two more grenades and tossed them in front of the Humvee. Yellow and purple smoke obliterated their position.

"Moving out!" he yelled, grabbing Cassidy from the ground and shoving him forward, leading them, exactly where, Ford did not know.

HIGHWAY 19 NEAR SAN VICENTE VILLAGE
BAJA, MEXICO

ALEX DIRECTED THE cabdriver north on Highway 19. She knew her gimmick to separate them from the two men would only offer a short reprieve. Access in and out of Cabo San Lucas was limited to two roads, and they quickly merged into one. Highway 1 went north to Los Barriles, then cut inland to La Paz. Highway 19 connected to Highway 1 just past Todos Santos, about an hour outside of Cabo. Ideally Alex would have preferred to travel to La Paz, the capital of Baja and a city of nearly 200,000. It would be easier to get lost in a crowd. But the drive was two hours, too long to remain on the same stretch of road. Two men could each take a road and, traveling at a high rate of speed, easily overtake them. She was not eager to get into a shootout.

Todos Santos was closer, but significantly smaller, just a few square blocks with a limited number of hotels. That wouldn't work either. Instead, she directed the driver to turn off the highway onto a dirt road, looking back to make sure no car followed them.

"Aquí," she said.

The driver stopped and looked about the desolate desert. *"Aquí?"*

"Sí." She stepped from the taxi into the warm sun. Tina and Jake followed.

"What are we doing here?" Jake asked.

"Give me a minute," Alex said. Tina walked Jake away from the taxi.

Alex leaned in the driver's window. The fare was nearly $80. Taxis in Cabo were not cheap. She handed the driver three hundred-dollar bills, continuing to speak to him in Spanish, telling him that when he got back to the road, she wanted him to continue driving north to La Paz as quickly as he could.

"Cuando regresemos a la carretera continua manejando hacia el norte rumbo a La Paz. Ve lo mas raido que puedas."

The driver gave her a perplexed look.

She handed him a note. "Give this to the person at the registration desk at the Grand Plaza hotel and they will give you an envelope. Inside is another three hundred dollars. That is also yours to keep. If anyone stops you on the drive back, tell him you took us to the Grand Plaza in La Paz. You can't get in any trouble if you tell them that. *Me haces ese favor?"* she asked.

The driver nodded. *"Sí, señorita. No hay problema."*

Alex thanked the man and stepped back, watching the taxi make a U-turn and depart, kicking up dust as it left them in the desert.

Tina and Jake stood looking forlorn.

"Are you ready?" Alex asked Jake, trying to sound upbeat.

The boy shrugged. "Ready for what?"

"A hike."

"Is this another one of those things I'm supposed to do without question?"

Tina said that it was.

"Then I guess so."

Though nearly dusk, it remained hot. The cactus and scrub brush offered no shade. They also had no water. As they neared what appeared to be a small farming village of cinder-block and adobe homes Alex left the path, giving the village a wide berth.

Tina spoke into her ear. "Why don't we go and at least get some water?"

"I don't want anyone in town seeing two women and a boy."

"Then, where are we going?"

"Trust me."

Clear of the village, she looped back to the path and continued walking for another half an hour. Just as she was beginning to think she had screwed up, they came to the campground in the foothills of the Sierra de la Laguna mountain range. The woman at the first motel had told her about the camp, an option Alex had stowed away, though hoping not to have to use.

Jake surveyed the handful of tents pitched in the shade of an organic orchard of mango, avocado, and grapefruit trees. "Is this the surprise?" He didn't sound or look happy.

"Your mother and I thought we might camp for a night," Alex said.

Jake turned to his mother. "But you hate camping."

Tina shrugged. "We always talk about trying things outside our comfort zones."

"We don't have any camping equipment."

"We can rent it here," Alex said. "Why don't you look around while I talk to the owner. I'm told there are all kinds of lizards, Jake."

That perked his spirits a bit. "Cool. Come on, Mom, let's find one."

As Alex approached the open-air kitchen, a woman ducked out from beneath the flap of a green canvas tent. "Can I help you?" American, she was decidedly of the Whole Earth crowd, in baggy shorts, Mexican sandals, a tank top, and a wide-brimmed hat.

"We need a place to stay for the night, maybe two."

The woman eyed Alex with suspicion.

Alex nodded to Tina and Jake. "Her husband is a very wealthy man in Southern California. He's also abusive. My organization helps women and their children hide until the divorce is final, and court decrees are in place. His men have tracked her to Cabo. They cannot find her. I'll pay cash, double the rate. We won't be a problem."

The woman shook her head. "That's not necessary. They're welcome here. I'll see what I can round up in the way of sleeping bags and some extra clothes. Are you hungry?"

AFTER GETTING JAKE to bed, Alex changed from the maid's uniform and the two women sat outside the tent talking. Alex did her best to fill Tina in on what had transpired since she first noticed the men at the dock.

"Tomorrow morning take Jake up into the mountains. The owner says there's a pool up there to keep him occupied. The trail is not well marked, so take a machete with you and make an X at the base of the trees as you go. I'll find you."

"Shouldn't we stay together?"

"I've only bought us time, and maybe not a lot at that. On the walk in I saw what looked like a large cattle ranch to the south of the village. I'll go and see about arranging for some permanent transportation out of here, then come back and get you."

CHAPTER
ELEVEN

Jenkins sat slumped in his seat, tired from the boredom and inactivity. His legs ached, but each time he adjusted, it caused a stabbing jab in his back. By his count, the two doofusses in the truck had stopped at nine drugstores, backtracking as far south as Auburn. He was ready to just pull them over and tell Cassidy to "go home," like a misbehaving dog, but then the white Chevy jumped back on Highway 18 in the direction of Maple Valley.

"Thank God," Jenkins said, relieved.

They eventually wound their way back to Valley Painting. The brown truck was still not there. Kroeger's son unleashed the dog, but rather than open the tailgate to ease her out, he tugged the chain collar and forced her to jump over the truck bed. With her leg muscles weary from being forced to stand the entire trip, the animal tumbled and hit her head. She rose shaking the water from her coat. Freedom was brief. Kroeger opened the hatchback of the Corolla, yanked the dog by her collar into the cramped space, and slammed it shut.

When Cassidy backed out to leave, the Corolla followed. Jenkins couldn't catch a break. He would have to be really careful. Following a car on rural residential streets without being seen was difficult enough. Doing it as part of a convoy would be even more so.

About ten miles outside of town, Cassidy made a left and ascended a mild grade. Jenkins slowed to give the two cars a head start before he turned and started the climb. Cresting the top, he quickly realized his problem had just become worse. Densely forested on each side, the road was sparsely traveled. He turned off the headlights, hoping that dusk, the weather, and the bends in the road would help to conceal the Buick. After another half a mile, he lost sight of both cars over a rise in the road. When he descended the other side, the stretch of asphalt was empty.

"Damn."

He couldn't slow for concern the two idiots weren't as stupid as he thought and had pulled off the road to determine if they were being followed. He drove until another bend in the road took him out of the line of vision, saw signs for a quarry, and made a two-point turn so he could back down a gravel driveway, facing the road. When the two cars didn't drive past, he started back the other direction. If they had pulled off, it had to have been within a short distance of the crest in the road.

Proceeding slowly, he saw what he was looking for, a dirt road partially overgrown with brambles of black-berry bushes and Scotch broom. He stopped on the side of the road and got out, feigning interest in a front tire but really looking at the muddy road. The tire tracks were fresh.

Back in the Buick, he turned off the asphalt and crept up the road, the bushes scraping the sides of his car. He sensed a creek bed to his right and tried to hug the left side of the road, but foliage on that side scratched the door panel. Cassidy sought serious solitude, and Jenkins sensed why after the daylong pharmaceutical trips.

When Jenkins came to a small clearing big enough to park the Buick, he killed the engine and let the car glide into tall grass and foliage. The front wheels dropped slightly, indicating an embankment. He stepped down on the emergency brake, grabbed the binoculars from under the seat, and slid out the door.

The rain had lightened to a drizzle, but judging from the darkened sky, the storm had not yet passed. He walked up the road, which inclined for another hundred yards, and started down the other side. The road bent sharply to the right. Unsure what lay ahead, he decided to get off the path and pushed through foliage. The ground was muddy and the underbrush thick. Then it cleared, revealing a large field of waist-high grass. Jenkins slowed, unsure of his footing. Dampness began to seep through his ankle-high boots, but the ground seemed hard enough to hold him.

Halfway across the field he knelt and raised the binoculars. The night-vision made the landscape glow a ghostly gray-green. Across the field someone had buttressed a weathered mobile home against a hillside. It sat amidst piles of junk, a toilet, propane tanks, beer cans, gas cans, wood, and a mound of miscellaneous garbage near which Cassidy and Kroeger had both parked. A light, tempered by a curtain, leaked from the trailer's window.

"No place like home," Jenkins said.

He surveyed the surrounding area. The road, had he stayed on it, continued around the field perpendicular to the trailer before turning again and running parallel to it, like a horseshoe. Just past the trailer Jenkins focused on an aluminum shed. The dog lifted her head at the sound of a coyote yipping. They'd chained her to the side. Jenkins saw no bowl for water or food.

He crept in for a closer look. The darkness and tall grass would cover his advance, though he'd have to be careful not to alert the dog. As he crossed the field his boots began to sink deeper, making a sucking sound each time he pulled free. He got within sixty yards, knelt again, and refocused the binoculars on the trailer.

The door opened.

The effect was like a flashbulb popping, though the binoculars were designed to shut down upon sudden light exposure to prevent blinding the user. Still, instinct caused Jenkins to lower them and look away.

Car doors slammed. An engine cranked to life, followed by another. Back-up lights lit up the night.

Evidently this was not home sweet home, Cassidy

and Kroeger weren't staying, there was only one road out, and it went right past where Jenkins had parked his car.

Even Dumb and Dumber would notice it.

THE TIN ROOM
BURIEN, WASHINGTON

COLONEL BO GRIFFIN had candidly admitted that the military's sudden interest in settling James Ford's claim was because of Sloane's involvement.

"You changed things."

"Why?"

"You didn't serve in Vietnam, but the drug and alcohol problem there was very real," Griffin said. "We tried to minimize that impact in Iraq by banning alcohol from base. Unfortunately, it has created quite a black market."

"You're saying Captain Kessler's squad didn't get lost in a sandstorm."

"There was a sandstorm, but the chances of a squad getting lost with the technology now employed inside the vehicle makes it highly unlikely the storm caused them to veer off course that far."

"So how did they end up in that village?"

"What do I know happened? Or what do I suspect happened?"

"Either."

"I know for certain that Captain Kessler and his men were bringing supplies to their FOB. Most of those supplies were basic staples to people like you and me, but to people living in the middle of a war zone they become considerably more valuable. We're talking about cartons of cigarettes, household supplies, and MREs—meals ready to eat. The squads protecting those convoys would have had ready access to those supplies. Things get lost, unaccounted for. It isn't difficult."

"You're saying they can be stolen and then sold or traded?"

Griffin nodded. "The Iraqis understand bartering very well. It's not a fortune, but it's not about what they're trading, it's what they're seeking in return."

"What are they seeking?"

"Drugs. Cocaine, hashish, opium, heroin. And alcohol and Iraqi pornography. We've become aware of soldiers falsely reporting an inability to sleep or to cope with the stress in order to get prescribed tranquilizers, antidepressants, and pain medication like Valium and Percocet, or modafinil, which is like speed but without the aftereffects. Those have a much higher street value."

"So they drive into these small towns, open up the back of the Humvee, and trade on the streets?"

"The sandstorm would have been the perfect cover for Captain Kessler to stop his vehicle, let the convoy proceed ahead, and divert into the local towns. He wasn't far from base, and the insurgency wasn't as well organized or widespread. Unfortunately, he picked the wrong town on the wrong day. He drove directly into that ambush."

"If you suspected that to be the case, Colonel, why didn't you push this matter further? Why not conduct an Article 32 hearing? If what you're saying is true, Captain Kessler was directly responsible for James Ford's death."

Griffin's voice hardened. "You saw the reports. What evidence did I have to pursue it? What evidence will you have?" Griffin crumpled a napkin and put it in his glass of melting ice. "And what good would have come from it? Why did you take your flak jacket off in Grenada and then lie about it? Who were you protecting, and why were you protecting him?"

The question was rhetorical. Sloane didn't respond.

"An investigation would have led to Captain Kessler and every one of those men being court-martialed. And it would have changed absolutely nothing, not a damn thing that we're doing over there. Don't you think Kessler was punished enough?"

"It would have sent a message to other soldiers."

"More than the message that ambush sent? More than the message James Ford's body sent when it came back to base in a bag?" Griffin shook his head. "Word spreads quickly on a base, Mr. Sloane. The message got out loud and clear. How do you think I heard the rumors? And what about the families of those men? Was I going to be the one to pull those medals off their chests?" Griffin cleared his throat and took a minute to calm down. "Besides," he said, softer. "I had no other avenues. As long as they all stuck to the same story, I had nothing to pursue. Kessler knew that. He knew it when I ended my investigation and James Ford's claim was denied. It was over—until you got involved."

"So *you* reopened the claim."

"We had no choice. It must have spooked him. He must have thought we were onto something."

"Kessler?"

Griffin nodded. "I wanted the chance to convince the chain of command to settle Ford's claim. I wanted to allow Ford's family to maintain their dignity. I never envisioned they would turn the money down. And I never envisioned it would lead to this."

"Good intentions aside, Colonel, you can't ignore this. Captain Kessler is no longer just guilty of misguided judgment. He killed Ferguson and Thomas, and he's using Argus's security forces to do it."

"How do you know?"

"I've seen their operation, Colonel. They made Ferguson's death look like a suicide and Thomas's death a drug killing. The man who came to my house also made it clear that if I kept looking into Argus, they'd take a greater interest in my family. There's another soldier out there from Kessler's squad still alive. If I'm right, he's a marked man. We need to find him before they do."

AS JENKINS LUMBERED across the uneven ground, his leg sank to his shin, as if something below the surface had grabbed hold of his foot and yanked down. When he pulled up, the heel slipped and he stepped out of the shoe. Off balance, he hopped once, then tumbled into the mud and wet grass. He turned back and searched through the weeds, but in the darkness he couldn't see a thing. He tried the night-vision but had no better luck.

His shoe was lost somewhere beneath the grass and mud, and he didn't have time to find it.

The two cars turned the bend in the road, proceeding around the field, one behind the other. Jenkins rose and hobbled across the field. At the edge of the thick underbrush he lost sight of the headlights. The cars had turned the corner. He pushed through the brush, protecting his face with his arms. Pain jabbed the bottom of his shoeless foot. Stepping free of the entanglement, he limped and shuffled down the road, blocking out the pain. His only hope was that Cassidy and Kroeger had to drive cautiously on the narrow road.

When he reached the Buick he glanced back, but did not see the approach of headlights. He slipped behind the wheel, started the engine, threw the car into reverse, looked over his right shoulder, and hit the gas. The back tires spun but did not grip. Instead, the front end slipped farther forward. Jenkins looked to his left. Beams of headlights shimmered high in the trees. Cassidy's truck was about to crest the hill. Even if Jenkins could get the car unstuck, he could never back it down the road without being seen. Cassidy and Kroeger would make him, and if they were doing what he suspected, they would be armed. He didn't want to start shooting people and likely kill Sloane's lone witness.

The beams of light grew brighter. The truck drew near.

Jenkins looked at the front of his car, now engulfed in foliage to the windshield.

He had no other choice.

THREE TREE POINT, WASHINGTON

THE HEADLIGHTS DESCENDED Maple-wild, and slowed just past the convenience store. Jenkins had called and told Sloane to wait out front, withholding any further details. He sounded pissed about something, but also said a picture was worth a thousand words, which Sloane assumed meant he'd explain later. The car turned out to be a tow truck, the Buick suspended behind it, back end off the ground. Caked in gunk, it looked like it had been driven through a mud hole. Reeds of grass and branches hung from the front bumper and grille.

The second surprise came when Jenkins stepped from the cab of the truck and limped toward Sloane barefoot, holding only one shoe. He looked as bad as the Buick, his pants covered in mud to mid-thigh.

"What happened?" Sloane asked. "Where's your other shoe?"

"Somewhere beneath three feet of mud."

"The car looks like it was beneath three feet of mud."

"That's because it was."

Sloane circled the car as the driver backed it into a spot in the easement. "Did you crash? Drive off a cliff?"

"Actually, this was self-inflicted." Jenkins explained how he had followed Cassidy and Kroeger for the better part of the day, and how they had led him to the trailer hidden in the woods, before their sudden decision to leave. "My only choice was to go forward and hope the foliage hid the car."

"So you drove into a ditch?"

"I didn't know it was that steep. Besides, I didn't exactly have a good explanation for what the hell I was doing up there, and I didn't want to end up in the same place as my shoe or have to shoot either of them."

"What are they doing?"

"We'll talk about that in a minute. Did you meet with Griffin?"

"He had quite the story to tell."

"How did it end?"

"Same way it started. Cassidy's dead if we don't get to him first."

"Then we need to go back there tonight."

"You said they left."

"They'll be back—one of them at least."

"How can you be sure?"

"Because they got something cooking and have to keep an eye on it. You got any camping equipment?"

"Some."

"Get out what you have. I'll throw my clothes in the wash and take a shower while you make me something to eat."

"What about your shoes?"

"I'll pick up a pair of boots when we go for supplies. Good thing my employer gives me an expense account." Jenkins started down the easement toward the gate. "Come on. We'll only get one shot at this."

THEY STOPPED FOR supplies at the Fred Meyer store in Burien. Jenkins pushed a cart through the aisles, grabbing headlamps, batteries, wool socks, waterproof gloves, long-sleeved thermal shirts, backpacks, camouflage floppy hats, two heavy green tarps, a bolt cutter, two sixteen-ounce water bottles and a size 14 pair of black combat-style boots. At the counter he grabbed a handful of health bars and packages of beef jerky.

In the parking lot Jenkins hid their purchases under the tarp in the back of Alex's Explorer. Alex had brought down his guns from Camano Island when he called at Sloane's request and asked her to get to Three Tree Point and stay with Tina and Jake until he or Sloane could get there. She'd brought his 12-gauge shotgun and an AR15 rifle, the civilian equivalent to an M16, which Jenkins had fitted with a Leupold scope. She also brought extra rounds for his Smith & Wesson and Glock.

Inside the car, Jenkins provided Sloane an overview of the terrain. "We can't approach the trailer from the front; it's two hundred yards of open space. The grass is tall, but the footing is bad from the rain, as you know, and there's no good place to park the car, which you also know. Besides, if someone else has found Cassidy, we don't want to get pinned in that grass."

"So what do you suggest?"

"There's a quarry up there that looks to have been closed for some time. We can hide the car there and hike in over the foothills. It's only about a thousand feet in elevation, but the foliage is thick and nasty. Without a defined path it's going to be slow going. But the vantage point will also be better up high. If anyone has found Cassidy, we'll be looking down on them."

Half an hour later, Jenkins exited the freeway and drove east through Maple Valley. He slowed the Explorer and turned up a hill, the road heavily wooded on both sides. With no street lamps or ambient light, the Explorer's headlights bored two funnel cones through the darkness.

"The road is up here on the right," Jenkins said, slowing. He turned off the asphalt onto dirt and gravel and drove for about ten yards, stopping at a metal gate across the road and shutting off the headlights.

"You drive," he said, sliding out the door with the pair of bolt cutters.

Sloane slid behind the wheel and watched Jenkins snap a chain locking the gate to a concrete embedded post. When he pushed the gate open, Sloane drove through and waited on the other side while Jenkins closed it and wrapped the chain back around the pole so it again appeared locked. Then he slid into the passenger seat.

Sloane followed the road into what looked like a crater on a distant planet. The surrounding hillside had been scraped and scarred by heavy equipment, leaving piles of upended tree stumps and boulders. The quarry was a good spot to leave the car.

At the back of the car they filled the two backpacks with the supplies and slipped on the headlamps. The glow illuminated a six-foot path but not much more than that. Jenkins slung the strap for his rifle over his shoulder and carried the shotgun. He gave Sloane the Glock and the Smith & Wesson.

As they descended the paved path and approached the main road, they turned off their headlamps, crossed the asphalt pavement in darkness, and stepped into the woods.

Jenkins had accurately described the terrain. Judging from the size of the trees and height of the branches, the area had been logged perhaps twenty years earlier, giving the undergrowth plenty of sunlight to grow thick and dense. And the recent rains had made the ground covering, ferns and composted leaves, slippery and unstable.

"They have bears out here?" Jenkins asked.

"I don't know, why?"

"I don't like bears."

"I read that you're supposed to wear bells on your hat to scare them off," Sloane said, struggling to catch his breath and find a rhythm to his breathing.

"Yeah, I've read that too," Jenkins replied. "Only my mother used to ring a bell to call my brothers and me to dinner."

They pushed on, the going slow. Jenkins led, holding each branch until Sloane could grab it. Neither spoke much, concentrating instead on his footing. The cool night air felt sodden and the waterproof hooded ponchos restricted air circulation. Sloane had soon perspired through his clothes. They stopped twice to drink water and allow Jenkins to check the compass. The smell of pine was strong, and the air buzzed with insects, the chirp of crickets, and the occasional hoot of an owl. After an hour of uphill hiking, the terrain flattened and the trees thinned. They had reached the top.

"If I did this correctly," Jenkins said, taking a gulp of water and breathing hard, "we should drop down just behind Cassidy's trailer. How're you doing?"

"I'm fine," Sloane said, though the hike had been harder than he had expected. He could feel the strain in the muscles of his thighs.

"All downhill from here."

But hiking down was as difficult as hiking up. The wet compost gave way unexpectedly, causing them to stumble frequently. Each landed on his ass once. Sloane picked up a branch to use as a walking stick, jabbing it into the ground in front of him for support and balance.

After another thirty minutes, Jenkins stopped and turned off his headlamp. Sloane did the same, plunging them into darkness. Jenkins lowered his backpack and lifted the binoculars, taking a moment to scan the area.

He handed Sloane the binoculars and pointed. "Bottom of the hill, follow the tree line about two hundred and fifty yards north."

With the night-vision the forest glowed green—so did a dilapidated shed, and next to it an equally dilapidated mobile home amidst a mound of junk. "What a dump."

"Didn't I tell you?"

Jenkins took back the binoculars and methodically scanned the area. When he was finished, he handed Sloane back the binoculars, spread a tarp on the ground, set the alarm on his wristwatch, and lay down. He pulled the poncho tight around his collar and lowered the brim of his hat over his face. "You get the first watch."

Sloane sat on his own tarp, chewing on a health bar. "What if he sticks to his story?"

Jenkins tilted back the hat. "You're not one of those Chatty Cathys in bed are you?"

"What if Cassidy sticks to his story?"

"Then we're no worse off than we are now, except for less sleep. Besides, nothing loosens lips like the knowledge that someone you trusted is trying to kill you."

Sloane shook his head. "Something is wrong. I'm missing something."

Jenkins sat up on his elbow. "Maybe it's like the guy in L.A. said—Argus was dirty over there. Hell Kessler could be using the Argus security force to continue the business he started, selling drugs. He could have made any number of contacts during his first tour. Or maybe it's like Griffin said, a man takes a bullet to his spine and finds himself confined to a wheelchair. He gets bitter and angry. He begins to believe he's entitled to a lot more than the military will otherwise provide. We can speculate until the cows come home. Why don't we just wait and find out what Cassidy knows."

Jenkins lay back down and again pulled the brim of the hat low over his face.

"I'm missing something," Sloane said.

Then he thought of Tina and Jake. He would not sleep, and he knew Jenkins wouldn't either.

SAN VICENTE VILLAGE
BAJA, MEXICO

THE TWO MEN drove the black SUV through the tiny village. Early in the morning, three boys walked along the road without shirts or shoes. One dangled a stick behind him, leaving a line in the dirt. A dog followed at another's heels.

The driver of the SUV slowed and rolled down the window. *"Buenos días, muchachos,"* he said.

The boys stopped and admired the car, smelling money. The dog barked and bounced around the vehicle.

"Estoy buscando a tres gringos," he said, telling the boys he was looking for three Americans. He adjusted the blue cap on the back of his head, speaking fluent Spanish. "I'm looking for my wife and son, a boy about your age. They're traveling with another woman. I'm afraid they could be lost." He asked if they had seen them. *"Los has visto?"*

The boys shook their heads no.

He held dollar bills out the window. *"Es muy importante que los encuetre,"* he said. "Is there any place else around here, any other villages I could check?"

The tallest of the three boys stepped to the window and pointed down the road.

"Para alla," he said, pointing down the road. "Maybe down there."

The man looked down the road. "Yeah? What's down there?"

"Un campemento," the boy replied, adding, "A gringo lady owns it."

The driver looked to his partner in the passenger seat, then back to the window. *"Gracias."*

He took his foot off the brake and let the car roll slowly down the road, still dangling the money out the window. The boys gave chase, shouting, but the man kept the dollars fluttering just beyond reach until he tired of the game and let loose, watching in the side mirror as the money scattered, sending the boys into a frenzy.

"Just like a pack of dogs," he said.

A mile down the road they came to what was presumably the campground, a handful of tents pitched in a small orchard. Why anyone would travel to Baja to stay in a tent, he hadn't a clue, but it would be a good place to hide.

The two men parked and exited the car. A woman, presumably the American the boys spoke of, stepped out from beneath a large canopy to greet them. "What can I do for you?" She smiled, but it did not look genuine. It looked forced. He pulled out credentials that identified him as a private investigator. "We're looking for two American women who've kidnapped a boy from Seattle. Have you seen them?"

The woman shook her head. "No."

Her eyes betrayed her. They registered fear. In his experience innocent people had nothing to fear. "We spotted them in Cabo but they evaded us. We believe they headed north, possibly hiding in one of the villages along the way."

"Did you check the village down the road?"

He nodded, looking about the camp. "Would you mind if we looked around?"

"I have guests here," the woman said.

He shrugged and stepped toward the tents. "We won't disturb anyone."

She moved into his path. "But I told you they're not here."

"Then you have nothing to worry about, do you?"

She grew defiant. "You have no authority here."

He removed his sunglasses. "You know about authority? They're fugitives from justice. If you're harboring them, that makes you an accomplice. Or are you a fugitive? You can hire a lawyer and sue me if I'm wrong. How's that for authority?"

The woman stepped back. "I told you they're not here."

They divided the task, searching the tents, going through the belongings. When they returned, the woman sat drinking a cup of tea, trying to appear calm.

"Will you be leaving now?" she asked.

The driver sat down at the table across from her. "Actually, we think we might like to stay a night. Do you have any openings?"

She shook her head. "We're full."

"That's too bad." He pulled out the blue hotel uniform and placed it on the table. "I've never stayed at a camp with maid service."

MAPLE VALLEY, WASHINGTON

JENKINS SAT UP and took the binoculars from Sloane but did not raise them. There was no need. The two cones of light across the grass field flickered behind the trunks of trees and shimmered in the branches before disappearing as the vehicle turned at the bend in the road. A few seconds later the lights reappeared and proceeded toward the trailer. As the vehicle neared, Sloane saw that it was a white truck.

Jenkins stood. "I love it when I'm right."

The dog tugged at the end of her tethered leash, tail wagging with excitement. Her bark echoed up to them, scaring birds from trees.

"Amazing," Jenkins said. "They treat her like shit. Don't feed her. No water. Leave her out in the cold all night, and she still just wants to love them."

A young man stepped from the cab, one hand thrust into the pocket of his blue jeans, the other holding a cigarette to his lips.

"Cassidy," Jenkins said.

Using the binoculars, Sloane watched Cassidy shiver against the dawn cold, shifting from one boot to the other as he sucked on a cigarette and blew out a cloud of smoke. In a flannel shirt, he looked like a construction worker inhaling as much nicotine as possible before rushing back to the job. Cassidy looked up the hill, causing Sloane to lower the binoculars.

"Relax," Jenkins said. "No way he can see us."

Cassidy flicked the butt at the dog, walked to the edge of the grass, which was covered by a thin layer of mist, and unzipped his fly. Steam rose where he urinated. Finished, he jumped up and down to zip his fly, pushed the bangs of hair from his face, and walked up the dilapidated trailer steps searching a key ring. He unlocked one lock, flipped through the ring for a key to a second lock, and repeated the process.

"A lot of security for a trailer nobody would ever find. What's the guy making, gold?" Sloane asked.

"Not far from the truth," Jenkins said. As Cassidy stepped inside the trailer Jenkins gathered their things. "Time to go pay him a visit."

"What about the dog?"

"Dog won't bother us."

"What if she starts to bark?"

"Dogs bark, David. No way to keep a dog from barking. We'll use it to our advantage. Just remember what we discussed."

At the bottom of the hill they split up. Sloane reached a designated spot in the trees about fifty yards from the trailer and waited. The dog's ears perked and she turned in his direction, sniffing the air. When the dog appeared to lose interest Sloane shuffled closer, slow and quiet. The tree line ended about twenty-five yards from the trailer. He squatted, checked his watch, waiting until the exact time he and Jenkins had agreed. Then he stood and stepped from the trees. The dog's head snapped in his direction and she lunged against the rope barking and growling. Sloane swung his approach in a wider arc to avoid her.

A curtain pulled back inside the mobile home. Cassidy pressed his face to the window. Then he disappeared. A second later the door to the trailer swung open and Cassidy stepped out onto the porch, the butt of a handgun protruding from the waist of his jeans.

"Hey! This is private property. You're trespassing!" He looked and sounded like a punk kid.

Sloane put a hand to his ear as if he couldn't hear over the dog's barking and slowed his approach. He needed Cassidy to step away from the door and down the steps. "What's that?"

"I said, this is private property. You're trespassing."

Sloane raised both hands. "Wow. I'm sorry about that. Someone told me there's a lake around here. I was hoping to do some fishing. I must have taken a wrong turn."

"A big wrong turn. There's no lake around here. So just turn around and go back the direction you came or I'll unleash the dog."

"No reason to get hostile, friend." Sloane took a couple more steps toward the trailer. The dog's bark grew more forceful. "It was an honest mistake."

"I ain't your friend, and I don't believe in honest mistakes." Cassidy stepped down off the porch and started toward Sloane. He pointed to the trees. "So just get the fuck out of here." He paused, a thought apparently coming to him. "Where's your fishing pole anyway?"

Cassidy's hand went for the butt of the gun, but before he reached it, Jenkins had come from around the backside of the trailer and swept the young man's legs out from under him. Cassidy lay on his back, the shotgun leveled at his face.

"Easy there, partner."

For a second it looked like the idiot might reach for his gun.

"Don't!" Jenkins warned. Cassidy froze like a bug on its back unable to right itself. "Don't . . . do . . . anything . . . stupid. Put your hands on the back of your head and interlock your fingers." Cassidy complied. "David, come around here." Jenkins handed him the shotgun. "Put a bead on this shithead; if he so much as flinches, shoot him. You don't even have to aim. It will cut him in half."

Sloane aimed the shotgun at the ground, not comfortable pointing it at Cassidy.

"Who are you?" Cassidy's bravado had been replaced with a staccato quiver.

"We're the guys holding the shotgun to your head. That's all that matters at the moment. So shut up." Jenkins pulled the gun from Cassidy's pants, a nickel-and-dime nine millimeter. The damn thing felt like plastic. "Anybody ever tell you not to shove a gun down the front of your pants, son? Good way to blow your dick off. You hold it at your side or put it at the small of your back." Jenkins threw the gun into the tall grass. "When you go looking for that, see if you can find a shoe while you're at it."

Cassidy looked at Jenkins like he was crazy.

Jenkins ran his hands over the rest of Cassidy's body, finding a sheathed, serrated knife strapped to Cassidy's leg just above his boot. "You have any more weapons on you, Butch?"

Cassidy shook his head. Then his eyes widened. "How do you know my name?"

"Your name isn't Butch. It's Michael. You a fan of *Butch Cassidy and the Sundance Kid*?"

"Never seen it."

"Figures. I know everything about you, Michael. You and me, we spent the day together with that other dirt-bag, Kroeger."

Cassidy looked confused. "I don't know you."

"I didn't say *you knew me*. You got any more weapons inside the trailer?"

"No."

"Liar. Let's all go inside and look, shall we?"

"Can I put my hands down?"

"Yeah, but if you so much as fart I'll come down on you like a hammer. You got it?" Jenkins took back the shotgun. "David, you go in first. Just be careful not to touch anything and don't take any deep breaths."

The steps sagged under Sloane's weight, rotted. He ducked inside the trailer. The smell nearly overwhelmed him, like a huge litter box for cats. His eyes watered and burned. He covered his nose and mouth with the sleeve of his shirt, fighting a gag reflex. After a moment the smell was less like cat urine and more like ammonia.

The inside of the trailer looked a lot like the yard. Mason jars filled with a clear liquid atop an inch of white or red solid material were scattered about the room. The cabinet doors had been removed, revealing bottles of iodine, and sulfuric, muriatic, and hydrochloric acid. Other unlabeled bottles contained a reddish-purple powder with rubber tubing protruding from the top. Cans of camp fuel, paint thinner, acetone, lithium batteries, and propane tanks, some with blue nozzles, littered the bare plywood floor.

Jenkins ducked inside behind Cassidy, his head inches

from the ceiling. "Well, well, well. What have we here?" He walked down a narrow hall to what was presumably the bedroom before returning to where Sloane and Cassidy stood. "This is quite the operation you have going here, Mike. You're a regular chemist. You ever see a crystal meth lab, David?"

Sloane shook his head. "No, but this would be my vision of hell."

"Oh, no," Jenkins replied, speaking as if Cassidy weren't in the room. "Hell is for the people who become addicted to this stuff." His voice hardened. "You a junkie, Michael, or are you the devil ruling over hell?"

Cassidy tilted back his head and thrust out his narrow chin, making it even more prominent. With angular, thin features, an equally prominent Adam's apple, and a nose that looked to have been broken and not set, he resembled a Midwest scarecrow. His eyes blinked rapidly—a tic. "I don't have to say nothing. I know my rights. I want to talk to a lawyer."

"Well, you're in luck there, Mike. David here is a lawyer."

Cassidy looked to Sloane. "You're not a cop?"

Sloane shook his head. "Lucky you."

Cassidy turned back to Jenkins. "Who are you?"

"A guy who really hates drug dealers and dog abusers."

"What do you want?"

"Believe it or not, we're your guardian angels," Jenkins said. "Surprise! We came to save your life. You can thank us later."

Cassidy's brow furrowed. "Say what?"

"We need some information," Sloane interjected. "And we have some information to give in exchange."

"About what?" Cassidy bit the nail of his index finger.

"James Ford."

The name seemed to momentarily catch Cassidy off guard, though not because he didn't recognize it. It likely didn't fit with Cassidy's current predicament. He pulled the finger out of his mouth. "Jimmy Ford? The dude in Iraq?"

"That's right."

"What's he got to do with this?"

"He's got nothing to do with this." Sloane gestured to the inside of the trailer. "I represent his family. They're suing the government for the way he died. I'm trying to find out what happened that night. I need you to tell me about it."

Cassidy laughed. "You ain't here to bust me?"

"We're still debating that," Jenkins said.

"Not if you cooperate and tell me what I need to know," Sloane said.

"About what?"

"Get the wax out of your ears, Michael," Jenkins said. "About what happened the night James Ford died."

Cassidy went back to nibbling on his nail. Sloane knew he was thinking like a drug dealer, wondering what the information could be worth even though he had no idea why Sloane needed it. "How much are you suing them for?"

"Oh, Christ," Jenkins said.

"You looking to make a deal?" Sloane asked. "Okay, here's a deal. You tell us what we want to know and we don't call the police so you can spend the next twenty to thirty years in jail. And if that's not enough to motivate you, then how about we keep you from getting killed?"

Cassidy scoffed. "Right. Who would be trying to kill me?"

"First things first," Sloane said. "Tell me what happened over there."

Cassidy's face momentarily hardened, but he knew he was screwed. He just didn't like it. "Hell, I would have told you anyway. You could have just asked me."

Sloane doubted it. "Start at the beginning."

Cassidy leaned his back against the counter and gripped the edge. "It was fucked up from the start."

"What was?" Sloane asked, remembering Katherine Ferguson told him that her husband had said something similar. *They never should have been there.*

"The night Jimmy got shot. The whole thing was fucked up."

"In what way?"

"In every way."

"I'm going to need more specifics. What were you doing away from your FOB?"

Cassidy looked like he was momentarily constipated. "They had us protecting a supply convoy. I hated that."

"Why?"

"Because the fucking Hajjis over there couldn't wait to blow our asses up with a bomb shoved up a donkey's ass, is why." His voice escalated. "Or else they hid under tarps along the side of the road to shoot at us."

"You boys ever take some stuff off those supply trucks?" Sloane asked.

Cassidy shrugged. "Sometimes. Hell, everyone did it—pack of smokes or an extra MRE. It wasn't any big deal."

"Your witness statement says you got stuck in a sandstorm."

Cassidy nodded. "It's like having a whole mountain of sand blasting at you. It comes out of nowhere like that. You can't see shit."

"So Captain Kessler gave the order to stop."

"Nothing more you can do."

"And then what?" Sloane asked.

"What do you mean, 'Then what?'"

"What did you do after the storm passed?"

"Nearly got ourselves killed," Cassidy said. "Drove into a fucking Hajji ambush."

"Tell me what you were doing in a town off the main highway, off your designated course."

Cassidy paused.

"What were you doing, Butch?"

"Give me a second," he said.

Sloane thought Cassidy's reticence was because he didn't want to incriminate himself. "Fine, we'll let the police handle it."

"This shit isn't exactly pleasant to remember, you know." Cassidy's eyes had watered. He turned his head, wiping away tears.

SIERRA DE LA LAGUNA
BAJA, MEXICO

TINA WATCHED JAKE climb the granite boulders, stopping every few seconds to hitch up his shorts. The weight of the soaking-wet fabric had caused them to sag below his hips.

She called up to him. "Not too high."

He waved down to her, smiling, and proceeded to step higher.

She sat on a rock letting her legs dangle in the pool and eating fruit from the camp trees. Occasionally she dipped her bandana and squeezed water onto her neck and chest. The hike into the mountains had been harder and longer than she had anticipated, but that could also have been because she had not slept the night before and had eaten little. The stress made her legs leaden, and the lack of food made her weak. Though only in the mid-eighties, the temperature felt hotter to them hiking up the mountain trail, which, as the camp owner had said, was partly overgrown with scrub brush. The dry air had sapped the fluid from her body and she had made Jake stop frequently to drink from the canister provided by the owner.

The topography at the lower elevations reminded her of areas around Phoenix, with red-tinted soil, cacti, palms, ironwood, and prickly shrubs. As they climbed higher, they encountered more oak trees and green vegetation, apparently watered by mountain streams. Tina had let Jake lead, giving him a wide berth as he hacked away with the machete, thinking it just about the coolest thing. Every so often she'd borrow the blade to mark the trees at the base with an X as Alex had instructed.

After about an hour of hiking, they heard the trickle of the stream and descended into a shallow valley where they found the pool. Jake had undressed and jumped in before Tina had even found a place to sit and rest her feet. He came out screaming with exhilaration.

"Okay, watch this one." Jake's voice echoed down to her as he stepped onto a flat rock that jutted out above the pristine blue pool. He inched forward until his toes curled over the edge.

"Be careful," she said. "Make sure you jump out."

He stood rigid, arms at his sides, chin thrust forward. Then he bent his knees, lifted his arms to a cross position, and jumped up and out like an Acapulco cliff diver. But rather than lean forward, entering the pool like a jack-knife, Jake grabbed his knees, pulled them to his chest and shouted.

"Cannonball!"

Tina had little time to react. Jake's bottom hit the surface with a thud and sent a pillar of water cascading over her, as if tossed from a bucket. She screamed.

Jake breached the surface spitting water and laughing so hard he was choking.

"Jake Andrew Carter! That's it," she shouted, standing. "You are going down."

"I dare you." He treaded water in the center of the pool.

She hesitated, reconsidering the water's temperature. "You'll have to get out sometime," she said.

"Chicken. Come on, I dare you."

"Who are you calling chicken?"

"You. You're a big chicken." He started clucking. "You would have jumped in when you were young."

"That's it. Calling me chicken is one thing. Calling me old . . ."

She leapt from the rock. The cold shot needles across her skin and momentarily took her breath away. She breached the surface screaming and swam after him. Perhaps shocked that she had actually jumped in, Jake got a late retreat and was now struggling to reach the other side of the pool. Tina wasn't about to let that happen. She hadn't braved the cold for nothing. She grabbed him by the ankle and jerked him under the water. They surfaced laughing, wildly splashing one another.

"Who's chicken now?" she asked, clucking like a hen. "Huh? Who's chicken now?"

She continued to splash back until she realized Jake had stopped his return fire. He treaded water, looking up at the rock formation from which he had jumped.

"Hello, Jake."

Tina turned, looking up, blinded by the bright sun, but seeing a shadow on the rock.

"Mr. Williams," Jake said, shading his eyes. "What are you doing here?"

CHAPTER
TWELVE

Michael Cassidy's story was a classic double-edged sword. If it was to be believed, somebody was covering up what actually happened the night James Ford died. But if true, it also appeared to confirm that Ford had been acting incident to his service at the time he was shot, which left Sloane without a case.

Sloane was right. He was missing something.

"We can't help you if you lie to us, Butch," Sloane said.

"I ain't lying."

"Phillip Ferguson and Dwayne Thomas were both murdered."

The information seemed to catch Cassidy off guard.

His eyes narrowed. "Now I know you're bullshitting. I heard Fergie committed suicide."

"You knew him. You tell me, did he seem like the type to kill himself?" Sloane asked.

"No, but I heard he was blind. I might kill myself too. You guys are making this shit up."

"Somebody put a bullet in the back of Dwayne Thomas's head," Sloane added. "That was definitely not a suicide."

Cassidy shrugged. "So? He probably deserved it. He was an asshole." He went back to biting his nails.

Jenkins said, "Sure, Mike. It could all be just one big coincidence."

"Except the Tacoma police don't have *any* suspects," Sloane said.

"And if *we're* right, it makes him the last of the three amigos," Jenkins added. "But he thinks using P.O. boxes and not paying taxes is going to hide him forever."

Cassidy's eyes shifted back and forth like a spectator at a tennis match.

"We found him. If we can, they can," Sloane said.

"He's definitely next on the hit parade," Jenkins concluded.

"What about Captain Kessler?" Cassidy blurted.

"Kessler might be the guy trying to kill you," Jenkins replied.

"What?" Cassidy shook his head. "I *know* that's bullshit. Why would Captain Kessler want to kill me?"

"Because he doesn't want what really happened that night to come out," Sloane said.

"I just told you what happened. There's nothing to hide. Hell, we were god-damned heroes."

Sloane thought so too. "We don't know why," he said.

"But we just climbed a freaking mountain to get here to save your ass," Jenkins said. "So the least you could do is be grateful."

Cassidy turned back to Sloane. "What would I have to do? What do you want?"

"I'll need you to come to federal court and tell a judge exactly what you just told me," Sloane said

"That wasn't part of the deal." Cassidy started to twitch again.

"We had no deal," Sloane said. "The deal was you do what we tell you, or you spend the next thirty to fifty becoming friendly with your cellmate."

Cassidy closed his eyes, inhaled slowly, and blew out a burst of air. "What time?"

Jenkins groaned. "What, do you have an appointment, Michael? You need to check your BlackBerry to find out what time you're getting your nails done? Or is there a large venture capital company looking to invest in your nifty operation here?"

Sloane put up a hand to tell Jenkins to back off. "I'd need you there next Tuesday."

Cassidy looked pale, and Sloane didn't think it was from the dull lighting inside the trailer. "Will it help Jimmy's family?"

Sloane didn't know. At present it would likely hurt his case, but the game had changed and he needed to adapt. This wasn't about winning. It was about surviving. "It might," he said.

"Fine. Give me an address and I'll be there."

Jenkins laughed. "Sure. You're about as dependable to show as the horses I bet on."

"You need to come with us now," Sloane said.

"Where?"

"Someplace safe, a hotel."

"I'm not going with you to no hotel."

"If you stay here, or run, they'll find you, and they'll kill you."

"So, much as I don't like it either, looks like you and me are bunking together," Jenkins said. "I hope you don't snore."

"After you testify, you can disappear," Sloane said.

Cassidy looked like he might cry. "Fine," he blurted. "Okay. Fine."

They decided to drive Cassidy's truck back to the quarry to retrieve the Explorer. Jenkins would drive with Cassidy to a hotel. Sloane would retrieve his laptop computer and meet them back at the room to draft an affidavit in case Cassidy got squirrelly or changed his story.

"What about the dog?" Jenkins asked.

Cassidy looked at him like he didn't know what he was talking about. "What about the dog?"

"She doesn't look like she's eaten or had any water in over a day."

"So? It ain't my dog."

Jenkins took a deep breath. "So? So how about I tie

you to a leash in that hotel room and not feed you or give you any water?"

"Hey, I said it ain't my dog. It's Kroeger's dog."

"You have any food around here?" Jenkins asked.

"No."

"When is Kroeger coming back?"

"He's painting with his dad. He's supposed to meet me at four when he gets off."

"Fine. When we get in the car you're going to call him and tell him to bring dog food and make sure the dog has water. Got it?"

Cassidy frowned. "Mellow out. It's just a dog, dude."

Jenkins lunged forward and lifted Cassidy off the ground, holding him by the neck. "So, asshole, she's a living, breathing creature, which means she doesn't deserve to be tortured, kicked, or starved."

Sloane grabbed Jenkins's forearm, but it was like grabbing a metal bar. "Put him down, Charlie! We can drive into town and get the dog food and water."

Cassidy dropped like a bag of flour and crumpled to the floor coughing and gagging.

Jenkins pushed open the door to the trailer with such force it flung off its top hinge and slammed against the siding. He stepped down into the yard, where the dog continued to bark, and paced, blowing off steam. He turned toward the dog, and realized she wasn't barking at him. She faced in the direction of the grass.

Cassidy had stepped out from the trailer onto the wooden step, Sloane behind him.

Jenkins rushed at them. "No!"

Cassidy's eyes widened as Jenkins slammed into him. Then his head snapped back as if he'd taken an invisible punch to the face.

A split second later the retort of the rifle echoed across the valley.

SAN VICENTE VILLAGE
BAJA, MEXICO

THREE YOUNG BOYS, their skin tanned a rich bronze, stepped into the street as Alex walked into the village. Their smudged but happy faces reminded her of her friends growing up in a suburb of Mexico City, though she had been considered relatively wealthy and these boys were dirt poor. They wore battered jeans and fraying shorts. Without shirts or shoes they rushed out to greet her, smiling and calling her "pretty lady." One asked her if she was "The Blessed Mother." These kids knew how to work a mark.

Alex explained that she was not interested in buying anything, but that she would pay the one who could take her to the family who owned the cattle ranch in the distance.

"Me tienes que llevar el dueño del rancho," she said.

The boys stepped back. "No," their leader said, speaking Spanish and looking concerned. "He shoots trespassers."

Alex produced several dollar bills. "Take me," she said, "and I'll give you each a dollar."

The leader considered the offer, taking a moment to whisper to his compadres. *"Tres."*

"*Dos,*" Alex countered.

He looked to his friends, who nodded.

They led her down the road, chattering at her, asking her where she had come from and why she did not have a car. Outside of town, a paved road intersected the dirt path. The boys took her as far as a wooden post and barbed wire fence. "*Aquí. Aquí,*" they shouted, holding out their hands to get paid.

She handed each two dollars. The leader tried to negotiate for an additional fee, but when he realized that wasn't about to happen, he reached into his pocket and pulled out a wad of dollar bills, showing them off.

Alex grabbed his wrist. "*De dónde sacaste eso?*"

"No. No," he cried, trying to pull away.

No way these poor boys had that kind of money, American dollars no less. "Tell me where you got the money."

"A man gave it to me," he said, eyes wide, voice pleading.

Her heart pounded. "*Por qué?* Why did he give it to you? What did he ask you?"

"*Es mío,*" the boy said, struggling to free his arm.

She held on. "What did he want to know? Tell me."

"He was looking for his wife and son," another of the boys said.

Adrenaline rushed through her. "*Que le dijiste? Que le dijiste?*"

"Leave me alone," the boy said.

"What did you tell him?"

"I told him to go to the camp. I told him to talk to the gringo lady."

Alex felt her legs go weak. "*Cuando?* When was he here?" she asked, but one of the boys rapped her across the arm with a stick, breaking her grip, and he and his friends ran off, frightened.

Alex turned and looked down the dirt road. It would take too long to get back to the camp, even if she ran the distance, and she would still have to climb the mountain and try to find the pond.

She slipped beneath the barbed wire, feeling the heat from the pavement through the thin soles of the sandals the woman at the camp had allowed her to borrow, along with a pair of shorts and a shirt. In the near distance a two-story yellow adobe home—surrounded by palm trees, with two cars parked in a turnabout—shimmered in the heat like a desert mirage. Behind it was what had caught her attention on the way to the campground—a swath of dirt through the brown grass and scrub stretched the length of the property, leading to a barn—a landing strip for a private plane.

As she hurried toward the house, a dog ran up the road, circling and barking. A man stepped out the front door dressed in crisp blue jeans and a red cotton shirt with a bolo tie. He donned a white cowboy hat to shade his face from the sun.

"*Buenos días,*" Alex said, introducing herself and apologizing for disturbing him. "*Disculpe la molestia.*"

"This is private property," the man said. The clasp of his tie was an ornate turquoise and silver design.

"I'm sorry," she said. "But I need your help."

The man asked how he could help. *"En que le puedo ayudar?"*

"A woman and her son are in the mountains," she said. "They are in grave danger."

MAPLE VALLEY, WASHINGTON

SLOANE LAY SPRAWLED on his back, his shirt covered in blood, Cassidy on top of him.

Jenkins scrambled to his knees, rifle in hand. Before he could get off any shots, bullets tore through the open door of the trailer, embedding in the walls with pings and tings. Outside, the rifle's retorts echoed across the grass valley. The gutted trailer wouldn't provide them much cover.

Sloane looked down at Cassidy. The young man's lifeless eyes remained open, but the right side of the top of his head was a matted mess.

Jenkins pulled and dragged Sloane out from under Cassidy and behind the counter. They lay flat on the ground while the assault continued. "You all right?"

Sloane nodded.

"If a bullet hits one of those propane tanks or gas cans, this place is going to go up like a bomb. We have to get the hell out of here," Jenkins said.

"That's a problem," Sloane said, "since we only have one door and they have a couple hundred yards of cover. We don't even know where they are."

"Just one guy," Jenkins said. "He's in the grass."

"How can you be sure it's just one guy?" Sloane ducked his head at the sound of glass bottles shattering in the cabinets above them.

"Because they couldn't have anticipated we'd be here, and they didn't need more than one guy to kill Cassidy. If there was more than one guy, I wouldn't be standing here and neither would you. The first guy would have waited to get a shot at Cassidy, but the second and third would have had their scopes set on you and me. We'd all be dead. A lone shooter had to make sure he killed Cassidy first, or risk giving himself away without getting his target. Now he can pick us off one at a time."

"We screwed this up," Sloane said.

"No, we didn't. He didn't follow us. If we'd been followed, they would have brought more than one guy. And Cassidy would still be dead if we hadn't come. We were his only chance. We did our best. Nothing we can do about it now."

More bottles in the cabinet shattered, spraying glass and acid.

"He thinks he's got us pinned down here," Jenkins said.

"He does have us pinned down."

"Wrong. He doesn't know who he picked a fight with." Jenkins handed Sloane what looked like a Costco-size mayonnaise jar. "Fill the jar with whatever gas you can find."

As Sloane poured what was left of the gas from the cans into the jar, Jenkins grabbed one of the propane tanks by the handle and unleashed it like a discus through a window. Then he picked up the AR15 and sprayed several blind shots into the grass, buying them some time.

"That's all of it." Sloane slid forward and handed him the jar, which was about half-full with gas.

"That'll do."

Jenkins yanked down the stained and torn curtain, and used Cassidy's knife to tear off a strip. He punched a hole in the lid of the jar, stuffed the fabric into the hole, and tilted the bottle so the gas wicked up the cloth. Then he crawled again to where Cassidy lay and reached into the young man's pockets, pulling out his lighter.

"I'll yell 'light it' from the bedroom. You have three seconds to get it lit. When you hear me shooting, stand and toss it."

"Grass is too wet to catch fire," Sloane said.

"We're not trying to burn him out. We need a diversion. Aim for the back of the truck. If the bottle doesn't break, shoot at it until it does, but get down if you hit it."

"What are you going to do?"

"I need to get back there." He pointed with his thumb to the back of the trailer. It meant getting past the open door. "And get us a better fix on where the guy is. When he pokes his head up at the explosion, I'll have him."

Another series of bullets blew out overhead fluorescent tubes, glass spraying. Jenkins grabbed his shotgun and rifle and crab-walked to the edge of the cabinets. Sloane lifted the Glock to the window and shot at random until Jenkins had darted past the door and down the short hall. A moment later Jenkins yelled.

"Okay, light it."

The lighter sparked a blue flame. The piece of curtain lit.

Sloane counted. The flame grew bigger. "Three," he shouted.

Sloane heard multiple shots from the back of the trailer, stood, and threw the jar out the window. It exploded in the back of the truck with a burst of flames, lighting a tarp. As the cloth burned, Sloane saw what was beneath it. Cassidy had restocked—cans of acetone, a gas can, two propane tanks.

Not good. Not good at all.

"Charlie?"

SIERRA DE LA LAGUNA
BAJA, MEXICO

THE MAN WHO called himself Mr. Williams wore a blue ball cap and sunglasses. He had come down the ledge and taken the machete. The other man remained on the boulders above them, looking down from under a wide-brimmed straw hat. Tina sat on the rocks beside the pool of water, an arm wrapped around Jake's shoulder, holding him close.

"I heard you caught a fish," Mr. Williams said. "What was it, thirty-three pounds?"

Jake glared at him.

"Don't be like that, Jake. I'm your friend. Didn't I help you catch that salmon?"

Jake shook his head. "You're not my friend."

"Maybe we can go fishing again. Would you like

that? Would you like to go fishing with your friend, Mr. Williams? Just tell me where the other woman is hiding and we'll all go fishing."

"She's gone," Tina said.

"I don't think so. The woman in the camp said you all came up here. So tell her to come out."

Tina considered that information, but was unsure why the woman would have lied. "I told you she's not here."

"And I told you to tell her to come out. Now."

Tina shouted. "Alex? Alex, come out." She looked at Mr. Williams and shrugged.

"That's a shame," Mr. Williams said. "Maybe she doesn't care about you as much as you think."

"She isn't here," Jake said.

"We're going to find that out, Jake." He looked to Tina. "Get in the water."

"What?"

"Get in the water."

"I'm not getting in the water."

"Fine. Jake, you get in the water."

"No," Tina said, pulling Jake closer.

"It's going to be one of you, Mrs. Sloane. Count on it."

Tina stood. Jake grabbed her arm. "No, Mom."

"It's all right," she told him. "It's going to be fine." She removed his arm, stepped to the edge of the pool, and dropped in, feeling the rush of cold.

"Swim out to the center."

Tina did as instructed. Mr. Williams sat down on the rock next to Jake. "What do you think, Jake, is your mother a good swimmer?"

"Get away from me," Jake said. "Leave us alone."

"If I were you, Jake, I'd start calling Alex, because I have all the time in the world to wait, and I don't think anyone is that good a swimmer, do you?"

MAPLE VALLEY, WASHINGTON

JENKINS BUSTED OUT the bedroom window facing the grass field. Keeping his head behind the wall, he pointed the AR15 out the window and fired randomly over the blades of grass in the general direction of where the dog had been looking. On Sloane's count of three Jenkins looked through the scope. It was sighted to zero at 200 yards, which meant he could put the crosshairs on the man's head. He heard the glass jar explode in the back of the truck and waited.

"Come on. Come on, you son of a bitch."

Nothing appeared over the blades of grass. It hadn't worked. The man was well trained.

"Charlie?" Sloane yelled from the bedroom.

Jenkins ducked back behind the wall, frustrated. "What?"

"Got a problem."

"I know."

"Cassidy restocked. There's gas cans and propane in the back of the truck."

Crap, Jenkins thought.

"You hear me?" Sloane asked.

"I heard you. Hang on."

Another idea came to him. Jenkins hated to do it, but it

was the only other way he could think of to get the man to give away his position. He lowered the rifle, picked up the shotgun, and busted out the window facing the shed. The dog, now struggling so hard with her collar she looked to be strangling herself, stopped to bark up at him.

"Charlie!"

Jenkins fired the shotgun, obliterating the tie ring embedded in the side of the shed along with the chunk of the aluminum to which it had been bolted. The dog flinched at the blast, flopped onto her side and somersaulted back to her feet.

"Go," Jenkins said. "Go."

The animal looked up at him, then took off like a shot across the grass, the rope trailing behind her.

"Charlie!"

Jenkins dropped the shotgun, quickly picked up his rifle, and hurried back to the window. He wedged the butt of the rifle firmly against his shoulder and lowered his eye to the scope, watching the blades fold as the dog's brown head crested the tops of the grass, anticipating her destination.

She surprised the man, as Jenkins had hoped. He rose from his crouch. When he did, Jenkins scoped him in the crosshairs, and fired. He looked up from the scope and watched. The dog popped up, circling and barking. The man did not reappear.

He picked up the shotgun and rushed down the hall. Sloane was waiting by the door. "Let's go."

Sloane bolted out the door and down the steps, running for the tree line, Jenkins behind him. Halfway there he heard the explosion behind them. He felt a rush of energy, like a shove to his back that propelled him forward and off balance.

Sloane lay on the ground with his head down. When he didn't feel anything fall on top of him he rolled over. Jenkins lay next to him. The white truck had been flipped upside down and crashed through the side of the trailer, like footage of a mobile home park after a Midwest tornado. Paint cans and debris fell from the sky along with the burning embers of the tarp. Smaller explosions began inside the trailer.

"The whole thing is going to go up," Jenkins said. "And it will look like the dumb son of a bitch burned himself up in a methamphetamine lab."

"What about the guy in the grass?" Sloane said, scrambling to his feet and still struggling to catch his breath.

"He's dead."

"Maybe he has some identification, something that would tie him to Argus."

"You saw their operation. What do you think the chances are of that? The body will be gone by the time the police and fire get here. We need to get out of here."

Sloane stood and looked at the trailer.

His last witness lay dead inside.

SIERRA DE LA LAGUNA
BAJA, MEXICO

JAKE'S VOICE GREW hoarse as he became more and more upset, crying. He shouted. "Alex!"

"I'm fine, Jake." Tina continued to reassure him, but her arms and legs had become heavy and her right calf had developed a persistent cramp. Each time she tried to float on her back to rest, the man above her dropped a rock into the water, a subtle reminder of their first warning—Jake would join her. With each passing minute it became more difficult to keep her head above the water.

"Let her out," Jake yelled. "Why are you doing this?"

"I'm not doing anything, Jake. As soon as Alex comes out from wherever she's hiding, your mom can get out of the water, and we'll all go fishing together. I told you that, and I always keep my word. Better call out again."

"Alex!"

Tina went underwater for a moment, holding her breath and hoping to rest her arms. When she came back up, Jake was kneeling at the edge of the rock, Mr. Williams holding him to keep him from jumping in.

"Mom! Mom!" Jake swung a fist at the man, but Mr. Williams blocked it and grabbed hold of his wrist.

"I'm fine, Jake. Leave him alone."

"You're wasting time, Jake," Mr. Williams said.

Tina opened her mouth to shout and swallowed water. She gasped, coughing and gagging, trying to recover her breath. It caused her to exert more energy she didn't have and she slipped beneath the surface, this time not on purpose.

"Mom!"

She came up gasping. "I'm . . . all . . . right . . . Jake."

"Let him go."

Alex appeared from the scrub on the rim of the ridge. She held no gun.

Mr. Williams stood, keeping hold of Jake. "Alex, nice of you to join us. You've proved the old adage about better late than never. Don't you think so, Mrs. Sloane?"

"Shoot him," Tina said, tired and out of breath.

"Yes, Ms. Hart, shoot me," Mr. Williams said, mocking her. "There's no need for violence. No one needs to get hurt. Walk down and we'll all leave together."

"I don't think so," Alex said. "I have another suggestion."

"Yeah, what's that?"

"You're going to let Jake go. Tina's going to get out of the water, and you and your partner are going to put down your weapons and get in. Then we're going to walk out of here without you."

Mr. Williams laughed. "You're quite the optimist. Meanwhile, as we have this debate, I'm not sure how much longer Mrs. Sloane can hold out."

"Mom," Jake cried out.

The cramp in Tina's leg worsened. She slipped underwater to massage it and came back up gasping for air.

"Don't be stubborn, Alex. That stunt you pulled at the bar was clever and resourceful, but you're outgunned and outmanned." Mr. Williams's partner pointed a handgun up the mountain at Alex. "I'm not interested in hurting women and children."

"That's good to know. It will make it easier for me to kick your ass."

"Really? Did you somehow manage to charm the entire fraternity to come hiking with you?"

"Not the fraternity," she said. *"Amigos, ya pueden salir."*

The Mexican rancher emerged on the ridge wearing a cowboy hat and holding a rifle. Another appeared beside him, then a third and a fourth. Others appeared on horseback, ringing the pool, each armed. Two men came out of the path behind Mr. Williams. One cocked a shotgun and leveled it at the man's back.

Alex smiled. "You better hope you swim as well as you fish."

CHAPTER THIRTEEN

MILLER RANCH
ELLENSBURG, WASHINGTON

Charles Jenkins pointed up at flashing lights, one red, one white, and one green amidst the multitude of stars in the night sky. "Here they come."

Friday night, he and Sloane stood on the private landing strip on the ranch in Ellensburg, Washington. The woman who had sold Jenkins the two Appaloosa horses did not hesitate when he asked her about using the ranch's airstrip. A widow, she spent much of the winter and spring in Florida. The caretaker would assist him with the lights for the landing strip, and provide access to the two guest homes, one green, the other yellow. The property also included several barns, a main log cabin, a bunkhouse, and a stocked trout pond, something Sloane hoped would make Jake happy and keep him occupied.

As the Beechcraft jet approached, the caretaker hit a switch on the side of one of the barns, and a string of white bulbs lit up each side of the asphalt pavement.

When Alex finally called, Sloane had felt an over-whelming rush of relief. That relief was replaced by anger when he learned that the man who had come to Three Tree Point, Mr. Williams, had followed through on his threat. That Alex had left the man and his accom-plice treading water in a mountain pool guarded by armed men from a nearby ranch did not relieve Sloane's anger. They all knew it would be naive to believe the two men would be detained long. Argus officials would eventually get them out of Mexico.

As the plane continued its approach, Sloane con-sidered the expansive property. A heavy locked gate at the entrance prevented anyone from driving onto the single access road. Unlike western Washington, which was lush and green nearly year-round, Ellensburg was arid and barren, with open fields of brown grass to roll-ing hills. Fields of recently harvested hay and alfalfa sur-rounded the three houses. No one would easily sneak up on them. Not that Sloane was overly concerned. The pilot had filed a flight plan from Baja to San Diego, with Boeing Field the plane's final destination. He omitted the stop at the private landing strip in Ellensburg, and there was also no discernable connection between the property and either Sloane or Jenkins. Argus would have had a difficult time locating it even if motivated to do so.

Sloane doubted they were. With Michael Cassidy dead, there was no reason for Argus to continue its pursuit of Sloane. Cassidy was the last person who could have testified that the official witness statements were not what actually occurred the night James Ford died, and Sloane had no other evidence to prove that Ford was not acting incident to his service. Come Tuesday, Judge Jo Natale would dismiss Ford's complaint, and the matter would be closed.

"You all right?" Jenkins asked.

Sloane nodded.

"It was the right call. Don't beat yourself up. Hindsight is always twenty-twenty."

"I want someone to pay for what they did, Charlie."

"You make it personal and you make stupid decisions."

"They made it personal." Sloane took a deep breath and exhaled. "I'm just not sure how she's going to react, what she'll want to do."

"About what?"

"About us. About staying together."

Jenkins frowned. "You're talking crazy. Tina loves you."

"She has a son to think about."

"*You* have a son to think about. Jake loves you too."

Sloane watched the plane circle the property, lining up for the approach. A minute later the high-pitched roar of the Beechcraft's engine broke the country silence. The back wheels hit the runway with a skid, the front wheel dropped to the ground, and the plane rolled past where they stood, down the strip. It circled at the end and rolled back toward them, stopping. A door on the side of the plane lowered and a staircase unfolded. Sloane watched the doorway. His heart felt like it was stuck in his throat.

Alex appeared first. She ducked and made her way down the stairs. Jenkins left Sloane's side, walking at first, then breaking into a run. Alex leapt two stairs from the bottom, wrapping her arms around his neck as Jenkins swung her in a circle.

When Sloane looked back up the stairs, he saw Jake in the doorway, Tina behind him. They stepped out slow and cautious. Sloane walked to the foot of the stairs. Despite what must have been a thrill to ride in a private jet, Jake looked somber.

"Are you okay?" Sloane asked, searching Tina's face for some answer.

Jake lunged at him, wrapping both arms around Sloane's midsection and burying his face in his chest. The boy's shoulders heaved, and tears he had apparently been holding back released in sobs. Sloane felt horrible. He knew what the boy had been through. He knew the trauma and the fear Jake had endured watching his mother suffer, thinking she was going to die.

Sloane had experienced that same fear as a boy. The nightmare still haunted him.

From the dirt ground, hidden beneath the bed, he watched the horror in silence as each man forced himself upon her, violating her. Blood from the beatings trickled from the corner of her mouth and her eye had become a swollen red pulp. But the other eye found him beneath the bed, imploring him to remain silent, to say nothing. Then she closed it and turned her face away from him.

When the last of the men had finished, a gloved hand pulled her from the ground by a tuft of her long, dark hair, her body hanging limp as a rag doll.

"Dónde está el niño? Dónde está el niño?" Parker Madsen had shouted at her repeatedly. "Where is the boy?"

But she had not answered him.

Madsen squatted to stare into her face, screaming his question. Still, she did not verbally respond. With what little energy and saliva she could muster, she spat, her final act of defiance, her final motherly act being to protect him.

The blade caught the flickering light of the moon as it sliced the darkness like a sickle through wheat, nearly decapitating her.

Sloane pressed Jake's head to his chest. Tina stepped to his side, resting her head on his shoulder, an arm still wrapped around her son. Sloane held them, no one speaking. Jake and Tina's sobs mixed with the sound of the crickets and insects in the fields, and the occasional croak of a bullfrog.

SLOANE, TINA, AND Jake stayed together in the yellow farmhouse. Alex and Jenkins would stay in the green house. Sloane opened the front door and led Tina and Jake inside.

"Jake, come with me," he said. "I want to show you something."

Sloane slid open a glass door and stepped out onto

a wraparound porch. Tina and Jake followed. Sloane pointed. Though it was dark, the light from the moon and abundant stars outlined the trout pond, a small pier, and the reeds surrounding it.

"Can you see it? A trout pond." He held his hands apart. "I'm told there are some trout in there that are five to six pounds and nearly two feet long. They've never been caught. Not once. Are you up for the challenge?"

Jake stared out into the darkness.

"We could get up early and let these country fish see what a true fisherman is really like," Sloane said.

Jake took a tentative half-step forward, and a sense of relief rushed over Sloane. Then the boy pivoted and turned away, his voice barely audible. "No, thanks."

Sloane felt his heart sink. "I brought poles and I picked up earthworms in town. The man told me the bigger fish can't resist them. Everything's all ready to go. I did it myself. I have the hooks on, weights."

Jake spoke to his mom. "I'm tired. Can I go to bed?"

Tina rubbed the boy's shoulder. "Sure, honey. Go on upstairs. We'll be up in a minute."

Jake started into the house, stopping at the sliding glass door. He looked back at Sloane. "You're staying, right? You're not leaving?"

Sloane nodded. "I'll be in the room right next door."

Jake turned and went inside.

Sloane closed his eyes and shook his head. All the progress he had made over their two years together to gain the boy's confidence had been squandered. Jake no longer trusted him.

"He'll be okay," Tina said. "It's just going to take some time."

How long? Sloane wondered. It had taken him a lifetime and still the dreams occasionally haunted him. Even now, he would awake in Tina's arms, sweating, crying out.

He did not wish that on anyone. He did not want that for Jake.

"How about you?" he asked. "How are you doing?"

"It will take me some time too," she said. "I'm not sure when I'll swim again."

"Tina, I'm sorry. I—"

She pulled him to her.

He smelled her beauty as he buried his face in her hair. "I should not have let you go alone."

"You didn't. Alex was there. It was the right decision," she said. "Don't excuse what they did by blaming yourself."

He pondered his next question, not sure he wanted to hear her response, not wanting to see her face for fear it would provide an answer he could not take.

"If this is too much for you and Jake, if you decide this isn't what you wanted, for either of you—"

She pulled back. "What are you talking about?"

"What happened in San Francisco, now this. If you wanted something more . . . I don't know. Stable."

She looked wounded. "You don't get it, do you?"

He looked at her, uncertain of the cause of her pain.

"*You* are all that I want." She wiped a tear from her cheek. "You were all that I thought of the entire time I was away. I was worried sick about *you*, and I felt awful for leaving the way I did."

"But what they did to you, the fact that I wasn't there to stop it, the fact that I caused it."

"You didn't cause anything, David. Don't start blaming yourself again for the world's evils."

"I should have listened to you. I should have never taken this case."

She put out her hands and he was uncertain whether she wanted to cradle his face or strangle him. "And so you think I'd want to leave you? Do you think that little of me, of my commitment to you?"

"No, I don't doubt that."

"Do you know how long I waited for you? Ten years. And I would have waited another ten if I had to. I love you. I've loved you from the moment I first set eyes on you, and these past two years I've only grown to love you more every day. What hurts most is that you don't understand that."

He felt a sense of relief, but also the numbing, hollow emptiness much like he used to feel. "I've never had this before. I've never loved any two people as much as I love you and Jake. I'm afraid of losing that. I'm afraid of being alone again. I can see the pain in Beverly Ford's face. Her loss is irreparable. She'll never be over it. She'll never stop loving him."

Tina pulled him close. "I'm not going anywhere, and neither is Jake. This is our family, and we're not going to let anyone take that away from us the way they took it away from her."

Later, they sat in the dark on a porch swing covered by a wool blanket. Tina rested her head on his chest, the porch swing creaking rhythmically, the sound of the insects in the fields reverberating around them.

"What happens now?" Tina asked.

He rubbed her shoulder. "The hearing on the motion to dismiss is Tuesday. That will likely be the end of it."

She lifted her head and sat back to look him in the face. "So they're going to get away with it?"

"All the witnesses are dead," Sloane said. "I have no evidence."

"That's not good enough," she said. "I know you— you can find a way."

Sloane smiled. "You're remarkable, you know that? After all that happened, you still want me to pursue this?"

"No. I want you to pursue this *because* of what happened. I might not like it, but you were right. This is what you do. If an injustice was done to that man and to his family, someone needs to stand up for them, just as you said."

Sloane blew out his frustration. "I don't know how at the moment."

"You'll figure out a way," she said.

"I don't have a lot of time to do it."

"Then you better get started."

She put her head back on his chest and they swung in silence. Sloane thought of Argus and Robert Kessler and Mr. Williams. He thought of revenge. Then he thought of Beverly Ford and her children, Althea with the bright smile beaming up at him, and he realized this wasn't about revenge. He'd been down that path before, a path that grew darker with each step, and without end. He thought instead of justice.

SUNDAY MORNING, SLOANE and Jenkins walked out into a field. Sloane outlined his plan, starting with the hearing on the motion to dismiss.

"It's risky," Jenkins said. "Too many things could go wrong."

"Who's raining on the parade now?"

"This is different. The stakes are higher. You could get killed. You have a wife and son to think about."

"So did James Ford."

"I told you, don't make it personal."

Sloane looked away. "I'm not. I've thought this through. This is the best option."

"Sounds like the only option."

"Maybe," Sloane said. He turned to the man who had become his best friend. "I need your help, but I understand you also have someone else in your life now to consider."

"Are you kidding? You haven't seen personal until you've seen Alex angry. And she is pissed."

Sloane chuckled at that. "What about you?"

"Oh, I've been pissed for a long time."

"I thought you said not to make this personal."

"I told *you* not to make it personal," Jenkins said. "I'm part Cherokee. It's always personal."

Sloane smiled. "Did you and Alex set a date?"

"Summer, probably August. I'll need a best man. You know anyone?" Jenkins said.

"No one who would stand up for you," Sloane replied, smiling.

They turned back toward the houses. Sloane caught a glimpse of someone walking across the lawn. "Look at that," he said, pointing.

Jake walked across the field toward the pond carrying what looked like two fishing poles.

"Looks like you're going fishing," Jenkins said.

Sloane smiled. "Looks like I am."

"He'll be fine," Jenkins said. "Kids are resilient." They started in the direction of the pond. "Just one question. How are we going to do this without a witness?"

"We still have one," Sloane said.

Jenkins stopped walking. "Kessler? He won't talk to you."

"He won't have a choice."

"What are you thinking of doing?"

"It's time to beat them at their own game," Sloane said.

CHAPTER
FOURTEEN

The following Tuesday, Sloane stepped back through the metal detector into the lobby of the Federal Building. This time he wore a suit and tie. Different marshals gave him the same spiel about emptying his pockets.

He exited the black marble elevator on the fourteenth floor to find Tom Pendergrass standing in the lobby outside the courtroom in his dress-green uniform, several rows of medals adorning his left breast pocket. Next to Pendergrass stood U.S. Attorney Rachel Keane, wearing a navy-blue pantsuit and looking like she'd stepped from a St. John catalogue.

Pendergrass made the introductions. "This is David Sloane."

Keane had a firm handshake. "Any chance your client will reconsider the government's offer?" she asked.

Sloane shook his head, his demeanor reserved. Inside red flags waved furiously. Having the U.S. attorney present in court for a simple motion to dismiss was more than overkill—it was like shooting a squirrel with a cannon.

"I'll let the clerk know we're here." Pendergrass turned toward the twelve-foot glass doors to the courtroom. Silver block letters on the wall to the right of the doors identified it as the courtroom of Judge Jo Natale.

"Tom?" Sloane said. Pendergrass stopped. "A word?"

Keane and Pendergrass exchanged a nod and Keane walked through the doors alone.

Pendergrass turned back

Sloane asked, "Did you ever stop to ask yourself why the government is willing to pay one hundred thousand dollars for a case they expect you to have dismissed this morning?"

Pendergrass shrugged. "My job is to convey the offer," he said. "Your client should have taken it. You're not losing confidence, are you, Mr. Sloane?"

"Then have you also considered that a hundred thousand dollars was well within your settlement authority?"

"What's your point?"

"My point is, why didn't the army convey the offer itself, before I filed my complaint?"

Pendergrass didn't have an immediate answer. Then he said, "It's irrelevant. Your client should have taken the offer. Everyone has to lose sometime." He turned and walked into the courtroom.

Sloane's cell phone rang.

"It's done," Jenkins said. "But it will be close. Stall."

ATTORNEYS STOOD IN an entryway checking the daily calendar for the order in which the court would hear their cases. Tracing his finger down the sheet of paper, Sloane found that the government's motion to dismiss was last on the calendar, an indication Judge Natale intended to give it more time, which is what Sloane needed.

He pushed through an interior set of wooden doors and entered a cavernous courtroom with a ceiling sloped like the roof of an underground amphitheater. Narrow windows fifteen feet off the ground and recessed, incandescent lighting lit the room. At the front of the room Pendergrass talked to the judge's clerk, who stood in the well area beneath the judge's red oak bench, presumably to let her know that his motion would be heard. Then Pendergrass returned and took a seat in the front pew next to Keane.

Having never appeared before Judge Natale, Sloane had done what research he could. Natale had risen through the ranks of the U.S. Attorney's Office at roughly the same time as Rachel Keane, though handling mostly criminal matters. Unlike Keane, she had forged her reputation in the courtroom rather than the newspapers. Quiet and reserved, she never discussed her cases with the media. She used a relentless and well-orchestrated plan to bring criminals to justice. Since ascending to the bench, her demeanor had not softened.

At nine o'clock sharp the judge's staff filed out the door to the left of the bench, and the clerk called the courtroom to order. Judge Natale took the bench, sitting directly beneath a large, brushed silver coin replica of the United States eagle, an olive branch clasped in one of its talons, arrows in the other. Natale wore her raven-colored hair past her shoulders and a string of pearls to accentuate her black robe. She adjusted stylish black-framed glasses and set to work disposing of the first two matters quickly, asking direct questions. Though she gave counsel the opportunity to speak, she kept all on a short leash, and everyone was on best behavior. Stalling was not going to be easy.

The calendar took thirty-seven minutes before the clerk called, "In the matter of James Ford versus the United States of America."

Sloane stood and looked to the doors behind him but did not see Jenkins. He pushed through the swinging gate, turned, and held it open for Pendergrass and Keane. As he let the gate swing shut and turned to the bench, he noticed Judge Natale raise her head and watch Keane take her place beside Pendergrass at the government's table. Apparently Sloane was not the only one surprised by Keane's presence in the courtroom.

The government's table faced the judge's bench, the defense table perpendicular to it, facing the jury box across the room. Each table, the judge's desk, the witness stand to the judge's immediate right, and the jury box to the right of it, were all equipped with computer screens.

Positioning himself at counsel table, Sloane opened his briefcase and removed Ford's file and the opposition to the government's motion. He heard the courtroom doors open, turned, and to his considerable surprise Beverly Ford walked in, followed by her four children, Lucas carrying Althea. He looked like a prep school student in a blue-and-gold-striped tie, blue blazer, and khakis. His brother and sisters were equally well dressed. They stopped, uncertain where to go or what to do. Judge Natale looked out over the top of her glasses.

"Your Honor, may I have a moment?"

Natale nodded.

Sloane walked to the back of the courtroom.

"It was Lucas's idea." Beverly Ford nodded to her son. "He thought you could use some support."

"He was right."

Sloane led the children to the pew just behind counsel table. Beverly Ford took a seat next to him at counsel table. Sloane remained standing.

All were in place. Pendergrass faced the bench and stated his appearance. Keane followed, then Sloane, who asked the court to note the presence of Ford and her children.

Wasting no time, Natale turned to Sloane. "Mr. Sloane, how do you expect to get past the exceptions to the Federal Tort Claims Act or the Feres doctrine? Your complaint alleges that Mr. Ford was a member of the Washington National Guard shot and killed during combat in Iraq. As tragic as that is, and this court has great sympathy for the sacrifice our soldiers and their families continue to make, do not both preclude this claim?" Natale did not wait for an answer. "I could dismiss your complaint as premature, given that the government contends the claim remains open, but what would be the point? What evidence can you marshal to overcome those hurdles?"

Sloane needed time. "Your Honor, we are well aware of the hurdles posed by the Feres doctrine. The application of that doctrine, however, has far exceeded the spirit and the intent of the original position espoused by Justice Jackson. The government now uses it as both shield and sword. The question in applying the Feres doctrine is whether the service member incurred his injuries while acting incident to his or her service. We've cited authority in our brief to support that position."

"Be that as it may," Natale said, cutting through Sloane's hyperbole. "I'm obligated to apply the law. What evidence exists that Mr. Ford's injuries were not incurred incident to his service?"

"Your Honor, we just filed this case. According to the government, Private Ford was killed in an ambush that took place several miles away from the rest of a convoy."

"So?"

"So at this point we don't know if that was because his squad was on a planned combat mission, which seems unlikely, or was ambushed while doing something not incident to their service. We don't have enough facts."

"How does the government explain it?"

Pendergrass started to answer, but Sloane cut him off. "The government has withheld documents pertinent to Mrs. Ford's claim in the interests of national security," he said. "In fact, their decision to reopen the claim prevents us from conducting discovery, further impeding our ability to determine exactly what Mr. Ford was doing the night he died."

Natale turned to Pendergrass. "Mr. Pendergrass?"

Pendergrass did not answer the question. "It is undisputed that Mr. Ford was a member of the Washington National Guard deployed in Iraq. It is undisputed that the United States is at war. It is undisputed that Mr. Ford was shot during that war and that he died from those wounds. What additional evidence do we need? I would suggest that counsel is stalling to avoid the inevitable. And the government did not classify *all* of the documents."

Sloane waited, silent.

"We provided counsel with witness statements taken from each of the soldiers serving with Mr. Ford the night he was shot," Pendergrass continued. "Those statements are conclusive evidence that he was shot incident to his service." Natale looked to be turning to Sloane for a response when Pendergrass quickly added, "I would like to submit those statements at this time."

He picked up the statements and stepped toward the judge's clerk. As he did, Sloane noticed Keane subtly reach out for his arm, then stop herself. Pendergrass handed the documents to the clerk and moved to introduce them.

"Any objection?" Natale asked.

"Your Honor, evidence submitted during a motion to dismiss turns it into a motion for summary judgment," Sloane responded. "If the government had intended to submit the witness statements, it should have provided us twenty-eight days' notice to provide a response. I would request that the court continue this matter to allow us to consider the additional evidence."

"Are you claiming prejudice?" Natale asked. Before Sloane could answer, she turned to Pendergrass. "When did the government provide these statements?"

Pendergrass remained smug. "Mrs. Ford was given these statements months ago. Presumably she gave them to her counsel. In fact, Mr. Sloane and I discussed them last week. Furthermore, Your Honor, the statements can be admitted to support our motion that the plaintiff's case is premature without the necessity of providing the plaintiff twenty-eight days' notice."

Natale looked to Sloane. "Mr. Sloane?"

Sloane heard the courtroom door open behind him. Charles Jenkins walked in and gave Sloane a slight nod. If he had been waiting to time the moment he could not have stepped through the doors on better cue.

Sloane tried to sound resigned. "Captain Pendergrass is indeed correct, Your Honor. The witness statements are admissible. I withdraw my objection."

"Very well," Natale said. "The documents are admitted into evidence."

"In which case," Sloane continued, "the plaintiffs wish to call a witness."

Pendergrass's head snapped in Sloane's direction.

"A witness?" Natale asked, looking up. "To testify about what?"

"About the statements that the government just introduced."

Natale sat back, considering Sloane. Obviously sharp, she had likely just realized that Sloane had set up the young government attorney, but with her hand obscuring her mouth, he couldn't tell from her expression if she was impressed or annoyed.

"Whom do you wish to call?" Natale asked.

"We wish to call Captain Robert Kessler."

Keane stood. This time she did not hold back. "Your Honor, the government objects. We were given no notice of a witness being called this morning."

"My investigator served Captain Kessler with a subpoena this morning," Sloane replied. "We were unable to serve him earlier. I'm told he's in the building and on his way to this courtroom as we speak."

"Your Honor, this is inappropriate," Keane said.

"It was counsel for the government who represented to the court that the witness statements are relevant to this hearing," Sloane said. He had baited Pendergrass into introducing the statements when they met on the observation deck of the Federal Building, suggesting that Pendergrass could not get them into evidence. Pendergrass struck Sloane as smart, but inexperienced. His ego had taken the challenge. Now the door was open to put Kessler on the stand.

"Which makes the testimony of Captain Kessler relevant," Sloane continued. He held up all of the witness statements. He had a second reason for baiting Pendergrass into introducing them. He placed them on the table as he said each name. "I would have also subpoenaed Phillip Ferguson but he has died since returning stateside. Dwayne Thomas has also died after returning home." Sloane looked to Pendergrass. "Michael Cassidy? Also recently dead. It seems Captain Kessler is the only member of the squad still alive."

Judge Natale looked to Pendergrass, but it was Keane who spoke. "Your Honor, we would ask the court's indulgence to speak with Captain Kessler before he takes the stand."

"We have no objection," Sloane said. "We're happy to accommodate the government."

KESSLER SAT IN his wheelchair at the witness stand looking anything but pleased to be there. Jenkins had caught up with him in the driveway of his Tacoma home, where he had camped out early that morning. Sloane and Jenkins both concluded that once Kessler got onto the Argus compound, they would never get the chance to serve him with the subpoena to appear in federal court that morning.

During the break, Jenkins had advised Sloane that although polite, Kessler had voiced his annoyance that the subpoena required his immediate appearance. Sloane had instructed Jenkins to not serve Kessler until the morning. He did not want the government to have advance notice that he intended to call Kessler as a witness. Meanwhile, Sloane had spent the better part of the prior day working on a direct examination of the captain.

Once Kessler settled behind the microphone, Pendergrass stood and requested that the hearing be closed to the public, and that the court reporter's transcript be sealed in the event Captain Kessler discussed information sensitive to national security. Again Sloane raised no objection. By closing the courtroom and sealing the transcript, the government would be hard-pressed to make any valid objections to Sloane's questions. Besides, other than Ford and her children, who had a right to be there, the courtroom was already empty, theirs being the last matter of the morning.

Sloane stood at the podium between the two tables. "Would you state your name for the record?"

"Robert Wilson Kessler."

"Captain Kessler, where do you work currently?"

"Argus International, Inc."

"And what is your job at Argus?"

"I'm head of security for Middle Eastern operations."

"Specifically Iraq?"

"Correct."

"And why would Argus need a Middle Eastern security force?"

Pendergrass stood. "Objection, Your Honor. Irrelevant and mischaracterizes the witness's response. He didn't say 'security force.'"

Natale looked to Sloane. "It's merely background, Your Honor. I'll rephrase. Captain Kessler, as head of security for Argus in Iraq, what are your daily responsibilities?"

"I oversee the safety of Argus employees working in that region to ensure they can accomplish the tasks Argus has contracted to perform, and are not in harm's way."

"And what type of harm's way would that be?"

"We're a global business. We have projects under way all over the world. Unfortunately, there are persons out there we are required to guard against."

"Terrorists?"

"Yes."

"Does Argus currently have projects under way in Iraq?"

Pendergrass stood again. "Objection, Your Honor. Relevance."

Natale nodded. "Mr. Sloane, I'll give you some freedom here, but I want you to move this along quickly. Captain Kessler, you may answer the question."

"Argus has been awarded several contracts in the reconstruction of Iraq."

"Lucrative contracts?"

Kessler shrugged. "I suppose."

"Since the start of the war those contracts have exceeded one point two billion dollars, have they not?"

"That's my understanding. It doesn't change my salary, however."

Everyone in the courtroom smiled. "And Argus had a contract at the outset of the war to provide and service chemical detection equipment."

"Yes, it did."

"And does Argus keep any offices, if you will indulge me that term, at forward operating bases in Iraq?"

"It does."

"And did it keep an office at forward operating base Kalsu where you and Specialist James Ford were stationed during your tour in Iraq?"

"Yes, it did."

"Mr. Sloane?" Natale asked, starting to look and sound annoyed. His leeway was up. Sloane needed to get to the point.

"Captain Kessler, you were James Ford's commanding officer while he served in Iraq."

"He was a member of my squad, correct."

"As his captain, you expected him to follow any order you gave."

Kessler nodded. "To the extent it was a lawful order, yes, I expected him to follow it."

"Well, did you ever give Specialist Ford an unlawful order?"

Pendergrass was on his feet. "Objection. 'Unlawful' is vague and ambiguous."

"I disagree," Natale said. "The witness used the term. I assume he understood what he meant. He can answer."

"No," Kessler said, "I did not."

"So we can assume that James Ford never disobeyed an order that you gave him."

"I can't think of any."

"He would have trusted that any order you gave was a lawful order, correct?"

Again Pendergrass stood. "Objection, Your Honor. The question is asking the witness to speculate about James Ford's state of mind."

"I'll rephrase," Sloane said. "Did James Ford ever object to any order that you gave?"

"No," Kessler said.

"And you would have never given an unlawful order, would you, Captain?"

"No, I would not."

"So we can all conclude that James Ford would have trusted that any order you gave was a lawful order and followed it without question."

"Your Honor . . ." Pendergrass said, raising his arms in exasperation.

Natale looked over her reading glasses at Sloane, admonishing him. "Mr. Sloane, I think we all get the point you're trying to make."

"Then I'll move on. Captain Kessler, on the evening James Ford died, your squad was returning from escorting a convoy of supplies back to forward operating base Kalsu, correct?"

"Correct."

"And in the course of those duties, your convoy was struck suddenly by a sandstorm so intense you could not see the truck in front of you, nor could you communicate by radio with the other trucks in your convoy."

"That was the case, yes."

"And where in the convoy was your squad located?" Sloane asked.

"Rear support."

"The last vehicle?"

Kessler nodded. "Yes."

"How was that position determined?"

"It came down the chain of command before the mission."

"When you say the chain of command, who specifically do you mean?"

"My commanding officer was Colonel Bo Griffin."

"So with the sandstorm raging and your vehicle being last in the convoy, no one would have known if you had driven off in another direction."

"No. They likely would not have."

"Captain Kessler, during your time in Iraq, have you ever known any soldiers to take items from a supply convoy for their own personal use?"

Kessler shrugged. "Maybe a pack of cigarettes or an extra MRE."

"So it was possible for a soldier to do that and to get away with it."

Kessler frowned. "He wasn't getting away with it. The supplies were for the soldiers."

"But if those soldiers took those supplies for other purposes, say to trade them on the black market for alcohol or Iraqi pornography, it would be improper, would it not?"

Pendergrass nearly jumped from his chair. "Objection, Your Honor. Calls for speculation. There's no evidence to support that hypothetical. Nor is it relevant."

"I'll allow it," Natale said. She looked to Kessler. "Answer the question if you can."

"It would be improper, yes."

"Did you ever do that, Captain Kessler?"

"No," Kessler said, adamant.

"Did you ever order your men to do it?"

"No," he said, equally adamant.

Sloane picked up Kessler's witness statement, flipping through it. "And according to your witness statement"—Sloane paused as if reading—"you suffered a spinal injury in the same engagement in which Specialist Ford lost his life. Isn't that true?"

"It is."

"Can you tell us what happened that night?"

Kessler sat back and cleared his throat. Beads of perspiration shimmered on his forehead.

"Captain?" Sloane asked.

Pendergrass put his palms on the table, started to stand, hesitated, and remained seated.

"Captain, please answer the question," Judge Natale said.

"No, I'm afraid I can't."

Sloane asked, "You can't provide us any of the details of what happened that evening, about how you were shot and James Ford died?"

Now Pendergrass stood. "Your Honor, the witness statement can be used to refresh the witness's recollection."

Sloane never took his gaze from Kessler. "Only if the witness had a recollection to begin with. Otherwise, there is nothing to refresh."

"Overruled," Natale said. "Repeat the question."

"You can't provide any details about what happened that evening, about how you were shot and James Ford died?"

"No."

"Because you don't remember what happened that night, do you, Captain Kessler?"

"No. I mean . . . correct. I don't remember what happened that night."

"Keep your voice up for the court reporter, Captain," Judge Natale instructed.

"You've never remembered what happened that night?" Sloane asked.

"I never have."

"According to your statement you were knocked unconscious by an air strike that blew up the building you and your men were directed to reach as your landing zone. Isn't that correct?"

Pendergrass flipped rapidly through the witness statements, perplexed by where Sloane was getting his information. Cassidy had provided it, but with a bullet in his head and his body incinerated, he couldn't testify to any of it. Sloane knew he had to get it from Kessler. The game had changed, but that had not meant the game was over. Sloane just had to find a different way to get the information into evidence.

Kessler lowered his head. "That's correct," he said.

Natale looked over at him. "You'll have to speak up, Captain Kessler."

Kessler cleared his throat. "That's correct. I don't recall."

"So your witness statement does not reflect *your* recollection."

"It does not."

"It was drafted for you by someone else."

"Yes."

"And you signed it."

Kessler nodded. "Yes."

"Would you consider that an honest act, Captain Kessler?"

"Objection," Pendergrass said, but it lacked fervor.

"It goes to this witness's credibility," Sloane said.

"No," Kessler said, not waiting for the judge to rule. "I would not consider it an honest act."

"The other men in your squad that evening—Phillip Ferguson, Dwayne Thomas, Michael Cassidy—they all signed witness statements that have been submitted to this court as evidence of what happened that night. Did you ever speak to any of them about the substance of their statements?"

"No, I never did."

"Have you read their statements?"

"Yes."

"Would you consider them similar in substance to the statement you signed but did not write?"

"I guess I would."

"More than similar?"

"I don't understand."

"Would you agree that the statements are nearly identical in terms of their content?"

"They're similar, certainly."

"Very similar?"

Pendergrass stood again. "Vague and ambiguous."

"Your Honor, the witness agreed the statements were similar. I'm trying to determine whether he has ever considered *how* similar those statements are to one another."

"I'll allow it," Natale ruled.

"I don't have an opinion other than that the statements are similar," Kessler said.

Sloane went back to his table and picked up the four highlighted statements. "Your Honor, I'd like to submit into evidence the same four statements, but these with highlights I will represent I added." He handed Pendergrass a copy and gave a set to the reporter.

"Any objection?" Natale asked.

Pendergrass flipped through them, considering the highlights. Keane leaned over and whispered something in his ear. "No objection," he said.

The clerk stamped the documents as exhibits and handed them to Kessler.

"Captain Kessler, would you take a moment to consider the highlights I've made on your statement?" Sloane said. Kessler did. "Now would you take some additional time to consider the highlights I've made on the other three witness statements?"

Again Kessler did as instructed. More important to Sloane, so did Judge Natale and Tom Pendergrass.

Sloane asked, "Would you agree, Captain Kessler, that each of the words highlighted on each of the statements is repeated at least once in the other three statements?"

"I can't say for certain. It does appear that the same words appear on each of the statements. Yes."

"In fact, I found forty-two words, not including conjunctions, prepositions, and pronouns that were repeated, substantive words used to describe the events. Would you agree?"

"I didn't count them," Kessler said. "I'll take your word for it."

"And you already testified that you did not provide the words that are included in your statement, correct?"

"No, I did not."

"So . . . who did?"

THE IMPLICATIONS OF Sloane's question hung in the courtroom. All eyes were now fixed on Kessler.

"Colonel Bo Griffin," Kessler said.

Sloane paused as if to consider his notes, letting the captain's answer reverberate with the implications. "And since you don't remember what happened, you don't know if the content of the other statements is accurate, or whether Colonel Griffin made them up as well—"

Pendergrass shot out of his chair. "Objection, Your Honor."

"Sustained." Natale shot Sloane a glance, clearly unhappy.

"Captain, are you aware that Phillip Ferguson, one of the men in your squad that night, is dead?"

"I'm aware that Fergie committed suicide. I attended his funeral."

"And are you aware that Dwayne Thomas is also dead?"

Another nod. "I read it in the paper. There was no service for him."

"So you're aware that Mr. Thomas was shot in the back of the head and that the Tacoma police suspect he was killed during a drug deal, except Mr. Thomas wasn't known to deal or use drugs, was not a known member of a gang, and there has been no indication of a drug war among gangs in that area?"

Sloane watched the captain's reaction closely. "No, I didn't know that."

Sloane held up a copy of the paper. "And are you also aware that Michael Cassidy, the last surviving member of your squad that night, besides you, died last week when his methamphetamine lab in Maple Valley exploded?"

Kessler shook his head.

"You need to answer audibly," Judge Natale said.

"No," Kessler said, looking dazed. "I was not aware of that."

"How many men under your command did you lose in Iraq, Captain?"

"James Ford was the only one."

"And that occurred during an ambush, a firefight involving several dozen insurgents, correct?"

"Correct."

"And yet, it seems, every other man who served in

your squad the night James Ford was shot and killed, and who managed to survive that peril, has died since returning to the States. Do you find that a bit odd?"

"Objection, Your Honor," Pendergrass said, though it sounded obligatory and without enthusiasm. "It's irrelevant what the captain believes."

"I'll withdraw the question." Sloane had made his point. "Captain Kessler, did you ever order your men to steal supplies from the convoy they were guarding and sell or exchange those supplies on the streets—"

"Objection," Pendergrass interrupted. "Your Honor, there is no—"

"—of Iraq for alcohol, narcotics or pornography—"

"—evidence to sustain such an unfounded accusation."

"—and would that not have constituted an unlawful order?"

Judge Natale banged her gavel. "Enough. Enough. Mr. Sloane, do you have any evidence to back up a question like that?"

"Any evidence I would have had, Your Honor," he said, locking eyes with Kessler, "died with those other three men."

OUTSIDE THE COURTROOM, Sloane huddled with Beverly Ford and her four children. After the hearing, Judge Natale had called counsel into chambers, though Rachel Keane had not attended. Sloane was explaining to Beverly that Judge Natale had dismissed their case.

"That's the bad news. The good news is she dismissed it as premature."

Judge Natale had no choice once Pendergrass submitted the witness statements. The difference, Sloane explained to Beverly, was that he could re-file the complaint if he found evidence that James Ford was not acting incident to his service.

"Is there any?" Beverly Ford asked.

"That's what I hope to find out," Sloane said.

"They're all dead?" Beverly Ford asked. "All those men who served with James?"

"Not all of them," Sloane said. To his right, Captain Robert Kessler wheeled himself to the bank of elevators, Pendergrass at his side. Kessler looked demoralized. As the elevator door opened, he turned his head and looked at Sloane, then wheeled his chair inside.

A few minutes later, Sloane rode the elevator with Beverly and her children to the lobby and escorted them to the pay parking lot across from the courthouse. He told Beverly he would keep her advised of anything that happened. After they drove off, he walked back to the courtyard. Charles Jenkins stood near the cast aluminum fist sculpture.

"He took the bait," Jenkins said, referring to Pendergrass.

"His ego took the bait."

"How did you know Kessler's statement was false?"

"You remember that day in his office when I handed it to him?"

"He never looked at it," Jenkins said.

"And if someone wanted to coordinate statements to reflect not what happened, but his version of what happened, wouldn't he start with the commanding officer's statement?"

"If you're right about this, Argus will come at you hard."

Sloane nodded. "I'm counting on it."

CHAPTER FIFTEEN

Tom Pendergrass sat behind the desk that wasn't his, in the office that wasn't his. His had been a single assignment—get the court to dismiss Beverly Ford's claim—and he had succeeded. Judge Natale had dismissed Ford's claim as premature. She didn't have a choice. She couldn't rule on the merits, not after he had boldly admitted the witness statements.

Stupid.

It had been a stupid mistake, a move blinded by his ambition. Worse, Sloane had set him up, and he'd been so confident that Pendergrass would fall for it, he'd gone so far as to subpoena Kessler to the courtroom. It was embarrassing, and had likely ruined any chance Pendergrass had of joining the U.S. Attorney's Office after his commitment.

But what bothered Pendergrass most was he could not figure out how Sloane could have known what Kessler would say.

Pendergrass distinctly remembered Sloane telling him that Kessler had refused to talk to him once the claim had been reopened. So how had Sloane known that Kessler didn't prepare his own witness statement? Where had he obtained all the information about soldiers stealing supplies from convoys? And those were not even close to the most nagging question Sloane had skillfully left for all in the courtroom to ponder: What were the odds that all of those men in James Ford's squad would die after returning stateside and all within six months of one another?

About the same as the odds that four witness statements could be so similar, particularly when one witness had no recollection of the events. Pendergrass opened his file and reconsidered the highlighted statements. If Colonel Bo Griffin had written Captain Kessler's statement, then he had also coordinated the other statements. There was no other logical conclusion.

But why?

"Those were some fireworks this morning." Pendergrass closed the file as Rachel Keane entered his office, closed the door, and took a seat. "I thought you conducted yourself well."

"I don't know about that," Pendergrass said. "It was a mistake to admit those witness statements. It opened the door for Sloane to put Captain Kessler on the stand."

Keane shrugged as if unconcerned. "Maybe, but what did it get Sloane in the end?"

"That's what I've been sitting here trying to figure out," he said. "What did you make of it?"

"Make of what?"

"Sloane's suggestion that the soldiers were stealing supplies and selling them on the black market?"

Keane shrugged. "I'd say Mr. Sloane was trying to create a hypothetical set of facts so Judge Natale wouldn't dismiss the claim. Personally I think he could have picked a better story—it bordered on the fantastic, don't you think? Jo knows that. She just didn't want to embarrass him in front of his client. You've been through the files. You prepared the litigation report. Did you find any evidence to support such a theory?"

"No, I didn't," Pendergrass said.

But he had not conducted the investigation. Command had done that, Colonel Bo Griffin, to be precise. The file to which Pendergrass had been given access was limited.

"Sloane was desperate," Keane continued. "He knows he can't prove his case, so he slung mud hoping something might stick. He overreached and Jo shot him down."

Pendergrass nodded.

"Something else bothering you, Captain?"

"What about those other three men?"

"What about them?"

"They're all dead. What are the odds of that?"

Keane leaned forward. "Higher than you might initially expect."

"I don't—"

Keane stood. "It's a lawyer's trick, Tom. You put three completely unrelated events together, find one common fact, and it makes it look like something unusual has occurred. We do it all the time, and Sloane is obviously a very skilled lawyer. But when you consider each case individually, they're not unusual at all. Phillip Ferguson's suicide sounds as though it was directly related to his being blind. The other two sound like deadbeat drug dealers. That's a dangerous business. I know—I tried a lot of drug cases. It's only a matter of time before bad luck catches up to you. Don't get sucked into Sloane's mind games."

Pendergrass nodded. "Yeah, I guess you're right."

Keane put an envelope on his desk. "This is for you, for all of your hard work."

The envelope was embossed. Inside was an invitation. Pendergrass was dumbfounded.

"Have you ever met a president?"

The invitation was to the reception for Senator Johnson Marshall at the home of Houghton Park Jr.

"I don't know what to say."

"Say yes. You've done an excellent job, Tom. You have all the skills I look for in my trial attorneys."

Pendergrass read the fine print on the invitation. "Black tie. I'm afraid I don't own a tuxedo."

"Don't be silly. Tuxedos are common and boring.

You'll wear your dress uniform. You earned that right. Besides, I simply won't accept common for my escort."

Pendergrass felt his face flush. "Your escort?"

"Would you mind? I don't have a date for the evening."

He thought of Keane riding in his Ford Taurus with over 100,000 miles on it.

"I'll meet you there," she said. "I'm in meetings out of the office the rest of the day. Unless you don't want to . . ."

"No," he said. "I mean yes, I do."

Keane stood and opened the door to leave.

"I'll submit a final memorandum to the Tort Claims administrative staff," Pendergrass said, "to let them know the file can be closed."

Keane turned back. "Don't worry about that. I'll have someone here take care of it. You have more pressing business. You need to get your medals polished." She winked and walked out.

Pendergrass sat back down, feeling like what a convict on death row must feel like upon receiving a reprieve.

The telephone rang. When he answered he didn't recognize the voice.

"Captain? This is Joann Cox with the Tort Litigation administrative staff."

"Thank you for getting back to me." He had called to request James Ford's file to complete the memorandum necessary to close it. "I guess I won't—"

"Don't thank me yet. I think there might have been a mistake."

"A mistake?" Pendergrass asked.

"About the name of the claimant you provided to my staff."

"What about it?"

"We can't seem to find a file matching that name."

ARGUS INTERNATIONAL

AS THE GUARD stepped from the booth, Sloane thrust his driver's license out the window. "I'm here to see Robert Kessler."

The man hesitated. This was a break in routine. He held up his clipboard. "I don't see your name."

"Get on the damn phone and tell Kessler I'm at the front gate. I don't have time for bullshit from some petty-ass rent-a-cop."

The guard's smug expression vanished. He froze momentarily, then turned and started back to his booth, his movements stiff and robotic, as if he were holding himself together and could literally explode, showering the area with springs, wires, and circuits. Inside his booth he picked up the telephone and appeared to be explaining the situation to someone on the other end. After another moment he hung up the phone, took his time doing something in the booth, and emerged carrying a visitor's pass.

He handed Sloane the white plastic card. Sloane threw it on the seat and looked up at the guard, challenging him. When the man's thumb remained hitched in his belt, Sloane said, "Either you open it, or I drive through it."

The guard's thumb slid to the button.

Sloane parked in front of the third building, not surprised to see Anne, Kessler's assistant, waiting to escort him. Ordinarily he never abused staff, but he was here to make an impression, and not a good one. The only thing Charles Jenkins hadn't liked about Sloane's plan was that Sloane had made himself the bait. Jenkins had likened it to a "crocodile hunt," an expression he said he learned in Vietnam from a soldier from Florida. Apparently, when you hunted crocodiles, you set out bait, waited for the crocodiles to take it, and killed them.

"Mr. Sloane—"

He waved her off. "I know I don't have an appointment. I assume he's in?"

"He is, but it's company policy that you wear the white visitor's card."

Sloane had left the card on the passenger seat. "I don't care about company policy. I don't like people keeping tabs on me. You know where I'm going, and I suspect with all the security goons you employ that I wouldn't get far if I wandered off without an escort, which appears to be your sole purpose in this operation."

Anne stiffened.

"So are you going to take me to Captain Kessler or fail at that as well?"

"I'd be happy to take you," she said, neither looking nor sounding happy.

At Kessler's office Anne knocked twice, opened the door, and stepped aside. Kessler sat behind his desk with his eyebrows knitted and worry lines creasing his forehead.

Kessler turned his wheelchair and came around the edge of the desk.

Sloane turned to Anne. "Thanks for showing me the way. If I need to use the bathroom, I'll have someone call you."

Anne looked to Kessler, who nodded, turned and pulled the door closed behind her.

Sloane never gave Kessler the chance to speak. "I'm not here for pleasantries, Captain, so we can cut the tours and cute jokes." He jabbed a finger at Kessler's face. "Why would you sign a report saying you got lost in a sandstorm when you did not?"

"I told you I don't recall—"

"Bullshit. You know exactly what happened. Your lack of memory is a convenience."

"A convenience? I'm in a wheelchair because of that convenience."

"You're in a wheelchair because you were selling and buying drugs on the black market and it caught up to you."

"You don't really believe—"

"I know all about it, Captain. Colonel Griffin filled me in."

"Colonel Griffin—"

"You were stealing supplies off that convoy along with whatever narcotics you could get on base to sell or to trade."

Kessler opened his mouth but Sloane again cut him off.

"Griffin told me everything—what you were doing

and how you got all of your men to agree on what to say in those reports."

"Griffin?"

"But it wasn't Griffin who made up the story, it was you. I spoke with Cassidy just before one of your men shot him."

"What?"

"He told me about your operation, Captain. He told me you gave the order to drive into that town. Only you picked the wrong town on the wrong day and—"

"He couldn't have—"

"And I recorded it. That's right, Captain. I recorded everything Cassidy had to say. And it will prove that Ford was not killed incident to his service."

Kessler looked as though he were fighting a migraine.

"I was also there when the bullet took off the top of Cassidy's head. I know he didn't blow himself up. You had him killed, just like you had Phillip Ferguson and Dwayne Thomas killed."

Kessler gripped the handles of his wheelchair, his knuckles white. "I brought them home. I brought them all home alive. Ford was—".

"You gave an unlawful order and led those men into that ambush. Then you convinced them to lie for you, to say it was the sandstorm. Griffin told me all about that too."

"That's not true."

"Everything was fine until Beverly Ford began to question what happened to her husband, and I became involved. But I'm not going away. I know the truth."

He pulled open the door before Kessler could respond. "This isn't the end. It's the beginning. I'll have the Justice Department and the FBI all over you and Argus." He stormed back down the hall, shouting for others to hear. "The hammer is going to drop, Captain, on you and everyone else."

Outside, Sloane walked quickly to his car, started it, and pulled from the parking spot. As he drove back down the access road to the gated entry, he let out a sigh of relief, though he also looked in his rearview mirror.

He had played his part. Now he just had to wait for the crocodiles to take the bait.

LAKE WASHINGTON
SEATTLE, WASHINGTON

TOM PENDERGRASS HAD only seen pictures of Houghton Park Jr.'s home. Built on the shores of Lake Washington, it looked like a chalet from the Italian Alps, which the newspapers and magazine articles indicated was just what Park had intended. Park had apparently visited Bolzano, Italy, and became so enamored with its ancient castles that he had dispatched architects and engineers to study the finer architectural attributes. He bought and tore down multimillion-dollar structures on the lake, brought in cranes, and began laying stones. The process took more than two years to complete, with crews working under a cloak of secrecy and behind a large mesh screen erected along the shore to keep boaters from taking pictures. Rumors spread about lavish luxuries, including tunnels under the home where Park kept, among other things, a submarine he could launch into the lake.

The rumors only made the entrance to the property, which Pendergrass saw from the window of a bus shuttling guests to Park's home from a designated parking area, more disappointing. There were no imposing gates or walls, no guards—nothing to give away the fact that the property belonged to one of the richest men in the country, if not the world. The entrance was a simple one-lane drive with two four-foot-tall brick columns, a nondescript light fixture atop each. Still, Pendergrass didn't doubt that the property was equipped with sensory devices that when tripped unleashed a horde of security personnel.

The invitation had included directions to the designated parking area three miles from Park's home. Pendergrass knew the arrangement was to minimize having to search so many cars, but he was just grateful to leave his Taurus behind, parked amidst cars that cost nearly as much as a down payment on a home. However, as the bus descended the road, Pendergrass noticed the owners of those luxury automobiles also subtly craning to look out the tinted windows at the manicured lawns, fountains, and pristine gardens. It reminded him of the moment in the movie *Willie Wonka and the Chocolate Factory* when the lucky Gold Ticket winners and a family member first entered the inner sanctum of the chocolate factory.

The bus stopped beneath a porte cochere where

women in black evening gowns greeted each guest and directed them into an enormous hall. Massive wood beams crisscrossed the ceiling, from which hung three enormous chandeliers. Pendergrass estimated the room could accommodate two full-sized basketball courts. He soon felt adrift amidst a sea of black- and white-clad guests, and trays of champagne, wine, and hors d'oeuvres. Not seeing Rachel Keane, he wandered toward French doors leading to a stone patio over which a large white tent had been erected. The one thing Houghton Park couldn't dictate was the weather, and it didn't look about to cooperate. Dark clouds had amassed to the south, and the winds indicated they were blowing north. Pendergrass stood as if considering the storm, trying not to feel self-conscious.

"Tom, I'm so glad you made it."

Rachel Keane approached in a stunning, form-fitting white evening gown. "And I'm even more glad that you wore your uniform."

Pendergrass reached out to take Keane's hand, but she stepped past his arm, pressing her cheek to his, kissing it lightly. "A man in uniform can be such a turn-on," she whispered.

THREE TREE POINT, WASHINGTON

SLOANE ARRIVED HOME later than he had intended. After his performance in Kessler's office, he had returned to his firm in Seattle, wanting to stick to routine. He called Tina and Jake from a pay phone in the lobby of the building. Both were fine. They had spent the day in Ellensburg after picking up supplies. Jake found a tack shop and became enamored of a black cowboy hat. Tina bought it for him. She said when they returned to the ranch, Jake put the hat on and the caretaker gave him a lesson on an Appaloosa.

"I hope he doesn't take to horseback riding the way he did fishing," Sloane had said. "We'd have a heck of a time with the neighbors if we kept a horse in the back-yard."

He could tell from the moments of silence in their conversations that Tina was worried about him, but they both knew he had to finish what he had started and that she was in his corner. There would be no going back.

With the heavy cloud layer continuing to roll in from the south, it was dark as he parked in the easement next to Jenkins's mud-caked Buick. They had agreed it unwise for him to park in the detached garage because when the doors closed, he would be momentarily lost from Jenkins's view.

Exiting the Jeep, Sloane fought his instincts to look about and pushed through the gate to the back porch. Jake's fishing pole leaned against the barbecue on the lawn. A light wind brought the briny smell of the Sound. The tide was in.

As he stepped inside, Bud jumped onto the counter, but Sloane didn't want to linger in the kitchen with all the windows. He walked into the front room. The shades remained down. Bud followed him upstairs, meowing and winding between his legs, making a pest of himself. Sloane changed into jeans, a black T-shirt, and dark, rubber-soled shoes. Returning downstairs, he turned on the lamp near the couch, and sat across the room in a leather chair with the Glock in his lap and his cell phone pre-dialed to Jenkins's number.

Then he waited.

FROM THE UNDERBRUSH on the hillside Jenkins scanned the area surrounding Sloane's home as Sloane pulled into the spot beside the Buick. Jenkins didn't like Sloane being in the open, though it was unlikely Argus would try to kill him with a sniper shot. Their first priority would be to recover the fictitious tape recording of Michael Cassidy's confession. It had been a smart play by Sloane. It would buy him time. If Argus stuck to their prior MO, they would make Sloane's death look explainable—a suicide like Ferguson, an accident like Cassidy, or a random killing, as with Dwayne Thomas.

Jenkins also didn't like being this far from the house, but no other alternative afforded him a view of the property and surrounding area. To the east and north the house faced the street and the public easement. The beach and the Sound were to the west. To the south, across an expanse of lawn, Sloane's neighbor illuminated a flag atop a pole with a bright spotlight. That left the hillside behind Sloane's property. Jenkins parked the Explorer on the street above Maplewild and accessed the hillside by cutting through yards.

Sloane disappeared from view as he passed through the gate and reappeared atop the back stairs. He lingered a moment, then pushed inside. Shortly thereafter a muted light reflected through a shaded window, the sign they had agreed upon that everything inside the house was all right. Jenkins knew exactly where Sloane would be sitting.

Sweat rolled down his forehead into his eyes. The humidity, unusual for the Northwest, had built all day, and the dark cloud layer gave the impression of a paper bag filled with water, capable of bursting at any moment. The lighting on the street was poor. A lamp on a utility pole cast the easement in an orange glow. Otherwise the street lamps were few and far between. Apparently the homeowners on Three Tree Point valued their privacy.

As the evening wore on, the wind began to gust out of the south, stiffening the flag on the neighbor's pole. Moments later the cloud layer flashed a brilliant purple and white, followed by a rumble of thunder that shook the ground.

And the paper bag burst.

Jenkins reached into his backpack and pulled out one of the camouflage ponchos he and Sloane had bought for their trek to Cassidy's trailer as great globules of water fell from the sky. They had put the ponchos away damp, and the plastic had stuck together as if melted. Jenkins fought to unravel it without ripping holes. When he had finally succeeded, he slipped it over his head and pulled it around his torso. Then he picked up the binoculars to scan the area, though he did not need them to see that a van had parked in the easement, directly beside Sloane's Jeep.

. . .

PENDERGRASS FELT HIMSELF blush, but before he could respond—not that any words came immediately to mind—Keane pulled away.

"Rachel."

Keane turned to the sound of her name being called. Pendergrass recognized Houghton Park Jr. from images in the media.

"Houghton, how are you?" Keane kissed Park on the cheek, then turned to introduce Pendergrass. "This is Captain Thomas Pendergrass."

Park's gray hair was slicked back off his forehead with a liberal dose of gel. "The young man you were telling me about?" He extended a hand. "Houghton Park. So very glad you came."

"Captain Pendergrass served in Iraq and is the newest member of my civil litigation team."

"A soldier and an attorney," Park said. "Is that like an officer and a gentleman?"

Pendergrass smiled. "I'm still a JAG lawyer at present," he said, though he had not missed the fact that Keane had apparently spoken to Park about him.

Keane slipped her arm through the captain's. "But he's going to consider a full-time position in the U.S. Attorney's Office, aren't you, Tom?"

Pendergrass smiled. "I certainly hope it will be an option." He suddenly remembered that he wanted to let Keane know about his conversation with the Tort Claims staff, and their inability to find James Ford's file, but decided the issue could wait until they were alone.

"Good for you," Park said, smiling. "Never come cheap or easy, my father used to say."

They all smiled politely.

"Thank you for having me," Pendergrass said.

"It's my pleasure. We are all indebted to you for your service. The president will be arriving shortly. Have you ever met a president, Captain?"

"I've never had that pleasure," Pendergrass said.

"I think you'll find it a memory that will last a lifetime." Park turned to Keane. "There are some people I'd like you to meet." He looked to Pendergrass. "Could I steal the U.S. attorney from you for a few moments?"

"Certainly," Pendergrass said.

As Keane walked off, the wrap across her shoulders slid, revealing a toned and muscled back. Pendergrass's eyes did not stop there. They continued lower, to her toned and firm butt.

Keane suddenly looked back over her shoulder, catching him. She winked.

A burst of light illuminated the clouds rolling in quickly, thunder just seconds behind it. Pendergrass felt the first drops of rain and, along with the other guests, moved quickly for cover inside what he was already calling the "the Great Hall." Despite the weather, for whatever the reason, tonight it certainly appeared that fortune had smiled on him. A few days ago he had been pushing papers around a desk at Fort Lewis. Now it appeared he was moving toward his long-term goal. He'd heard others talk about their lives changing in an instant. Soldiers knew it well. Maybe this was his instant.

Feeling emboldened, he made eye contact with a woman carrying a tray of hors d'oeuvres, took two, and plucked a glass of wine from another passing tray. He then stepped toward a conversation, introduced himself, and soon found that he mingled easily among the rich and famous, his uniform an obvious icebreaker. Before he knew it, he was knee-deep in half a dozen conversations.

"Did you serve in the war?"

"How long were you in Iraq?"

"Will you have to go back?"

"Is it as bad as the media is portraying?"

Others simply thanked him for his service. Pendergrass did not downplay the attention by explaining that during his tour he had never left the Green Zone and spent most of his time sorting through legal claims by angry Iraqi civilians seeking compensation for damage inflicted to their homes or other property by American forces. He tried to sound humble, opining that the real heroes were those soldiers who had given their lives. It made him think of James Ford. He had meant it when he told David Sloane that he wished he could compensate every family who lost a relative in Iraq, that he was, at heart, still a soldier. He wished Beverly Ford had taken the money.

In need of a bathroom, he excused himself from a conversation. Not seeing any signs—this was after all, despite its immensity, still a man's home and not a public facility—he wandered to the edge of the room and started down a hall, turned another corner, and found himself lost. Approaching the end of another corridor, he heard voices and slowed, embarrassed that he may have strayed into an area not intended for guests. He came to a room with a large stone fireplace, high ceiling, and fresco paintings, but the décor was not what caught his immediate attention. What caught his immediate attention was the sight of the shawl draped across the toned bare shoulders. Rachel Keane stepped through a doorway into an adjacent room, Houghton Park's hand pressed gently against the small of her back.

Pendergrass was about to turn away when a third person, already inside the room, moved to close the door behind Park. Catching a glimpse of the man's profile just before the door shut, Pendergrass went numb.

THE WIND-DRIVEN RAIN splattered on the roof and skylights, the water pinging through the overwhelmed gutters and downspouts. A spark of light pulsed blue against the window blinds and momentarily lit the living room. Seconds later, thunder rattled the windows.

Then something banged.

Sloane stood from his chair, Glock in one hand, his phone in the other. Another bang.

This time the noise had a familiarity to it, and Sloane placed it—the screen door off the kitchen slamming against the house. When unlatched, the wind caught the door and flung it against the siding. The first time Sloane had heard the noise, it had startled him and Tina from a dead sleep.

He walked to the kitchen and watched as the wind caught the screen again and whipped it backward against the siding. The rational side of his brain told him to let it be, but he also didn't want the noise to distract him from other possible sounds. He had forgotten to disable the bulb over the back door illuminating the porch and didn't relish the thought of standing in the spotlight even for a moment, Jenkins's theory that Argus wouldn't snipe him notwithstanding.

He crept below the marble counter, put the gun on the floor, and pulled the door open a crack. The wind howled. He slid forward but couldn't reach the screen door handle and his fingers could not grip an edge to pull the door closed. Not wanting to linger on the porch, he stepped out, grabbed the handle of the screen, pulled it closed and latched the eyehook. Then he closed the kitchen door. Though it took only seconds, his heart hammered in his chest and his hair dripped as if he'd been sprayed with a burst from a garden hose.

He walked back through the living room, shaking the water from his hair, when he noticed the shadow on the cloth blind, what he initially thought to be a bush beneath the windowsill rustling in the wind. Then the shadow moved across the blind right to left, the top of someone's head ducking just beneath the sill.

Sloane watched as the shadow progressed from one window to the next, perhaps trying to see inside by looking beneath the blinds.

The crocodiles had come.

The hunt was on.

He pressed the send button as the shadow turned the southwest corner of the house. A moment later it reappeared on the blind of his den window. Sloane lost the shadow a second time as the person turned the southeast corner to the front of the house. Jenkins's phone rang a second time.

Jenkins did not answer.

"Come on. Come on," Sloane said.

The shadow crept past the window to the right of the front door but did not appear in the window on the other side. Again Jenkins's phone rang.

Again he did not answer.

Sloane dropped to one knee and pressed an ear to the door but heard only the whistle of the wind and the beating of the rain. When Jenkins did not answer after the third ring, Sloane hung up.

He forced himself to remain calm, to think clearly. The police were not an option. Sloane had one shot at this, and for it to work, Argus had to think they had the upper hand at all times. He suspected they would send more than one man. The first time had only been meant to warn; this time their intent would be to kill. Were they planning to come through the back, hoping to flush him out the front door? That was information Jenkins was to provide. Not any longer, though why, Sloane did not know.

He decided he could not stay in the house. His paths of escape were limited and could be directed. Outside he would have the cover of darkness, the weather, and the advantage of knowing the terrain. But that presented two problems: getting out, and deciding which direction to run.

He wouldn't make it across the neighbor's lawn, not

with the floodlight illuminating the flagpole and everything around it. To the west, the high tide had narrowed the beach to a six-foot strip that would force him to run in a straight line and not very fast in the rocks and shells, a bad combination if someone was shooting at him. That left the front door, where the man waited, and the easement off the back porch, which was basically a dead end.

Not if you can reach the Indian Trail.

In his mind Sloane recalled Jake stepping behind the blue community Dumpster while cleaning up fireworks after the Fourth of July and seeming to disappear. Following him, Sloane had pulled back a hedge and discovered an overgrown footpath that led through and behind the yards of the homes perched on the hillside overlooking Puget Sound. Further inquiry revealed the path to have been originally used by Native Americans to access the beach a century before man carved Maplewild in the hillside.

If Sloane could reach the trail he would be well concealed.

That was well and good, but it did not solve his first problem, getting out of the house. If Argus had stationed a man at the front door, they likely had one or more at the back.

The room again pulsed blue light, followed by a near simultaneous clap of thunder. It shook the house, nearly masking another sound; this one not the product of nature, but an explosion that plunged Sloane into total darkness.

.   .   .

JENKINS SLIPPED AND slid on the wet ground, hurrying up the hillside from his hiding place. Three steps into the neighbor's backyard he heard the command.

"Freeze."

Jenkins froze.

"Hands. Show me your hands."

He held up his hands, the backpack in one, his cell phone in the other. Rain sheeted off his camouflage poncho.

The police officer had his gun drawn, as did his female partner, standing to Jenkins's right. The male officer continued to shout, but Jenkins was having difficulty hearing him over the storm. Water dripped down his face. "What?"

"Drop the backpack and keep your hands where I can see them."

Jenkins dropped the backpack.

"What's in your left hand?" the officer shouted.

"Cell phone."

"Drop it!"

Jenkins looked down at the puddle at his feet.

"Now! Do not lower your hands. Let it fall."

The phone landed in the puddle.

Then it rang. Sloane.

Jenkins nearly reached for it, but his instincts to not get shot prevailed.

"On your knees. Keep your hands above your head. I want to see them at all times."

Jenkins complied. "I'm a private investigator," he shouted. "I'm armed."

The officer shared a look with his partner. "Where's your weapon?"

"My right hip, under the poncho."

The phone rang again. He and Sloane had agreed they would only call if necessary. Sloane was in trouble, and capable as he was in and out of a courtroom, he would be no match for Argus's commandos alone.

"Are you carrying any other weapons?"

"No."

The shotgun and the AR15 rifle remained hidden in the back of Alex's Explorer parked on the street.

Again the phone rang.

The officer signaled to his female partner. She approached Jenkins from behind and grabbed his right wrist. The cuff pinched the flesh. The officer pulled his arm behind his back and quickly snapped the second cuff. Then she felt along his side and reached beneath the poncho to remove his gun.

Lightning crackled, this time the thunder nearly simultaneous.

Then something exploded.

Jenkins jerked his head to look over his shoulder, but he could no longer see Sloane's house behind the foliage. He half expected to see flames leaping into the sky.

He looked down at his phone. The screen had gone black. "My investigator's license is in my back pocket."

Sloane had insisted Jenkins get the damn license, worried about potential liability. Jenkins had called him a namby-pants. He hoped he had the chance to take it back.

"We'll get that all figured out." The male officer helped Jenkins to his feet and led him through the yard. Jenkins looked again, but could not see Sloane's home. The female officer carried the backpack and cell phone as they crossed the yard. Frightened faces peered from behind curtained windows.

Jenkins leaned against the back of the police cruiser and spread his legs without being asked, hoping to move things along.

"What were you doing in the bushes?" the male officer asked.

"Watching a client's house. He's received anonymous threats. It's the only place with a view. I should have asked the neighbor for permission, but you know people get squeamish about those kinds of things, especially when the request is made by a large black man."

"Who's your client?"

"David Sloane. He lives in the white colonial next to the easement."

"What kind of threats?"

"Threats to his wife and children. He's a lawyer," Jenkins said, keeping his response vague. "My license and identification are in my back pocket. I have a permit to carry a concealed weapon."

The male officer pulled out Jenkins's wallet and opened the back door of the car. "Okay, take a seat out of the rain."

"Could you rush it?" Jenkins asked.

He debated asking the officers to go to the house and check on Sloane, but Sloane had been adamant about not involving law enforcement. Law enforcement would only spook Argus, and that would give them time to destroy whatever evidence could still exist. Argus was also a trained combat force, and Jenkins could be sending two police officers unprepared into an ambush.

"It will go as fast as it goes," the officer said.

Jenkins sat on the edge of the backseat, folded his knees to his chest, and squeezed into the car. His knees pressed against the hard plastic, and the handcuffs forced him to lean forward, putting a strain on his neck and back.

The male officer directed his partner to go and reassure the homeowner, then slid in the driver's-side door out of the rain, typing on a computer. He would run a Department of Licensing check to confirm that Jenkins did have a concealed weapons permit, and also check to ensure the gun wasn't stolen. He'd also search for outstanding warrants.

It was routine, but routine took time, and that was the one thing Jenkins feared Sloane did not have.

CHAPTER SIXTEEN

Pendergrass slipped inside a bathroom, locking the door. He stood at the sink, staring at his reflection in the oval, gold-leaf mirror, feeling sickened and lightheaded. He lowered the toilet seat and sat.

Someone knocked.

His head snapped to the sound. Another knock. He stood.

"Just a minute." He turned on the faucet and splashed cold water on his face. Then he dried his hands and face on a hand towel, checked his appearance again in the mirror, took a deep breath, and pulled open the door.

A well-coiffed woman leaned against the doorframe, breasts swelling over the top of a low-cut, sequined gown. Her eyes widened as if she had discovered something she liked on the menu. "Hello, soldier," she said, words slurring. "Don't you look yummy."

He stepped past her.

"Hey, don't run off."

Walking back into the Great Hall, Pendergrass did not see Park or Keane, although the crowd had thinned, most now outside under the tents. He hurried quickly to the tent and surveyed the faces. The crowd buzzed with anticipation. Pendergrass looked at his watch. The president was due to arrive at any moment.

He needed to leave quickly. He needed to warn Sloane.

Houghton Park exited the French doors to the wing of the house and approached Johnson Marshall. The incumbent senator stood on the patio in spit-polished shoes, a navy-blue suit, white shirt, and red tie. Keane emerged through the same doors a discreet moment later.

Park raised his hands. "Ladies and gentlemen, I'm advised that the president will be joining us very shortly. At this time, however, it gives me great pleasure to introduce to you Washington's own senator, Johnson Marshall."

Marshall stepped forward to applause. Pendergrass didn't wait to hear the speech. He stepped back into the Great Hall, now deserted but for the staff, and moved quickly across it to the porte cochere. The bus was not there. He'd have to walk. He started up the driveway on foot. Halfway up the road, four police motorcycles descended toward him, lights flashing. Pendergrass walked back down and stepped to the side as the president's motorcade arrived. Secret Service exited black

Town Cars and fanned out across the property. Two agents moved directly toward Pendergrass.

"I'm going to have to ask you to return to the party," one of the men said. "We need to secure this area."

Pendergrass didn't bother to debate. He walked down the road and back inside the Great Hall. Starting across it, he had a thought and veered in a different direction, retracing his earlier steps. He found the corridor that led to the room with the stone fireplace and frescoes, crossed to the door into which Keane and Park had stepped, and reached for the handle.

"Tom." Pendergrass subtly pulled back his hand, turned. "I've been looking for you," Keane said.

Pendergrass maintained a calm demeanor. "I was looking for the bathroom. I must have got turned around."

"Certainly understandable in this place," she said. "You missed the announcement. The president has arrived."

"That would be just like me to miss it." He smiled. "Story of my life."

Keane took his arm. "Well, I'm not about to let that happen to my escort."

Walking back to the Great Hall, Pendergrass thought of the three dead guardsmen. Astronomical. What were the odds of all three dying so close to one another? Astronomical.

He thought of Captain Robert Kessler.

Then he thought again of David Sloane.

THE IDEA CAME suddenly.

Sloane did not question it.

He ripped open the door and aimed the gun. The man had turned his head to the reverberating echo from the explosion, giving Sloane the split-second advantage he had sought. The only thing that kept him from pulling the trigger was he had aimed too high. By the time he corrected, the synapses in his brain had ordered him not to shoot.

Captain Robert Kessler turned back and flinched, but otherwise sat motionless staring up at Sloane through the rain.

"I'm alone," Kessler said. "And I'm unarmed."

"What are you doing sitting out here in the rain?"

"I can't stand." Kessler smiled. "I couldn't get up the steps to reach a door."

Sloane scanned the yard but did not detect anyone else. "What do you want?"

"I know Cassidy didn't tell you we were selling supplies on the black market."

"Yeah? How do you know that?"

"Because it's a lie. And because Cassidy would have had no reason to lie. You also had to know Cassidy. That boy began to twitch the second we left base. He wouldn't have sold a pack of cigarettes for a million dollars if it meant staying off our FOB longer than necessary. So I'm guessing you came to my office to let me know it was Griffin who told you that story, just like you put me on the stand to let me know he coordinated the witness statements."

Sloane lowered the weapon, stepped off the porch, and helped Kessler up the steps.

Inside, Sloane pulled back the blind to look out the den window to his neighbor's yard. The light remained out. As with the screen door banging against the house, Sloane had recognized the sudden explosion to be the transformer atop the pole in the easement. It had exploded twice before, including that winter when the Point actually got snow for the first time in many neighbors' memories.

He grabbed two towels from the bathroom and tossed one to Kessler, then went to his study and returned with his boom box, which ran on both electricity and batteries. The shadow on the blinds wasn't someone creeping past the windows. It had been Kessler struggling to wheel the chair on the saturated lawn.

Sloane turned on the boom box and Kessler nodded his understanding, keeping his voice low. "Did you actually talk to Butch?"

"Right before he was shot. He said Griffin's story was bullshit, but I already knew that."

Kessler gave him a look.

"I knew James Ford would never have done it," Sloane said. He had been suspicious of Griffin the moment he met the colonel in the Tin Room and Griffin recounted Sloane's history as a marine, including removing his flak jacket in Grenada. Sloane had deliberately fed the information to Pendergrass on the observation deck of the Federal Building, knowing someone was listening to their conversation through the bug in his jacket. He had hoped it might help him figure out who that person was. Griffin also had no good reason to research Sloane's background. His statement that he liked to know who he was meeting didn't fly. Neither did his story about Kessler selling contraband on the Iraqi black market. It had been intended to convince Beverly Ford to settle the case and save her husband's reputation. Sloane had dealt with the tactic before. But Griffin had been lazy. Had he truly done his homework, he would have known how far out of character it would have been for James Ford to do what Griffin was proposing.

Sloane's problem was how to feed the information to Kessler without Griffin learning that Sloane knew the story was a ruse. Sloane needed Kessler and Pendergrass to take a closer look at the witness statements. He had suspected Kessler did not write his own statement when he had refused to consider it. He confirmed it when Cassidy told them Kessler had been knocked unconscious and later told Cassidy that he had little recollection of the events. The only logical conclusion was that Griffin had coordinated all four statements. Sloane also wanted Pendergrass and Kessler to know that Ferguson, Thomas, and Cassidy were all dead.

Getting Kessler on the witness stand was act one of his plan. His tirade in Kessler's office, which he suspected was also bugged, was act two.

"You were very convincing," Kessler said.

"What happened after I left?"

"I told everyone you were crazy and tried to maintain a normal routine. It wasn't easy. At four I told Anne

I was leaving to watch my son's Little League game. She asked again if I was all right. I assured her you were a nut job. After the performance you gave, I had little trouble getting her to believe me."

"You weren't followed?" Sloane asked.

"I don't think so," Kessler said. "Argus knows where I live. They'd have little trouble finding me and no reason to follow me thanks to your performance. I stopped at a restaurant and used a pay phone to call the JAG officer who handled Ford's claim. You made an impression on him in court as well."

"What did he say?"

"He said he became suspicious when Ford's claim was reopened and that his suspicion increased when the U.S. attorney instructed him to settle. He checked after court and said the administrative staff has no record of a settlement offer. I don't know what that means exactly, except I assume they should have had such a record."

"The settlement offer made no sense," Sloane said.

In the legal case Pendergrass had provided, the secretary of defense had used his discretion to settle the claims, but it had required congressional approval. Argus would not have wanted such publicity.

"There was no settlement offer, not from the government," Sloane said.

"Then where's the money coming from?"

"I suspect Houghton Park."

"How?" Kessler asked.

"I'm not sure yet, but Keane also has some interest in this, given her appearance in court. She would need to make it look like the money was coming through the Treasury Department, and I suspect Argus could call in enough chips to make it appear that was the case."

"They didn't anticipate Beverly Ford turning it down. She sounds a lot like James."

"How much do you actually remember about that night?"

Kessler's gaze dropped to the floor. "Bits and pieces. I remember trying to get my men to safety. I remember the ambush." He looked up. "I don't remember much before or after that."

"You didn't get lost in a sandstorm, Captain."

"But I remember the sandstorm."

"There was a sandstorm," Sloane said, "but it isn't what caused you to go off course. Michael Cassidy remembered it very well. You received a call for help, another unit in trouble, an ambush. You and your men responded to that call and found yourselves in one hell of a firefight."

SHIMRAN AL MUSLO, IRAQ

ALL HIS LIFE James Ford had looked to the Cross to save him. Now he prayed it didn't get him killed. He needed to secure the gold crucifix beneath his uniform; any shimmer of light could be a target for the insurgents. But to do so would require that he take a hand off the M249. And he wasn't about to do that, not with the staccato chatter of AK-47s all around him. The Lord would forever be his savior, but prayers wouldn't keep him alive this night. The machine gun just might.

He fired three-round bursts into the doorways, windows,

and holes in the buildings. With each block the resistance became heavier, as if they were running into the teeth of the ambush, rather than from it. His chest heaved for air. He felt weighted carrying the big gun and the extra drums of ammunition. Each step his boots sank in the ankle-deep mud and sewage flowing down the street, making a sucking sound when he pulled free.

Ten meters in front of him, Captain Robert Kessler drop-kicked a battered metal door, springing it inward, then crouched in the doorway and sprayed the surrounding buildings until Dwayne Thomas and Michael Cassidy ducked inside. Ford set up opposite Kessler and fired the big gun down the alley. When Fergie slipped in, Ford followed, and the captain slammed the door shut.

Ford pressed his back against a cinder-block wall, gulping for air. Adrenaline caused his heart to jackhammer in his chest. He kissed the crucifix, tucked it safely beneath his perspiration-soaked T-shirt, and looked about. The absurdity of their situation nearly made him laugh. They had ducked into the building for cover, but only two to three feet of crumbling mud and brick remained of the back wall.

"Can't stay here, Captain." Ford gestured to the gaping hole.

"Don't intend to," Kessler replied. "Man that sector." He turned to Thomas. "DT, give me the radio."

Thomas sat with knees pulled to his chest, sobbing. Cassidy sat beside him, wide-eyed. Vomit stained the front of his vest.

"Thomas!" Kessler yelled.

Ford pulled the radio from the pouch on the back of Thomas's rucksack and handed it to Kessler.

"Wolverine six, this is Alfa one-two. Over." Kessler called

their tactical operations center using the convoy's designated name. "Wolverine six, this is Alfa one-two. Request alternate LZ." The captain sought an alternate landing zone at which to rendezvous with air transport. "Wolverine six. We are encountering heavy resistance. Say again. Requesting alternate LZ. Over."

The radio burst static. Then it went silent.

Ford looked over his shoulder as Kessler began another transmission. "Wolv—"

"Captain!"

Kessler looked at him.

Ford pointed to the mouthpiece. "It's broken, Captain. They can't hear you."

For a moment it looked like Kessler might throw the radio to the ground, but he calmly handed it to Ford, who slid it into the slot on his own pack.

"What do we do, Captain?"

"We push on."

"We've got heavy resistance coming from the end of the block, Captain. We'll be running into it," Ford said.

"You want to let me finish, Private?" Kessler snapped. "We push on to the LZ. We don't have a choice with the radio out. They probably have an evac en route. Once we reach the traffic circle we'll send up a couple of clusters." He turned to Ferguson. "How many white stars do you have?"

"At least three."

Kessler took a deep breath, gathering himself. Then he shouted, "Everybody up!" He pulled Thomas and Cassidy from the ground. "Get up! Move your ass! Remember your training." He pointed out a hole in the wall, yelling at Thomas. "When we go out that door, you fire at the rooftops. You got that?"

Thomas nodded.

"I want to hear you say it, Private. 'I fire at the rooftops.'"

"I fire at the rooftops," Thomas repeated, voice cracking.

He wrapped Cassidy's hands around the stock of his M16. "You suppress those windows and doorways."

"I suppress the windows and doorways," Cassidy said.

"Fergie, you got an HEDP in the tube?"

Fergie held up the M203 grenade launcher. "Locked and loaded, Captain."

"On my call, put one in the storefront window across the alley. Put a second in the storefront beside it."

"Roger that."

"I'm going to drop smoke. We move out on my call. Ford, you got our backs."

Ford nodded. "Rules of engagement, Captain?"

They had been trained to consider everyone in Iraq a potential hostile, but the military rules of engagement prevented them from firing unless fired upon.

"No friendlies here," Kessler said

He pulled open the door just wide enough for the M203 barrel. The first sound, a rush of air, launched the 40-mm high-explosive dual-purpose grenade.

Poomp!

An explosion followed.

Ferguson ejected the casing, loaded the second round, slammed the tube shut, and fired again. On the second explosion Kessler tossed two grenades into the alley. Thick green and red smoke quickly obscured everything.

"Move!"

Kessler darted out the door behind the deep retort of his

M16. Cassidy and Thomas followed, each firing three-round bursts. Ford sprayed bullets back down the alley through the thick cover of smoke, brass shell casings dropping at his feet. After Fergie exited, Ford turned and followed, darting between the buildings and alleys. But the resistance continued to intensify, forcing Kessler to again seek cover inside a building.

"What the fuck?" Kessler yelled in frustration. "Where are they coming from?"

Ford pointed to the tallest building at the end of the block. "That's got to be the granary."

"We have to get up on that roof. That's our LZ," Kessler said. The taller buildings afforded the insurgents the high ground, and Mogadishu had taught that Black Hawk helicopters were susceptible to rocket-propelled grenades.

"Thomas, give me your grenades." Thomas handed Kessler two grenades. Kessler looked to Ford. "I'll empty the building, then suppress for Thomas and Cassidy. You and Fergie follow."

"Too far to go, Captain."

"You got your handheld?"

Ford pulled his walkie-talkie from his vest. They confirmed a frequency. Then Kessler crouched close to the door.

"Captain," Ford said again.

"On my order."

Unable to deter him, Ford took up his designated position near the hole in the wall that afforded a view of the circle. Kessler took a deep breath, nodded, and burst out the door.

Ford pulled back the trigger on the M249 and sprayed the building, dust and debris obliterating much of the second floor, while Kessler zigged and zagged across the courtyard. When he had reached the building he lobbed a grenade through the open *doors and was about to launch a second when it looked like he stumbled, and dropped to the ground.*

The reverberating blast of the grenade and gunfire momentarily drowned out all sound. As it passed, Ford heard something else.

"Cease fire," Ford shouted. "Cease fire."

Kessler's voice poured from the handheld. "I'm hit! I'm hit, God damn it!"

"AND NEXT THING we know we're in the middle of a fucking ambush," Cassidy had told Sloane and Jenkins.

Not fully understanding Cassidy's explanation, Sloane said, "Back up and tell me again."

Cassidy leaned against the counter, speaking as if with great effort. "We get a call over the radio Bravo three-sixteen is screaming about needing to be evacuated. They were low on ammo and fuel and had casualties. While we're listening, Ford turns to the captain and points to the plugger. There's this blue square with an X through it."

"What's a plugger?"

"A screen that provides satellite images."

"And what does a blue square with an X through it signify?"

"What does it what?"

"What's it mean?" Sloane asked.

"That means friendlies, our guys. Bravo three-sixteen. If it had been a red X that would have meant Hajji."

"So what happened next?"

"Captain called it in to ask what we're supposed to do. But like I said, we couldn't even communicate with the other guys in the convoy 'cause of the storm."

"So how did your TOC hear the transmission from Bravo three-sixteen?"

Cassidy shrugged. "I don't know. Captain had to make the decision on his own."

Sloane found that even more interesting. "You didn't get orders from your forward operating base?"

"Nope."

"Then who sent the image on the plugger?"

Cassidy's brow furrowed. "Had to be TOC."

"Does that make sense to you?" Sloane asked.

Cassidy thought for a moment. "I don't know."

Sloane paced the trailer, changing thoughts. "You liked Captain Kessler."

"*Like* is a little strong for the military. I'm not sure I *liked* anybody."

"Respected?"

"Hell, yeah. Captain was better than most. He wasn't the rah-rah type, you know, but he knew his shit. Yeah, we all respected him."

"Enough to lie for him?"

"I don't have to lie for him."

Sloane pulled out a copy of Cassidy's witness statement and handed it to him. "You told Colonel Bo Griffin that you got off course in the sandstorm and drove into that ambush. There's nothing in your statement about getting a radio transmission."

Cassidy flipped through the statement, shuffling his

feet. He made a face like he'd just caught scent of something foul. "This ain't my statement."

"That's your signature."

"Yeah, but this ain't what I put in my statement."

"You didn't get stuck in a sandstorm?"

"The sandstorm part is right, but after that . . . what it says in there, that's not what happened. I just told you what happened."

"To protect the captain?"

Cassidy scowled. "Protect him from what?"

"A court-martial for selling supplies out the back of the Humvee, dealing drugs and other contraband on the black market."

"Who told you that?" Cassidy laughed. "Stealing from the convoy? Why would we? They gave you anything you wanted, and smokes were cheap. We had no reason to steal. He shook his head. "I don't know who's feeding you your information, but that's bullshit. Once we got off base, the only thing we wanted to do was get back *on base* and the faster the better."

He explained that their missions were well coordinated and that while a convoy could get off course, that was usually if a road suddenly became inaccessible, or a bridge was bombed overnight, requiring they take a different route.

"But to do it on purpose? Hell no," Cassidy said. "Captain gave the order because he was trying to save lives. Whoever told you otherwise is lying." He chuckled. "Did they say Ford was dealing drugs? Because *that* would be funny. Ford was religious, always kissing his cross and praying."

That's when Sloane realized Griffin had wanted to present him with a quandary: a factual scenario that would prove Ford had not been acting incident to his service, but would also ruin his family's memory of him as a man of faith and principle. Griffin wanted to force Sloane to have to make a moral decision: take the money and drop the case to protect the family's memory, or pursue the complaint and ruin that memory.

"How many of the vehicles proceeded to assist Bravo three-sixteen?" Jenkins asked.

Cassidy held up a single finger. "Just us."

"How many ultimately responded?"

"Until they blew up the building, no one."

"Did you ever find out why not?" Sloane asked.

"I talked to some of the guys when we got back to the base. You know, I asked, 'Where the hell were you?'"

"What'd they say?"

"Just said they never got the transmission."

"How could only you have heard it?" Sloane asked, beginning to suspect he knew the answer.

Cassidy shrugged. "I don't know. Maybe they'd all left by then, or maybe the storm had something to do with it. Or they were on a different frequency. I don't know. All I know is next thing we're knee-deep in the shit and running for our lives. Then, ka-boom! Shit started falling all around us, chunks of cement and barrels flying everywhere, exploding."

"Barrels? I thought you said it was a granary."

"That's what they told us." Cassidy shrugged. "Apparently they were wrong. When all the smoke cleared it was just rubble and all these barrels burning, and Ford and Fergie and the captain all laying there."

"Who called in the air strike?" Sloane had asked, recalling that Katherine Ferguson said her husband had told her something similar.

"The captain, I guess." Cassidy paused, looking like he was trying to silently solve a physics problem.

"What?" Sloane asked.

"Except our radio was broke."

"What do you mean, broke?"

"I mean broke. The captain couldn't have called in an air strike because the mouthpiece was crushed. I remember we could hear but we couldn't talk back." Cassidy looked confused. "What's going on?"

"Did you get a better look at the barrels, see a label on them, anything at all?" Sloane asked.

Cassidy shook his head. "I was just glad to be alive, man. I wasn't worried about nothing else. Besides, we weren't allowed to go near the building."

"Why not?"

"They secured it."

"Who?"

"Contractor types."

"Military contractors?" Jenkins asked.

Cassidy nodded. "But hell, I don't know. I couldn't tell those guys apart half the time anyway."

THE FEMALE POLICE officer pulled open the passenger-side door and slid in out of the rain. "Anything?" she asked.

"Last one coming back now." Her partner read the screen. "Okay, Mr. Jenkins, you're good to go." He pushed open the door, stepped into the rain, and walked around the car to open the back door for Jenkins. "You can't just walk through private property because it's convenient," he said, helping Jenkins out of the car and removing the handcuffs.

Jenkins wasn't in the mood for a class on property rights. He rubbed his wrists and grabbed his backpack and phone.

"You want us to go with you to make sure your client is all right?"

"No," Jenkins said. "But thanks."

He ran down the street to where he had parked the Explorer, climbed in, and started the engine. Pulling into the street, he flipped open his phone. The interior window remained black. He pressed the power button. Nothing happened. The water had killed the battery. He tossed it on the seat and drove.

At the bottom of the hill he was relieved to find Sloane's home still standing, and even more relieved to see the transformer atop a utility pole sparking and emitting a small blue flame. He deduced it caused the explosion. Still, that didn't explain why Sloane had called. Perhaps he had spooked at the explosion. No. The phone rang first, then the explosion. Jenkins stepped from the car into a steady drizzle and retrieved his shotgun and rifle from the back. He crept along the side of the van and glanced through the passenger-side window. The drive shaft had been modified to accommodate a man no longer able to use his legs, the seat pushed close to the steering wheel and an arm protruding from the column to allow the driver to use his hands to accelerate and stop the vehicle.

Kessler.

Jenkins worked his way around the van with his rifle slung over his shoulder, shotgun at his hip. He quietly unlatched the gate, took a moment to survey the yard, and ascended the first porch step.

Movement caught his attention. He stopped, considering the beach, letting his eyes roam the area. With the cloud layer and no artificial light he could not distinguish anything from the shadowy movement of the waves on the surface of the water.

About to turn back to the house, he again sensed movement. He lowered the backpack and shotgun and raised the binoculars, scanning the surface of the Sound. He was about to lower the binoculars when he saw something protrude from the surface of the water. It looked to be the rounded head of a seal. Jenkins had heard the animals bark at the Point but had never seen one. Another rounded head surfaced close by, followed by a third. One seal would have been unusual. Three was implausible.

One of the heads rose from the water revealing a face mask and breathing apparatus. The other two divers followed. Jenkins refocused further out into the Sound. A boat sat anchored offshore, a dangerous thing to do at night with the massive cargo ships that used the passage as a shipping lane.

The crocodiles had reached the beach. If they made it to the house they would kill Sloane and Kessler. Sloane had deliberately given them the scenario they needed. Witnesses would talk about how an enraged Sloane burst into Kessler's office that afternoon and threatened to expose Kessler in the killings of three guardsmen to cover up an illegal drug operation while in Iraq. The implication would be that Kessler went to Sloane's home, killed him, then turned the gun on himself.

Jenkins couldn't let it get that far.

KESSLER TURNED TO Sloane. "Butch was right. I didn't call in an air strike," he said, keeping his voice low. "The radio was broken. The mouthpiece was crushed. I could receive transmissions, but I couldn't respond."

"Someone wanted to blow that building. You were the excuse to do it," Sloane said. "It wasn't a granary."

"Chemicals," Kessler said.

"Argus supplied Saddam with precursor chemicals he used to build his chemical weapons, and they made a lot of money doing it." Sloane explained how UN inspectors had found chemical and biological agents in Iraq as late as 1998, long after it became illegal to supply them.

"But it's a highly regulated industry," Kessler said. "How could Argus hide the shipments?"

Sloane explained what Mills had learned about the chemicals being shipped through Jordan or Syria and then through the free-trade port of Aqaba to a middleman who was falsely identified as the end user. The middleman would then load the shipments onto trucks and illegally drive them into Iraq.

"As you know, there were no border checks."

Kessler asked, "What about the payments?"

Sloane continued to repeat what Mills had learned, explaining that even after the embargo, Jordan continued to import 300 million dollars' worth of Iraqi oil every year. Syria, too, purchased the oil.

"A middleman could have presented an invoice for food or other supplies approved under the oil-for-food program to a commercial attaché at Iraq's embassy in Jordan. The attaché would then pay him out of the proceeds from the sale of Iraq's oil shipments. Similar scams could have been run through Syria, which was making a billion dollars a year from the Iraq-Syrian oil pipeline, all of it outside UN control. Saddam just had to find a way to hide the chemicals."

"That's not a problem," Kessler said. "Iraq is a huge ammo dump. We'd find explosives everywhere. An abandoned granary would have been perfect because it would not normally have been a military target."

"And Argus couldn't take the chance of an officially sanctioned military mission," Sloane said.

Kessler agreed. "If we had found the chemicals, it would have gone a long way toward the administration's justification for the war, that Saddam had weapons of mass destruction or at least the capability of manufacturing them. No way Argus could have kept that information from leaking."

"It would have exposed one of the largest military contractors, and several members of the president's administration," Sloane said. "The public outcry would have forced the administration to pull every Argus contract."

"Billions of dollars," Kessler said.

"And not even Argus's friends in the administration could have protected it from a Department of Justice or congressional inquiry. In fact, I suspect they would have distanced themselves," Sloane said.

Kessler looked stricken. "Griffin used us to target the building to make it look like a military mission."

Sloane nodded. "James didn't die on a military mission."

"But how could Argus fake the transmission? What about Bravo three-sixteen?"

"I think I can explain that," Sloane said. "The problem is I can't prove any of it, and without proof, we're both vulnerable."

"You didn't tape Cassidy."

Sloane shook his head. "That was just a ploy to hopefully keep us alive. They won't kill us if they think we have evidence to implicate Argus."

Sloane's cell phone rang. He checked the number, expecting Charles Jenkins, but didn't recognize it. He didn't immediately recognize the voice either.

"Mr. Sloane? This is Tom Pendergrass."

"*YOU SAID YOU* taped Cassidy?"

Aboard the fishing vessel anchored off Three Tree Point's shore, Mr. Williams cupped the headphones to his ears. Up to that moment, he had heard only music. Sloane and Kessler must have moved to a room closer to the transmitter in Sloane's jacket. He slid to the computer screen and read their conversation as it simultaneously appeared on the screen while continuing to listen.

"I didn't have time," Sloane responded. "You're the last witness."

The transmission again went silent. Then Kessler said, "The FBCB2."

Mr. Williams sat up.

"What about it?" Sloane asked.

"It would have recorded the transmission from Bravo three-sixteen. It would prove that Cassidy told you the truth."

"But you destroyed it. Your witness statement said you climbed back inside the Humvee and burned the hard drive."

"But we both know I didn't write that statement."

"You didn't burn it?"

"I didn't have to. When I dropped back down the hatch, the FBCB2 had been split open."

"It was destroyed."

"Yes and no. As I said, it was split open. So I just yanked the hard drive out and shoved it in my rucksack. I didn't give it a second thought."

"What did you do with it?"

"After I got shot they put me on a transport to Germany and I spent several weeks in a hospital rehabbing before they sent me back to the States. I had completely forgotten about it. I didn't realize I still had it until I got back to Fort Lewis and was preparing for discharge."

"You still have it?"

"They sent my stuff there. It was still in my rucksack."

"They didn't confiscate it?"

"I've heard stories of guys getting their M16s home, knives, all kinds of stuff. Nobody was going to question something no bigger than a PalmPilot. Hell, it would have been easy if I'd been trying."

"And you've kept it? You still have it somewhere?"

"Not remembering bothered me," Kessler said. *"I felt guilty about Ford's death. I thought someday I might get the courage to listen to it, see if I screwed up. Eventually I guess I didn't have the courage to find out."*

Sloane's voice became more urgent. *"Where is it? What did you do with it?"*

"That's the problem," Kessler said. *"I put it in the most secure place I could think of."*

"Where's that?"

"It's in a safe in my office at Argus."

There was a pause in the conversation. Then Sloane spoke. *"We need that hard drive. We need to get it tonight."*

"I can get in," Kessler said. *"But if Argus is onto me, the problem won't be getting in. The problem will be getting back out."*

Mr. Williams smiled and picked up the phone. Colonel Griffin answered on the first ring.

"Colonel," he started. Then he heard a concussive blast and turned to look out the window of the boat. A fireball rolled into the sky.

CHAPTER
SEVENTEEN

The plate glass window exploded. The blinds ripped from their hinges. Propelled backward, Sloane landed hard on the floor. Kessler toppled from his chair and landed beside him. They waited a moment, then Sloane shook the cobwebs and scrambled to his knees, Glock in hand.

"Are you all right?"

Kessler nodded.

"Wait here." Sloane crept to the window, careful to stay below the sill. He had limited ammunition and would have to use it sparingly to hold off Argus. Ideally he wanted one man alive, one chance to maybe get information to prove Argus was complicit in the killings of Ferguson, Thomas, and Cassidy. He slowly rose and peered over the window ledge.

A fire burned on his lawn.

A TRUCK HAD backed down the easement, a city employee standing in a bucket at the end of an extension arm. The man had managed to restore temporary power to the area; the lights in the neighbors' homes and the street lamps again cast an orange hue on the wet pavement. Sloane stood in the easement finishing a conversation with a Burien police officer. A neighbor had called the police upon hearing the explosion from Sloane's property and seeing the fireball. Sloane had kept to the story Jenkins had earlier told the police.

"While I was living in Northern California someone broke into my apartment and trashed it. There's a report on file with the Pacifica Police Department. It was ultimately the reason we moved. Seattle was supposed to be a fresh start."

"And now you think that same person has followed you here?"

"I don't know," Sloane said. "I thought I'd put it all behind me. Then I started to receive the threatening phone calls again. I sent my wife and son away and hired Mr. Jenkins."

When the officer completed his questions, he told Sloane a detective would be contacting him to discuss the matter further. Then he got back in the vehicle and drove off.

Sloane walked down the easement into his backyard.

Jenkins stood on the lawn, the binoculars focused on the water. "Boat's gone," he said.

Sloane looked at the twisted and charred remains of his barbecue. "That was your plan, shooting my barbecue?"

Jenkins shrugged. "I was making do with what I had. Besides, it worked, didn't it? They spooked and left."

"How many came?"

"Too many for us to handle. This way is better. Where's Kessler?"

"Making phone calls."

"What do you think the response will be?"

"I don't know, but Griffin said Kessler was well liked, that his men were loyal to him." He looked out over the water. "Does this remind you of anything?" Sloane was thinking of the bluff in West Virginia where the two men had met. It was that bluff on which Jenkins had explained that Sloan was the boy from the mountains in Mexico, and that Jenkins had been partially responsible for the massacre that had orphaned him.

"I was thinking the same thing." Jenkins turned and looked at Sloane's house. "Is Kessler up for this?"

Sloane nodded. "He's a soldier. It means a lot to him, what happened to his men."

"What about you?"

"No turning back now."

"You can always turn back, David."

Sloane thought of Beverly Ford and her four children. He thought of James Ford, Phillip Ferguson, and Dwayne Thomas, whom he never knew, and he thought of Michael Cassidy, a punk drug dealer. Even he had deserved better. He thought of Tina being forced to tread water in a mountain pool while her son watched her slowly drown, a memory the boy was not soon to forget.

"Not always," he said.

ARGUS INTERNATIONAL

ROBERT KESSLER ROLLED down the window and gave a friendly wave as the security guard stepped down from his booth.

Didn't this guy ever go home?

"How are you doing, Mel?"

"What are you doing here this late, Captain?"

Kessler had never seen the guard's eyes. He was surprised they were blue. "I spent all day at Little League games," Kessler said. "You know how that goes."

"Not me, Captain. I'm not married."

"Still playing the field, huh?"

"Right now I'm dedicated to my job."

"That's admirable," Kessler said. "I better do the same."

The guard smiled. "No rest for the wicked."

"I have a presentation to the board of directors tomorrow on how we intend to protect our workers administering that new contract in Egypt. How about you? Don't you ever go home?"

"I'm working a double shift. I like the long hours." Mel passed Kessler the clipboard through the window.

"I'll have to ask you to sign in, Captain. It's regulations after-hours."

"I know all about regulations," Kessler said. He scribbled his name and time of entry and handed back the clipboard. The guard pressed the button on his belt, raising the wooden arm.

"You have a good night, Captain."

The plant was lit bright as day. Kessler parked in his reserved spot closest to the back entrance to his building. The spot was marked by a handicap placard, a man in a wheelchair. Kessler shut off the engine, unlocked the seat, and swiveled to lift himself onto the wheelchair. Getting situated, he pushed a button, the van doors slid open, and the platform lowerd him onto the ground. For all of his rehab, and his determination to live some semblance of a normal life, to be a role model for his kids, he couldn't even get in and out of a car on his own. He had rationalised his loss as an honorable reminder of his service to his country. Now that, too, had been taken from him. It made him bitter. It made him angry.

He rolled up the concrete ramp to the back door, punched in the code on the security keypad, heard the steel latch slide, and pulled open the door.

Though the halls and cubicles were deserted, nearly every light in the building shone brightly. Kessler rolled inside his office and shut the door behind him, now acutely aware that his office was bugged. He moved behind his desk and reached beneath the wood chair railing along the wall, feeling for the button. When he pressed it, the map on the wall pulled apart, revealing a wall safe. Unfortunately, it had been installed for a man of average height. Kessler loosened the leg straps and used his upper body to lift himself from the chair, leaning his weight against the credenza. He entered the computerized code and pulled the door open.

As he sat down, the door to his office opened behind him. Colonel Bo Griffin walked in, flanked by two men from Argus's security forces, each carrying an automatic weapon.

"You're here awfully late, Captain," Griffin said.

Kessler settled into his chair. "Did I miss the memo, Colonel? Has Argus hired you?"

Griffin smiled. Then he nodded to the hard drive in Kessler's lap. "A soldier can be court-martialed for stealing military property, particularly if it contains sensitive information."

"I'd be happy to go forward with that hearing, Colonel."

"I'm sure you would."

"So Sloane was right. It has been you all along. I never would have believed it, Colonel."

Griffin held out his hand for the hard drive.

Kessler shook his head. "I don't think so."

"Don't make me take it from you. It would be undignified."

"You talk to me about dignity? You put me in this chair. That's right, I know all about that too, how you sent us to target that granary so you could order the air strike. How you expected that all of us would die. How you conducted the investigation to cover it up. I know you were behind it all. The only thing I haven't figured out is the transmission. How'd you do it? How did you send it so only we could hear it? You didn't send it from the TOC because it would have been recorded at the base and others in the area could have picked it up."

"Fortunately, the equipment Argus uses to communicate with its security forces is more sophisticated than what we'd been using," Griffin said.

Sloane had told Kessler he suspected as much. "You sent it from Argus's communication center on base. Was it a tape?"

"Bravo three-sixteen had been ambushed two months earlier. They never reached the building," Griffin said. "The forces loyal to Saddam remained stronger then."

"And you couldn't call in an air strike because they didn't reach the building, Sloane was right. He figured it all out."

"Sloane is a very bright man, and resourceful. But it won't get him anywhere. He has no evidence to prove anything, and he never will."

"We're still debating that now, aren't we, Colonel?"

"Not much of a debate, Captain."

"Then tell me why," Kessler asked. "Why put good men in harm's way? Why not just blow the building?"

"You know why. We heard you talking it over with Sloane tonight in his home. If the military had found the chemicals, we would have had to go public with the information. It was too valuable to bury, and you can't keep information that big from leaking, especially with the press embedded over there and so many soldiers keeping private blogs. It would have come out eventually."

"And a formal military mission would have raised too many questions about the nature of the target in the pre-mission meetings," Kessler said.

Griffin agreed. "They would have wanted to know why the hell we were concerned with a granary."

"But the men, Colonel, how could you do that to us?"

"There's a war going on, Captain. Casualties are a part of war. You told Mr. Sloane that in this very office."

"Those were American soldiers."

"I did it for the American soldier."

"What?"

"I saw it in Vietnam," Griffin said, bitterness creeping into his voice. "Do you know how many men died over there because we couldn't get the political support we needed to do the job? We lost fifty thousand men. What would have happened if the American public and the politicians found out that some of the chemicals we were looking for in Iraq were manufactured by American companies and shipped while members of the president's administration held offices in those companies? The American public would have abandoned the cause just as it did in Vietnam, and the soldiers would have suffered for it. You erode support for a war's justification and you erode support for those fighting it. That's how they end up getting killed. How many men would have died as a result?"

Kessler shook his head. "Spare me the patriotism speech, Colonel. You didn't do this for the country or for the men. You did it for the money. Houghton Park's only motivation was to save his ass. Argus was facing a public relations nightmare. They stood to lose billions of dollars in reconstruction contracts, not to mention the potential liability from lawsuits. The company stock would have plummeted, and its officers would have faced significant jail sentences. They paid you, handsomely I would guess."

"Believe what you want, but I would have done this for free."

Kessler scoffed. "Then you're even crazier than I thought."

"I'll take that hard drive now."

"Sloane knows everything. He's not going to let this go. He'll keep at it."

"Sloane is a lawyer. He knows he has no evidence—that's why he sent you here tonight. Without that hard drive he has no case. He can't prove what happened that night. We both know that's why you risked coming here. Mr Sloane won't be a problem. You are."

Griffin nodded. The two men stepped forward.

Kessler pulled his hand from the pocket of his jacket, fingers wrapped around a grenade. The two men stopped.

"He's bluffing," one said. But neither man moved.

Kessler pulled the pin.

"You can't get out," Griffin said. "You know that."

"What does it do to a man, Colonel?"

"What?"

"To his psyche? What does it do to a man to suddenly find himself confined to a wheelchair?"

Griffin's eyes widened.

"He becomes bitter and angry and he begins to believe he's entitled to more than the military will give him." Kessler smiled. "You misjudged me, Colonel, again. This isn't just about the hard drive anymore. You killed my men. You tried to kill me. You put me in this chair for the rest of my life. Did you think I'd let you get away with that?"

Beads of sweat glistened on Griffin's upper lip.

"You want to call my bluff, Colonel? You have the guts when it's your life on the line? Come on, I'm giving you the chance to die for something you just told me you believe in. Give the order. Give the order for them to shoot and we all die, and nobody ever finds out what happened. Argus walks away."

One of the men looked as though he might take that step.

"No!" Griffin ordered.

Kessler smiled. "I didn't think so. You're a coward, Colonel." He gestured to the two men to stand to the side. Griffin told them to comply.

"Put your weapons on the floor," Kessler instructed. They set the rifles down. "Now step away from them."

Kessler rolled to the door and motioned the men to move further into the office. He rolled forward, picked up the weapons, and laid them across his lap. Then he rolled backward down the hall, watching them. "I release my grip and the funnel blast down this hallway will kill us all."

"You have nowhere to go, Captain," Griffin said. "Your vehicle has been disabled."

Kessler entered the code on the keypad. The red light lit. The door unlatched. He pulled it open. "You're wrong, Colonel. I'm going back to Iraq."

He tossed the grenade down the hallway and let the steel door slam shut behind him.

KESSLER KNEW HE had only a few seconds' head start before the men realized the grenade was disabled. He tossed one of the automatic weapons in the darkness and kept the other across his lap. It wouldn't do him much good at present. He needed his arms to push and steer his chair through the dirt roads, his progress slowed by the potholes, debris, and darkness. His advantage was that he knew the streets intimately. He'd designed them. He hoped that would be enough of an edge to make it out. He wheeled past the burned-out shells of vehicles and the scarred walls of the courtyards surrounding the Iraqi houses, eerily similar to the real thing. Behind him he heard the metal door to the warehouse open and slam closed. His pursuers would move faster than he could roll, but he also had the advantage of knowing where he was headed.

He spun the chair down a narrow alley, continuing through the maze, arms burning, breathing labored. He turned again and pushed down another passage that would end near the rolling gate at the front of the building.

HE TOSSED THE *first grenade into the building and was preparing to throw the second when he felt the sharp, stinging pain in his back, just below his vest. It felt like someone had kicked his legs out from under him. He toppled forward onto the ground. Dust and debris from the first grenade rolled over him.*

Get up, he told himself. Get up.

But his body was not listening. His legs would not move. He heard Ford's voice over the handheld.

"Captain, you have to get out of there. Move on my call. We'll suppress. Over."

"I can't," Kessler said, groaning in pain.

"Captain, they've called an air strike on the building. They're going to blow it."

"I can't move."

"Captain—"

"James, I can't feel my legs."

HEAVY FOOTSTEPS SOUNDED behind him. Kessler looked back over his shoulder.

The two men rounded the corner.

He turned his attention back to the road. Too late. He saw the pothole but could not change his course or slow his speed. He swerved, but the wheel caught the depression and the chair pitched. Kessler fought to remain upright, struggling against gravity, unable to right the chair. He toppled headfirst onto the dirt, the chair on top of him, and reached for the automatic weapon. Finding it, he grabbed the handle. Then a boot came down hard, pinning the weapon to the ground. Griffin.

The two men had also reached Kessler quickly, weapons trained. Griffin bent down and took the gun, pulled the chair off Kessler, and tossed it aside. He held out his hand. "Enough. The hard drive, please."

Kessler hesitated.

"You're going to die either way, Captain. We both know that."

Kessler tossed the drive at Griffin's feet.

Griffin stepped back and fired several rounds into the drive, shattering the casing. The men jumped backward, fearful of the ricochet. Kessler covered his face. What remained Griffin battered with the butt of the rifle, grinding it to pieces.

"It doesn't have to end this way, Colonel," Kessler said.

Winded and sweating from the temperature in the building, Griffin handed the gun to the man to his right and turned to leave. "I already gave you that choice. Now it's too late."

The interior of the building began to rattle and shake as if struck by an earthquake.

"I meant for you," Kessler shouted.

"ROLL!" SLOANE SHOUTED to the driver. "Roll!"

The treads of the Bradley gripped the ground and the big machine lurched forward. Within seconds it was moving more swiftly than Sloane would have imagined for something so heavy. He watched their progression across the open field on a small screen from the passenger seat. The vehicle bounced onto a dirt and gravel road, turned again, and continued toward Argus, the security booth directly in its path.

The guard stepped from the sanctuary of his perch with a perplexed expression, mouth agape. Then the idiot stepped forward, thrusting out a hand like a traffic cop stopping cars.

"What do we do?" the driver asked through the headset.

Sloane had a feeling about a man who hid his eyes behind sunglasses.

"What do we do?" the driver asked again.

"Keep going."

The driver shifted. The Bradley geared down, gaining speed.

The guard looked like a statue, frozen with his hand out.

The driver glanced at Sloane. "Sir? Sir?"

Sloane watched.

At the last moment, the guard's eyes widened, he dropped his hand, took three hurried steps, and launched himself out of the Bradley's path. The big machine hit the booth at full speed, glass and fiberglass shattering. It snapped the arm of the gate like a twig and ripped through the Cyclone fencing as if it were fish netting.

"Where?" the driver asked.

"Third building from the left," Sloane directed.

In his headphones Sloane heard Kessler and Griffin talking.

"*It doesn't have to end this way, Colonel.*"

"*I already gave you that choice.*"

"*I meant for you.*"

The driver shouted at Sloane. "The door's not up."

Sloane looked to the screen. The rolling gate was still down. Kessler had not reached the switch.

"What do we do?" the driver asked again.

"Can you take it down?" Sloane asked.

"Roger fucking that," the driver shouted. "Brace yourself."

GRIFFIN'S EYES NARROWED. The air-conditioning ducts and equipment hanging from the overhead steel rafters swayed violently. The building exterior rattled and shook. He looked down as the wall exploded inward, emitting an awful sound of metal ripping. The rolling door tore from its runner and waved like the tongue of some giant serpent, crashing to the ground.

The sheer force of the assault knocked down Griffin and his two men. By the time they had recovered, the gunner sitting atop the huge machine had trained the Bradley's 50-mm gun on them, and half a dozen armed guardsmen were spilling out the back.

Griffin's men put up no resistance.

Sloane stepped from the vehicle and helped Kessler to right his wheelchair. The plan had been for Kessler to get out the front of the building and raise the door for the Bradley. "You all right?" Sloane asked.

Kessler nodded as he got back atop his chair.

Sloane looked to the two men getting up off the ground. He recognized one to be Mr. Williams, the fisherman who had come to Three Tree Point and later forced Tina to swim in the mountain pool. Argus had got them out of Mexico unscathed.

Griffin stood defiant. "You're too late, Mr. Sloane. You have no evidence."

Sloane reached down and picked up a piece of the shattered hard drive, considering it.

"Are you referring to this? This is the hard drive from my son's computer, Colonel. Nothing on here but some really violent video games his mother doesn't like him playing anyway. He'll be upset, though; he doesn't take disappointment too well. How about you?"

Griffin looked to Kessler, then back to Sloane.

"We knew you were listening to our conversation at the beach house," Sloane said. "So we told you what you wanted to hear." Sloane turned to Kessler. "You look good in my jacket, Captain."

Kessler wore Sloane's leather jacket.

"We reset the transmitter, Colonel. Everything you just said in Captain Kessler's office and this warehouse has been recorded."

Griffin did not wilt. "It's illegal. Argus's attorneys will eat you alive. You'll never get into court."

"I wouldn't make that bet, Colonel. Besides, I don't have to get it into court, do I? I can just get it to the press and to the local authorities. And I'm sure the Justice Department will be very interested in it as well."

"What do you want, Sloane? Park will pay you anything. He'll pay the widow whatever she wants. Name the price."

Sloane looked to Kessler before addressing the colonel.

"There is no price. That's what you don't understand. There is no amount of money to compensate her for what you took." He stepped toward Mr. Williams. "I warned you not to come back," he said. He turned to leave. Then he stopped. "What the hell." He spun, hitting the man hard across the jaw, knocking him down. "And I warned you about threatening my family."

"It's illegal to use the military to conduct a civilian operation," Griffin said. "How are you going to explain this?"

Kessler wheeled forward. "What civilian operation are you talking about? These men are from my former unit, and I can guarantee you there will be no record whatsoever of any civilian exercise. This was a training mission." Kessler turned and looked up at the guardsman behind the 50-mm gun. "You appear to have driven off course, Sergeant."

"Seriously off course, Captain," the soldier agreed, smiling.

Kessler turned back to Griffin. "You know how a storm can wreak havoc with communications."

CHARLES JENKINS REMOVED his headset and turned off the recorder. The re-coded transmitter had worked perfectly; so had Sloane and Kessler's plan, with a few minor glitches. From the Explorer, Jenkins had watched the Bradley take out the security guard's booth like a balsa-wood fake, then tear through the gated entrance. It had given him a perverse sense of satisfaction, and he couldn't help but wish that *Cool Hand Luke* had ended in a similar manner, but the producer and director had gone for a more subtle ending.

During his self-imposed exile on Camano Island, Jenkins had read the biographies of Mahatma Gandhi, Nelson Mandela, and Lech Walesa, men who had taken down walls of injustice without ever firing a bullet or picking up a sledgehammer. But they were extraordinary people. Sometimes you had to physically destroy the walls. The world needed to see it, as with the Berlin Wall. But those men had been correct in their core belief. Injustice was not built of stone and mortar, or of metal. It was built of greed, inhumanity, and man's thirst for power.

Jenkins stepped from his car and walked to where the guard booth now lay splintered and ruined. Bits of glass crunched beneath his boots and reflected the overhead lights on the security poles. Something hummed, a high-pitched whine that sounded like a motor straining. He heard a different sound to his right and turned to see the security guard rising unsteadily to his feet, his pristine uniform dirty and ripped at the knee. The guard looked to Jenkins, then back to the booth, dumbfounded.

Jenkins picked up the clipboard lying on the ground with the pen still attached by a chain. He tore off the page with Captain Kessler's name, and tossed the clipboard at the man's feet. Walking away, he heard something else crunch beneath the sole of his boot, stepped back, and bent to pick it up.

The guard's sunglasses.

They were twisted and misshapen, both lenses shattered, just like the boss man's glasses in the ending to *Cool Hand Luke*. Jenkins smiled. He might just have to start believing in coincidences after all.

BEVERLY FORD OPENED her front door. Her children stood beside her. "Please come in," she said.

Sloane stepped in and made the introductions. "Beverly, I'd like to introduce Captain Robert Kessler, James's commanding officer in Iraq."

Beverly stepped forward and bent to wrap her arms around Kessler's shoulders. "It's a pleasure having you in our home, Captain Kessler."

Kessler bit his bottom lip, fighting his emotions. He looked up at her, their faces close. "James was as fine a man as any I've ever had the pleasure to serve with."

She hugged him again, both crying now. They moved into the living room where she had set a pitcher of iced tea on the table. Lucas sat in the recliner holding Althea on his lap. James junior and Alicia sat on the carpet near Kessler's wheelchair. Sloane stood off to the side. This was not his show.

"I'm sure you all have a lot of questions," Kessler said, clearing his throat. Beverly poured a glass of iced tea and handed it to him. He sipped it. Then he said, "I don't know where to begin."

They sat in silence for a moment.

"I'd like to know how my dad died," Lucas said.

Kessler nodded, and took another moment to compose himself. "A hero," he said, his voice catching. "Your father died a hero."

SHIMRAN AL MUSLO, IRAQ

FORD LOWERED HIS walkie-talkie. "He's hit. Captain's hit."

The men sat, confused and uncertain what to do.

Static broke the silence.

Ford lifted his walkie-talkie, then realized it was coming from the radio in his rucksack. He pulled it out. All four men gathered to listen.

"Alfa one-two, this is Talon. I have the granary in sight. Coming in hot. Over."

Panicked, Ford grabbed the handset. "Talon, this is Alfa one-two. Abort. I repeat. Abort."

No response.

"Talon, this is Alfa one-two. Abort! We have a man down inside the building! Abort!"

The radio crackled. "Talon, you are cleared hot."

"No!" Ford shouted. "Talon, you are not cleared."

Ferguson grabbed his arm. "James."

"Roger, Alfa. Talon is hot. Understand danger close. Out."

Ford started again, but Ferguson yelled louder. "James, it's broke! The mouthpiece is broke."

Ford looked down at the crushed mouthpiece. They couldn't hear him. God, they couldn't hear him.

He threw the radio to the ground and yelled into the hand-held.

"Captain, you have to get out of there. Move on my call. We'll suppress. Over."

"I can't," Kessler said, groaning in pain.

"Captain, they've called an air strike on the building. They're going to blow it."

"I can't move."

"Captain—"

"James, I can't feel my legs."

Sweat rolled down Ford's face. Cassidy, Thomas, and Ferguson stared at him.

"I can't move them, James," Kessler said again.

Ford slipped the M249 over his head and handed it to Ferguson along with the remaining two-hundred-round canisters. "Lay down suppression on that rooftop."

"What are you going to do?" Fergie asked, alarmed.

"I'm going to go get the captain."

"You'll never make it."

"Have to," he said matter-of-factly. "You heard. They've ordered an air strike on the building."

"James—"

"I'm not going to leave the captain," Ford shouted, then regained his composure. "We're getting out of here. All of us. That includes the captain. Now give me your rifle." Ferguson handed Ford the M16 and two thirty-round magazines. Ford handed one back.

"You need ammunition," Ferguson insisted.

"One to get me there." Ford held up the second magazine. "One to get me back. If I don't make it, I won't need a third. You might." He tapped Thomas on the shoulder and shouted into his ear. "I want you trained on those windows. Three-round bursts."

DT nodded.

Ferguson stepped in front of him. "James—"

"We don't have time to argue. Butch, get your ass up here!" Cassidy slid forward. "Either DT or Fergie runs out of ammo, you take their sector while they reload. You got that? I want sustained suppression on that building."

Cassidy nodded. His nostrils flared. "Fuck it. Time to get me some Hajji."

Ford tapped him on the helmet. "Good boy. Just don't shoot me in the ass."

Ferguson retook his position behind the big gun as Ford spoke into his handheld. "Captain, hang on. I'm coming to get you."

"No," Kessler responded, emphatic. "Ford, that is not approved. Have Fergie send up a flare and get everyone out."

Ford dropped the handheld into the dirt with the captain still talking. "Ford? Ford?"

He released the bolt on the M16, hit the forward assist, and slid the selector to automatic. "When I get back with the captain, get behind that wall and get your heads down." He paused, looking each man in the eye. "Then we're going to go home. Do you hear me? All of us, we're all going home."

At the doorway he looked back to Fergie. "On my call."

He took a breath, closed his eyes, and lifted the crucifix to his lips. "Dear Jesus," he said. "My lord and my savior." Then he tucked the crucifix safely back beneath his uniform, turned back to Fergie, and drew in a deep breath. "Go!"

The roar of gunfire deafened all other sound. Purple and

green tracers crisscrossed the insurgents' red. Though Ford knew it best to zigzag, there wasn't time. He ran in a straight line, bulling his way forward, head down. Halfway across the circle he pulled back the trigger and unleashed three-round bursts. When he neared the building he threw his body down beside Kessler, rolled onto his back, pulled out the empty magazine, and slammed the second in place.

Kessler had his head up, firing his weapon, the rounds pinging off rusted metal drums inside the building. "Ford, I gave you an order," he said, but for the first time in the seven months Ford had served under the captain, he saw fear in the man's eyes.

"Sorry, Captain. Radio must not be working. Time to get you out of here. Can you stand?"

Kessler shook his head. "I can't feel my legs, James."

"Don't you worry, Captain. I'm going to be your legs. But we have to go now. Air strike is on its way."

"Who called in an air strike?"

"Don't know, but it's coming in hot."

An insurgent jumped out from behind a barrel, hell-bent on seeing Allah. Ford shot the man twice in the chest, knocking him backward, but not down. He was set to fire another burst when a tracer passed overhead and dropped the insurgent. Ford looked back. Cassidy gave him a thumbs-up. Other insurgents also crept forward, using the drums as cover. Ford pulled a grenade from his vest, tore at the electrical tape holding down the spoon, pulled the pin, and hurled it inside the building. The explosion sent drums airborne. One exploded.

Using the diversion, he scrambled to his feet and lifted Kessler onto his shoulders in a fireman's carry, setting his feet beneath him. Another explosion erupted behind him, and he allowed the force to push him forward, the M16 in his right hand.

Across the courtyard Ferguson and Thomas continued to lay down a firestorm of suppression fire. Cassidy beckoned to him from the hole in the wall, the young man's mouth open, silently urging him on.

Kessler moaned with each step, his body bouncing on Ford's shoulders. The tracers continued to light up the courtyard, but Ford shut out everything around him, focusing only on the building, on going home.

"You take us with you, James Ford," his wife whispered in his ear. "And you bring us all home with you."

He pressed on, one step after the next, then felt as if his body had suddenly burst into flames. He took one more step, and half of another before pain buckled his legs. He collapsed to his knees, breathing heavily, struggling to remain upright, the captain still across his shoulders. A searing heat filled his chest and enveloped his limbs.

Across the circle, Fergie, DT, and Butch screamed in silence, waving for him to get up, to keep moving, to make it back to the building so they could all go home. That's what he had promised. He had promised to bring back the captain, and when he did, they would all go home.

Ford rose to one knee, but his body betrayed him. Turning his shoulders, he gently slid the captain down his back onto the ground. Kessler's weight rotated Ford's upper torso, pulling him down also, the back of his helmet coming to rest atop the captain's body armor. He gazed up at the Iraqi sky and saw flickering shimmers of light, feeling at peace, and struck by the *thought that he could not distinguish the starry sky from the one above his own backyard. How little he knew about this country or its people. So much history, he thought, thousands of years before the United States had ever become a nation. And he knew nothing about it.*

The fire in his chest no longer burned, replaced now by a numbing cold. Ford removed his helmet. His hands shook as he slid the photograph from the envelope. He laid eyes on his wife and children, hearing her soft voice whispering again in his ear.

"Let us bring you back home."

Hands gripped him about the shoulders. Ford looked up from the photograph. Fergie stood above him, his face straining as he struggled to drag Ford and the captain across the ground to the building. Ford wanted to tell him it was all right. He wanted to tell Fergie that he could let go. But no words came, and the sky descended like a shroud. Just before everything disappeared in a brilliant burst of light. And at that moment James Ford smelled it, the sweet fragrance of his wife and children. He inhaled deeply, breathing in their beauty, allowing them to carry him home.

"YOUR FATHER SAVED my life," Kessler said, openly weeping. "He got me home. I'm so sorry I couldn't bring him with me. I'm so very sorry."

CHAPTER EIGHTEEN

This time Charles Jenkins did not stop to watch the cinder-block building from a distance. He didn't care who was inside. He parked beneath the faded sign next to the brown truck and walked through the double-wide entrance. The pit bull sat up from her place beside the plywood counter, but did not bark or lunge at him. In fact, she cocked her head slightly as if to ask, Don't I know you?

"Can I help you?" Chuck Kroeger's son sat with his boots propped on the counter, a cigarette between his lips, a baseball cap perched on the back of his head.

"Mr. Johnson?" Kroeger senior emerged from the back of the building with an outstretched hand. "You finally back to get that house painted? Been a couple weeks, hasn't it?"

Jenkins shook his head. "Actually, Mr. Kroeger, I don't own any house, and I don't need a painter."

Kroeger's brow furrowed. "I don't understand. Who are you?"

"I'm just a guy who hates to see an animal mistreated." Jenkins directed the comment to the dull young man sitting at the counter.

"Come again?" Kroeger asked, looking to his son.

"The dog," Jenkins said to the son. "I came for your dog."

The young man lowered his legs. "Like fuck you did."

"Let me ask you something," Jenkins said, "because I'm always curious. Why bother? You don't feed her. You mistreat her. You obviously don't give a lick about her. Why keep her at all?"

Chuck Kroeger looked to Jenkins, then back to his son. A good sign it was a legitimate question.

"I keep her 'cause she's mine," the son said, defiant. "That's why. So why don't you take a walk."

Jenkins knew the kid was just talking brave; his body language wasn't backing him up. He twitched and avoided eye contact. "You know what I think? I think you keep her for security. You know, to guard something."

Chuck Kroeger stepped forward, palms raised. "Listen, mister, I can guarantee you that dog does not guard this building. I don't even like having it around here. So if it bit somebody or something, I don't have any liability here. This isn't my problem."

"I know that." Jenkins kept his gaze on the boy. "And I'm not here to cause you any trouble. Your son knows what I'm talking about. Don't you?"

The boy shook his head, but the panic in his eyes and stutter in his voice again betrayed him. "I . . . I don't know what you're talking about."

"Sure you do. That little operation you and Michael Cassidy had going in that trailer in the mountains."

"What is he talking about, Lloyd?" Chuck Kroeger asked.

The boy looked to his father. Then he turned to Jenkins. "Cassidy is dead."

"I know that too," Jenkins said. "He blew himself up in that trailer according to the news article. Except the coroner has since said an autopsy revealed he had a bullet hole in his skull, which likely makes it a homicide. You were his business partner. I'm sure the police would like to talk to you in detail about that relationship."

The boy shot forward. "I didn't have nothing to do with that."

"Lloyd, what the hell is he talking about?"

"Maybe you did. Maybe you didn't." Jenkins held out the leash he'd brought. "Like I said, I just came for the dog."

Lloyd Kroeger hesitated, thinking through his options, of which he had none. He tossed his cigarette and snatched the leash from Jenkins's hand. "Fine. Take the bitch. What do I care? You're right; I don't even like the damn dog." He snapped the leash on the ring of the dog's collar and threw it back at Jenkins.

Jenkins gently coaxed the dog outside. Behind him he heard Charles Kroeger and his son begin what Jenkins assumed would be a protracted and heated conversation.

Though he had brought a muzzle, Jenkins didn't think he'd need it. The dog wasn't mean. She was scared. Still, he had expected her to at least put up a struggle, to be recalcitrant. She was neither. She padded forward without prodding, head low.

Jenkins opened the door to the Buick. It had cost a small fortune to get it cleaned and to get the engine running again, but some things you just didn't throw away. He coaxed the dog in the driver's door. She jumped up and padded across to the passenger seat, and sat on her haunches, watching him.

Jenkins slid in, closed the door, and backed out of the driveway. "You'll be the third woman in the house," he said. "Alex runs the show, but really the one you'll need to win over is Sam. She can be aloof when you first get to know her, and I imagine she'll be a bit jealous, but she'll come around."

The dog circled on the seat, then lay down and lowered her head to her paws, looking up at him with the same sad brown eyes Sam used to get what she wanted.

"Oh, boy," Jenkins said. "You're going to get me in a lot of trouble too, aren't you?"

THREE TREE POINT, WASHINGTON

SLOANE WALKED THROUGH the side door and hooked his keys on Larry Bird. Bud, like clockwork, jumped onto the counter, purring. Sloane picked him up and cradled him as he walked through the kitchen.

"Anyone home?"

"Out here."

Tina knelt on the lawn outside the other door off the kitchen. Sloane pushed through the screen and walked to her. She had a shovel in her hand and several plants in plastic containers at her feet, lined up to be planted.

"Rhododendrons," Sloane said, putting Bud down.

"Can you help me dig a couple of holes?"

He kissed her and took the shovel, driving the spade into the ground with the heel of his shoe. In the intervening month since the assault on Argus, Tina and Jake were continuing to recover. Neither liked being in the house without him, so Sloane had been working more from his home office. Jake had nightmares, and would awake screaming, but the last one had been four nights before, and the trauma not as intense. What bothered Sloane the most was that he could not make the dreams stop, that he couldn't push the rewind button and change the past.

Life was about coping in the present.

"Did you get everything done?" she asked.

"We'll find out tomorrow," he said in between jabs with the shovel.

Articles about Argus and Houghton Park had filled

the local and national newspapers, and nightly news. The Tacoma Police Department and the U.S. Justice Department had each executed search warrants on the company, seizing documents that, as Kessler predicted, proved to be a veritable gold mine of information. Argus had covered its tracks well, using a maze of subsidiaries and illegal couriers to transport chemicals into Iraq through Jordan, Syria, and other Middle Eastern countries. It would make the task of tracing the end users more difficult, but not impossible, Sloane knew. He had been working closely with the Department of Justice.

As Kessler had also predicted, in a heavily regulated industry, Argus had been required to account for every ounce of every chemical it produced. With the help of Argus's accountants and shipping personnel, granted immunity from prosecution, the Justice Department was confident it would ultimately get it all sorted out.

Defense Secretary Frederick Northrup had come under heavy fire for his involvement with the company. Many of the illegal shipments had taken place during his watch as Argus company president. Northrup had declined to comment, and his lawyers were predictably saying the defense secretary had no knowledge of the activities, but the pressure on Northrup to make a statement built daily.

Sloane had re-filed the complaint on behalf of Beverly Ford and her children. This time it did not lack for allegations. A sixty-six-page torne, he had written it with a lot of help from Ken Mills, who had become a nightly fixture on CNN, Fox News, *Larry King*, and other nationally syndicated shows. In it Sloane had detailed Argus's illegal shipments, as well as allegations of a conspiracy involving Northrup, Houghton Park, Colonel Bo Griffin, and unnamed others, to conceal those shipments, and to murder national guardsmen James Ford, Phillip Ferguson, Michael Cassidy, and Dwayne Thomas. Sloane alleged that on the night James Ford was killed, Argus had paid an as-yet-undetermined sum of money to Griffin to send a false radio transmission that ultimately led Kessler and his squad into an ambush. The transmission's purpose had been to target a building filled with some of the illegally shipped Argus chemicals, as well as Iraqi records documenting those shipments. Sloane argued that, under the circumstances, Ford had not been acting incident to his service at the time of his death, since the order had been illegal and had no military objective.

The government had again responded with a motion to dismiss, and the hearing was set for the morning. It promised to produce still more fireworks.

Sloane built up a sweat digging the holes and helping to plant the rhododendrons, then put down the shovel and grabbed the hose to water them.

"This time next spring they'll be in full bloom," Tina said, gathering the plastic containers and her gardening tools. "I'll finish here. You grab Jake. I'll get dinner going."

He kissed her, shut off the hose, and walked down to the beach. Jake had stayed closer to the house since his experience with Mr. Williams and remained leery of strangers. To Sloane it was sad that kids had to initially fear an adult, and that Jake had a better reason to do so than most.

"How are they biting, Hemingway?"

Jake smiled halfheartedly. "Nothing yet." He cast out and waited for the lure to plunk into the water before clicking over the reel. "Mom says you have a big motion tomorrow. Are you going to be on the news again?"

"I don't know." Sloane smiled. "Probably."

"Cool."

"Your mom's getting dinner ready. Better reel in."

Jake began to reel. The top of his pole suddenly yanked forward, jerking him a step toward the water as the line on his reel whizzed. The big fish had struck quickly and was now running with the bait.

"I have one," Jake yelled, eyes wide in disbelief. "Dad, I have one."

Sloane smiled. "Play with him, son. Be patient. Let him tire himself out."

U.S. DISTRICT COURT
SEATTLE, WASHINGTON

JUDGE JO NATALE looked down from her seat behind the bench.

"Mr. Sloane, you're back."

Natale spoke as if Sloane had simply stepped out of line at a bank and returned to make a deposit, seeming to ignore the overflow crowd in her gallery that included local and national news media, law enforcement, and attorneys from the Justice Department in Washington, D.C.

"I am, Your Honor," Sloane responded, "and I've brought co-counsel."

The man to Sloane's right introduced himself in a deep baritone voice. "John Kannin, also appearing on behalf of the plaintiffs."

When Sloane called to ask for Kannin's assistance, he'd laughed. "I told you to kick up some dust," he'd said, "not create a tornado."

Beverly Ford sat between them at counsel table, Lucas and his three siblings in the first pew behind them. Sloane introduced them.

Tom Pendergrass again stood at the table perpendicular to Sloane, wearing his dress-green uniform. This time he was far from alone. Although Rachel Keane had opted not to sit at counsel table, she sat in the pew behind the railing, and a chorus line of blue suits two rows deep stood next to Pendergrass. Lawyers from national law firms stated their appearances on behalf of Colonel Bo Griffin, Argus International, Houghton Park, and a number of other current and former Argus executives, including Northrup.

When the attorneys had finished, Natale looked to Sloane. "I've read your amended complaint, as well as the government's motion to dismiss, joined and supplemented by each defendant. Does the government wish to provide any further evidence?"

Pendergrass had attached the four witness statements to his motion to dismiss. One of the designated blue suits stood and objected that the introduction of the statements was improper. The others joined in.

Pendergrass looked chagrined. "Your Honor, I am perplexed by my colleagues' objections. The statements are already a part of the court record. Besides, they unequivocally state that Mr. Ford was killed incident to his service, while engaged in a military exercise. They prove there is no basis for Mr. Sloane's fantastical allegations of a civilian conspiracy."

Although the blue suits vehemently objected that the admission of the additional information was improper, Sloane knew, and he suspected Judge Natale did also, that their real concern was not the witness statements, but the smoking gun Sloane was prepared to use: the taped confession of Colonel Bo Griffin that the statements were false.

Judge Natale listened to their objections before turning to Sloane. "The real prejudice would be to you, Mr. Sloane. Do you object to the admission of these statements?"

"I do not, Your Honor, so long as the government will indulge me the same courtesy."

Pendergrass looked to the bench. "The government has no objection."

Again the blue suits objected. Again Judge Natale overruled them.

"Mr. Sloane, how many witnesses do you intend to call?" Natale asked.

"Two, Your Honor. We anticipate the testimony of the first witness to be lengthy. The second witness we don't anticipate will take much time at all."

"Very well, call your first witness."

"Plaintiffs call Captain Robert Kessler."

Every head in the room turned as the courtroom doors opened and Kessler wheeled himself down the aisle in full-dress uniform, the medals on his chest glistening. Jenkins and Alex, who had been protecting Kessler and his family, slipped silently into the room behind him.

The intervening weeks since Kessler had gone to the newspapers as an Argus whistle-blower looked to have taken its toll on him physically. Thin through the cheeks and neck, he had dark circles beneath his eyes, indicating he had not slept much. The Justice Department and FBI had subpoenaed him to testify before a grand jury, and Congress, too, had indicated it would subpoena him to appear at hearings. Sloane had agreed to represent him.

With Kessler positioned at the witness stand, Sloane moved to the podium and gently walked him through his background. Then he asked Kessler about the admissions made to him by Griffin. Concluding, Sloane asked, "Captain Kessler, these are rather incredible statements. Do you have anything to support your allegations that Colonel Griffin made them?"

As rehearsed, Kessler said simply, "I do."

"And what evidence would that be?"

"The statements were recorded."

The blue suits leaned forward, like swimmers on starting blocks, as Sloane casually returned to counsel table and John Kannin handed him the tape. Kannin had performed the research on the admissibility of the recording in a Washington federal court. It was a dicey argument. Natale could go either way.

"Your Honor, plaintiffs wish to move into evidence a tape recording made the night in question as authenticated by Captain Kessler, and further wish to play that recording here in court."

The blue suits dived from their blocks, objections flying. They argued that the tape was inadmissible because Griffin had been surreptitiously recorded.

"Mr. Sloane, are you prepared to authenticate the tape?" Natale asked.

"I am, Your Honor. The operator is in the courtroom," he said, referring to Jenkins.

"And what of the defendants' objection that the tape is inadmissible?"

Sloane turned to Kannin, who handed him the legal brief containing the argument, though Sloane had committed it to memory. He presented the brief to Judge Natale and a stack of copies to the opposing counsel. "The exclusionary rule is a product of the constitutional protections of the Fourth Amendment, Your Honor. It is a constitutional limitation on the admissibility of evidence otherwise probative. The Supreme Court has therefore restricted its application, as has the Ninth Circuit, which governs here. So long as the Fourth Amendment has not been directly violated, a recording obtained with the consent of one party to the conversation is admissible in federal court. Captain Kessler agreed to be recorded, and defendants have not argued a Fourth Amendment violation."

Judge Natale turned to the blue suits. "Do you have some evidence that the tape was obtained in violation of your clients' Fourth Amendment rights?"

They did, of course, given that Sloane had ridden through Argus in a Bradley and busted through the warehouse wall. But the men had no way to prove that a regiment of national guardsmen had stormed Argus under the cloak of night. The guardsmen, to a man, feigned ignorance of any such maneuver. They had all filed statements that they had driven off course while performing an exercise. Their superiors supported them. The two Argus guards with Griffin that night were also cooperating with the investigation and apparently had no desire to hurt their deals by standing up for the colonel. Besides, Griffin couldn't very well call upon them, since he had no way to justify his presence at the company the night in question without admitting to being part of the civil conspiracy.

After the chorus line of lawyers fumbled with their responses, Natale turned to Sloane. "I'm going to rule that the tape is admissible. You may play it, Mr. Sloane."

For the next ten minutes the only sounds in the courtroom were the recorded voices of Griffin and Kessler. When the recording ended, there was deafening silence. The blue suits sat with their heads down, either rethinking their strategy, or thinking of a way out of the case. Beverly Ford sat stoically.

"Captain Kessler," Sloane said, "do you believe James Ford was a hero?"

No one objected. No one dared.

Kessler looked to Beverly Ford. "I believe that every man and woman who serves is a hero. We might not agree with the philosophy of the war, but as soldiers that is not our job. It's about service. James Ford, Michael Cassidy, Dwayne Thomas, and Phillip Ferguson served with honor. They are all heroes."

AFTER A MORNING recess, Judge Natale retook the bench. "Mr. Sloane, you indicated you have a second witness?"

"We do, Your Honor. Plaintiffs call United States Attorney Rachel Keane."

The announcement brought still further astonished expressions and utterances. Keane, who had sat calmly to that point, went ghostly white.

Pendergrass rose. "The government objects. We had no prior knowledge of plaintiffs' intent. As a matter of courtesy, counsel should have notified us of this clearly unorthodox request. The United States attorney represents the government. She is extremely busy."

Sloane had to give Pendergrass credit. The objection sounded almost sincere.

"The United States attorney is in court, Your Honor," Sloane countered. "And we don't intend to keep her long. Nor do we intend to ask her any questions that could violate the attorney-client privilege or the work-product doctrine."

Natale looked to Keane. "The U.S. attorney has been present in the courtroom all morning. Therefore I see no prejudice," she said. Sloane thought he noticed a slight lilt in Natale's voice. "Ms. Keane, please take the stand."

Keane stood and proceeded up the aisle while reporters scribbled furiously in their notepads. After Keane had been sworn to tell the truth, Pendergrass stipulated that Sloane could dispense with the usual preliminaries concerning Keane's occupation and other personal information.

"I think we're all aware of Ms. Keane's background," Natale agreed, and this time Sloane was certain he detected a hint of sarcasm.

Sloane stepped back to the podium. "Ms. Keane, as the United States attorney for the Western District of Washington, you have authority to make offers of settlement on behalf of the United States so long as those offers do not exceed a certain dollar limit. Is that correct?"

"That is correct," she said.

"And in this particular matter you authorized a settlement offer to Mrs. Ford in an amount within your authority. Isn't that correct?"

Pendergrass stood, his timing perfect. "Objection, Your Honor. Offers of settlement as well as all settlement discussions are inadmissible pursuant to Evidence Rule 408."

"Mr. Sloane?" Natale asked.

"Counsel is correct. An offer of settlement is inadmissible for the purposes of implying guilt or liability. We are not offering it for either reason. We are offering this evidence only to show that an offer was made. If the court will grant me some indulgence, I can finish this quickly."

"I'm going to overrule the objection," Natale said. "I'll allow you some leeway, Mr. Sloane. I believe the court is sufficiently capable of differentiating between the many reasons why an offer of settlement can be made other than liability. Answer the question, Ms. Keane."

Keane looked up at Judge Natale. "Yes, I authorized an offer of settlement."

"Was there a demand?" Sloane asked.

"No, there was not," Keane said, still poised, though looking less and less in command.

"Is it unusual for the United States attorney to make a settlement offer when the plaintiff has not made a demand?"

"It happens," Keane said, calm.

"Can you remember another occasion?"

Keane shrugged. "Not off the top of my head, no."

"So we can assume it's not frequent."

"No, it's not frequent."

"And you did not seek authority from your superiors to make this settlement offer because, as you said, the amount was within your authority, correct?"

"That is correct."

"Did you request that a Treasury check be issued from the Department of the Treasury?"

Keane smiled. "There was no need, Counselor. Your client turned down the offer."

Sloane paused, nodding. Then he asked, "I take it, however, that you advised the Federal Tort Claims staff that Mrs. Ford had filed a claim and forwarded a copy of the complaint to them for processing?"

"I don't do those kinds of things, Counselor. Someone on my staff handled that," Keane said, dismissive.

"And when would that have been done?"

"I'd have to have my staff check the file. I really wouldn't know."

"Was it within the last week?"

"Yes," she said. "Most likely."

"Actually, you have a good memory," Sloane said. "It was one week ago today," he said, holding up another document. "But perhaps you didn't hear my initial question, Ms. Keane. I didn't ask whether you forwarded a copy of Mrs. Ford's *amended* complaint to the Tort Claims division. I asked whether a copy of the original complaint was forwarded to that division."

Keane squirmed in her chair. "I don't recall."

"I think we've just established that that would have been standard procedure, would it not?"

"Yes, it would have been."

"Would there be any good reason why that standard procedure would not have been followed in this instance?"

"I can't think of any. Perhaps administrative oversight."

"In that case, I would request that the government be ordered to turn over their file for Beverly Ford."

Pendergrass stood. "Objection, Your Honor. That request violates the attorney-client privilege and contains the government's work product."

"Your Honor," Sloane said. "I'm not interested in any of the government's work product. I'm just interested in whether the United States attorney ever notified the proper divisions within her office that Mrs. Ford filed a complaint before the offer of settlement. I'm happy to allow the government to provide that file to the court for an in-camera inspection for that purpose."

"I'll grant the motion," Natale said, now seemingly on Sloane's wavelength or at least damn interested in where he was heading. "The government will provide the court with its file immediately following this hearing."

Pendergrass sat.

"Mr. Sloane, do you have any further questions of Ms. Keane?"

"No, Your Honor."

Keane started from the stand.

Sloane turned back. "Actually, I'm sorry, I do have just one more."

Keane begrudgingly retook her seat.

Sloane took a moment, as if studying his notes before looking up at the U.S. attorney. "Ms. Keane, have you ever met with Argus CEO Houghton Park and Colonel Bo Griffin at Mr. Park's residence on Lake Washington to discuss how Argus could pay a hundred thousand dollars to Mrs. Ford so that no settlement offer would have to be communicated through the Tort Claims staff?"

The courtroom erupted. This time Judge Natale did not seek to calm it. She turned and looked to the witness chair.

Keane's face had faded to an ashen white. Her eyes shifted across the room to Pendergrass, urging him to stand and object.

But Pendergrass remained anchored in his seat, eyes locked on Rachel Keane. To the rest of the courtroom he looked like a statue, unmoving, frozen, but Sloane saw the nearly imperceptible movement, and he knew Keane did as well.

Pendergrass winked.

OUTSIDE THE COURTHOUSE Sloane finished with the last of the news media interviews. As technicians rolled up yards of cable and packed equipment back into news vans, he unclipped the microphone from his suit coat and met Beverly Ford in the courtyard out front of the Federal Building. Beverly wore the same modest skirt and jacket as when Sloane first met her in the King County Superior Courtroom. She called it her lucky suit.

At the end of the hearing Judge Natale had not taken the matter under submission, as was her normal routine. Instead, she had read from a carefully prepared statement. She said that the evidence of wrongdoing on the part of Argus and its directors, as well as Colonel Bo Griffin, and perhaps Rachel Keane, was overwhelming.

Keane had never answered Sloane's final question. She pleaded the Fifth Amendment.

Natale also said there was significant evidence the mission that had resulted in James Ford's death was not a military operation at all, and therefore that James Ford had likely not been killed while acting incident to his service.

Then she granted the government's motion to dismiss.

While the rest of the courtroom sat in wide-eyed shock and disbelief, Judge Natale explained that despite the evidence, under the Feres doctrine, as currently interpreted by the U.S. Supreme Court, Beverly Ford's complaint was barred, and Natale was duty-bound to apply it.

God bless her! It was the only time Sloane could have kissed a judge for ruling against him.

Addressing Beverly Ford, Judge Natale had said, "If ever there was a case that cried out for justice, Mrs. Ford, this would be it. I hope you find it."

Ford had turned and smiled at Sloane. "I have hope, Your Honor. And faith."

Natale had then turned to Sloane. "I suspect my ruling will cause you to appeal this matter to the Ninth Circuit Court of Appeals, Mr. Sloane."

Sloane nodded. "It will, Your Honor, and perhaps beyond."

Natale nodded. "Perhaps." Then she stood and left the bench, and the onslaught of reporters converged on Sloane and Kannin for nearly an hour.

Ford handed Sloane a wrapped package. "I got you something. And I want you to know, win or lose, I won't forget what you've done for James and our family."

Sloane unwrapped the package. Inside was the framed painting from Beverly Ford's mantel, the one of the dove and the prayer about houses being built not of wood and stone but love. He smiled. "I'll put it on the mantel in my home. And it will remind me of what you've done for me as well."

"What I did?"

"You taught me about hope, Beverly."

Sloane gave her a hug. When they separated they started toward Beverly's children, who stood on the grass beneath the fist sculpture in the middle of the court-yard, along with Charles Jenkins, Alex, and John Kannin. Sloane would not allow Tina or Jake to be at the hearing. He did not want either one of them appearing on film or in the papers.

As Sloane and Ford approached, Althea broke free of Lucas's hand and ran across the cement toward them. Beverly Ford reached out to greet her daughter, but to Sloane's considerable surprise, Althea veered at the last second and ran to him, wrapping her arms around his legs.

When she released her grip, he lowered to her eye level and asked, "What was that for, angel?"

Althea turned and looked over her shoulder at her brother. Lucas nodded. Then she turned back to Sloane.

"Thank you," she said.

ACKNOWLEDGMENTS

AS ALWAYS THERE are many to thank. If I miss any-one, you know who you are and how grateful I am for the help and support.

My thanks to those who allowed me to use their names or likenesses, either to benefit charity or just for the heck of it. Among those are King County Superior Court judge Anthony P. Wartnik (retired), who allowed me to sit in his courtroom and pick his brain. Thanks also to John Kannin, a good friend and excellent trial attorney; and to Charles Jenkins, my law school roommate and friend. I'd like to say I made Charles larger than life, but those who know him, know he is larger than life. To Jo Natale and her husband Scott Cameron for their generous contribution to the Bellevue Boys & Girls Clubs in exchange for my use of her name. Thanks also

ACKNOWLEDGMENTS

to Johnson Marshall, a Canadian but with such a cool name I
had to make him a United States senator. And thanks to Dan
House, aka Dan the Sausageman, owner of the Tin Room, a
great restaurant in Burien.

To Colonel Drew Blazey, United States Army
(retired), for putting me in contact with those who served
in Iraq who were willing to share their experiences. To
Command Sergeant Major (retired) Bill Barkley (Washington National Guard) for taking the time to give me a
tour of Fort Lewis and Camp Murray and to introduce me
to JAG officers and other soldiers who served in Iraq and
who have handled the claims of soldiers and their families, including Major Matt Cooper, Judge Advocate General–Washington National Guard, for taking the time to
explain to me some of the intricacies of the claims process
and Feres doctrine.

Thanks also to W. L. Rivers Black, Esq. (Navy Reserve),
and Joseph C. Misenti, Jr. (JAG, Captain, Navy Reserve), for
their help in sorting through and understanding the claims
process and the Feres doctrine.

To Sergeant Jack Lewis (Army Reserve) who generously
gave of his time to help me understand his experiences on
the ground in Iraq. I couldn't have written this novel without his help. He provided me with much of the information
for the fictional account of the guardsmen set forth herein,
corrected my mistakes, and helped to make real the fictional
events portrayed herein. I am indebted for his kindness. And
to those other soldiers, U.S. Army and national guardsmen,
who provided me with their experiences serving in Iraq, but
who for personal reasons wish to remain anonymous, thank

you for your time and for your service. Any mistakes in the portrayal are mine.

To Mr. Michael T. Hurley, supervisory special agent, Drug Enforcement Administration (retired) who always goes out of his way to provide me with numerous contacts, all of whom made the book infinitely better, among them Daryl Higgins, Tacoma Police detective, Special Investigation Division; and Sergeant Tom Davidson, CID/Homicide/Robbery/Assaults, Tacoma Police Department. I'm grateful for the tour of the Hilltop in Tacoma, and for their insights.

To Ignacio Davila, for helping to translate my sometimes poor English into proper Spanish; and to Dr. Shane Macaulay, for proofreading the manuscript and educating me on rifles, handguns, shotguns, and just about everything else that fires a bullet.

To Cherie Tucker, the grammar guru of Grammar-Works, for giving the manuscript her critical eye.

In addition to the dozens of legal cases, treatises, and magazine and newspaper articles I read on the Feres doctrine, the military contractor defense, and the issues of body armor and Iraq's chemical weapons program, I also read a number of blogs of soldiers serving in Iraq, as well as first-person accounts published, including: *The Gift of Valor*, Michael M. Phillips, Broadway Books, 2005; *Just Another Soldier*, Jason Christopher Hartley, HarperCollins, 2005; *My War: Killing Time in Iraq*, Colby Buzzell, G.P. Putnam's Sons, 2005; *In the Company of Soldiers*, Rick Atkinson, Henry Holt & Co., 2004; *Operation Homecoming*, the award-winning anthology of stories written by military personnel and their families and edited by Andrew Carroll about military service in Iraq and

Afghanistan; Michael Yon's Online Magazine, http://www
.michaelyon-online.com, on Fallujah; Columbia: Journalism
Review Dispatches from Iraq, www.cjrdaily.org/dispatches_
from_iraq.

While the information concerning the history of Iraq's
chemical weapons program comes from newspaper and
magazine accounts, the events portrayed in this book and
the characters are all fictional. None of the above persons
breached any confidences or privileges in lending me their
names, likenesses, or assistance. To the extent anything in
this novel reflects a true account, it is coincidence. Again, all
mistakes are mine.

I am also grateful to all of the people at Touchstone for
making *Wrongful Death* as good as it can possibly be. Thanks
to publisher Mark Gompertz and deputy publisher Chris
Lloreda for believing in the manuscript; to publicity director
Marcia Burch and publicist Ellen Silberman for getting the
book and me out there and for their creative means to publicize it. To art director Cherlynne Li and production editor Josh
Karpf for making the book look and read better than I could
have hoped. To Louise Burke, Pocket Books publisher; and
Pocket Books associate publisher, Anthony Ziccardi, thanks
also for believing in the manuscript. Special thanks to Trish
Grader, my editor. It can be a thankless behind-the-scenes
job, but without her deft touch in helping me to improve the
manuscript, keep the story moving, and ratchet up the sus-
pense, I would not be writing this acknowledgment. Thanks
for your guidance and your support. And if things in Trish's
office work the way they do in mine, thanks also to her assistant, Meghan Stevenson, for taking care of the little things

that make the big things work. Finally, to all on the Simon & Schuster/Touchstone sales force, without whom no one would be reading this book, thanks for your hard work and dedication promoting and selling *Wrongful Death*.

To Jane Rotrosen, Donald Cleary, Mike McCormack and everyone else at the Jane Rotrosen Agency for continuing to take an interest in all aspects of my career and for taking such good care of me; and especially to my agent, Meg Ruley. Meg is the rare person who, as talented as she is at being a literary agent, is an even better person. Meg, I couldn't do this without your guidance, tenacity, enthusiasm, humor, and patience. I am truly grateful for all that you do for me.

And always, to my wife, who puts up with the mood swings of a writer, and makes everything else in our lives never skip a beat. I've said before you are more talented than I, and I grow to appreciate and love you more each day.

ABOUT THE AUTHOR

ROBERT DUGONI IS a *New York Times* bestselling author of the legal/political thrillers *The Jury Master* and *Damage Control*. His exposé *The Cyanide Canary* (Simon & Schuster, 2004) was a *Washington Post* 2004 Best Book of the Year Selection, and the Idaho Library Association's Book of the Year. He is a two-time winner of the Pacific Northwest Writers Association Literary Award for fiction. Mr. Dugoni lives in Seattle, Washington, where he coaches basketball and Little League baseball. For more about Robert Dugoni, visit www.robertdugoni.com.

Turn the page for a sneak peek
at the next exciting novel from
New York Times bestselling author

Robert Dugoni

BODILY HARM

Coming soon from Touchstone

IT HURT TO BLINK.

The light stabbed at his eyes, shooting daggers of pain to the back of his skull. When he shut them, an aurora of black and white spots lingered.

Albert Payne had never been one to partake liberally in alcohol; not that he was a complete teetotaler either. He'd been hung over a handful of times during his fifty-six years, but those few occasions had been the result of unintended excess, never a deliberate intent to get drunk. So although he had little experience with which to compare it, his pounding head seemed a clear indicator that he had indeed drunk to excess. He'd have to accept that to be so because he could remember little about the prior evening. Each factory owner, in conjunction with the local officials in China's Guangdong

Province had insisted on holding a reception to make Payne and the others in the delegation feel welcome, no doubt hoping their hospitality would ensure a favorable report. Payne recalled sipping white wine, but after three weeks the receptions had blended together and he could not separate one from another.

Coffee.

The thought popped into his head. He seemed to recall that caffeine helped a hangover. Maybe so, but locating the magic elixir would require that he stand, dress, leave his hotel room, and ride the elevator to the lobby. At the moment, just lifting his head felt as if it would require a crane.

Forcing his eyelids to remain open, he followed dust motes floating in a stream of light to an ornate ceiling of crisscrossing wooden beams and squares of ornate decorative wallpaper. He blinked and pinched the bridge of his nose, then looked again, but the view had not changed. He felt a cold sweat envelop him. The ceiling in his room at the Shenzhen Hotel had no beams or ornate wallpaper; he'd awakened the previous three mornings to a flat white ceiling.

With a sense of dread he shifted his gaze. Cheap wood paneling and a dingy, burnt-orange carpet confirmed his fear: this was not his hotel room and, by simple deduction, this could not be his bed.

He slid his hand along the sheet, fingertips brushing fabric until encountering something distinctly different, soft and warm. His heart thumped hard in his chest. He turned his head. Dark hair flowed over alabaster shoulders blemished only by two small moles. The woman lay on her side, the sheet draped across the gentle slope of her rounded hip.

Payne felt himself starting to hyperventilate and forced

deep breaths from his diaphragm. Now was not the time to panic. Besides, rushing from the room was not an option, not in his present condition, and not without his clothes. Think! The woman had not yet stirred, and judging by her heavy breathing she remained deep asleep, perhaps as hung over as he, perhaps enough that if he didn't panic, Payne might be able to sneak out without waking her, if he could somehow manage to get up.

He forced his head from the pillow and scanned the carpet along the wall to the foot of the bed where he spotted a shoe and felt a moment of great relief that just as quickly became greater alarm. The shoe was not his brown Oxford loafer, but a square-toed boot and a leg.

Payne sat up, but the room spun and tilted off-kilter, bringing fleeting, blurred images like a ride on a merry-go-round. The images did not clear until the spinning slowed. When it did, Payne was staring at a man sitting in an armless, slatted wood chair.

"Good morning, Mr. Payne. You appear to be having a difficult morning." Eyes as dark as a crow, the man wore his hair parted in the middle and pulled back off his forehead in a ponytail that extended beyond the collar of his black leather coat.

"Would you care for some water?"

Not waiting for a response, the man stood. At a small round table in the corner of the room he filled a glass from a pitcher, offering it to Payne. If this were a bad dream, it was very real. Payne hesitated, no longer certain his hangover was the product of alcohol.

The man motioned with the glass and arched heavy eyebrows accentuating the bridge of a strong forehead. Dark stubble shaded his face. "Please. I assure you it's clean, relatively speaking, and your throat does sound as if it will be appreciated."

Payne took the glass but did not immediately drink, watching as the man returned to the chair, crossed his legs, and folded his hands in his lap. The man again motioned to the glass. This time Payne took a small sip. The glass clattered against his teeth and water trickled over his bottom lip and chin onto the sheet. When the man said nothing, Payne asked, "What do you want?"

"Me? *I* want nothing."

"Then why are you—"

The man raised a single finger. "My employer, however, has several requests."

"Your employer? Who is your employer?"

"I'm afraid I'm not at liberty to divulge that information."

The woman emitted a small moan but her body continued to rhythmically rise and fall. Payne looked from her back to the man, an idea occurring. "I've been married for more than twenty years; my wife will never believe this."

But the man responded with a blank stare. "Believe what?"

Payne gestured to the woman. "Her. It's not going to work."

"Ah." The man nodded. "You believe that I am here to blackmail you with photographs or videotapes of the two of you fornicating."

"It isn't going to work," Payne repeated.

"Let me first say that it is refreshing to hear in this day when more than fifty percent of all marriages end in divorce that yours remains strong. Good for you. But look around you, Mr. Payne; do you see a camera or a video recorder any-where in the room?"

Payne did not.

"Now, as I said, my employer has several requests." For the next several minutes the man outlined those requests. Finishing, he asked, "Do we have an understanding?"

Confused, Payne shook his head. "But you said you weren't here to blackmail me."

"I said I was not here to blackmail you with photographs or videotapes. And as you have already educated me, such an attempt would not be productive."

"Then why would I do what you're asking?"

"Another good question." The man pinched his lower lip. His brow furrowed. "It appears I will need something more persuasive." He paused. "Can you think of anything?"

"What?"

"Something that would make a man like you acquiesce to my employer's demands?"

"There's nothing," Payne said. "This isn't going to work. So if I could just have my clothes back . . ."

"Nothing?" The man seemed to be giving the problem greater consideration. He snapped his fingers. "I have it."

Payne waited.

"Murder."

The word struck Payne like a dart to the chest. "Murder? I haven't murdered anyone."

With the fluidity of a dancer the man stood, a gun slid-ing into his extended left hand from somewhere beneath his splayed black coat, and the back of the woman's head exploded, blood splattering Payne about the face and neck.

"Now you have."

THE EDGE OF YOUR SEAT IS WAITING FOR YOU

Pick up a thrilling bestseller from Pocket Books!

TED BELL
TSAR

Once again, Russia is a threat to democracy . . .
And only Alex Hawke can save the world.

STEPHEN FREY
FORCED OUT

Three men. Three secrets. One chance at redemption.

MARK ALPERT
FINAL THEORY

The solution to one of Einstein's greatest puzzles
could save the world—or doom it.

GEORGE D. SHUMAN
LOST GIRLS

Sherry Moore may be blind—but a special
gift allows her to "see" the final 18 seconds
of a murder victim's life.

Available wherever books are sold or at
www.simonandschuster.com

Don't miss these riveting thrillers from Pocket Books!

Joy Fielding
CHARLEY'S WEB
An ambitious South Florida journalist is in a heart-pounding race to save her children and herself from a killer's deadly designs.

Robert K. Tanenbaum
ESCAPE
District Attorney Butch Karp takes on a controversial defense in the courtroom, as a deadly terrorist plot unfolds in the heart of Manhattan.

Robert Ferrigno
SINS OF THE ASSASSIN
Radical forces battle for control of a nuke-ravaged nation...the land once known as America.

Bob Reiss
BLACK MONDAY
A worldwide epidemic—affecting not humans, but oil—causes civilization to descend into chaos.

John Connolly
THE REAPERS
A chain of killings is obscurely linked over a long passage of years, and it is time for the blood debts to be settled.

Available wherever books are sold or at www.simonandschuster.com

"Part of what makes *What Now?* such a special read is Yael's ability to take meditation out of the ephemeral and make it real-life relevant. Yael does this through her unflinching honesty in sharing her own anxieties, challenges, heartbreaks and triumphs. Never arrogant, deeply humble and always purposeful, *What Now?* makes a strong case for why meditation can help anyone better understand a moment or a life, one lived and one still unfolding. It's clear that meditation has helped Yael become whom she always was meant to be——and helped her write an absolutely beautiful book."

—Chelsea Clinton, Vice Chair of the Clinton Foundation, *She Persisted* and *It's Your World*

"*What Now?* is a wonderful book, straightforward, personal, and engaging. Its grasp of basic Buddhist teachings and meditation techniques is impressive, and it extends them into areas of interest for young people, all the way up to activism, relationships, and even sex. I can't think of a better guide for young people in search of honest spirituality than Yael Shy."

—Norman Fischer, former Co-Abbot of the San Francisco Zen Center and Founder of The Everyday Zen Foundation, *What Is Zen?* and *Training in Compassion*

"The key question is how do you have an integrated life? In this book, Yael brings us through her own struggles and joys of living a life of attention, compassion and awareness. It is refreshing to read and a joyful offering to the world."

—Sensei Koshin Paley Ellison, Co-Founder of the New York Zen Center for Contemplative Care, Editor of *Awake at the Bedside*

WHAT NOW?
MEDITATION FOR YOUR
TWENTIES
AND BEYOND

WHAT NOW?

MEDITATION FOR YOUR
TWENTIES AND BEYOND

By Yael Shy
Foreword by Lodro Rinzler

**PARALLAX
PRESS**

BERKELEY, CALIFORNIA

Parallax Press
P.O. Box 7355
Berkeley, California 94707
www.parallax.org

Parallax Press is the publishing division of
Plum Village Community of Engaged Buddhism, Inc.
Printed in the United States of America

Text design by Gopa & Ted2
Cover design by Jess Morphew
Cover art by Katie Edwards / Getty Images
Author photo by Erika Scott

ISBN: 978-1-941529-82-9

Library of Congress Cataloging-in-Publication Data
is available upon request.

1 2 3 4 5 / 21 20 19 18 17

CONTENTS

Foreword by Lodro Rinzler   vii

Introduction   1

1: Suffering: You Aren't Crazy and
   You Aren't Alone   9

2: Learning to Meditate   31

3: Mindfulness In-Between   63

4: Feeling Emotions, Not Being Emotions   87

5: Mindful Relationships   135

6: Changing the World Without
   Burning Out   161

7: Your Hair Is on Fire and Everything
   Is Okay   181

Appendix: A Basic Meditation Guide   189

Acknowledgments   207

About the Author   211

FOREWORD

UNTIL WE DIE, we are constantly in a state of change and evolution. As Benjamin Franklin said: "When you're finished changing, you're finished."

The question of "What now?" feels especially potent when you are at an age where everyone and their mom (literally) is asking you what you are going to do with your life. Yet this question continues to haunt us throughout our years—it doesn't go away. A few years after college, you may begin to wonder what you *really* want to do for a career. Perhaps you begin to wonder about whether you should stop dating so casually and find someone to settle down with. When you think you've figured some things out, you might begin to question whether those things actually make you happy or get thrown a curveball where those things fall apart and you have to start fresh. "What now?" is a question you must return to over and over again.

In 2015, I was approached by a friend with a request to learn meditation, and that conversation gradually spiraled into a business idea. Her "What now?" questions around seeking a new spiritual path and deepening her meditation practice joined with my "What now?" questions of finding the next step in my livelihood, and spiraled into MNDFL, our network of drop-in studios where stressed-out seekers take thirty- and forty-five-minute meditation classes in a wide variety of traditions.

As MNDFL was getting off the ground, I shot an email to a friend, a Zen teacher in New York City, and asked if he was interested in joining our faculty. I told him that we were looking for teachers who embodied the wisdom of their traditions and were completely accessible and kind to people walking in off the streets, people who had never meditated before. He politely declined due to his own workload, but said that I had completely described someone he knew. He asked if I had heard of someone named Yael Shy. I had not and immediately agreed to sit down with her.

From the moment I met her, I knew, from her very presence, that she was a home run in terms of what we were looking for, and I brought her on to our teaching staff. Yael is a bit of a unicorn: she was raised in the Jewish faith, yet has practiced and studied Zen from a young age. She can speak to both (and has, beautifully, in this volume) in a way that makes these ancient traditions relevant for our modern world.

When I first met Yael, I saw that she embodied the very qualities we teachers strive to promote through meditation: equanimity, gentleness, and strength. In the years of our friendship since then I have seen her go through many

"What now?" life moments: marriage, pregnancy, work transitions, and motherhood, and while she is open about none of it being easy, she does it all with grace and charm. She is the real deal.

In this volume, she speaks to the basic insecurities that plague all of us: whether we're on the right track in life, whether we will find love, whether we are good enough for x, y, or z. She talks about times she has given in to strong emotions and the havoc that can wreak on one's life. She provides a roadmap for us to follow so we feel less alone and have the support we need to answer life's big questions.

Here's an interesting thought experiment: name five women Buddhist teachers under the age of forty who have produced a book. I can't. This is slowly changing, but prior to now we have not had a lot of young, well-trained meditation teachers sitting down and offering their thoughts, not as the guru-on-a-mountain, but as a peer in the world.

In my tradition we have a term: *kalyanamitra*. It can be translated as "spiritual friend." It is not the sort of teacher who gives you some tools to work with your mind and sends you on your way—that's known as an instructor. It's also not the teacher who has mastered their mind so that to look upon them shows you your own enlightened nature—that's the guru. It's the person who is a bit farther down the path than you, who has been in your shoes, knows the mistakes and pitfalls you are going to encounter as you traverse your own journey, and will stick around to make sure you avoid them, or, at the very least, will pick you up and help you keep going. Yael is that friend who has done the work. And let's be clear, this whole meditation thing isn't about being blissed out on a mountain: it is hard work to get to know and ultimately befriend ourselves. But she's done it. I am so glad that we have a sincere, young, frank, wise teacher like Yael to pour her years of meditative understanding into a book so that we can all access such a spiritual friend ourselves.

For anyone in transition—and let's be clear, we are all always in transition—this is a book that will help. Witty, insightful, and kind, *What Now?* is not the book we read and put away; it's the book we carry around with us and continue to reference in the many moments when life feels uncertain, wild, and chaotic. To read and revisit this book often is to have a delightful spiritual friend with you, so that you continue to navigate life's choppy waters with ease and grace. Thank you, Yael, for this tremendous gift.

Lodro Rinzler
June 2017

INTRODUCTION

DURING MY JUNIOR year of college at New York University, I ducked into a clothing store on Broadway and Thirteenth to find some quiet as I dialed my friend Sasha. "I can't breathe again," I said in short gusts, as my chest constricted. I felt lightheaded and dizzy, and I was covered in a cold sweat. I was having a panic attack—my third that month.

Sasha told me to focus on what was in front of me. "Touch the clothing," she said, "How does it feel?"

"Soft," I responded, still struggling with my shallow breath.

"What do you notice in the store?" she asked.

After describing my surroundings to her for the next twenty minutes, my breathing finally calmed down. I broke down in tears of gratitude and exhaustion.

"Yael," Sasha told me gently, "you have to get help."

The next week, I nervously attended a workshop on anxiety run by the university health center. The facilitator mostly talked about the stress of classes, homework, and exams.

I thought to myself: *Stress? About homework?* The word "stress" seemed to fall short of capturing what I was feeling. Homework was the least of my worries.

I was stressed because I wasn't sure if I would ever find love, or if love was even real. Earlier that year, my parents had announced that they were getting a divorce after thirty-five years of marriage. And earlier that month, my long-distance boyfriend had broken up with me because of what he called "other temptations."

I was stressed because I had taken out tens of thousands of dollars in loans to attend college and had no idea how I would pay them back after graduation.

I was stressed because on September 11th of that year, 2001, more than two thousand people were killed less than fifteen minutes from my residence hall. The world felt like it had gone insane. Despite having friends, I felt lonely. Despite doing well in my classes, I felt exhausted and burnt out.

I was experiencing more than just "stress." I was deeply, existentially anxious. I was hungry for instruction and guidance on how to *be*, not just how to take deep breaths. I wanted to live a good life. I wanted to love and be loved. I wanted to make a difference. And yet I felt like I didn't have the right tools for any of those things.

My mother, noticing my state, gave me a flyer for a seven-day silent meditation retreat in upstate New York. I thought it sounded nice, like a relaxing spa vacation. Turns out it was nothing like a spa. It was seven days of complete silence. We could ask questions of the teachers, but otherwise even eye contact was discouraged. We practiced sitting and walking meditation all day long. In the evening, the teachers gave talks about mindfulness and something everyone kept referring to as "the practice."

I cursed and cried my way through the first three days. The meditation was physically excruciating on my back and knees. I could not get comfortable. Unable to talk to anyone, I felt completely alone. Moreover, I continued to fail miserably at "the practice." I could not pay attention to my breath for more than ten seconds at a time. I couldn't pay attention to my food after the second bite. My mind was a self-recriminating, panicky, anxious mess, and my body hurt everywhere. At night, I devised elaborate escape plans wherein I would hotwire one of the cars and drive off into the woods, where I was sure life would be better than at the meditation center.

On the third or fourth day of the retreat, it was finally my turn to meet with one of the teachers. When I had pictured this moment during the days prior, I imagined that I would ask a deep philosophical question about the meaning of life and my place in it. Instead, as soon as I sat in front of him, I burst into tears. "I feel afraid all the time," I heard myself say. That's it. That's all I seemed to want to say after days in silence.

The teacher paused for a minute, and then said, "You

know, the interesting thing about fear is that it doesn't like the light. The more you bring a flashlight to your deepest fears, the more they won't be able to survive."

I skipped the next period of meditation and walked down to the creek. Sitting at its edge, I concentrated on breathing slowly and imagined shining a small flashlight on my insides. *What are you afraid of?* I asked myself, and waited to see what the light beam would reveal. *That I'm ugly, that I'm stupid, that nobody loves me, that nobody will ever love me, that I'm a disappointment. And also war, terrorism, environmental disaster, apocalypse . . .*

I tried all of these fears on for size, but none felt like the whole truth. None quite resembled the kernel of fear in my gut that was causing so much grief.

I'm afraid of dying.

Now I was closer. I was afraid of dying, but I had never died. How could I be afraid of something that hadn't happened to me yet? What did I imagine dying to be?

No longer existing. Being worthless and empty to the point of invisibility.

And there it was: the feeling of being invisible and worthless. That was the core fear I carried with me without knowing it, the foundation of pain on which an entire shaky structure of identity was built. I knew this was only the beginning. It would take years of meditation and exploration to unpack this core fear. But my teacher was right—meditation provided a steady light to shine on my anxieties and a container in which I could examine them. I felt lighter during the rest of the retreat. My mind settled and the tension in my body eased. I felt broken open, and, simultaneously, entirely whole.

Studying meditation and mindfulness have offered me a path to understanding how to be in the world, how to work with difficult and painful emotions, how to live life authentically and honestly, and how to find a way to work toward justice without burning out.

Today I teach meditation to thousands of college students each year as the senior director of MindfulNYU at New York University, the largest campus-wide mindfulness initiative in the country. I witness the struggles of young people and listen to them as they grapple with the same existential questions that I struggled with as a college student. The students who come to my office are often far more resourceful and knowledgeable than I was, but their essential questions remain the same: How do I balance all the pressures I am under? How do I forge my path in the world? How do I deal with heartbreak and loneliness? Who am I?

Young people today report higher levels of stress and lower levels of emotional health than ever before. A *New York Times* article from 2015 reported that suicide among fifteen- to twenty-four-year-olds has been rising steadily since 2011, from 9.6 deaths per one hundred thousand students to 11.1 in 2013.[1] The article suggests that this increase may be a result of the pressures young people are feeling to maintain perfection in school, relationships, and work with very few healthy opportunities for release and rest.

Fortunately, studies have shown the significant positive effects of mindfulness on the mental health of young people, including improved overall health, and decreased stress.[2] We at NYU have seen these positive effects firsthand. Our Global Spiritual Life Center hosts four thousand people per week, with over five thousand students trying at least one yoga and meditation class per year. Our meditation events and programs regularly fill to capacity, reflecting a national trend of young people passionate about meditation and mindfulness.

Young people in their twenties and thirties are rapidly becoming the "meditation generation," and yet there is a lack of books and resources geared specifically to their experiences. This book hopes to fill that gap, offering key practices and teachings from Buddhism and other mindfulness traditions that have transformed my life and the lives of my students over the years.

1. Julie Scelfo, "Suicide on Campus and the Pressure of Perfection," *New York Times*, July 27, 2015. Accessed April 25, 2017.
2. Cheryl Regehr et al., "Interventions to Reduce Stress in University Students: A Review and Meta-Analysis," *Journal of Affective Disorders*, 148, no. 1, (2013): 1–11.

I use plenty of examples and stories throughout the book in an attempt to demystify mindfulness and to disabuse you of any notion that it is outside of your ability to practice. As you will read, I was never a "star" meditator. I have never been a naturally relaxed, present, or particularly spiritual person. For most of my life, I have been a jumpy, anxious, neurotic mess. I offer my story to you because I have come to believe that any happiness and freedom I have experienced has come from *within* the mess, not from overcoming it. Everything I ever hated about myself, everything I tried to get rid of, has turned out to be the rich soil of my liberation. My neediness, my anxiety, and my anger have all been manifestations of my capacity for intimacy and connection. My traumas have softened my heart and enabled me to understand other people's pain. Freedom, for me, comes not from changing myself, but from growing ever more expansive and loving toward all of the darkness within.

"What now?" is a question to which we are forced to return many times in our life, but it takes on particular urgency in our twenties and thirties. No matter the circumstances that brought you here, there is no better moment and no better time to create and sustain a meditation practice for yourself than right now.

Your unique messes contain the seeds of everything you need. They hold within them real love for yourself and others. They contain the path to healing and to liberation. By returning to who you are in meditation, by deeply understanding your emotions, your suffering, and your interconnection with the larger world, you water these seeds. Eventually, they break open, revealing your strong and vulnerable heart, able to hold all of your pain and all of your joy.

1: SUFFERING: YOU AREN'T CRAZY AND YOU AREN'T ALONE

THE FOLKSINGER Cosy Sheridan once sang, "It's a hard life, but there are very soft days."[3] In my twenties, the hard days were much more common than the soft ones. There seemed to be so much that was uncertain and so much that was constantly changing. I was trying to figure out who I was and what I wanted with the vague sensation that there was more to happiness than succeeding in the "rat race" of life. There seemed to be a hollowness at my core, an incessant ache that I could not figure out how to fix. Was there something wrong with me? Why did I feel so alone all the time? And what was the *point* of being alive, if everything died in the end?

After my eye-opening experience on my first meditation retreat, I began taking Buddhism classes, reading books on Buddhism and meditation, and learning as much as I could. I sought answers to these questions about the purpose of life and the emptiness and sadness I felt at the core. When I

3. Cosy Sheridan, "Too Much Time," *Solo Songbook*, CD Baby, 2013.

learned about the three marks of existence (impermanence, unsatisfactoriness, no separate self) in a class at the end of my senior year of college, it felt like a piece of the puzzle in my mind clicked into place. It felt like the Buddha himself, alive over two thousand years ago, was sitting me down and seeing me and my predicament (and the predicament of all humans!) with clarity and kindness. "You are suffering," he was saying, "let me explain why."

According to early texts, the Buddha said that all of existence as we know it is "marked" by three qualities: impermanence, "unsatisfactoriness," or the tendency to cling to pleasure and to avoid pain, and "no separate self." Suffering happens, according to the Buddha, when we resist or deny any of these truths in our life. Let's take these one by one.

IMPERMANENCE

In Buddhism, the first mark of existence is "impermanence," or the fact that everything changes. *Everything.* Every plant in nature, every drop in the ocean, every cell in your body is constantly moving, transforming, changing, dying, and being born. Nothing is static, and nothing is permanent. This is not so much a belief as a fact of life, and one that has been borne out by modern science.

When life is filled with pain, we sometimes wonder if the pain will ever end and if anything will ever change. If we have accepted the truth of impermanence, we know that things will change. It is much harder to deal with impermanence when we resist its truth, grasping hard to the things of this world that we love and want to keep, only to have them slip through our fingers.

There is a famous Buddhist story of a woman whose only child died. The woman lost her mind, screaming and clutching her dead baby to her chest. She went from house to house in the village, demanding a cure from her neighbors that would bring her child back to life. Finally, she landed at the Buddha's door, who said, "I can cure your baby, but first, you need to bring me a mustard seed from the house of someone in this village who has never experienced the death of a loved one." The woman went door-to-door, but could not find anyone who had never had someone dear to them die. They all told her, in one way or another, that "The living are few, but the dead are many." The woman came to realize the universality of death and the truth of impermanence. She buried her son in the forest and became a follower of Buddha.

The first few times I heard this story, I hated it. It seemed like the opposite of good grief counseling. If someone has suffered a catastrophic loss, such as the death of a child, probably the worst possible thing you could say to that person is, "Oh well! Death happens to everyone!" As I have gotten older, however, I've started to see the story of the woman and her dead child as a story about all of us. We humans struggle and pound our fists against a basic, fundamental truth of existence: all life in this world is impermanent. We learn that everything arises and falls in its own time, in its own season—and we *really* don't want this to be true. So we resist. We cling with all our hearts to the things we love. We try with all our might to fight loss and change. We, like the mother in the story, want to find a "cure" for death and impermanence. We want to find a way to subvert the rules and gain control over our environment and our lives. And when that fails, when we are forced to confront our lack of ultimate control, we avoid it. We steer clear of relationships and experiences that might cause us to get attached.

In *Open to Desire*, Mark Epstein tells a story about Sigmund Freud and his fellow psychoanalysts out for a walk on a beautiful spring day.[4] Freud keeps pointing out beautiful flowers to his friends, who seem annoyed and want to continue with their heady conversation. After he returns home, Freud hypothesizes that his friends couldn't take in the beauty of the flowers because by doing so, they would have to acknowledge the fleeting nature of the flowers' lives. They would have to accept the death right in the middle of the life, and say "Yes" to the whole process. Freud's friends, like many of us, were missing out on so much life by trying to keep their hearts safely shielded from death.

This resistance is natural. Without it, how would we

4. Mark Epstein, *Open to Desire: Embracing a Lust for Life Insights from Buddhism and Psychotherapy* (New York: Gotham Books, 2005), 176.

have survived as a species? Of course we are scared of change and death. The trouble is, impermanence will always win, and our resistance to this essential part of existence will always fail. And this resistance hurts. Resistance to suffering causes additional suffering, on top of the pain and disorientation of the change itself. Relationships end. People we love die. Friendships dissolve. We grow older. This is just true. When I acknowledge this and let it deeply penetrate my understanding of things, something within me relaxes. I stop fighting.

I had a mentor when I was in law school whom I admired deeply. He was a funny, brilliant, and compassionate leader in the field of restorative justice. He was also a health nut, biking to and from work every day, maintaining a strict diet, and even taking naps each afternoon instead of drinking coffee. A few years after I graduated, I found out that he was diagnosed with a rare form of stomach cancer. Although he fought the cancer with a mix of Eastern and Western remedies, he died a few years later, leaving behind three daughters in their twenties, a devastated wife, and a community that loved him.

When I heard the news, I felt a distant sort of sadness, but my brain seemed to be more preoccupied with the problems in my own life. Namely, my tumultuous relationship with my boyfriend. All day long, my mind chewed on horrible things my boyfriend had said to me and how I was going to respond. Our fights played on repeat in my mind, like a terrible movie I was forced to watch over and over again. It was not until the very end of the day, as I was sitting in meditation, that it hit me: thinking about my boyfriend all day was a strategic move by my mind. Thinking and worrying kept me away from feeling. Once I sat down and was able to let go of my looping boyfriend thoughts for even a moment, my sadness and grief about my mentor came rushing in with the force of a tidal wave. I broke down in tears. I was finally able to touch my sadness and feelings of loss for someone who was so special to me. Although I fought that sadness all day with a great deal of energy, afraid of what it would do to me, it was actually the *resistance* to the sadness that was the most painful feeling, not the sadness itself. The sadness felt like an opening and a relief.

On a retreat I attended, a woman raised her hand and said to the teacher, "I'm so tired of fighting myself all the time." The teacher responded, "Let yourself win." This is how I feel when I remember that everything is impermanent. Rather than fighting with life, I exhale and let life win.

What remains in the aftermath of this acceptance and letting go? In my experience with my mentor, I was left with grief and love. Grief as the heart mourned that to which it was attached, and love for the opportunity to have become attached in the first place.

There is another beautiful story about a Buddhist abbot

of a monastery who loses his son suddenly one night. The abbot spends the night after the death shrieking, crying, and wailing in his grief. The other monks become disturbed by the abbot's behavior. One of the monks finally approaches the abbot and says, "Teacher, why are you acting like this? Didn't you teach us that all of life is impermanent and that a solid, unchanging idea of human life is an illusion?"

The teacher nodded and said, "Yes. And the loss of a child is the most painful illusion of them all."

Just because we accept the truth of impermanence doesn't mean we don't feel the pain associated with it. In fact, the acceptance catapults us right into the center of our grief. This is a good thing. This is where healing and processing can happen. This is how we find our way back to love.

UNSATISFACTORINESS

According to the Buddha, the second mark of existence is "unsatisfactoriness," or suffering itself. Suffering, or *dukkha* in Pali, describes an axle that doesn't fit properly into the axle hole of the wheel, so it makes for a bumpy ride. Something isn't fitting. Something feels off. This is how the Buddha describes the suffering of everyday life. It is a quiet but persistent hum underneath all of our interactions. It is a baseline unsatisfactoriness. Clearly, when things are going wrong, we are unhappy, but even when things are going well, there is a feeling that it could end at any time—that it might be taken away from us. Happiness is fleeting in this situation. There is nothing we can hold on to—everything is constantly shifting. What we humans do in the face of this ever-changing, impermanent world is to grasp after the things we want and to push away the things we do not want.

This constant grasping and pushing is not a character flaw; it is a part of existence itself. Like our denial of death, this human trait is a survival strategy. If the fire burns us, we don't put our hand in the fire again (aversion). If the food tastes good, we want more food (clinging). The trouble is that because the world is uncontrollable and impermanent, this endless grasping and pushing causes us suffering.

When I started falling in love with Ben, the man who would later become my husband, I experienced a curious mix of happiness, excitement, and fear—a fear so deep it felt like a hundred-pound weight sitting on my chest. It took me a while to understand what that was about. Everything was going so well in the relationship, so why was I feeling such dread? Why the sleepless nights, nightmares, and sudden shortness of breath? It seemed like each time we inched closer in our intimacy, I got a little more scared. It was not like my prior relationships, where there was always an inner voice saying, "get out," or "this is bad." Instead, this time, this inner voice said, "loving someone this much is dangerous." I could feel my heart grasping for solid ground. Was this for *sure?* Could I still get hurt? What if I let myself get completely involved in the relationship and it ended? What if I loved with all my heart, and then he died?

My fear began to cause problems in our relationship. I became hyper vigilant about everything—worrying that it was a sign of the doom to come. If he didn't tell me I looked pretty one day, or neglected to notice a new haircut, I took it as a sign that I was more attached to him than he was to me. Any small argument made me question whether I should cut my losses and end the relationship before it went any further. I was in the best relationship of my life, and yet I was suffering and causing my boyfriend to suffer also.

When I identified this suffering as *dukkha*, or the suffering born of grasping, the whole situation began to soften and ease. I began to have compassion for myself and my vulnerable heart. When I would feel jealous, I tried to touch my face or my heart, saying, "Poor thing, you are very scared of losing him." I started to see my clinging and grasping as a sign of how much I loved this person and how much I was opening up. Each time I noticed a new attack of fear and clinginess, I tried to take a breath and physically relax my body. Relaxing my body helped me to loosen the grip on my mind. I reminded myself of what I could control (my own behavior) and what I could not (my boyfriend's behavior, his feelings, and the truth of impermanence). Gradually, the risk of loving became less terrifying over time. I am still not crazy about the fact that either he or I will die someday. I am equally not happy about the possibility that he or I could fall out of love at some point and leave. Acknowledging impermanence and the ever-changing nature of reality, however, helps me to appreciate what I have right *now* and release my fantasies and fears of what the future might hold.

In a June 2000 episode of *This American Life*, the author Nick Hornby told a story about his autistic, then-six-year-old son, Danny. Hornby describes Danny's love of long car rides, and Danny's anger when Hornby drives Danny only a short distance away from their home to go to the park.

> The yells get louder when we stop, and reach a sweat-inducing pitch when I open his door. "Come on, Dan," I say, in my best fun voice. "We're going to the park, the swings, the seesaw!" He just turns the yellometer up to eleven. I try to lead him out by the hand, but he snatches it away and grabs hold of something, the seat belt, anything that will anchor him inside. So we're fighting, the car and I, for custody of this small boy. . . . I end up dragging my son out by his ankles. A couple look at us as they walk past. They don't say anything, but one day I'm sure someone's going to report me and I'll be arrested.

Hornby then describes Danny's readjustment and subsequent delight when he fully realizes he is in a park, there are empty swings, and it's a lovely day:

> And there's no trace whatsoever in his face of the ankle-pulling trauma to which he was so recently and cruelly subjected. And I want to find the couple who may or may not have had a disapproving look on their faces when they saw me commit awful acts of violence, and show them just how joyful he is now. But of course they're not around, which is maybe just as well, because in a while, I'm going to have to find a way to get him out of this swing.[5]

Danny's response to impermanence is deeply relatable. Internally or externally, we do the same thing. We scream, cling, and resist change. We often have to be dragged to the next stage of our lives, only to discover that the next thing is exactly what we needed. It held treasures we did not even know how to think about or to conceptualize.

5. "Million Bubbles," *This American Life*, originally aired June 2, 2000, accessed April 24, 2017, https://www.thisamericanlife.org/radio -archives/episode/161/transcript.

Reminding ourselves of this takes practice. There are Tibetan Buddhist monks who practice dying each morning for a significant period of time, entering into a meditation so deep that they slow their heart rates down to a level that approaches death. Once they emerge out of the meditation, their bodies remember the truth that all of their daily grasping and aversion will not protect them against death. They remember who they are and what's important.

Even if we aren't Tibetan monks, we can accomplish something similar through meditation. We can watch our grasping mind try desperately to hold onto the things and people we love and want. And we can practice letting go over and over again.

No Separate Self

Every year during orientation at NYU, I tell the following story to the incoming first-year students: There were two waves traveling along the ocean together. One of the waves was small and one was quite tall. As the waves were getting closer to the shore, the tall wave could see, way off in the distance, that all the waves that had traveled before him were crashing as they came to the shore. With horror, he realized that there were no exceptions, and that neither he, nor his little friend, would be able to travel backward. That meant that both of them would eventually crash and disappear when they got to the shore.

Once he absorbed this information, the tall wave began to cry inconsolably. The little wave, unable to see the same view, was concerned for his friend. "Why are you crying? What's wrong?" The tall wave shook his watery head. "I can't tell you. I'm seeing a horrible sight right now. If I told you what it was, you would be as depressed as I am." The little wave continued to press him, however, and eventually the tall wave relented and told the little wave about the crashes at the shore, and the fact that there seemed to be no escape for them or any of their wave compatriots. The little wave was quiet for a while as they traveled along. Suddenly, he turned to his friend and said, "Tall Wave, I can tell you in seven words why this situation that you observe is not a problem." The tall wave was doubtful but told his small friend to go ahead with the seven words. The little wave said, "You're not just a wave. You're water."[6]

We are not just waves either, although we walk around most days believing we are. We believe we are distinct, separate, self-operating creatures, encased in skin, who may interact with other distinct, separate, self-operating creatures, but who are fundamentally separate from them. On some level, this is true. Looking at the ocean, we do see separate waves. Each wave has its own existence. Each wave

6. Adapted from Mitch Albom, *An Old Man, a Young Man, and Life's Greatest Lesson* (New York: Doubleday, 1997), 179.

has its own life span, and its own unique characteristics that make it different from every wave that has come along before and after it.

Learning to love and accept our own unique wave configuration is essential for our development as full human beings. So many of us, from a very young age, absorb messages from our parents and our society saying that there is something defective about us. For some of us, this may be because of the color of our skin, our sexual orientation, our gender, or some way in which we are subtly (or not so subtly) told we aren't as special or precious as others. For some of us, this may be because of painful, destructive messages we absorb about our worth being tied to our productivity, our wealth, our likability, or other things that are essentially outside of our control.

For me, my placement as the middle child of a large and loud family created the conditions for me to feel invisible and abandoned during a lot of my childhood. Although I always knew my parents loved me and they took care of my daily needs, I had to create a framework to manage the fear and loneliness of not feeling fully seen. Like most children, I could not implicate my parents in the problem because my literal survival depended on them, so I believed the problem stemmed from me. The story I came up with went something like this: There is something essentially lacking and empty in me that makes it impossible to be truly seen and loved. If, however, I work *really* hard to trick/convince others to pay attention to me, I may be able to redeem myself and find relief from my own flawed position.

The premise of the story was that there was a core problem with me, a way in which I was not worthy of love without having to *do* something. With that core pain as the base, any positive attention I received over the years eventually felt hollow, or like a tiny drop of water in a parched desert. And yet the story I created told me I just needed to try harder, and keep going the way I was going, or else risk something much worse. I couldn't tell what was on the other side of letting go of my story, but I was too terrified to find out. Who would I be without it?

The psychotherapist and author Adam Phillips wrote about an agoraphobic client he had who was terrified of crowds. "I think if I were to go into a crowded theatre," the client exclaimed, "I would die." Phillips finds himself thinking, "Why not agree to die and see what happens?"[7] For me, learning to love myself has been a practice of agreeing to let my story of myself as unlovable die, and seeing what happens. Because this is scary and destabilizing, I have had to do it in teeny tiny pieces. In therapy and meditation, I have tried to see the role the story has played in my life and witness when it arises. When I catch it, I practice

7. Adam Phillips, *On Kissing, Tickling, and Being Bored: Psychoanalytic Essays on the Examined Life* (Cambridge: Harvard University Press, 1998), 18.

asking myself the question, "What if I am actually deeply loveable, just as I am? Without having to do or perform anything? What if I am worthy of being here, alive, as myself?" Hypothetically, I imagine: if this were unassailably true, how would I feel? How would I speak to others? How would I walk or spend my time?

Usually, this imagining helps me feel strong and full. I notice I stand up straighter, and I look people in the eye. Slowly, these exercises have given me a taste of what true self-acceptance feels like. They have helped me to reprogram my brain to challenge its default self-hatred and to build alternative narratives through which I am learning to love my wave configuration, exactly as it is. In returning back to myself, just as I am, over and over again in meditation, I practice self-acceptance, the same way a weight lifter at the gym builds her muscles.

The story doesn't end there, however. We are waves, and it is important we love our particular wave shape, color and characteristics. But *at the very same time*, we are water. We are composed of materials—carbon, water, cells, oxygen, etc.—that we did not invent and that we do not own. As Vietnamese Zen teacher Thich Nhat Hanh says, we *inter-are*. We only exist in conjunction with billions of forces that are allowing for our continued existence, every second of every day. Our physical bodies are deeply interpenetrated with our environment, taking in oxygen, nutrients, and energy, and releasing waste.

Our minds and hearts are also porous to other people, taking in ideas, traumas, narratives, and information. This book is written in my voice and tells many of my stories, but both my voice and my stories have been molded and shaped by my family, friends, teachers, the books I have read, the media I have consumed. The folksinger Ani DiFranco sings:

> We can't afford to do anyone harm
> because we owe them our lives
> each breath is recycled from someone else's lungs
> our enemies are the very air in disguise[8]

It isn't just that I am "water," interdependent and co-arising with all things; *all* people are water, interdependent and co-arising with all things. The worst people who have ever lived, and the best.

When I reflect on my interconnected nature, I feel a sense of relief, like the little wave in the story. The huge problem of death and suffering is lighter, somehow. This is not because I don't want to stay alive, but because what I thought of as "my life" (separate, distinct, happening on a linear timeline) is only one part of the whole picture of life itself.

It is hard to wrap our heads around this way of thinking.

8. Ani DiFranco, "Looking for the Holes," *Not So Soft*, Righteous Babe Records, 1997, CD.

When I teach this concept of no independent, separate self to my students, many of them resist. "But I feel separate!" they say. "There does seem to be someone here, making decisions, reliving memories, having a different life than the person next to me."

When we sit down in meditation, however, I challenge these students to find exactly the place that is *them*. I ask them to watch their mind, to follow their thoughts, to search and to find the solid, unchanging core of their personhood. "Find the 'I' underneath," I challenge them. Neither they, nor anyone I know, can do this, because it doesn't exist. What we find instead are clusters of memories, imaginings, conditioned patterns of thoughts, and emotions that are constantly morphing and changing in a close, porous relationship to our world.

Even our bodies, which seem like *ours* (i.e., separate and distinct from the rest of the world), are continually undergoing change, shedding cells, aging, and are in constant communication with our environment. What I call "Yael" is a momentary grouping of cells and processes firing together in time, constantly in flux, to which I am affixing a label for a brief period of time. The cells of which I am composed will die and regenerate many times over in the course of my life. I gained allergies to pollen, cherries, and almonds when I was around twelve years old, and then miraculously lost them when I was around age twenty-five. My skin gains wrinkles each day and changes its form. The chronic anxiety and panic I experienced from a very young age has lessened to an almost indiscernible level in the past few years. "Yael" the wave is composed of water, was water before it was "Yael," and will be water again after "Yael" has fallen apart.

When I first learned about the concept of no separate self, I, like my students, felt a strong sense of resistance to it. Focusing on my water-like nature felt too much like letting the "me" I was trying to understand and love slip through my fingers. I was already so used to feeling invisible and worthless, that accepting the "oneness" of interconnection felt painful—I was somehow on the outside of the oneness and couldn't experience myself as a part of it. I remember laughing and crying in recognition when a woman on a retreat told the teacher, "I am just learning to love myself, and now you want me to let go of everything I thought was myself in the first place? I'm going to miss me!"

There is another great danger when we focus too heavily or exclusively on our water-like nature: what psychologist and Buddhist practitioner John Welwood calls "spiritual bypass." Spiritual bypass is the tendency to use meditation and/or spirituality to "sidestep or avoid facing unresolved emotional issues, psychological wounds, and unfinished developmental tasks."[9] One young man in my meditation

9. John Welwood, "Human Nature, Buddha Nature: On Spiritual Bypassing, Relationship, and the Dharma," *Tricycle Magazine*, Spring

class, when asked why he wanted to learn to meditate, said that he found himself to be "rotten" and wanted to find a means to transcend himself. Most of us have experienced this at one point or another—the desire to escape our lives or jump out of our pain and conditioning through spiritual practice, rather than tackle it head-on.

Spiritual bypass of thorny issues such as racism, sexism, ableism, and other "isms" is another common danger for meditation practitioners and spiritual communities who become attached only to the "water" understanding of themselves. Many people of color report that white leadership and white practitioners in meditation communities wave away any accusations of bias or racism in their centers by claiming to have reached heights "beyond" such markers of identity. Zenju Earthlyn Manuel, a Zen teacher and writer, argues that not only is this a hurtful form of bypass, it ignores a fundamental truth about our interrelated reality.

According to Manuel, nobody can erase their identity in a relative sense. White people are white—they are not invisible, or race-less. She writes:

> If we have created "race," we are all involved in the lived experience of it, whether we individually view in terms of race or not. When we are treated

---

by others or act ourselves with a consciousness of
race, we can count on an impact of that consciousness on everyone we interact with. If oppression is
a particular kind of suffering for some, then it is a
general type of suffering for all.[10]

Since everyone is "raced" in the relative world, we are all
being impacted in different ways as a result of our race.
Rather than try to bypass this truth, or pretend we can
meditate it away, we can look at it deeply in practice and in
community, creating safe spaces and affinity groups where
those who have been marginalized can find companionship and community, and those who are white can learn
to unpack and understand their whiteness. This honest
approach is our best path toward healing from the pain of
oppression on an individual and a community-wide level.

In order to see the whole picture, we have to see the ways
in which we are responsible for the work of understanding
and developing our own little wave, even while we see and
recognize our water-like nature. The two are both always
true, at the same time.

In my experience, the three marks of existence are most
helpful in daily life when we reframe them as questions:
Am I suffering right now because I am resisting or for-

---

10. Zenju Earthlyn Manuel, *The Way of Tenderness: Awakening through
Race, Sexuality, and Gender* (Boston: Wisdom Publications, 2015), 44.

getting one of these truths? Am I resisting impermanence and change? Am I clinging hard to an outcome I want, or pushing away something I don't want? Am I believing that I am separate from life, and love, or clinging to a definition of myself that isn't true? Most of the time, when I am suffering, the answer is "yes" to one or more of these. Recognizing this, I can relax my resistance a little. I can take a breath. I can practice being with what is.

2: LEARNING TO MEDITATE

WHAT IS MEDITATION?

LODRO RINZLER writes that the word "meditation" in Tibetan comes from the word "gom," which means, "to become familiar with."[11] Meditation is a process of becoming familiar with life. We do this by training our mind to pay attention. Sometimes we pay attention to our breath. Sometimes we pay attention to what we are doing—walking, eating, or even using the bathroom. When we are completely focused on what is happening in real time, even for a few seconds at a time, we are not caught in the tangle of thoughts that constantly swing between the future and the past. We become intimate with the experience of life and are able to live it more deeply.

Meditation is also the practice of coming home to ourselves. When I have not meditated for a little while, I often tentatively approach the "door" of my heart and mind.

11. Lodro Rinzler, *The Buddha Walks into a Bar . . . : A Guide to Life for a New Generation* (Boston: Shambhala, 2012).

What is on the other side? What has happened while I was away? Maybe I left the house in a mess and it will still be a mess when I return. Maybe it has been so long since I've been home that the territory will be unfamiliar and scary. As I sit to meditate, I try to courageously prepare myself for whatever is on the other side of that door. I commit to being with what is, as it is.

This time spent practicing being present with our breath trains our attention to be present more of the time in "regular" life, off the meditation cushion. We begin to taste the food we eat, rather than mindlessly shoveling it in. We listen when people talk to us rather than gathering the "gist" and then tuning out. We notice as things arise and fall—in nature, in our emotions, in our bodies. Even as the chatter of our minds comes and goes, we stay rooted in life as it is happening, rather than get lost in repetitive thinking. We put down our distractions, our busyness, our ideas about ourselves, and turn toward our lives.

If you have ever tried meditating for a few minutes, one of the first things you've probably noticed is that paying attention to the breath is harder than it sounds. A critical part of the process of meditation is watching our attention fly away from our anchor, despite our best attempts to stay focused. One minute we can be softly paying attention to our breath and then, before we know it, we are planning dinner, analyzing our relationship (or lack thereof), regretting having said something to a friend, or we find ourselves halfway through a wildly imaginative dream. This does not mean you have failed. Distraction is an essential part of the process, helping us to see and understand the contents of our minds.

In my early years meditating, each time I noticed I was distracted from my breath, I felt disappointment and anger at myself. *Why couldn't I just stay focused? Why was I such a bad meditator?* My body tightened up. I shifted position. I looked at my watch and tried to locate the exit. I hated the ping-pong of my racing thoughts and the assault of outside distractions, and was exhausted by the fight to try and control them. The inner voice that berated me each time I got distracted was so unpleasant, and the attendant sense of failure and frustration was so deep, that I quickly began dreading sitting down to meditate.

During one particularly bad meditation on retreat, I could not get comfortable in my seat and kept shifting. *You are disturbing everyone,* my inner voice said. Feeling bad, I decided I would get up and quietly leave the meditation hall. On my way out, I accidentally let the door slam behind me. *You just destroyed the peace of the meditation hall,* I thought. Feeling even lower, I walked down to the river. I threw a rock in the lake. *Nice work. You probably just ruined the ecosystem,* my inner voice offered. After considering this for a moment, even I could tell that my mental critic was going a little too far and I laughed at myself out loud. For the first time that day I heard the way my inner voice was speaking to me, and it was *mean*. In fact, without my realizing it, it had been beating me up for most of my life. It told me I ruined every space I was in. It told me I was worthless and small. The inner voice made me miserable. It caused me to loathe myself. And the more I ran from it or tried to shove it down in meditation, the louder it got.

None of this was new. What was new was that this time, I was paying attention. I didn't just assume the inner critic was the voice of truth. The practice of watching my thoughts arise and fall in meditation had given me a sliver of space between the moment the inner critic attacked, and the moment I believed it. In that tiny pause, I had options. I could hate my inner voices. I could yell at them, argue with them, give them the middle finger in my mind. This is known in the meditation world as "stacking aversions on aversions." It usually made me feel worse.

Alternatively, I could try and be kind to the inner critic. I could welcome her in. I could allow her to be heard and seen, without becoming completely swallowed by her. I could try and understand her origins and logic. I could remind myself that, while this critical voice was a part of me, she wasn't the whole of me.

The distance we gain from our inner critic is one of the most rarely discussed treasures of meditation. When our minds wander, we can wake up and realize they are wandering. We can give a soft label to the place we wandered to: "past memory," "desire for food," "imagination," are some examples. As soon as we have gently labeled the thought, we return home to our breath. Through this practice of getting distracted and bringing our attention back, we become intimate with our minds and hearts—the good, the bad, and the ugly. We meet our inner critic and see the things our mind loves to think about. We witness the patterns and the questions that occupy our daily mental energy, as well as some of the buried pains that emerge from the depths of our consciousness. In this way, this practice teaches us how to love ourselves. As we return to what is *truly happening* in the present moment in our bodies and in the world, our hearts open. Love is presence, and the act of paying attention and returning is an act of love that we repeat over and over again.

WHAT IS THE POINT?

Inevitably, when we practice, especially if it is difficult, we ask, what is the point? Why keep returning to the breath? What is the connection between returning to the present and all of the struggles and questions that we face?

Ultimately, our goal in meditation *is* the reward—waking up in our lives. Whether it is our crazy wandering minds or the storm of emotions thundering within us, when we do not run away from what is happening in real time but return back to it again and again, we train ourselves to inhabit our life as it is. The practice of meditation helps us to break outside of the achievement-based paradigm most of us live in every day because it is not about getting anywhere or doing anything in particular. It is just about being with what is, as we are right now.

And yet, it can be very difficult to simply turn off our mind that wants to see results, achieve goals, and reap rewards. We have been trained this way our whole life! So with a nod to that very human part of ourselves, here are just a few of the many other benefits of meditation that often arise when we practice.

Relaxation

Perhaps meditation's most famous claim is that it has the ability to help us relax. In many of the meditations I have led over the years, as well as in quite a few in which I have participated, people have sat down to meditate, promptly fallen asleep, and not woken up again until the sound of the bell at the end. Once, I even tried to use the sound of a man's loud snoring as my present-moment anchor, as there was no hope of ignoring it. In the nonstop lives we lead, most of us are chronically exhausted, tightly wound, and sleep deprived.

If you are struggling with the pressures of coursework, being away from home, trying to maintain relationships, finding a job, or getting a good night's sleep, you are not alone. A *New York Times* article from 2011 reported that the emotional health of first-year college students was the lowest it had been in twenty-five years, according to the self-assessment surveys of more than 200,000 students from across the United States.[12] Women in the study reported significantly worse mental health than men, with the gap widening each year. Several other studies have pointed to the additional mental and physical stressors that students of color report experiencing as a result of daily overt and covert racism.[13]

Relaxing in this environment is more than just a luxury—it is a necessity. The everyday tension and stress that accompanies life in our twenties can be debilitating to our mental and physical health.

I first began meditating as a college student because I suffered from unrelenting anxiety that did not subside even when I went to sleep. Anxiety soon led to the panic attacks I described in the introduction, causing a serious disruption in my life and wreaking havoc on my body and mind.

Regular meditation helped retrain my brain and body to handle anxious thoughts when they arrived. It didn't

12. Tamar Lewin, "Record Level of Stress Found in College Freshmen," *New York Times*, January 26, 2011. Accessed April 13, 2017.
13. Kevin L. Nadal et al., "The Adverse Impact of Racial Microaggressions on College Students' Self-Esteem," *Journal of College Student Development* 55, no. 5 (2014): 461–474.

stop the anxious thoughts, but it helped short-circuit the trigger that connected the thoughts to the physical panic symptoms, such as shortness of breath, sweating, and fainting.

Meditation helps us ground ourselves more of the time in the here and the now, rather than in the "what-if." Panic lives in the "what-if." *What if this stalled subway is a terrorist attack? What if I never find love? What if I fail my classes, can't get a job, disgrace my family, and have to live on the street?* Panic doesn't take these as thought experiments. It actually makes the mind believe those things are happening *now.* The more we train our minds to stay present, the more we become able to meet these "what-ifs" with the distance of a witness, rather than as a victim.

Feel your chair or cushion supporting you, right now. Feel the stability of the ground beneath you. Feel the rise and fall of your breath. Yes, things in the future might not be okay. Yes, bad things might happen. But right now, and most of the time, you are okay. Even if you are sad, grieving, scared, or angry, there is an okay-ness that rests underneath, available for you to access when you take a breath and connect.

When my mind is wildly leaping between what was and what might be, or when I am overwhelmed with my to-do list and my body feels like a tightly coiled spring, something about sitting down, letting go, and returning to my breath feels like a release. It feels like drinking ice water on a hot day. The silence, stillness, and stability of the moment are so much vaster than even my most pressing problems and fears.

Wisdom

If you have ever been up late at night, tossing and turning with the difficulties of the day, lost in circular thoughts or obsessed with a difficult decision, you have witnessed the limited capacity of the mind to tolerate pain. In my experience, the thinking mind tries to pick apart, understand, and bring logic to painful or complicated feelings, without a great deal of success. The body, on the other hand, can work with a tremendous amount of pain. It can process and emote pain, leading to healing and release. When I have felt stuck, lost, or sad and opened up to feel these feelings in the body, allowing the emotions to move through me, I may cry, it may be profoundly uncomfortable, but I do not usually feel stuck for very long.

Psychologist Bessel Van der Kolk writes about the absolute necessity of incorporating body-based practices in the process of healing from trauma. Because the site of trauma is often the body itself, healing requires a loving return to "the scene of the crime." "In order to change, people need to become aware of their sensations and the way that their bodies interact with the world around them," he writes.

"Physical self-awareness is the first step in releasing the tyranny of the past."[14]

The body has deep wisdom, and our ability to process pain and confusion depends upon us being able to drop into the physical, energetic movements outside of the thinking mind. Meditation helps the body to access this wisdom by clearing away the top levels of chattering thoughts and allowing truth to emerge.

When our mind becomes quiet—when we hook into the depth of this moment and practice just being with our breath—a miraculous thing begins to happen. We start to notice the pattern of our thoughts without getting too attached to them. We start to hear with remarkable clarity the many voices in our head—voices of parents, of society, of the stories we have invented. We also make room for insights and truths to speak to us from unconscious realms within us. This inner listening and discernment *is* the definition of wisdom, or *prajña* in Sanskrit.

This is easier said than done. In my midtwenties, I went on a meditation retreat in the middle of a very tumultuous time in my working life. I had spent the previous six months creating a business with a friend of mine into which we had poured our hearts and our energy. Although the business was thriving, our friendship had been slowly com-

14. Bessel Van der Kolk, *The Body Keeps the Score: Brain, Mind, and Body in the Healing of Trauma* (New York: Viking, 2014), 101.

ing apart, with most of our interactions ending either in screaming fights or icy silences. I felt angry, dejected, and sick to my stomach.

Worst of all, I simply could not figure out what to do. I did not want to leave the business after giving so much time, money, and energy to it. I didn't want to live in tension with my friend. But try as we might, we could not reconcile our differences. I felt completely stuck.

When I sat down in meditation on the first few days of the retreat, I could feel the magnetic attraction of my work problems consuming my thoughts and not letting me go. I tried to follow the practice, returning my attention over and over again to my breath, pulling my thoughts out of the confused, addictive mess of what to do. I remember my mind telling me, *If you just think about this a little longer, you will solve it! Just a little longer!* Of course, each time I gave in, trying to decide what to do, trying to figure out who was to blame, nothing emerged except more agitation and suffering.

On one of the last days of the retreat, after a week of repeatedly getting caught up in thoughts and then repeatedly returning to my breath, suddenly my thinking mind surrendered. Exhausted, it let go. Out of nowhere, I heard an internal voice. It was a different voice than the endless, confused machinations of the mind I had been struggling with. It said quietly, with clarity: *You have to go.* As soon as those words had the chance to break through, I burst into tears. That was it. With four words, what I knew to be true, but didn't want to face, came to the surface. My friendship was broken. I needed to leave the business. The decision was made and all that was left was the grieving.

Nearly all the major insights I have had in my life have come from that place deep inside. Rarely have they ever come from "thinking things through." Perhaps you have noticed this in your life—times when your mind stopped fixating on a problem and an answer came to you from a different place. This is the nature of our mind's inner wisdom, and meditation is the fertile ground that enables it to emerge.

Compassion

Buddhist teachings describe awakening as composed of wisdom (*prajña*) and compassion (*karuna*). These two mind states are cultivated by deep and regular meditation practice. They are likened to the two wings of a bird, which enable it to fly. Compassion is the heart-opening feeling that occurs when we witness the ways we are interconnected with every being and thing in the world. Different from pity, which assumes we are better than the other person, compassion (when coupled with wisdom) sees the ways our liberation is bound up with the liberation of others.

At the end of meditation sessions, I often notice a desire to smile at people on the street and avoid killing bugs. The more I meditate, the more I feel motivated to fight for justice and to treat people nicely. Meditation cracks my heart wide open and softens me towards others. It is not something I logically think through. It feels more like a chemical response—a rush of love—that bypasses my defenses and tenderizes me for a period of time.

Interestingly, recent research supports this claim. A 2013 study from Harvard and Northeastern measured the results of eight weeks of meditation on compassionate behavior.[15] Researchers invited each member of the meditation group and the control group, one at a time, into a waiting room with two actors and an empty chair. They then hired a third actor to enter the room on crutches, appearing to be in great physical pain. The two seated actors had been told to ignore the person on crutches and to look at their phones or pretend to be reading a book. The researchers wanted to see if the study's participants would intervene and help the person on crutches, even if the others in the room were not doing so. Among the non-meditators, 15 percent of participants offered to help, while among the meditators, 50 percent did. The study suggests what meditation practitioners have felt for a long time: meditation opens the heart, builds

15. Paul Condon et al. "Meditation Increases Compassionate Responses to Suffering," *Psychological Science* 24, no. 10 (2013): 2125– 27.

compassion, and has the potential to inspire loving action which fosters positive change.

HINDRANCES: WHEN THE GOING GETS TOUGH

Meditation never came easily to me. I tried the practice for the first time when I was fifteen years old. There was a school assembly program about stress, and all of the students were encouraged to lie down on the hard gymnasium floor while someone led us in a relaxing body scan. At least that is what I heard later. I fell asleep approximately two minutes after lying down and woke up to the sound of the bell that ended the meditation. I enjoyed the nap but left the assembly believing I was a failure at meditating. I didn't try again for the next five years.

During and after my first meditation retreat, I continued to struggle with meditation. The teachers on the retreat told us to pay attention to our breath, and when our mind wandered, to gently bring it back. To me, "gently" consisted of hacking with a knife at each thought in my imagination every time I realized my attention had drifted away. I could not stay focused. It was painfully boring. I kept falling asleep. Between all the violent stabbing away at my thoughts and all of the effort it took to keep myself awake, I became discouraged. I constantly felt like a failure, which then made me want to give up. I liked the way I felt after meditating—calm, open, relaxed—but the process of "getting there" was so aggressive and forceful, I could not keep up the practice.

It was only much later that I came to understand that meditation is not about "getting" anywhere. It is about being with what is. If I am calm, I can be with the calmness. If I am angry or sad, I can be with the anger or sadness in my body and mind without getting lost in the story of what made me so. The practice of meditation certainly takes effort, but it shouldn't be a brawl between me and my mind. The Buddha described it as the process of playing a string instrument. If the strings are too tight, they snap and break. If too loose, they cannot be played properly. The balance between discipline and gentleness is what makes the music.

When we first sit down to practice meditation, most of us are greeted by certain "friends." The Buddha called these "hindrances." The hindrances are barriers—patterns of thought and/or energy that can be very unsettling and disappointing if we don't know what we are encountering. Once we name and understand them, however, they, like all thoughts and energy patterns, simply arise and fall away. Like weather patterns, we don't have to resist or fight them, and we don't have to think they are ruining our meditation. Noticing a hindrance and working with it *is* meditation.

There are five "classical," common hindrances to meditation (and daily life): grasping, aversion, restlessness, sleepiness, and doubt. In addition to those, I have noticed a "bonus" hindrance in myself and my students: boredom.

Grasping/Clinging

We have already seen grasping in a larger sense in the three marks of existence. As a hindrance to meditation, grasping is the mind's attempt to reach for things outside the present moment that will make what is happening right now more pleasurable. The grasping mind takes a look around and sees the potential for MORE! and BETTER! It is important to note that the desire at the root of grasping can be a beautiful and important thing (more on that later). The trouble with grasping is that it leads to suffering, narrowing our minds and hearts around an outcome that we cannot control and that we believe we need to control in order to be okay. At the root of grasping is the idea that the present moment is not enough.

Zen teacher Teah Strozer says that most people "major" in one hindrance over the others. It is the one they come back to most often when meditations get long or our mind itches for an escape. In my case, it is grasping. On one retreat, I changed the location of my cushion six times in two days when my grasping mind convinced me that the meditation would be so much more effective if I moved spots. During other meditations, I have spent hours and sometimes *days* avoiding paying attention to my breath and the present moment as my mind obsessed over a new crush or how I would decorate my apartment when I got home.

There are two ways of working with grasping when it arises. The first is to make the grasping itself the object of the meditation. What does grasping feel like? How do we know we are grasping? What are the sensations involved?

At one meditation retreat I attended, the teachers had a practice of, on the last day, allowing several people to share about their retreat experiences in front of the whole group. I had been attending this same retreat for several years and had never shared, so I decided that this year I would try. Of course, as soon as I decided I would do that, each meditation session was filled with my grasping mind planning every detail of what I would say, imagining people laughing at my jokes, being moved to tears by my poignant remarks, and generally falling in love with me. I kept trying to return to my breath, but the power of the fantasy was so intense, it was proving to be a very strong hindrance to me.

Finally, rather than fighting the grasping mind spinning these beautiful stories about how I was going to deliver the World's Best Post-Meditation Sharing, I decided I would try and notice what it felt like when mind escaped into the fantasy. I noticed that I was lonely in the meditation, and that my fantasy included a loving audience with whom I could connect. I noticed how strongly I wanted to see people's eyes on me—my lifelong wish for attention—which I felt mostly in my stomach and my heart area. Every time I noticed my mind slipping into the grasping, I tried to let go of the perfect final words and stay instead with that desire in my body. It was lucky that I did, because at the end of the week, the teachers were late in ending the retreat, and they decided to skip the sharing section. After all those hours crafting and perfecting my remarks, there was nowhere to share them! I was glad that I had begun to stay in the present with my experience rather than spending the entire week grasping at a fantasy.

In classical Buddhist teachings, the antidote to grasping is either visiting or visualizing a charnel ground where dead bodies are left to decompose. Why? Because remembering the truth that we all die—and remembering how unglamorous and icky it is when it happens—might help us cling less tightly to the fleeting wants that hinder our meditations. Can't get a crush out of your mind? Picturing their rotting flesh and decomposing bones might help. Feeling distracted by desires for tasty food or a perfectly decorated apartment? Remembering the grisly reality of the death we will all face might put things in perspective. The practice is meant to help us release the powerful hold our mind has over us when it *has* to have something.

A few years ago, a meditation center in New York City called the Interdependence Project sold T-shirts that said in big letters across the front: "This Body Will Be a Corpse." I remember feeling jarred when seeing it for the first time.

Dark! Intense! Such a downer! It stayed with me, floating around in my head like a refrain: *This Body Will Be a Corpse. This Body Will Be a Corpse.* You couldn't really argue with it. You couldn't fight it. My body and your body and every body that ever lives will be a corpse at some point. When I really remember this and let it soak in, I see the wisdom in the Buddha's suggestion to go to a charnel ground when we get caught up in lust and grasping. Whatever it is that we want cannot be taken with us, including our body and the bodies of others. All we have is what we have, right now.

One final suggestion for working with grasping in meditation is to balance the object of grasping against the larger truth. If the grasping is for something that is harmful to you (cigarettes, alcohol, sugar, an ex-partner), it sometimes helps to see the fantasy all the way through. Imagine eating the sweet and then feeling sick afterward. Imagine drinking to the point of being sick. Imagine calling your ex, having a rush of happiness when you connect, and then feeling lonely, sad, and angry afterward. Try to play the whole scenario out, all the way to the end, and then see if the grasping has the same force in your body as it did before. It can be scary to allow ourselves to feel the full force of our desires, but pledging to look honestly at the results of that desire can sometimes ease us out of a period of obsession or clinging.

Aversion

Aversion is the flip side of grasping. Aversion is the desire to push away an experience in favor of an easier, more pleasant or comfortable one. Aversion says "no" to life. It causes us to tighten up and constrict as we reject the pain or difficulty of what is happening to us in meditation, as well as in daily life. It can make us feel like the circumstances for the meditation are wrong, or that someone or something is "ruining" the moment for us.

Working with aversion is similar to working with desire. The more we become aware of it and we drop into its sensations in the body, the less of a hold it has over us. Where does aversion live? What happens in the face, in the chest, or in the belly when we are locked in aversion and resistance? We can bring our attention and breath to these constrictions, rather than to the object of our mind or the environment that's triggering the aversive response. We open to the fullness of our aversion so that we may truly understand it, instead of trying to get rid of it or believing the stories it tells us.

Another way of working with aversion is to send love and well wishes to ourselves and others. On one long meditation retreat, I was seated next to someone who sniffled. Sniffling doesn't sound like a terrible crime, but in the silent hall, when I was struggling to concentrate, her sniffling soon became a thorn in my side that kept me from relaxing. Every time I brought my body to ease, every time I settled into a pattern of following my breath, without fail, I would hear (what sounded to me) like an ear-piercing, mucus-filled sniffle. Unlike the soothing rhythm of the heater turning on and off at regular intervals in the meditation hall, it was impossible to predict when the next sniffle would arrive to assault me. I had no way to protect or prepare myself. I began to gently nudge a box of tissues in her direction, hoping she would take the hint. Alas, nothing. I started sighing loudly after each sniffle, shifting my position or staring icily at my new antagonist, "Sniffles." At one point it took all my energy of restraint not to jump up and yell in Sniffles' face, "BLOW YOUR NOSE!" I was very deep in aversion.

When I realized this, I tried to send compassion to Sniffles, to wish her well, but I felt too agitated, too wound up in my own suffering. I had saved up my earnings for several months and taken several of my vacation days to attend this meditation retreat and Sniffles was *ruining it*! I was angry at her, and angry at myself for being so petty and judgmental. Once again, I began "stacking aversions on aversions."

In order to break the cycle, during one meditation period, I held my hands on my chest, where I could feel the anger boiling inside me, and said to myself, *Poor baby, poor sweetheart. This is really difficult. You are feeling really judgmental, upset, and irritated. This is really hard. May you feel at ease. May you feel peace. May you feel joy.* I repeated these lines over and over again throughout the session. I could feel some of the tightness in my body relax. I could feel myself breathe a little easier. Interestingly, toward the end of the retreat, when I had already stopped doing this practice, when I had somehow managed to absorb the reality of Sniffles into my meditation sessions, I looked over at Sniffles on our way to lunch and a feeling of compassion swept over me. Why was she sniffling so much? A cold? Allergies? A lot of crying? "I hope Sniffles is okay," I thought to myself. And to my shock, I really meant it.

Did I stop finding people annoying after this day? No. I still find people annoying all the time. In that moment, however, through the practice, I was able to find room to empathize and soften toward someone who had previously been the bane of my existence.

In the Buddha's day, he would send his monks to secluded locations in the forest in order to meditate. The monks would complain[16] about the dangers in the forest, the damp and uncomfortable conditions, the cold and the hunger. They were in deep aversion as they faced the prospect of their forest retreat. The Buddha instructed the monks to send out *metta*, or *loving-kindness*, to the world. I assume that the monks included themselves in those well

16. Acharya Buddharakkhita, "Metta: The Philosophy and Practice of Universal Love" on Access to Insight, accessed June 20, 2017 (2. The Background to the Metta Sutta), http://www.accesstoinsight.org/lib/authors/buddharakkhita/wheel365.html.

wishes. Something about bringing love and compassion to our experience, even when we are in a fog of judgment and aversion, even when we don't think we deserve it, releases the aversion and softens our hearts. From this soft place, we can be compassionate and loving to others—even those who are driving us crazy.

Try this out for yourself the next time you find yourself facing aversive thoughts, either about yourself or others. If you feel like a failure, if you feel like the person next to you is breathing *too loudly*, if you find yourself filled with fear, anger, or hate, just take a breath, and see if you can wish love and ease to yourself. *Poor baby,* you can say to yourself, *poor sweetheart. You are feeling really judgmental and upset and irritated. This is really hard. May you feel at ease. May you feel peace. May you feel joy.* Even if it is forced at first, try to keep going, repeating wishes of love and ease, over and over again. See if the nature of your experience changes.

Restlessness

Restlessness is the feeling of excess energy in the body and mind, making formal sitting meditation extremely difficult. Restlessness often has less of a storyline than grasping or aversion. It simply says: Go! Run! Move! Leave! Our minds can feel like a very small room with the bouncy balls of our thoughts ricocheting off each wall at crazy speeds. A friend of mine, meditation teacher James Jacobson Maisels, recounts how when he first started meditating, he felt so much restlessness he actually worried he might die if he didn't get up. I too have had sessions when the jumpy energy I felt was so extreme that I started sweating and shaking. My body wanted me to avoid the meditation at all costs.

Both James and I noticed that when we stuck through the meditation, taking deep breaths to expand our awareness *around* and *through* the restlessness, insight and the underlying emotion had the chance to break through.

Indeed, the antidote to restlessness is allowing the bouncy balls of our thoughts much more room to move around in our body. Rather than a laser-like focus on your breath as an anchor, allow your attention to expand, using the whole body as an anchor, or using the sounds in the room as an anchor instead. Breathe deeply and expansively to settle the mind and body. Invite and allow each muscle to relax. Do not try to stop the thoughts—just keep imagining them bouncing around in a larger, more spacious environment. You will not die of restlessness, and it will pass in time. Just keep breathing!

Sleepiness

College students have a serious problem with sleep. According to one study, approximately 50 percent report daytime sleepiness and 70 percent are not getting enough sleep. This has been shown to negatively impact learning, memory, and performance, and to increase depression and mood disorders.[17] The picture does not necessarily improve when we graduate. Approximately fifty to seventy million adults in the US suffer from a sleep disorder, causing the Centers for Disease Control and Prevention (CDC) to call sleep deprivation "a public health problem."[18] If you are repeatedly feeling sleepy during meditation, it is very possible you might be sleep deprived, and might actually need to take a nap. Your meditation practice will benefit over the long run, as will the other parts of your life, if you try to get between seven and eight hours of sleep per night.

If you have slept plenty of hours, however, and you are still facing sleepiness when you meditate, you are probably encountering the hindrance of sleepiness (also called *sloth* or *torpor*). Sometimes this manifests as "conking out" during meditation and sometimes it can just feel like a dense fog or a dreamlike state that settles over the mind, even if you are not actually sleeping.

Sleepiness is a stagnation or slowdown of energy that doesn't allow our mind to be clear or perceptive during meditation. Like the other hindrances, we can make sleepiness the object of meditation when it arises, becoming

17. S. D. Hershner and R. D. Chervin, "Causes and Consequences of Sleepiness among College Students." *Nature and Science of Sleep* 6 (2014): 73–84.
18. "Insufficient Sleep is a Public Health Problem," Centers for Disease Control and Prevention, accessed April 25, 2017, https://www.cdc .gov/features/dssleep/.

extremely curious about the texture of sleepiness feeling its sensations in the eyes, the breath, and the body. Sharpening our attention can help to focus our mind and not allow it to drift into dreamland. Opening the eyes (with a soft gaze) can be helpful if we are sleepy, and standing up can help prevent us from nodding off. You may notice meditating at certain times of the day makes you less prone to dream-like sessions. For me, any meditations after lunch are guaranteed to be very drowsy. If I am headed into a meditation at this time, I try to do several jumping jacks, move my arms around, and stretch my body beforehand in order to bring some fresh energy to the meditation.

Sometimes sleepiness is persistent when meditating because our mind is trying to protect us from something painful in our life that is living right underneath the surface of the conscious mind. This was the case with one of my students on a retreat who, try as she might, simply could not stay awake through a meditation session. She tried paying attention to the sleepiness, she tried moving around beforehand, she even tried standing up. Almost as soon as she started each session, her mind would go "fuzzy" and she would begin to come in and out of a dream-like state. By the third day of this persistent sleepiness, I encouraged her in the next session to gently ask herself what might be underneath the sleepiness? What might her body be trying to protect her from? I suggested she listen for the answer, without rushing to try and fill it in.

She reported to me that when she tried this, gently asking herself this question several times, the sleepiness cracked open and she faced an ocean of sadness and grief. Breaking down in tears, she realized that she had never processed her parents' divorce that had happened several years earlier, instead "sucking up" her feelings to appear supportive to her parents and siblings. Touching the pain and the sadness allowed her to begin a healing process which, while difficult, was much less painful and destructive than repressing those feelings into ever-increasing hours of sleep and numbness.

Sleepiness can feel like a sweet escape from our lives. There is a reason, however, that enlightenment is often referred to as "waking up." We must wake up in our lives if we are going to be fully whole. We have to courageously and gently peer beneath the desire to fade away into dreams and unconsciousness—and wake up, over and over again, to life.

Doubt

Doubt weakens our resolve to keep practicing. Often masquerading as "truth," it can derail our original intention to meditate by causing us to get lost in a spiral of blame and questioning. Doubt, like some of the other hindrances, is composed of thoughts, but doubts are particularly sticky and pervasive ones. We may feel confused and lost when doubt visits us in meditation.

Of course, having doubt is not necessarily a bad thing. Doubt can help us to discern scams, phonies, and charlatans. In college, we learn to sharpen our critical minds and to question everything. We should not suspend this questioning and blindly follow anyone who wants to teach us meditation. In fact, the Buddha famously said not to believe him on word alone, but instead to practice and see for ourselves what happens. A Zen saying goes even further, warning that if we meet the Buddha in the road, we should kill him. Any time we begin to deify or revere someone (or something) without personally experiencing it to be true, there is a problem.

Yet if we are lost in doubt, it can be hard to continue our practice at all. Doubt sometimes has a way of crowding the field, taking up all the space and stopping us from trying something new, difficult, and scary, in an attempt to protect us. The antidote to doubt in these situations is faith. Sharon Salzberg defines faith as "the willing suspension of disbelief."[19] If we are normally skeptical or critical, this definition does not ask us to cross the long bridge to believing. It just asks us to suspend disbelief long enough to keep practicing. Faith is the ability to open up the mind and heart and step out into the unknown in order to see what happens. It is remembering what brought us to meditation in the first

19. Sharon Salzberg, "Faith," SharonSalzberg.com, January 29, 2015, accessed April 13, 2017, http://www.sharonsalzberg.com/faith-2/.

place, and trusting the voice inside that urged us to explore this practice.

Perhaps the most beautiful story of doubt and faith is that of the Buddha himself. The Buddha, a historical prince named Siddhartha Gautama, left his home and palace at the age of twenty-nine, seeking a path to the permanent alleviation of suffering. After much wandering and many failed attempts to relieve the suffering within, the Buddha decided that he would simply sit down under a tree and not move until he woke up from all suffering. He had many insights and saw many truths while sitting. In the middle of the night, on his last day of sitting, Mara, a demon-like being, visited him and tried to disturb the Buddha's awakening.

Mara launched all kinds of attacks at the Buddha, trying to tempt him with sex or scare him by shooting hundreds of arrows at him. Nothing worked. Finally, Mara assailed Buddha with words of self-doubt that are stunningly familiar to anyone who has ever taken a risk or done something out of their comfort zone. "Who do you think you are to wake up?" Mara asked. "Many have tried to do this before you who have worked much harder than you. Who are *you* to succeed?"

The Buddha raised one finger and touched the earth in front of him. He called upon the earth and all its creatures to serve as his witness that he deserved to live a life free from suffering. With this gesture, it is as if he said, "I deserve this because I'm here, because I'm alive." If we feel consumed with self-doubt as we meditate, we can remember the Buddha's example. We deserve to be happy. We deserve to live a good life simply because we are here.

A Bonus: Boredom

Many of my students ask me about boredom as a hindrance. Although not a classical hindrance, boredom is extremely common when starting to meditate. After all, nothing is happening! In our hyper-wired, hyper-connected, nonstop world, boredom tells us to change the channel, check the phone, and reach for the next distraction. Consciously choosing to sit inside the boredom can be extremely uncomfortable at first.

If you investigate boredom like you do the more classical hindrances, however, some interesting things come to light. First of all, what actually is the sensation of being bored? The dictionary describes it as "feeling weary and impatient because one is unoccupied or lacks interest in one's current activity."[20] When I am bored in meditation, however, the feeling is not exactly *weariness*. It feels more jumpy and active—perhaps a blend of aversion, doubt, and restlessness. The thoughts that accompany boredom are hot and itchy (*there is so much else you need to do right now, this is a waste of time*) as are the feelings in the body.

20. Oxford Dictionary, accessed June 1 2017, https://en.oxforddictio naries.com/definition/bored.

Psychologist Adam Phillips described boredom in children as essential for their development. He defines it as " a state of suspended anticipation in which things are started and nothing begins, the mood of diffuse restlessness which contains that most absurd and paradoxical wish, the wish for a desire."[21] Out of that "diffuse restlessness," new, previously unimagined discoveries and insights emerge. Phillips goes on to say that "boredom is the impossible experience of waiting for something without knowing what it could be."[22]

If we understand boredom less as something to be feared and more as this essential pause in the action before a transformation, perhaps we can find the space to relax into it. When our mind shouts at us, "nothing is happening!" we can breathe, recognize that we are bored, and settle into the discomfort of waiting for our own life to emerge out of the mystery.

21. Adam Phillips, *On Kissing, Tickling, and Being Bored: Psychoanalytic Essays on the Examined Life* (Cambridge: Harvard University Press, 1998).
22. Ibid.

3: MINDFULNESS IN-BETWEEN

THERE IS a Zen story about a young girl who is running from a tiger and comes to the edge of a cliff. The tiger is in hot pursuit, but the girl looks down at the sheer drop-off and isn't sure what to do. Luckily, she notices that there is a vine hanging off the cliff that she can climb down to avoid the tiger. She scurries down the vine just as the tiger makes it to the edge of the cliff, roaring ferociously.

Suddenly, she sees several mice at the top of the cliff, gnawing away at the vine. She looks beneath her, at the immense distance she will fall. She looks above her at the tiger, perched at the edge of the cliff. She looks left and sees nothing but more cliff. She looks right, and sees a strawberry plant extending off the rock face, with one big, ripe strawberry. She picks the strawberry. She tastes the strawberry. She says, "So sweet."

The story ends there.

Whenever I tell this story to my students, they laugh at the abrupt, unatisfactory ending. How does the girl save herself? What becomes of her? The story is not meant to wrap up with a neat ending, however. It's meant to capture something about our own daily experience. How often do we feel like the girl in the story, as we race around from one stressful encounter to another? I have had many days where busyness, to-do lists, and planning have consumed so much of the day that I have lost touch with the actual experience of being alive. All of the tigers and cliffs and mice often cause me to miss the strawberry. ·

The strawberry, of course, is everything. Although in the story, in logical terms, the strawberry can't save the girl's life, the pause she takes from her stress and fear to taste it drops her into the richness and aliveness of her life. In this way, the vibrancy of her life is saved.

We can do the same thing. We can bring color and life back into our lives when they grow grey and alienated by bringing mindfulness, awareness, and attention to everything we do, as we do it.

I have notes stuck around my computer at work. They say things like, "Just This," "Breathe," and, "Right Here, Right Now." They are the visual cues I use to bring present-moment awareness into the craziness of everyday life. Some days it works wonderfully and I am able to take mindful minutes to breathe, center myself, and be present. Other days, when the phone is ringing, I am hundreds of emails behind, and I have a long list of meetings and deadlines looming, being present can get lost in the chaos. That is why I find that sitting meditation and daily mindfulness must go together. Without a regular practice of sitting meditation, it is too easy to get swept up in the current of our nonstop, crazy lives. We need a regular meditation practice to help our body and mind remember to climb out of the rushing river of our thoughts and return to what is happening in the *now*.

On the other hand, if we only care about our time spent "on the cushion," we may find the rest of our life just as confusing, alienating, unsatisfactory, and stressful as we did before we started meditating. We may end up using meditation as an escape from everyday life, rather than a heart-opening practice that helps us infuse our everyday life with clarity and meaning.

Ultimately, living a mindful life means paying attention all day, every day. When I first understood that, I felt baffled. *How?* When would I do my thinking? How would I work out the problems that occupied my mind all day long? I started by trying it out on a retreat. Between sessions, when my mind was on its usual treadmill of thoughts, I tried bringing my attention to the present moment—to my feet on the ground as they walked, my body in the shower as the water hit it, or the taste of food in my mouth during a meal.

I learned that I didn't need all of the "thinking time" I thought I did. My thoughts still operated well enough to get me to meals and meditations on time. I was able to figure out what I wanted from the dinner buffet. I was able to decide whether and when I would shower.

I also found that I didn't need my thinking mind to solve my larger problems for me or to help me understand my emotions. In fact, it became clear that my thinking mind is actually pretty terrible at those things, often sending me into looped, repetitive black holes. As I discussed earlier, most of the major problems and decisions in my life have been solved not by applying my mind to them, but by listening to a deeper truth within myself that emerges when it's ready.

Buddhist teacher Sharon Salzberg recommends practicing mindfulness by paying attention to: "Many moments, many times."[23] She recommends setting an alarm on our phone or computer, and taking a breath every time it rings as a way to focus your attention.

What does this book (or tablet) feel like in your hands right now? What are the physical sensations, textures, and temperatures of the book against your hand? What shape are your hands in as you hold the book? How is your body positioned as you read? What are your feet doing? What does the air feel like? What sounds are in the room around you? It is nearly impossible to be lost in anxious thoughts and to-do lists when dropping into our sensations, even if for a short time. Doing so helps us to experience our life

23. Sharon Salzberg, "Faith."

more directly, rather than living all of our time in thoughts *about* our lives.

In this way of practicing, there is no break at all from paying attention. In his outstanding book, *This Is Real and You Are Completely Unprepared*, Rabbi Alan Lew writes about the difference between looking through a window at the outside world, and turning the gaze to look at the window itself—the glass, the *schmutz* on the glass, the screen, etc.[24] For most of our lives we are looking through the window of our minds at the world. Living a mindful life means examining the mechanisms of the mind and the heart themselves. How does this machine work? How are emotions processed? What does it feel like to be alive right now? And what about now?

There is so much to notice when we try to be mindful in between sitting meditations. Walking, laughing with friends, texting, drinking, dancing, sitting in traffic, getting dressed, falling in love—our whole life happens in the in-between. The next few sections examine mindfulness in three "in-between" activities where most of us spend a lot of time: walking, eating, and using technology.

24. Alan Lew, *This Is Real and You Are Completely Unprepared: The Days of Awe as a Journey of Transformation* (Boston: Little, Brown and Co., 2009).

MINDFUL WALKING

I have lived in New York City for a long time. In New York City, walking is *intense.* People rarely stroll. Everyone has places to go, urgent appointments for which they are late, people they have to meet, and things that had to get done yesterday. New Yorkers pride themselves on walking extremely fast and knowing the absolute quickest way to get from point A to point B.

Walking meditation is pretty much the exact opposite of that. In walking meditation, it does not matter where you go and it does not matter how fast you get there. In fact, many people intentionally slow down their walking during this practice so that they can feel the muscles of their legs and body move as they walk, so they can be aware of their breathing or their surroundings. The point of walking meditation is to bring all of your attention to the walking itself. This can mean paying focused attention to every feeling your foot encounters as it contacts the floor, or it can mean opening up your awareness to the feeling of your entire body moving through space as you walk. It is being right here, right now, in motion.

In the Soto Zen tradition, in which I practiced meditation for many years, formal walking meditation is done in a circle inside the meditation hall. For ten-minute sessions between sitting meditation, each person tries to be completely present with each of their steps while slowly making their way around the hall. New Yorker that I am, walking meditation was often an infuriating practice for me. I always seemed to get caught behind a person moving at the speed of molasses. My mind would fill with judgments about this person. *What is wrong with them?* I would wonder at my walking enemy of the day. *Why can't they see that there is a huge gap of space in front of them and hurry up?* My frustration was comical, given that there was literally no place to go and no hurry to get there. We were walking in a *circle!*

It makes sense that aimless, destination-less walking has been hard for me. From my first year in school to every single year after, I was told that I must work hard and prepare for the following year, which would be *much* harder. Once I left elementary school, I had to work toward middle school, middle school to high school, high school to college. We were taught to always be forward thinking, always going somewhere, always on the move. I once heard Dan Siegel, neuroscientist and meditator, give a talk in which he commented on this phenomenon, saying: "We are all trying to get into the best colleges, to go to the best graduate schools, to get the greatest jobs, to make the most money, to buy the biggest houses, to get the best plots of the cemetery!" All of this striving is not about fulfillment or joy or meaning. It is about endless ambition, acquisition, and activity.

Walking meditation takes a monkey wrench to these values. It doesn't matter where we are going, or what the next step is. Our job is to be with this step. And then this one. Walking is no longer a boring, cumbersome way to transport our body to where "life" happens. Paying attention to walking—to our bodies and to the moment—*is* life.

Mindful walking takes formal walking meditation and moves it out to the "real world." What would it feel like to pay attention to the walk from our front door to our car/train/bus? How does it feel to be aware of my body and my feet when standing in line? How might life open up for me if I was actually present and aware during the multiple daily journeys from here to there? We feel the body shifting and stepping. We feel the wind against our face. We hear people talking, birds chirping. We smell flowers or barbeque or the nearest bakery. Yes, there is often a destination in this practice, but we do not zone out until we get there. Each step matters. Each step offers the chance to wake up and pay attention.

The best teachers of this practice are small children and pets. Walks for them are filled with so much wonder and joy that it is really hard not to absorb some of it. Taking what should have been a five-minute walk around the block with my former six-year-old babysitting charge would sometimes take twenty to thirty minutes as he stopped, stared, and wondered about so much that seemed mundane to my eyes. A fire truck! A squirrel! A man in a hat! Mindfulness is about recapturing and reseeing the magic in everyday life as a child or a pet does.

For most of us, it is rare to experience the world in this way when we're in our twenties and thirties. We have so much going on, it is hard to pay attention to the beauty and awe of everyday life. Of course there are always times, perhaps in nature or on a particularly beautiful night, when beauty hits us out of nowhere, and we are stunned and ecstatic. But those instances can be few and far between in adult life.

There is a saying that enlightenment is an accident, but meditation makes us more accident-prone. Mindful walking helps exercise our muscle of being present in the world during one of the most banal, overlooked times of our lives: moving from one place to the next.

MINDFUL EATING

Mindful eating is the practice of bringing all of our attention and awareness to the experience of consuming food and drink. This can begin before we take the first bite, noticing the smell, the feeling of hunger and anticipation in our belly, the awareness of how the food came to us, the feeling in our hand as we lift a mouthful from the plate, the way the food looks, etc. It continues through the first bite and sip until we finish, satiated.

Mark Epstein tells a story in his book *The Trauma of Everyday Life* of being on a long meditation retreat and craving fresh bread. One day, he wakes up and there is

freshly baked bread in the dining hall! He is delighted. He
quickly grabs a few pieces, butters them and brings them to
his seat. He very mindfully takes a bite, relishing it, savor-
ing it. He then writes:

> I have only a vague recollection of what happened
> next. I believe my mind wandered to the laundry
> I had to do the next morning. . . . The next thing I
> remember was that my toast was gone. "Who ate
> my toast?" my mind cried as I stared at my empty
> plate. And for a brief second, before the humor
> of the situation could take hold, the whole thing
> became a metaphor for my entire life. I was staring
> into a big, empty, devouring hole, where my toast,
> and my life, used to be.[25]

Mindful eating is a particularly rich practice, allowing
us to literally and figuratively experience the flavor and
nourishment of our lives by bringing as much awareness as
possible into each bite and swallow. Eating while distracted,
like doing *anything* while distracted, forecloses the opportunity to sink our teeth into the juiciness of this world.

The very act of paying attention to what we eat as we eat
it, often cracks open for us the myriad meanings we assign

25. Mark Epstein, *The Trauma of Everyday Life* (New York: Penguin
Books, 2014).

to food. Sometimes this can be intensely pleasurable. After partaking in an eating meditation with a tangerine, one of my students was so enraptured with her tangerine, so intoxicated with its textures, smells, and tastes, she ate the entire peel—and loved it! For some, however, practicing eating meditation can be very uncomfortable. So many of us have complicated relationships with food, whether in connection to our body image, our sense of security, or as a buffer against feelings we do not want to feel.

When I first started practicing eating meditation, I immediately noticed the anxiety that accompanied the early part of every meal. Previously, I would try to read or chat with someone through the meal to lessen my feeling of anxiety. Without these distractions, I noticed that the anxiety would often be about getting enough food. "Are you sure this will satiate you?" a voice would say. "Hurry up and eat . . . it may not last." Although I never went hungry as a child, I now realize that my parents' fears about food (and other types of) scarcity from their childhood were transmitted to me. I think that I forfeited the joy of tasting and enjoying many meals to avoid the lurking anxiety of a generations-old fear.

Eating meditation has also unearthed other feelings that I tend to eat, rather than feel. I have eaten loneliness, grief, fear, and longing. Going to the refrigerator or the cabinet in a daze, I have scarfed down food without tasting it, stuffing my belly so that no emotion had the space to fit.

Slowing down while eating makes it much harder to outrun feelings. I am there, in the moment, with my food and my heart. Somehow, the moments of biting, chewing, and swallowing bring me face to face with my emotional state even more intensely than sitting meditation. On one meditation retreat, I noted in my journal: "I cried for an hour this morning into my kale. I don't think it was about the kale."

Eating meditation also brings us face-to-face with the sometimes-uncomfortable reality of where our food comes from and how it is produced. Sadly, so much of our food in the US is made on massive corporate farms, poisoning the earth with pesticides. Most of the produce is picked, collected, and packaged by laborers who are often exploited. Our fisheries are depleted, our wild fish is filled with mercury, and animals are treated inhumanely on factory farms all across the country. Additionally, according to the Worldwatch Institute, 51 percent of all greenhouse gas emissions are caused by animal agriculture.[26]

Slowing down with food forces us to come to terms with these realities. It asks us to realize our interconnection with all beings that we eat, all beings that plant, harvest, prepare, and package our food, and the state of the soil and climate.

---

26. Jeff Anhang and Robert Goodland, "Livestock and Climate Change," Worldwatch Institute, accessed April 13, 2017, http://www .worldwatch.org/node/6294.

Opening our mouths, we also open our hearts to all parts of the process; it is all in each bite.

I have had many students for whom the experience of eating is triggering. Many of them are away from home for the first time without a kitchen, cooking know-how, or time to resist the unhealthy options at the local dining hall. Others find themselves gaining or losing weight at unhealthy levels in an attempt to control or bury their feelings about this tumultuous time in their lives. According to one large study in 2013, 32.6 percent of college females and 25 percent of college males develop an eating disorder while at school.[27] Developing a healthy relationship with food is often a life-long journey. For many of us, that journey is best undertaken with the help of therapists and nutritionists. Eating meditation can be a wonderful practice, however, allowing us to come back home to ourselves during this daily activity. Eating in this way can remind us of the preciousness of food as fuel for our bodies and minds, and allow us to take some time each day to truly "taste" our life.

27. National Eating Disorders Association, "Eating Disorders on the College Campus: A National Survey of Programs and Resources," National Eating Disorders Association, February 2013. https://www .nationaleatingdisorders.org//sites/default/files/CollegeSurvey/Colle giateSurveyProject.pdf.

MINDFULNESS AND TECHNOLOGY

If you are a millennial between the ages of eighteen and thirty six, you probably spend an average of eighteen hours a day consuming media, with approximately five hours of that time engaged in social media and peer-created content.[28] Those hours are consumed across a variety of platforms and may include simultaneous consumption of media. For example, if you spend two hours per day on Facebook, three hours texting, and an hour watching television, that adds up to six total hours, even though it may only translate to three or four "real" hours in your day, if you are doing some of those things at the same time. Media consumption includes texts, surfing the Internet, binge-watching Netflix and playing games on your phone. I reach for my phone at nearly every pause in my day, from the moment I wake up to the moment I fall asleep. Our phones are extensions of ourselves, connectors to others, portals to the world, and addictive tools. If we are going to take our goal of living a mindful life seriously, we have to consider our very intimate, ubiquitous relationship with our devices.

The key to mindful living "off the cushion" is building in a pause to check in with our intention, our body, and our

28. Kate Taylor, "Millenials Spend 18 Hours a Day Consuming Media," Entrepreneur.com, March 10, 2014, accessed May 9, 2017, https://www.entrepreneur.com/article/232062.

heart before we reach for our favorite distractions. Nowhere is this more palpable and powerful than in our relationships to our devices. When do you reach for your phone? When do you click on social media sites? How do you feel right before heading to your page on the site? What happens in your mind while scrolling or posting? How do you feel afterward?

For me, that initial reach toward my phone usually comes when there is any type of pause in the action. Aside from just being addicted to stimulation, some part of me suspects there might be loneliness, disconnection, and sadness waiting for me in the silence of phonelessness, and I am scared to face it.

The comedian Louis C.K. spoke profoundly about this on the Conan O'Brien show in 2014. When asked why he didn't let his young daughters have cell phones, Louis launched into a monologue about how cell phones are problematic buffers against feeling emotions. He explained:

> So I was in my car the other day . . . and I started to get that sad feeling and I started reaching for my phone and I said, "You know, just don't. Just be sad. Just stand in the way of it and let it hit you like a truck." And . . . I started to feel it and I was like, "Oh my god," and I pulled over and I just cried. Like a bitch. I cried so much. And it was beautiful! . . . And I had happy feelings because of it. Because

if you let yourself be sad, your body has antibodies; it has happiness that comes rushing in to meet the sadness. . . . And the thing is, because we don't want that first little bit of sad, we push it away for some little bit of phone jerk off or food and you never feel completely sad or completely happy. You just feel kinda satisfied with your products. And then you die.[29]

It is very hard to do what Louis did—to allow the emotions to "hit us like a truck" rather than distracting ourselves. For a long period of my life, I kept the Jewish Sabbath, which meant I didn't go on my phone or check email from sundown on Friday night until sundown on Saturday night. Even though it was hard to do, I loved the peace and relaxation that came from being apart from the craziness of my virtual life for those twenty-four hours. And yet, as time went on, when the Sabbath would roll around and I would feel the familiar hints of loneliness or emptiness descend upon me, I would start my Sabbath a little later and break it a little earlier. Soon I began sneaking peeks at my phone during the day, to see if I had any texts. Before long, like the addict I was, I was back on full phone usage on the Sabbath. Did the phone usage make me happy? Yes,

29. Team Coco, "Louis C.K. Hates Cell Phones," 4:50, posted September 20, 2013. Accessed April 24, 2017, https://www.youtube.com/watch?v =5HbYScltf1c.

but only as a quick fix. Like eating candy when I was hungry for a meal, it never fully satisfied the deeper need. Yet I lost my ability to keep from checking it for one whole day.

A few years ago, there was an excellent segment on NPR called "Bored and Brilliant."[30] It was an attempt to help people take control over their relationship with their phone. The show issued a challenge to listeners: delete the app on your phone that you feel is your biggest time waster— whether it's a social media platform or a game—and see how it felt. I immediately knew what my addictive app was: Facebook. I scrolled through Facebook constantly—sometimes even in a lull in conversation with my friends or partner. It was so automatic, I often didn't realize I was doing it until I had been scrolling for at least ten minutes.

I decided to take the NPR challenge. I took a deep breath and deleted the Facebook application off of my phone.

At first, I felt free and happy, like I was standing up to a bully that had come to dominate my mind and my time. Pretty quickly afterward, however, when standing in line or lying in bed on a Sunday morning, I felt the nervous, addictive energy of wanting to check Facebook. What are my friends doing? What is the newest meme that everyone is laughing at? What is happening in the world? And

30. "Bored . . . And Brilliant? A Challenge to Disconnect from Your Phone," *All Things Considered*, January 15, 2015, accessed April 24, 2017, http://www.npr.org/sections/alltechconsidered/2015/01/12/376717870/bored-and-brilliant-a-challenge-to-disconnect-from-your-phone.

lurking just underneath that, there was a feeling of discomfort, loneliness, and antsy energy that led me to want to escape. I asked myself the question, "Will checking Facebook really make me feel better right now? Will it satisfy my desire to connect to others? Or will it actually make me feel worse?" Sometimes I still checked it. Sometimes I shook myself out of my addictive trance and just breathed instead. Sometimes I called a friend or went for a walk. The extra time it took me to sign in to the site forced an important pause between impulse and action, which helped me to feel less like an alienated automaton and more like a human being using an electronic device.

I never reinstalled my Facebook app, but I have had periods of time when I forget the lessons I learned from "Bored and Brilliant" and sign in to the Facebook site mindlessly on my phone, looking for a fix. I do notice that the more I practice mindfulness of technology (pausing, breathing, finding my intention before clicking) the better I get at noticing when I am attempting to escape. Like sitting meditation, the muscle of staying present slowly builds, requiring less time running away, clicking on links, flying away into the Internet.

The Endless Scroll

Once I open my time-wasting app of choice—perhaps with some mindfulness, perhaps on autopilot—I immediately begin to tumble down the rabbit hole of posts, tweets, photos, videos, and memes. After twenty minutes (or more) of scrolling along, I begin to realize that I am lost in a scroll-and-click universe where I have the capacity to ingest endless thoughts, photos, and virtual lives of friends and acquaintances, post my own, and wait for the "likes" to roll in.

I deeply understand the pull of social media. I find pleasure reading about the goings-on of friends and family who live far away, appreciate the notifications about events and interesting articles, and I like getting affirmation for my posts and photos. I am pretty certain, however, that I could obtain all of those pleasures in about one hour on the site per day, or less. What I do instead is spend *hours* of my life scrolling, getting lost in articles, comment conversations, and other people's photo albums. Like staring blankly at a television screen, the endless scroll allows my brain to zone out from my life and float away.

There is nothing inherently wrong with this zone out, but after a certain period of time, I notice that—like a junk food binge—I feel pretty sick. I feel alienated and lonely, exactly the opposite of the reason I signed on in the first place.

There is a Zen chant that includes the words:

"Life and death are of supreme importance.
Time swiftly passes by
and opportunity is lost . . .

Wake up! Wake up!
This night your days are diminished
    by one.
Do not squander your life."

Every time I chant this, I think of the hours and days I
have spent on social media. I think of the precious time I
have squandered *after* I have checked in on my friends and
loved ones, *after* I have checked my messages and invites,
and *after* reading any interesting articles. The time spent
endlessly scrolling. It makes me sad. It makes me want to be
more aware, and to wake up from the social media trance
and interact in real time again.

Comparing Mind

One of the other dangers of too much social media is
engaging in what Buddhists call "comparing mind." This
is exactly what it sounds like—comparing our lives, our
looks, our achievements, and even our meditation abilities
to others to see how we stack up. Everyone engages in comparing mind sometimes, but in the world of social media,
where people only publicize the rosy moments, the filtered
photos, and the happy news, it is particularly easy to think
we are the only ones having a hard time.

I remember one particular day of college when I made
the mistake of Googling a young woman with whom I was
planning a conference. Even though this woman was only

a few years older than me, I found hundreds of articles she had written, awards she had won, and other accomplishments staring back at me on the screen. Tears streamed down my face as I compared it to what happened when I typed in my own name: Nothing. Nada. No results whatsoever. *I am a nobody,* I remember thinking, my comparing mind in full force. *I will never be as accomplished as this woman. I will never amount to anything.* I carried around this dreary view of my own worth all day, long after I had shut down the computer.

Comparing mind starts from a place of insecurity. It rests on an assumption of deficit or lack (I'm not lovable, I'm not worthy) that then looks to the outside world to prove or disprove that flawed assumption. "If I am better looking than Lilly, I am good looking," the logic goes. "If I have achieved more than Jim, I am successful." The trouble with comparing mind is that, resting on that shaky foundation of insecurity, it is never satisfied. It never successfully answers the question of whether we are lovable or successful. Even if we come out "on top" in one particular comparison, there is *always* someone who seems to have more or be more than us.

Additionally, even if we were to be deemed *the* best looking, *the* most lovable, *the* most successful by others, when the affirmation comes exclusively from the outside world and is tied to our sense of self, we will suffer.

The "self" is always changing, and is completely interpenetrated with everything else in the universe. Its very nature is instability. When I recognize this, how can I take credit for the good things "I" do, since "I" am constantly being influenced by the people and landscapes around me? How can I compare myself to anyone else in the world when every force in their universe and every force in my universe came together in very different, yet interpenetrating ways?

"Self-ing," the project of continuing to try and reify a separate, permanent, unchanging self, is a delusional project that I find myself trapped in over and over again, and it is what lies at the heart of comparing mind. In many ways, it also lies at the heart of social media, where we are all continually branding ourselves, polishing our images, curating our lives and then comparing ourselves to the "brands" of others.

Sometimes, to break out of comparing mind while scrolling through social media, or just looking around the room at a party, I ask myself, "What if I am okay and enough right now? What if the only standard I have to live up to is my deepest, most authentic self?"

One of my favorite Jewish Hasidic stories is of a Rabbi named Zusha (not coincidentally the name of my son) on his deathbed. He was crying and distraught, and his students asked him why, reminding their teacher of all the wonderful deeds he had done over the course of his life. Rabbi Zusha replied, "I'm afraid that when I get to heaven, God will not ask me 'Why weren't you more like Abraham? Or why weren't you more like King David?' God will ask, 'Why weren't you more like Zusha?'"

Why wasn't I more like Yael? When I get lost in a sea of measurements and comparisons, I try and return back to that central question.

Wise Consumption

Lodro Rinzler talks about checking email and using devices the same way he describes drinking alcohol. Alcohol, like phones, email, or social media, is not inherently bad or good, he says.[31] It just is. And realistically, it is a part of many people's lives— especially those in their twenties and thirties. How we relate to both alcohol and technology is what matters. Do we consume these things in unhealthy amounts? Do we ingest them first thing in the morning or last thing at night, just before we close our eyes? Can we use these platforms without losing our awareness, giving ourselves time to process our emotions and feel our loneliness or our boredom? Can we limit our time wasted online? Can we resist the constant comparing of ourselves to others?

The first step in mindful technology consumption is to pause and recognize the power these devices have over us,

31. Lodro Rinzler, "How to Love Yourself (and Sometimes Other People)," teaching at New York University, New York, NY, December 7, 2015.

to check in with ourselves *before* we reach for them, and to build in pauses, breaks, and (emotional) rehab when it all becomes too automatic, too addictive, and too much.

The magic of mindfulness in the "in-between" moments of our life is that we don't need any special gear, quiet space or complex instructions to practice it. We can bring meditation to meet us wherever we are, whatever we are doing, right in the middle of our crazy lives. It takes some practice to *see* the strawberry hanging from the vine, let alone to taste it in these moments. And yet, that is exactly when the strawberry—the juice of our lives—is most needed. Real life is lived in the in-between. Now is our chance to meet it.

4: FEELING EMOTIONS, NOT BEING EMOTIONS

WHEN I FIRST learned to meditate, I was taught—like most new meditators are—to focus on the breath as an anchor in sitting meditation, the feet in walking meditation, and to return to that anchor over and over again, no matter what is going on in the chattering mind. This practice made sense to develop a baseline level of concentration and to climb my way out of my thoughts and into my embodied experience.

At some point fairly early on, however, as I tried to hone that concentration on the breath, my emotions would make a racket within me, like a toddler who was being ignored. I knew I was not supposed to pay attention to my thoughts, but what was I supposed to do with this tidal wave of sadness? This bubbling pot of anger? This burning fire of longing? If I pushed them all away to focus on my breath, it felt like repression. But if I turned toward them, I quickly became utterly lost in the storylines connected to the emotions. What to do?

It was a question I was facing in my daily life as well.

Emotional cocktails of highs and lows, pains and pleasures, dominated life in my twenties. I waffled between drowning in emotions and trying to "rise above" them, which never really worked.

I was excited to learn the RAIN (Recognize, Accept, Inquire, Nourish) meditation from Tara Brach,[32] to help me navigate these waters in both formal practice and in my daily life. Used in tandem with my basic, pay-attention-to-the-breath practice, RAIN practice has helped me learn to *feel* feelings without being consumed by them. I have learned to be kind and accepting toward the emotions that arrive at my door, without giving them an undue amount of power.

RAIN begins with "R" for "Recognize." "Recognize" means to identify what is happening in the mind and body. In my case, that meant that before I traveled down the black hole of feeling worthless in the aftermath of a rejection, I would stop and recognize that thoughts of my worthlessness were arising in response to feelings of disappointment or sadness. Recognizing seems simple, but as a novice practitioner, sometimes hours would go by in a haze of telling myself I would never meet anyone, I was going to be alone forever, there was something wrong with me, etc., before I

---

32. Tara Brach, "The RAIN of Self Compassion," Tarabrach.com, accessed May 7, 2017. http://www.tarabrach.com/wp-content/uploads/pdf/RAIN-of-Self-Compassion2.pdf.

recognized: "Oh, I feel a weight on my chest. I feel a heaviness of heart. I must be lonely. I must be sad."

One of my teachers, Jeff Roth, used to say that until he was far along in his thirties, he would classify every sensation between his chin and his knees as "hungry." If he felt the emotions of sadness, anger, or fear, it all registered as hunger, and he ate to try and make it go away. Recognizing that we are experiencing an emotion is the first big moment of pause. It is the moment we step out of our looped thinking and conditioned responses and into what is happening in the present moment.

The next letter in the acronym is "A," for "Allow" or "Accept." Once we recognize that something unpleasant or intense is happening and we feel it, our natural tendency is to tense up and resist it. When I started getting migraines, for example, my face would contort and my muscles would tense in response to the pounding I felt in my head. It happened so quickly and automatically that I didn't even realize I was doing it. One day, I started getting a migraine in the middle of meditation. I noticed that each time I felt a throbbing in my head, and I met that throbbing with release rather than clench, my pain eased a little bit. It was then that I realized that the stress I was adding to the original pain of the migraine was making it much worse.

The same is true with emotional pain. The Buddha called this the "second arrow." The first arrow, pain, is shot at us by the world. Someone we love dies. We get dumped.

We don't get the job we wanted. Pain, the Buddha said, is inevitable. It is a consequence of being human. Suffering, he qualified, is optional. Suffering is when we take out a second arrow and shoot it at ourselves, after being pierced by the first. Suffering is fighting the pain through resistance and struggle. It is the abuse we inflict on ourselves after we are dumped or abandoned. It is the stories we tell ourselves about how it was all our fault or it was someone else's fault. Like my clenching during a migraine, this resistance always makes the original pain worse.

The alternative is *allowing* the feeling or emotion its time in our system. We can ease our resistance to it—not because we like it or want it to be there, but because it is there nonetheless. The poet Rumi described the heart as being like a guesthouse. Our job is to greet and welcome whatever emotional and mental "guests" visit that day. "Even if they are a crowd of sorrows," he writes, "who violently sweep your house empty of its furniture, still treat each guest honorably. He may be clearing you out for some new delight!"[33]

On a practical level, this might mean actually talking to ourselves in the midst of a strong emotion (silently or out loud), soothing ourselves with gentle and loving words when we are in pain or feel shaky. Meditation teacher Sylvia Boorstein is fond of using the term "sweetheart" when soothing herself in a moment of pain. Thich Nhat Hanh suggests saying to yourself, "Darling, I see you are suffering. I am here for you." Tara Brach recommends putting a hand on your own face or heart, offering yourself physical comfort through touch while trying to calm down and accept the emotion. I tend to imagine holding my pain like a newborn baby, cradling it with breath and with love, softening my heart toward myself and trying to relax all my muscles around wherever I am holding the pain.

The next letter is "I," for Inquire (with Kindness). This type of inquiry is not an interrogation. On the contrary, inquiry is the gentlest of approaches into the pain we are experiencing. It is a tender touch on a fragile wound that asks: What is underneath this? What might have caused this? It is a soft flashlight beam into the darkness. What might be the reasons this situation is so painful? Why is this triggering me? When did this first begin? What are my clues? Like good therapists, we listen more than we speak when we inquire into our emotions. Sometimes the answers don't come right away, and that is fine. When we inquire with kindness, we provide a safe container for answers to find their way to our conscious mind in their own time.

Finally, there is "N" for "Nourish." Nourish asks, while we are feeling this way, what can we do for ourselves? How can we take care of ourselves? Perhaps the best thing we can do is to take a walk. Perhaps it is to call a friend or to have a cup of tea. Nourishing ourselves respects the power and the force of strong emotions and helps us to be gentle with ourselves through the process.

When I was in the thick of post-traumatic stress disorder after September 11, I saw a therapist for the first time. I remember voicing over and over again that I wasn't sure *why* I was having panic-filled reactions to the slightest stimuli. A plane flying overhead or a police siren would make my heart beat so fast I thought I was having a heart attack. I remember asking the therapist how to feel better and what to do. "We will get there," she responded, "but in the meantime, rather than asking yourself, 'Why do I feel this way?' Ask yourself, 'What can I do for myself when I feel this way?'"

In her reframing of the question, she introduced me to the transformative act of nourishing myself while going through a difficult time. I gave it a try the next day. When I heard my mind start to go down the rabbit hole of "Why am I feeling like this? What's wrong with me? When will I get better?" I stopped and asked, "What can I do for myself right now?" Out of nowhere, I heard a voice that suggested I listen to a classical music piece I had always liked, and take a walk. So I did it. Each note of the music felt like a kindness and helped ease the pain. "I guess there is a time for working things out," I remember thinking, "and a time for just taking care." That afternoon, I took care, and it helped.

We can use RAIN to help us unpack emotions such as fear, desire, and anger in greater depth. Those are the "big three" that dominated my life in my twenties, and that my students tell me overwhelm them as well.

The Anatomy of Fear

My mother tells me that when I was a baby, I was very clingy and fussy. I needed to be held and comforted constantly. At the age of seven or eight, each time my mother left the house, I would pace up and down the driveway of our home, repeating softly to myself, "Mom, mom, come home now. Mom, mom, or I'll have a cow."[34] As a child, I walked around with an anxious ball of worry and anxiety in my belly and heart, sometimes making it difficult to breathe. The world was a scary place and danger was possible around every corner—particularly when I was alone.

As I got older, the knot of fear remained. I was so scared the night before school started each year that I found myself hyperventilating, sometimes even vomiting. I was so scared and overwhelmed by dating that I avoided it throughout all of middle school and most of high school. I was so anxious about getting into a good college that I spent many sleepless nights crying into my pillow in fits of exhaustion and worry.

In order to deal with my fear and anxiety in college, I began drinking. Before going to a party or a bar, I drank several shots of vodka or tequila to numb my fear and allow

34. This was the early 1990s. Bart Simpson was huge.

me to engage in social life. And it worked, except for the side effects. Although I fortunately never became an alcoholic, I did spend thousands of dollars I didn't have. I put myself in extremely dangerous situations, sometimes sleeping at strangers' apartments or dorm rooms, sometimes relying on people who were also severely drunk to get me home. I woke up nearly every weekend for the next few years with debilitating hangovers from the poison I was putting in my body. Even a few trips to the emergency room for dehydration and near alcohol poisoning didn't stop me from continuing to drink excessively each weekend. Although drinking allowed me to numb my social anxiety for parties, it was powerless against the hum of anxiety I felt during my nondrinking hours, and I couldn't bring myself to drink during the school week. By the time I reached my junior year of college, my anxiety had graduated to full-fledged panic attacks several times a week, leading me to seek out therapy and meditation in a desperate attempt to feel better.

Because fear and anxiety were such a constant, unpleasant part of my childhood and early adulthood, I became obsessed with understanding what fear actually is and how it operates, both within myself and in general.

What is fear? Of what is it composed? There is a Zen parable of a man who draws a picture of a tiger. He renders the details with such accuracy that, as he applies the finishing touches, he takes a look at it, screams, and runs away. In my experience, this is how fear works. The mind takes unpleasant (sometimes traumatic) past experiences, adds some facts from the world around it, and constructs an imaginary future filled with pain and suffering. Fear then convinces us that this image is real—a dispatch from the future rather than an invention of our own mind. The ferocious tiger seems to leap off the page, headed straight for us.

The truth, of course, is that we cannot see the future. This seems obvious but I remember the moment it first really sank in. I was sitting on a train from Manhattan to my parents' home in Long Island a week after someone mailed anthrax-laced letters to several news agencies and politicians in New York and Washington, D.C. At one point on the journey, I looked over to the left and saw a dusty white substance on the windowsill. In a few seconds, I realized that, sitting in such close proximity to the ledge, I undoubtedly inhaled anthrax. I was sure that in a few moments I would struggle to breathe. The other passengers would begin hacking and coughing. As people realized what was going on, there would be a stampede to exit the train. Parents would grab the hands of their coughing and crying children. Someone would pull the emergency brake. The train would come to a screeching halt. Too weak to walk, too wracked by coughing, I would know that my life was over. I would say a heart-wrenching goodbye to my family and friends in my mind. It was so sad. I was so young! I had so much I wanted to do before I died. Tears stung my eyes as I imagined the end.

I looked again at the anthrax only to realize that the "dust" I saw was actually some dried speckles of paint. I looked around at the other passengers. They were calmly reading or listening to their headphones. I looked down at myself. I was fine. I had made the whole scene up. None of it was real. I was shocked. *If my mind could see and hear something happen so clearly, without it actually happening,* I thought, *it could fabricate the other terrible things that I'm convinced will happen to me.* I realized that my mind was an unreliable narrator. My fear was really my imagination run amok.

Why does fear work like this? What is fear's reason for being? Evolutionarily, fear helps us to survive. Our memory stores experiences that are painful to help us recognize danger, generalize about the danger, and prevent being hurt again. In 1999, Gavin De Becker wrote a book called *The Gift of Fear*, arguing that fear is an evolutionary gift.[35] Fear helps us stay out of oncoming traffic, go to the doctor when something doesn't feel right, and avoid snarling animals (and people).

Anxiety, on the other hand, does not usually help us prevent danger. It *tells* us it is helping us, of course, and that is why it dominates our mind and turns us into a nervous wreck. "If I don't worry about the fact that I haven't met my soul mate," one of my students, Alex, asked me one day,

---

35. Gavin De Becker, *The Gift of Fear* (Prince Frederick, MD: Recorded Books, 2000).

"how will I find him?" Alex, like most of us, believed that worrying keeps us vigilant, safe, and wards off unwanted outcomes. When we have very little control over a situation, anxiety and worry can give us a false sense of power and cause magical thinking—imagining we can cause coincidences to occur and make something wished for come about.

The truth is, worrying about whether we will meet our soul mate will not help the person to materialize. Worry will not keep us or our family members safe from harm. It won't even help us do better on an exam, as the time and energy it takes to worry usually demands more of us than the actual studying would. When we acknowledge the truth of this, we weaken the grip that fear and anxiety have on us, and we can begin to work with these emotions in a very different way.

My meditation students over the years have come to me with worry and anxiety more frequently than any other emotion or problem. Although our world is safer now than at any other point in history, news media that focus on gun violence, terrorism, war, and global climate change have us anxious and afraid a lot of the time.[36] One of my students, a recent graduate named Amelia, told me about coming

36. "The World Is Actually Safer Than Ever, and Here's the Data to Prove That," *The Takeaway*, PRI Radio, accessed April 24, 2017, https://www.pri.org/stories/2014-10-23/world-actually-safer-ever -and-heres-data-prove.

home one day to find a terrifying headline on the front page of her newspaper. It read, in big red letters, "EBOLA, ISIS, AND OTHER THINGS YOU SHOULD BE AFRAID OF RIGHT NOW." Even though she recognized that the headline was over the top, Amelia noticed that her stomach dropped involuntarily when she read it. Her heartbeat sped up, and she had trouble breathing. "My logical mind knew that being afraid wouldn't help anything," she explained, "but my body was already afraid before I could process that thought."

Other students describe the daily pressures of trying to succeed in school or work, balancing a social life, and earning enough money to live as panic inducing, even without the added stressors of the wider world. Like I did, they carry their fear and anxiety around with them, self-medicating when they can, but the fear takes its toll on their physical, mental, and emotional well-being.

When we find that we are caught in fear, anxiety, or worry, we can use the RAIN framework to understand and process what is happening.

We begin with recognizing what is going on in our bodies. How do we know we are anxious or afraid? What are its manifestations in the body? Amelia described it as a combination of her stomach dropping and her heart speeding up. I often find my breathing becomes shallower and I may begin to sweat. Others describe a feeling of unraveling or free falling, or a feeling of being crushed.

In English, we say "I am afraid," or "I am anxious," but this language sometimes reinforces our feeling of being totally overwhelmed when we are in these states. We think we *are* our fear and our anxiety. Instead, I recommend we start saying, "Fear is here," or, "Anxiety is here," as a way of simply recognizing and acknowledging our visitor in that moment. Sometimes, just recognizing the fear and breathing can help soothe anxiety, as it did for me in the incident in the clothing store that I wrote about in the introduction. Even when it cannot, however, I have found it to be a critically helpful first step to help me to get my bearings in the midst of an anxiety attack.

After we recognize the anxiety, we allow ourselves to feel it. The one thing that always makes anxiety worse, in my experience, is trying to stop feeling it. Doing so is like fighting a rip tide by trying to swim against it, exerting a ton of energy as the wave's current sucks you under the surface. Instead, as with a rip tide, the key is to soften all resistance and swim *into* the current, rather than against it. We release and dive in, trusting that our bodies will not succumb, and that we will find our secure footing again on the other side.

In college, I babysat to make some extra spending money. I worked for one family with a two-year-old girl who had intense separation anxiety from her mother. When her mother would leave, the little girl would begin screaming, crying and pounding on the door, and would cry inconsolably for twenty minutes or more. She looked panic stricken, abandoned, and afraid. I tried everything I could think of to soothe her. I would try and reason with her, telling her that her mother would be back later that evening. I would try to distract her with another toy or even a cookie or sweet treat. I even tried to physically remove her from the door and put her in another room to help her "forget" her mother and become interested in playing with a toy instead.

Nothing worked. Exasperated, I confessed the problem to my sister one day, and my sister, with several years more babysitting experience than I, suggested I take a different tack. "Get on her level," she suggested, "so that you are eye to eye with her. When she begins to cry, look her in the eye and say, 'I know. It's really scary. You really miss your mommy.' My sister told me to mirror the little girl's affect, frowning and nodding and repeating how hard and sad it was when mommy left. This approach seemed counter-intuitive and risky to me. Wouldn't reinforcing her feelings only cause her to get lost in them even further? I had tried everything else, however, so I decided to give it a shot.

The next time I was babysitting, I employed my sister's method. I stared right at the little girl, getting to her level and looking into her eyes. "I *know*!" I said, "It's *so* sad. It's *so* scary when mommy leaves. It is *really* painful. You miss her so much." I didn't tell her not to be afraid and I didn't try to distract her. I just repeated what I thought she was feeling over and over again. The little girl stopped her screaming almost as soon as I started talking to her. Her eyes filled with tears, but she hung onto my every word. She stopped pounding on the door. She nodded her head and came over to me, continuing to stare at me. I repeated my refrain. "You miss your mommy. You don't like when she leaves. You feel afraid." Pretty soon, she climbed into my lap, picked up a toy and started playing with it. She was so soothed by seeing her feelings reflected in my voice and my affect that she didn't need to scream anymore.

In an old Buddhist story, the monk Milarepa returns to his cave one day and sees that it is filled to the brim with terrifying demons. Scared out of his mind, he tries to chase them out. He yells at them, throws things, and threatens them, but nothing works. They seem to multiply in number and in ferocity. Milarepa realizes that his approach isn't working, and so he calms down and decides that teaching the demons the Dharma (Buddhist teachings) might cause them to disappear. Instead they just sit there, staring at him.

Milarepa gives up. He realizes that he is not going to get the demons to leave through any force of will or reason. Although he is still scared, he summons his courage and looks at them one by one in their snarling, bloodthirsty faces. "Okay, you win," he says to them. "It looks like we are sharing this space together. I'll stop trying to get you to leave. I open myself to whatever you have to teach me." Suddenly, the demons start disappearing, until only one remains. The last one is the biggest and scariest of them all, with sharp fangs and evil eyes. Milarepa begins to shake and tremble. The demon will eat him alive! Just then it dawns on him what he has to do. He comes as close as possible to the demon, and, as the demon opens his mouth to shriek, Milarepa lays his head down into the mouth of the demon, surrendering fully. The demon bows low to Milarepa in respect, and disappears. Milarepa had to let go completely into the thing he was the most afraid of in order to learn and grow from the experience and move on.

When I first started dating my husband, I was consumed with jealousy and fear on a regular basis. I was filled with the conviction that he would leave me, that I wouldn't be enough for him. I instigated fight after fight when I saw him even talking to other women, convinced he liked them more than me, or that he thought them prettier than me. No matter how many times he reassured me that he liked me and wanted to be with me, it wouldn't stick. I struggled with insomnia. I would let my anxiety about losing him torture me through many tearful, fretful nights. The demons were taking up so much room in my heart and mind, I could barely breathe.

During this period, I met with my meditation teacher, Teah. I told her how afraid and jealous I was all the time, but that wasn't the worst part. The worst part was how ashamed I felt about that fear and jealousy. "I know they are ugly and unattractive qualities," I said, "but I can't seem to get rid of them, no matter how hard I try."

"You have to love them to death," she responded, employing Milarepa's wisdom. "You have to welcome them in like your sweet, dear friends. Stop fighting. Love them, love them, and then love them some more."

I wasn't exactly sure how to love my fear and my jealousy, but I knew that beating myself up every time I felt them was not helping. The next time I felt a wave of jealousy and panic arise in relation to my boyfriend, I caught myself before starting a fight with him. Instead, I went inside myself. I took a deep breath. I said to my jealousy, "I love you. I'm here for you." I said the same to my fear. All of a sudden, the scary demons of my fear and jealousy looked very, very young. In fact, they looked exactly like myself when I was around five years old. I saw all the fear, abandonment, and terror of that age in my own eyes. I felt it in my chest and my stomach. I put my hand on my heart and my stomach. I felt filled with compassion and sadness for the young me. "I love you, I'm sorry, I'm here for you," I said to myself, over and over again. This practice did not immediately eliminate my jealousy or my fear, but as I continued to *recognize* and *allow* the feelings over and over again during the following months, the emotions no longer had the power to derail me or my relationship.

Accepting our fear provides a safe environment to open up a gentle inquiry into its origins. What is at the root of this fear? When did it first begin to terrify me? What are its triggers? What might the fear be illuminating about my deepest desires?

One of my students, Will, once came to me and said that his anxiety was causing him to experience a crushing feeling in his chest. It didn't seem to matter what his anxiety was attached to—a grade in a class, a promotion at work, a first date—he felt all of it pressing on his chest, making it hard for him to breathe. Sitting with him in meditation, I helped him through the first few steps of RAIN, having him recognize the sensations (pressing, tightness) and the emotion (fear, anticipation), as well as to relax and try to accept them and welcome them in. He put his hand on his chest and we practiced breathing together for a little while. I then began the inquiry, asking if he happened to hear any stories or see any images associated with the feeling in his chest. He took a few breaths, and then began speaking slowly, "When I used to walk home as a kid, there was a bully, Ted, who would beat me up on my way home. One of his signature moves was to knock me to the ground and then sit on my chest, and I couldn't breathe." Will's eyes were closed but I could tell the memory was very painful. His brow was furrowed, and he put his hand on his chest, reflexively.

"Can you see your face when you were that age, during this period, when this was happening?" I asked.

"Yes," he said. "I look really scared. I was trying not to be afraid, but I thought I was going to die."

I suggested he send love to the scared little boy that he

was. He held his hand on his chest and breathed deeply for a few minutes. "Do you still feel the crushing pressure on your chest?" I asked.

"Yes," Will answered. I thought for a moment.

"Will, can you see Ted's face as he is sitting on your chest?"

"Yes, but I don't want to look," Will answered quickly.

"Can you stay with the little boy you were, holding his hand, giving him love, and look at Ted's face? How does he look? What do you see?"

"Ted looks . . . scared. Ted looks really scared." With this, Will broke down in tears.

Will told me that the pressure on his chest eased when he realized he had been walking around with Ted sitting on him for over ten years. He had absorbed Ted, believing that Ted had been right about him, that he was worthless and deserved to be bullied. The Ted within was his cruelest demon. He couldn't look directly at Ted, for fear of what he would find. When he finally did look, when he finally saw Ted's face, Ted's vulnerability and fear, the bloodthirsty demon just looked small and sad.

Many of our fears for the future are actually past traumas that still need attention and healing. This was the case with my fear-based jealousy and Will's anxiety. Sometimes, however, fear exists to help us illuminate our deepest wishes. Mark Epstein writes that the opposite of fear is not calm;

it is desire.[37] Looking closely at almost any deep fear we carry around, we can find a tender, earnest desire underneath that is afraid to see the light of day. For instance, if I feel afraid and anxious that I will do poorly on an exam, I can instead tap into how much I want to do well and let that desire grow bright. If I am worried I will never meet the love of my life, I can instead acknowledge how much I want intimacy and feel that desire. Connecting with the flame of desire and hope at the root of so many of my fears, big and small, feels so much better and more brave that trying to protect myself by living in the fear. Every time my mind starts to elbow in with, "But what if it never happens?! What if everything goes wrong?!" I try to respond compassionately to that fear, saying to myself, "You *really* want it. You are afraid because you have so much desire in you." I try to sit and breathe right into the heart of that desire and hold it close to me.

Nourishing ourselves when we feel fear might mean any number of things in the moment that fear comes to visit. Whether it is deep breathing to calm our nervous system, speaking to a therapist or a good friend about a past trauma, taking a walk in nature, or connecting to the desire within the fear, nourishing means welcoming the fear and bringing patience and love to ourselves while we experience it.

37. Epstein, *Open to Desire*.

Most of the time, healing and transformation happen so slowly that we don't always notice something has changed until a lot of time has passed. We are often the last to be aware of our own progress. I remember a moment several years ago when I was rushing to a graduate student meet-and-greet at NYU, where I was going to schmooze a little and talk up our meditation program to recruit students. As I was about to push the door open, I paused for a second and smiled to myself. In the past, a meet-and-greet of *any* kind would have sent me into a tailspin of hives, hyperventilation, and anxiety. Now here I was, with just a touch of nervousness in my stomach. I felt so grateful for meditation and for the power of healing and change. When my students ask me, "Do you think it's possible that I won't be anxious all the time?" I answer unequivocally, "Yes." I've seen it and experienced it firsthand.

THE ANATOMY OF DESIRE

When I was growing up, my parents were often exasperated with my seemingly endless demands. "Yael, stop whining!" was a refrain I heard repeatedly. I was told that if I didn't learn to be happy with what I had, I might become like my great aunt Liza, who, according to my parents, was an unhappy child and grew up to be a miserable and unhappy adult.

I didn't like being so needy. I felt ashamed and disappointed in myself. At the same time, I couldn't figure out how to stop. What my parents called "whining" was my attempt to get what I wanted. In my young mind, the thing my parents hated, the thing that kept people from liking me, was desire. If I could teach myself to stop wanting things, I could get more love and acceptance.

Additionally, as I grew up, wanting things over which I had no control felt terrible. I wanted attention in class, but wasn't always able to get it. I wanted boys to like me, which felt both shameful and futile. I wanted real friendship, where I would be seen and loved, and yet I did not have many friends.

I was attracted to Buddhism because I thought it would teach me how to stop having desire. After all, didn't the Buddha say that desire was the cause of suffering? Given how much suffering desire had caused in my life, Buddhism sounded perfect.

The more I practiced and studied, however, the more I started to encounter a very different understanding of desire in Buddhism and other wisdom traditions. I heard the following story, originally recounted by thirteenth century Jewish mystic Reb Isaac of Akko, on one of my first retreats.

There was once a princess riding through a town in her carriage. The town's fool caught a glimpse of the princess and instantly was overwhelmed with desire for her. He ran up to the window of the carriage. "Please, Princess, I'm in love with you and I must see you again! Please tell me where I can meet you again in private?" he said.

The princess contemptuously turned toward the fool and sneered. "I'll meet you in the graveyard," she said. With that, the carriage galloped away toward the castle.

The fool, being the fool, ran off to the graveyard, believing the princess would be on her way to meet him shortly. When nightfall came and the princess still didn't show up, the fool decided he would wait in the graveyard for her as long as it took for her to arrive. He slept in the graveyard. He ate what he could forage off the trees and plants in the vicinity. He waited for her each day and night for weeks, months, and years. As he waited, he concentrated on the princess and on his desire for her. He let the desire move through his body until there was no other feeling in his body *but* desire for her. He continued this practice day after day. Over time, this man became known as the wise man of the village who lived in the graveyard, and people would come from far and near for advice and counsel. Reb Isaac ends the story with the words: "Woe be to he who never desires a princess like that."

The princess never shows up, and this is somehow a happy ending? The fool becomes a wise man *through*, not in spite of, his longing and his unrequited love? This story turned my thoughts about desire on their head. It implies a power and energy in yearning, no matter whether the object of the yearning is obtained.

What is your princess? What are you still waiting for?

Have you ever allowed yourself to want that princess with every cell and every pore of your body, as the fool did? Is it love or acceptance from a parent? Meeting a partner? Achieving some level of success? Recognizing that desire and allowing it to exist within us is the first step to allowing desire to be our teacher.

One day, on summer break from college, I was at the beach with a group of friends, including the guy I had a huge crush on at the time. Unfortunately, we were also on the beach with his girlfriend. Every time I talked with my crush, I felt simultaneously excited and depressed. I liked him so much, but he only had eyes for his girlfriend. My longing and loneliness felt unbearable in their presence. I could hear my inner monologue comparing my body, looks, and charm with his girlfriend's. I could hear a voice telling me to stop liking him, and quit wanting what I couldn't have. Once again, I was trying to escape my desire and it was not working.

Suddenly, I thought about the story of the princess and the fool. I thought about how much desire I felt—not only for this guy, but for all of my unrequited crushes over the years. Rather than trying to forcefully stop the feeling, I tried to breathe in the desire, feeling it flood my body, and breathe out, trying to relax around it. Since I was at the beach, I made my way into the waves. I allowed each new wave to be a cue for opening up to another wave of desire, relaxing as each one receded back into the ocean. "I want to have a boyfriend I really like," I said into the first wave. "I want to be loved and get attention," I said into the second. "I want to be considered pretty and smart," I said into the third, and continued, allowing each "wave" of desire the chance to fully wash over me and through me.

Something unusual and wonderful happened as I continued this impromptu meditation. After I spoke my desire into the wave and let it crash into me, I had a strange feeling of fullness—as though I already had the thing I wanted. Of course, nothing changed in real life. I was still single. My crush was still happily snuggling with his girlfriend down the beach. And yet, rather than the painful, empty, tugging feeling of longing I'd associated with desire in the past, this time I felt *full*. Recognizing and acknowledging my wants, regardless of whether I ever achieved them, felt so kind and nourishing to myself.

I want to be clear that I am not advocating wallowing in obsession for people who do not see our beauty or our value, or who are involved with others. That kind of grasping hurts, and usually reinforces an inner story about ourselves that we are not okay as we are and that we need someone or something else to complete us. But in my experience, the way out of such obsessions and heartache is not through self-bullying, "tough love," or trying to clamp down on desire. It is by releasing the mind's tight grip on the *object* of the desire, and opening up to the feeling of the wanting itself.

In fact, one of the most curious myths about desire is that we think recognizing and allowing it will lead to complete lack of control. If I desire cookies, the logic goes, and I recognize and allow the desire to overtake me, I will eat the entire box and feel sick afterward. A closer examination of desire, however, shows that staying with the raw sensations of desire (the quickening of the heart, the pulling in the stomach, the visualization of happiness) rather than fixating on the object of the desire (cookies!) separates the two things from each other—the wanting of the cookies and the cookies themselves. Opening up to the *want* is expansive and rich. Clinging to the object is constricting and painful.

If you spend some time looking deeply into your desires, you may find that there is shame wrapped around desire. Many of us received messages in childhood or in adolescence that "neediness" was frowned upon, that wanting things put an undue burden on those around us. We were taught that showing our desire was unattractive and overwhelming to others. We were supposed to "play it cool," to avoid being desperate (or at least not to show it), and to act as if we were completely self-sufficient beings who didn't need love, connection, and intimacy with others.

In my twenties, I always tried to portray a breezy, no-need attitude with the men that I was dating (or wanted to date), despite, of course, wanting and needing them a great deal. You don't want to be weighed down with the terms "boyfriend/girlfriend"? No problem—who needs labels? You don't want to be monogamous in case someone "more amazing" comes along? I get it. Who wouldn't want to leave all their options open? The problem, of course, was that I didn't want to leave all my options open. I wanted real intimacy and connection, and yes, monogamy. I wanted someone to desire me above all others and to commit to me. I was terribly ashamed of these desires, however, and felt that if I ever let anyone know these things about myself, the rejection and shame would be instantaneous and overwhelming.

When I told my therapist this in a session once, he asked me to look critically at that shame and to see if there was any legitimacy to it. What was so gross about wanting someone more than they wanted me, or wanting something I could not have? What was so embarrassing about it? He used the analogy of going to the store to buy something, and, upon arriving at the store, realizing it was closed. Would I feel disappointed that the store was closed? Of course. Would I feel deeply ashamed of myself? Unlikely. What was the difference with romantic desire?

Years later, I saw a scene in the Charlie Kaufman movie *Adaptation* that echoed this idea. The protagonists of the film are twins: Charlie and Donald. Charlie turns to Donald and says:

Charlie: You know I admire you, Donald. I've spent my whole life worried about people not liking me, and you're oblivious.

Donald: I'm not oblivious.

Charlie: No, I meant that as a compliment. There was this time in high school I watched you flirting with Sarah Madison—

Donald: Oh god, I was so in love with her.

Charlie: She was being really sweet to you. And when you walked away, she started to make fun of you with her friends. You didn't even realize it.

Donald: I knew. I heard them.

Charlie: But you were so happy!

Donald: I loved Sarah Madison. That was mine.

Charlie: But she thought you were pathetic!

Donald: That's her problem, not mine. You are what you love, not who loves you.[38]

After watching the movie, I thought to myself, what if I was that unafraid to shine my desire out into the world? What if I believed that owning my desire made me *more* loveable, *more* attractive, not less? My friend Rachel once told me that she wished she could walk around with the word "desperate" on a T-shirt, letting people see it, emerging from

38. *Adaptation*, directed by Spike Jonze (Los Angeles: Sony Pictures DVD, 2002).

out of the taboo that word carries for so many of us, and reclaiming it. I knew exactly what she meant. Trying not to show needs and wants is exhausting. Shame is exhausting.

One evening, years after I had the revelation on the beach with the waves, I was leaving what I thought was a date with a colleague, only to find out that he was actually engaged to be married. On my way home, I felt the familiar darkness of shame and loneliness settle on me like a fog. "Everyone is taken. You will be alone forever. You are so pathetic and always will be," my mind spoke to me, taking me deeper down my spiral of misery.

Suddenly, remembering my intention to nourish my desire rather than my shame, I sat down on a stoop in the East Village where I'd been walking. I took a few deep breaths. I practiced allowing the warm flame of desire to burn brightly in my heart and my stomach. I said aloud to myself the things that I wanted deeply: love, a partner, to be seen, to be held. I imagined blowing softly into the flames of each of these desires, as if I was stoking a campfire to life. I was situated in my own body, giving myself full permission for desire to move in. I felt a vague disappointment about the colleague, but a much stronger sense of love and compassion for myself. After a period of time, I got up and walked the rest of the way home. I felt much more calm and at ease.

Nourishing desire takes practice. Like the fool in the graveyard, becoming completely and totally open to the sensations of yearning have helped me to begin to make friends with desire, and to see it as a source of energy rather than shame.

THE ANATOMY OF ANGER

Creating a positive relationship with your anger can be difficult if you are taught, as many young women are, that anger is unattractive, unfeminine, or flat out not permitted. People of color in this country are often taught that anger is dangerous, or will cause people to avoid or dismiss them. In these cases, anger is often buried in the body and becomes self-directed or shows up in explosive rage.

Like fear and desire, however, anger can be a valuable and important "friend" in the clubhouse of our emotions. Anger is like the whistle on a teakettle. It lets us know, as it grows louder and louder, that something is wrong and needs to be addressed. Anger brings the energy, when properly understood and harnessed, to address the wrong. Rage, which can be destructive, is the explosion that occurs when we do not know how to address and manage our anger, or feel powerless to do so.

For many of my early years in therapy, my therapist tried very hard to help me admit to the anger I was afraid to recognize in myself.

"I felt very *frustrated* at my father . . ." I would begin.

"Maybe you felt angry?" she would suggest.

"I was really *disappointed* at my boyfriend . . ." I would offer.

"Anyone would be angered by that," she would counter.

I resisted her nudges for a long time, terrified that naming my anger would take the lid off a carefully sealed vault that, once opened, would explode.

There was some truth to these fears. When I did start expressing my anger in therapy, it started emerging everywhere in my life, and I wasn't very graceful in working with it. I screamed at my brother for not giving me a ride to a friend's house. I lashed out at a customer service representative from the phone company. Anger had been released in my body like a fire, searching for someone or something to burn. It took some time and practice to figure out how to put distance between the rage and the response.

Thich Nhat Hanh writes that recognizing our anger is crucial for our well-being. He suggests seeing our anger as a newborn baby that is screaming out for our attention. As soon as we begin feeling the anger, we should put down whatever else we are doing and rush to the cries of our anger, gently rocking it, soothing it, staying calm as it moves through our bodies. If a person is making us angry, he suggests that we speak kindly to the person, telling them we are suffering and angry, and that we need to step away and tend to our anger for a little while before we return. Indeed, one of the best maxims I have learned is to "strike when the iron is cool." In my experience, this period of "cooling off" usually takes three times longer than I think it will, but it is always beneficial to wait for the flames to cool down before rushing into action. One of meditation's greatest gifts is elongating the time between stimulus of any kind—including the trigger of anger—and a response.

When we accept our anger, we're able to walk that careful middle path between knee-jerk reaction (usually causing more damage) and repressing our rage. What are the practices of this middle path? How do we accept and diffuse our anger without becoming completely lost in it? Thich Nhat Hanh does not advocate punching a pillow or "primal screaming." He argues that this behavior nurtures and stokes the violence of anger in our bodies. Instead, he suggests putting a hand on our heart, taking deep and steadying breaths, and pledging to relate to our anger with love. For me, that usually means pausing while trying to solve the problem and taking significant time to breathe, sending myself wishes of love and care. "Poor thing," I say to myself, "I'm not going to leave you. I know you are very angry. I know you are suffering. I'm here for you."

A *New Yorker* cartoon several years ago featured a family of tourists in the middle of the jungle. The father, scratching his chin, says, "O.K., I admit it, we're lost, but the important thing is to remain focused on whose fault it is." When I am lost in anger, all that seems to matter initially is who should be blamed. My mind is on hyperspeed, replaying the incident over and over, constantly flipping between blaming myself and blaming the other person.

Beneath anger almost always lies fear, hurt, and a sense of powerlessness. Anger arises as a response to the ego's attempt to regain power. To look deeply into anger, we have to escape the ping-pong of blame and fault and explore the underlying hurt.

As I mentioned earlier, my early fights with my husband involved a lot of anger and jealousy. He would mention something about another woman in a way that lit up my jealousy, even if it was fairly innocuous. Feeling hurt, jealous, and scared, and yet at the same time ashamed of those feelings, I would fire a passive aggressive statement back. He would become upset, feeling like I was taking his comment out of context and shaming him for simply noticing other women exist. I would become angry, insecure and upset that he was noticing other women. Logically I knew that everyone, including myself, noticed good looking people, but that didn't help. The fights would escalate, with screaming and crying, door slams, and eventually, make-ups. It was predictable and exhausting, and yet I couldn't seem to stop the train of the fight once it left the station of the trigger.

One evening, after yet another fight of this kind, Ben went to sleep and I stayed awake, brewing with anger. I replayed the fight over and over, tossing and turning and becoming increasingly furious and righteous. *How dare he talk about running into his ex-girlfriend in the park?* I fumed. *He clearly wishes he was still with her. He clearly takes me for granted.* At some point in the night, I said to myself, "What's the worst thing you are believing about yourself in these fights, that you are ascribing to Ben? What's the fear underneath?"

I listened for the answer. It came in a torrent of tears. *That you are garbage. That you are worthless. That no man will ever choose you over others. That you are not pretty or special enough to be someone's only love.* These were my darkest fears and beliefs about myself—they were not actually Ben's beliefs about me. Continuing to ascribe them to him was causing him to feel unseen and angry in his own right. Each time I was triggered, I needed to take it as an opportunity to nurture and love the young girl in me that felt unlovable and scared. That was the only way to break the cycle.

The next time I was triggered in this way, I had a little more awareness and was slower to react with a passive aggressive comment. It took some time, but gradually these fights I once thought intractable have become few and far between.

The most frequent and commonplace way anger arises in my life is when I have let a boundary be trampled and feel disempowered as a result. Perhaps someone treats me disrespectfully and I don't stand up for myself. Perhaps someone asks me to do something I do not want to do and I say yes out of guilt or obligation. In these circumstances, I find myself fuming with bottled up anger or bad-mouthing a person to everyone that will listen, in a poor attempt to gain some power back after having given too much of it away.

The best advice I have ever heard for working with this type of anger is contained in the following six words: "Don't get angry; draw a boundary." It seems so simple; and yet, as a people pleaser, I have often noticed myself knee-deep in fury before realizing that I have allowed a boundary to blur.

I once coplanned an event with someone who was a frustrating combination of anxious and disorganized. He called and emailed multiple times per day, expressing his stress and overwhelm and asking me each day to take on additional duties. I tried to set his mind at ease in each call and kept agreeing to do more—my own anxiety and resentment slowly ratcheting up in the process. One morning, a week before the event, he wrote me an email with a hint of recrimination about the way I handled the pricing of the tickets. I lost my mind with anger. All of the prior weeks of taking on too much without standing up for myself or drawing appropriate boundaries exploded into raw rage. Before I could stop my fingers, I typed a furious, defensive response, copied all of his supervisors, my supervisors, and several of our colleagues, in a poorly thought-out attempt to gain sympathy from outsiders. Immediately after I pressed "send," I regretted it. I felt deeply ashamed for losing my cool and failing to handle the situation professionally. I was sick to my stomach. He replied a few hours later, taking everyone else off the email chain and asking if we could speak by phone. We talked it through and the event ended up going well, but I learned from that experience to listen to the alarm of my anger *before* it blows up, seeing where I can draw a boundary, talk through my feelings, or find my power in a situation.

Sometimes anger is short lived and the situation is easily handled after some cooling off. Sometimes, however, the anger is deep, searing, and not immediately "solvable." This is usually the case when working with situations of personal or collective trauma and/or systemic injustices. Accepting anger in these cases means validating that anger is our body's *healthy* reaction to a situation that was/is wrong and that should not have happened. People we love and upon whom we depend should not hurt us. Our government and its police officers should protect us and not kill its citizens. We should not be discriminated against because of our race, our religion, our gender, or our sexual orientation. Anger in these cases reflects a heart that is open and tender and that refuses complacency with systems—personal or societal—which do harm.

The trouble with anger, however, is that it hurts, whether the anger is justified or not. It feels constricting and tight in the body. The damage of living in anger for too long without adequate processing can take its toll on our physical and emotional health. People who have prolonged, unaddressed anger are twice as likely to have a heart attack. Conditions related to anxiety and depression are exacerbated by anger, and one study suggests that members of a couple who hold on to anger have shorter life spans than those who process it together or individually.[39]

Despite functioning as an alarm system and alerting us to problems that require healing, anger is a very poor instructional manual. It doesn't provide *strategy*, apart from rudimentary fight, flight, or freeze responses. To find an appropriate response to problems that anger brings to light, we have to give ourselves time and space. We have to have patience. As Reb Anderson writes in *Being Upright:*

> Through patience, your vision clears and you see the dependent co-arising of pain, frustration, and anger. Practicing patience does not mean gritting your teeth and ignoring the pain, but developing and expanding your capacity for experiencing pain, opening wide enough to feel the pain without either running away or wallowing in it.[40]

39. Debbie Strong, "7 Ways Anger is Ruining Your Health," EverydayHealth.Com, accessed April 25, 2017, http://www.everydayhealth.com/news/ways-anger-ruining-your-health/.
40. Reb Anderson, *Being Upright: Zen Meditation and the Bodhisattva Precepts* (Berkeley, CA: Rodmell Press, 2001), 182.

Practicing patience has always been very difficult for me. Perhaps because I have spent most of my adult life in New York City, when someone tells me to "be patient," my anger and irritation usually grows. *I don't want to be patient,* my mind protests, *I want what I want now.* Patience is equated in my mind with repression and delay. Patience in the face of anger is the only effective response, however. It is the only way that the powerful (and important!) energy of anger can be held and cradled to reveal the grief, hurt, and fear underneath. It is the only practice that enables us to create enough space around a problem, not so we can repress it, but so we can find a wise response.

One of my students, Christina, told me that she hates to be late and she hates the feeling of powerlessness when the subway stalls, causing her to be late to class or a meeting with friends. She gets angry and agitated—a New Yorker's version of road rage. "Being patient in these cases feels like saying it's okay that this is happening," she told me, "And it isn't okay! It messes up my day and embarrasses me!"

I asked Christina if her impatience hurts the Metropolitan Transit Authority. I asked her if it causes the subway to stop stalling and move faster. I asked her if it makes her feel better about being late, or feel better in general. She smiled, and said, "No." Impatience in circumstances like these give us the illusion of control, but in reality, contracting in anger causes us suffering *on top* of the pain of being late. If, out of our anger and frustration, we then snap at other subway riders or even our friends and family members later on, the original harm of being late has now multiplied, causing more damage.

Patience, on the other hand, does not sanction the harm that is done, it simply acknowledges the limits of our ability to affect change in that moment. It causes us to come face-to-face with our pain and our confusion, as well as the unknowable future of how things will evolve and take shape. Patience is our capacity to be in a world that is outside of our understanding and control. When we realize that we are stuck in something, unable to change it, we can rest back into patience, remembering impermanence and breathing into the truth that everything eventually changes.

As we work through our anger and our rage, cultivating patience is the kindest thing we can do to nourish ourselves. As Rainer Maria Rilke writes in *Letters to a Young Poet*:

> I would like to beg you, dear Sir, as well as I can, to have patience with everything unresolved in your heart and to try to love the questions themselves as if they were locked rooms or books written in a very foreign language. Don't search for the answers, which could not be given to you now, because you would not be able to live them. And the point is, to live everything. Live the questions

now. Perhaps then, someday far in the future, you
will gradually, without even noticing it, live your
way into the answer.[41]

How do we have patience in the face of anger and confusion? How do we "live our way into the answer?" By
breathing deeply. By separating ourselves from the source
of our anger when we can, even for a temporary period
of time. By welcoming and trusting our anger as a friend,
here to deliver an important message about finding our
power, righting a wrong, and/or loving ourselves. By being
extremely gentle with ourselves through this process, like a
parent with a newborn baby, allowing our anger to expose
the other feelings that might be contained within it. Finally,
by remembering that all things arise and fall in their own
time, including the discomforts of anger and rage, which
can, with patience, be transformed into a force for powerful
and profound change.

FORGIVENESS

The path from anger to forgiveness is complicated. We all
know that forgiveness is positive and we want to be for-
given for our missteps. But for the times we have been *really*

---

41. Rainer Maria Rilke, *Letters to a Young Poet* (New York: Penguin,
2016).

hurt, when the other person isn't even remotely sorry or is a repeat offender, someone uttering the word "forgiveness" within a four block radius may cause us to feel a murderous rage. Or at least it does for me.

For small infractions and petty disagreements among friends and loved ones, most of us don't have too much trouble forgiving others. We bump up against each other, we hurt each other, we apologize, we ask for and grant forgiveness. In those cases, forgiveness feels good because it heals a relationship.

With major wounds, however, forgiveness is much more difficult. Very often, the person who hurts us doesn't issue an apology or doesn't admit that what they did was wrong. My good friend Lisa's father physically and emotionally abused her and her sisters for most of their childhood. Through significant therapy and meditation, my friend found the courage to confront her father and to let him know how much pain and damage he caused in her life. During the confrontation, Lisa's father kept interrupting her to defend himself, blame others for his behavior, or minimize her pain. When Lisa, exasperated, finally just asked her father if he could apologize and recognize what he did to her and the family, he paused for a few long seconds. "I did the best I could," he replied. Lisa's father is typical of so many people who hurt others, with egos so fragile that they cannot and will not apologize for the harm they cause.

Sometimes the person who hurt us cannot issue an

apology because they have passed away. Sometimes the person at whom we are angry is ourselves, or God, or nature, making an apology impossible. Sometimes the person is still alive but is so different today than they were when they caused the harm, it can feel like fighting with a ghost.

Even when we do receive an apology, sometimes forgiveness is still difficult. It can feel as though forgiving the person who harmed us means erasing the act, even while it continues to cause us pain. It can feel like letting the other person off the hook, or saying that what happened was permissible, when our body tells us it was not. Resisting forgiveness feels like a natural response in these situations.

Mark Nepo lays this out beautifully in his essay, "About Forgiveness!" He writes:

> The pain was necessary to know the truth but we don't have to keep the pain alive to keep the truth alive. This is what has kept me from forgiveness: the feeling that all I've been through will evaporate if I don't relive it; that if those who hurt me don't see what they've done, my suffering will have been for nothing.

We are afraid to forgive because we think it will erase or minimize the pain that occurred. This has been the case for me many times. Each time someone has really hurt me, and I consider forgiving them, a voice seems to scream at me from within: *They aren't sorry! They are living their lives, as happy as can be, while you suffer! If you forgive, you erase what happened! Nobody will affirm how much pain you are in!* It often feels like if I don't hold my ground in anger, I will be doing damage to myself again, on top of the original wounding, by not standing up for my pain.

But the validation I seek most likely will never come from the people who hurt me. It must come from myself. And in the meantime, the pain and the burden of holding on to my anger are damaging me, not those who hurt me. I am living with the weight and the constriction and the suffering of the anger, in addition to the original harm.

In the Dhammapada, one of the Buddha's most well known scriptures, the Buddha describes the importance of forgiveness for our own well-being—no matter how horrible the original wound. "If someone has abused you, beat you, robbed you," the text goes, "abandon your thoughts of anger. Soon you will die. Life is too short to live with hatred."[42]

Contrary to our fears, true forgiveness is actually the opposite of forgetting. It is turning towards the pain, the torn place within us, and really grieving its loss. It is the process of being brave enough to look at it and loving

42. The Dhammapada, translated by and cited in Jack Kornfield, "The Practice of Forgiveness," Jackkornfield.com, accessed May 7, 2017, https://jackkornfield.com/the-practice-of-forgiveness-2/.

ourselves enough to not continue to live with bitterness and resentment.

Eva Kor, a Holocaust survivor featured in the documentary film *Forgiving Dr. Mengele* (2006), has written and spoken about the liberation that comes with the forgiveness of unforgiveable crimes. Kor, along with her twin sister, endured brutal and inhumane medical experiments at the hands of Nazi doctors in Auschwitz. In 1995, she gave a speech at the fiftieth anniversary ceremony of the liberation of Auschwitz, forgiving the Nazis for what they did to her. She said of the experience:

> As I did that, I felt a burden of pain was lifted from me. I was no longer in the grip of pain and hate; I was finally free. . . . For most people there is a big obstacle to forgiveness because society expects revenge. It seems we need it to honor our victims. But I always wonder if my dead loved ones would want me to live with pain and anger until the end of my life.[43]

She goes on to explain that beneath that first level of forgiveness, a cascade of additional forgiveness followed:

43. Eva Kor, "Biomedical Sciences and Human Experimentation at Kaiser Wilhelm Institutes—The Auschwitz Connection" symposium, June 7, 2001, Berlin, accessed April 24, 2017, https://candlesholocaust-museum.org/learn/evas-2001-speech-on-healing.html.

> The day I forgave the Nazis, privately I forgave my parents whom I hated all my life for not having saved me from Auschwitz. Children expect their parents to protect them, mine couldn't. And then I forgave myself for hating my parents.

Desmond Tutu, in writing about his journey to forgive his alcoholic and abusive father, also writes about the multiple layers of forgiveness at play in any deep process of healing:

> When I reflect back across the years to my father's drunken tirades, I realize now that it was not just with him that I was angry. I was angry with myself. That small boy, trembling in fear, had not been able to stand up to my father or protect my mother. So many years later, I realize that I not only have to forgive my father. I have to forgive myself. [44]

My experience with anger and forgiveness has followed this trajectory. When I decided to leave a business that I'd poured my heart into building because of the difficulties I was having with my business partner, I spent days, weeks, and hours seething with anger in the shower, walking down

44. Desmond Tutu, "An Invitation to Forgive," *Huffington Post*, March 28, 2014, accessed April 13, 2017, http://www.huffingtonpost.com/des mond-tutu/an-invitation-to-forgive_b_5050747.html.

the street, and in meditation. I could not forgive quickly or easily. It took a while to process the fury, the pain, and the grief of the lost business and the end of the friendship. It didn't help when I judged myself for feeling angry. It didn't help to try and reason my way out of the anger. I had to walk all the way through the fury of anger, and live there for several months, to see the light of forgiveness on the other side.

When that crack of light came, I was sitting in meditation. I was getting tired and kept falling asleep, only to wake up again and replay my angry fights with my former business partner. Finally, toward the end of the period of meditation, I heard an inner voice say to me, "You have to forgive yourself." I was shocked. In all my months of going back and forth between trying to decide whether or not I wanted to forgive my former friend, I never considered needing to forgive *myself*. Examining the situation, I could now see that I was very angry at myself for allowing myself to get hurt so badly, for missing the warning signs, for failing to be able to make the business, and the friendship, work. I was deeply ashamed.

You have to forgive yourself. How can I do that? I remember asking myself. What are the steps? I had to start with trying to understand. What were my legitimate desires and fears that caused me to find myself in that difficult situation?

I was scared to start the business alone, scared of holding

exclusive authority. It was the first major public enterprise I had started—of course I would be scared! Once we were in the partnership and I started disagreeing with the choices we were making, I wanted my partner to like me, I wanted to be "easy" and to keep the peace.

As my understanding and compassion for myself grew, I could see, understand, and forgive myself for the whole situation. Forgiving my partner came somewhat more easily after that. If all of my behavior was a result of the causes and conditions of my whole life before the moment we founded the business, then it followed that hers was as well. All that was left, after accepting this truth, was grief for what was lost, and a decision to handle future situations with more awareness.

Forgiveness does not automatically equal reconciliation. When people hurt us—especially those who hurt us continually—the wisest course of action can sometimes be to separate from them if we possibly can. As Dr. Maya Angelou says, "I forgive people so they don't continue to have power over me. That does not mean that when a fire burns me, I put my hand back in the fire."[45] Setting boundaries and separating from those who repeatedly hurt us can be

45. Maya Angelou, "Mom & Me & Mom," Diane Rehm, first aired May 8, 2013, accessed April 26, 2017, https://dianerehm.org/shows/2013-05-08 /maya-angelou-mom-me-mom.

an important part of showing love and respect for ourselves and facilitating the forgiveness process as a whole.

Indeed, once we process and accept the past, forgiveness allows us to make clear decisions about how we want to move forward and what we wish to do with the pain we have been carrying. Perhaps this means we just let go and move on with our lives. Perhaps we take our hurt and anger and put it toward a new endeavor. Out of the ashes of my failed business, I took everything I learned and created MindfulNYU, which is currently the largest campus-wide mindfulness initiative in the country, serving and supporting thousands of students each year. I was still sad about the loss of the business, but I was so glad I was able to repurpose my grief and anger for a larger good.

Forgiveness cannot be rushed. It happens on its own time, after taking great care to validate the pain we have experienced and to accept the fact that it happened. If you keep introducing the intention to move forward into forgiveness, however, you may notice one beautiful day, as you walk down the street thinking of other things, that the bruise on your heart you are so used to touching is all of a sudden not there. In its place is new tissue with a new shape, stronger and more expansive than before.

5: MINDFUL RELATIONSHIPS

OFTEN, in the beginning stages of a new relationship, there is a "honeymoon" period when both parties are projecting onto the other and seeing everything through the rosy lens of lust and excitement. It can be fun and exhilarating, anxiety provoking and intense. Could this person be the *one*? Could they really like me? Could they be the answer to all of my problems? Once the rose-colored dust settles, you return to being you, and they return to being them. Do you like the person you have in front of you? Can you accept them as they are? Do you feel seen and accepted by them?

Perhaps the deeper question that real relationships pose is do we like ourselves? Do we believe we are worthy of love and belonging? Can we accept ourselves? Relationships are like a mirror. In real intimacy, the other person reflects back to you the parts of yourself you like, as well as the parts of which you are deeply ashamed.

When I was in my late twenties, I was in a tumultuous relationship with someone who I was not sure actually liked me very much. I was not sure if I liked him very much either, but I also didn't want to break up. It was one of *those* relationships. I was so nervous and uncomfortable when I was with him, that I often couldn't eat or sleep. His ambivalence about me reflected back to me the burning question at the center of my heart: Did I deserve love? Since he was not sure, I thought if I convinced him that I was loveable, perhaps I could settle the question once and for all.

One night, as the relationship was deteriorating, I was up tossing and turning in my bed until three or four in the morning with a sick feeling in my stomach and frantic circular thoughts about the relationship in my head. Finally, exasperated, I got up, drew a bath and climbed in. In the bath, I meditated.

I felt the sadness and the exhaustion. I felt my breath and my heartbeat. I tried to relax into the warmth of the water and the stillness of the very early morning. Each time my mind wanted to dwell on the impending breakup, I gently returned to the sensations of the bath and the feelings in my body. Suddenly, from within the meditation, a powerful voice said to me: *Yael, are you going to love yourself or not? Are you going to walk through this world with full acceptance of yourself, or not?*

I knew this was a watershed moment. All the years of returning to my breath and my body in meditation had brought me here, to this choice. The voice that asked me these questions was not stern or angry. It was the voice of someone who loved me and couldn't bear to see me suffer. *Life is so short*, I remember thinking. *How many more years will I spend with partners who don't treat me well? How many more boyfriends will I have who don't reflect my inner worth?* The commitment I had fostered in myself *to* myself through meditation was demanding more of me. Each time I returned to myself in meditation, I sent a message to myself that I was worth returning to. Each time I treated my inner critic with kindness, I slowly stopped believing its stories about me. Now here I was. I took a deep breath, feeling as if someone was asking me to marry them. *Yes, I'm in.* I said to myself. I decided to commit to myself for the long haul. I decided to go with love. That boyfriend broke up with me the next day. Although I didn't immediately meet my soul mate afterward, I never again dated someone who wasn't kind to me.

So many of my relationship struggles have been about learning to love and accept myself rather than outsourcing that struggle to a partner. To really see and connect with my partners, I needed to confront my own wounded and aching places.

We have a powerful need to project our inner struggles on to our partners. If we wish we were more successful, we may think our partners wish that about us too. If we wish we were smarter, we may idealize our partner to be the smartest person in the room, who, if we are worthy, might decide that we are smart as well. I don't think this is wrong or immature. I think it is human. Untangling what is mine from what is my partner's is a central practice of mindful relationships. We can be grateful for the mirror they provide without believing that the projections are originating from them.

The philosopher Martin Buber had a way of describing this situation with his concept of I-thou relationships, as distinct from I-it relationships.[46] I-thou, according to Buber, is when we relate to the other with respect and dignity. We see their fullness and their humanity. We notice where we end and the other begins. I-it, on the other hand, is when we relate to others as objects in our storylines. The other person is really just an extension of ourselves and is not fully seen or respected in their own right. We are so busy using them to affirm or deny some part of ourselves that we never get to know who they really are.

Susan Piver, the Buddhist author and teacher, writes about this beautifully in her book, *How Not to Be Afraid of Your Own Life*. She says:

> I wish I had known that when you live with someone for a long time, you will experience continuous mind-blowing irritation . . . when you try and replace your actual partner with a projection of a partner. He always figures out a way to tell you

46. Martin Buber, *I and Thou* (New York: Collier Books, 1986).

how unlike your ideal he really is, which once you pick yourself up, gives you yet another opportunity to choose between who this person is and who you sort of hoped he was . . . We have to throw away the script and begin to improvise. You're playing you and I'm playing me. Go.[47]

Both the person who is projecting and the person who feels unseen suffer. Our practice is to do our best to wake up when we notice this going on, attend to our pain, and try to remember the "thou-ness" of the other.

Our partners are different people than we are. I know this sounds obvious. Of course they are different than us! Otherwise it wouldn't be a relationship! But my experience is that the closer you get to someone in any relationship—whether romantic, platonic, or familial—the harder it is to see the boundary of difference between you. Identities begin to smash together, and pretty soon it becomes hard to see the separations.

I had a platonic friendship through most of my twenties with someone named Holly. Although we looked nothing alike, people used to think we were sisters. We spent so much time together, lived together as roommates, and

47. Susan Piver, *How Not to Be Afraid of Your Own Life: Opening Your Heart to Confidence, Intimacy, and Joy* (New York: St. Martin's Griffin, 2008), 115.

shared so much of ourselves with each other that we sub-consciously took on each other's vocal mannerisms. It was a beautiful and close relationship, and I felt like she under-stood the deepest parts of me, and I of her.

Over the years, however, the extreme intimacy of the friendship made it hard to see where she ended and I began, and both of us, without knowing or articulating it, began to chafe at the feeling of disappearing into the other. Although on the surface everything was the same, I began to grow silently jealous of the many other friends she had and the way she met and befriended guys effortlessly, when it was still such a struggle for me. Living together and being so close I also wanted space within our friendship, which I did not know how to ask for. The relationship blew up one night when I, out of pent-up competitiveness and jealousy, went on a secret date with a guy she had a crush on. When she found out about it a few days later and confronted me, I felt empty of words for how to account for myself. Why did I do that? What was wrong with me? I felt guilty and ashamed. She was furious and hurt.

The fight caused us to take a break from each other for several months, and it was only in that break that we both realized we needed to individuate from each other. The boy fights were just a convenient wedge to stick between each other so that we could find our own paths and our own identities.

This can happen frequently in close friendships and relationships. If healthy boundaries aren't there, someone will create them. Someone will drive a wedge in the relationship to find the space to breathe and individuate.

In Khalil Gibran's classic book *The Prophet*, he writes of this need for boundaries within intimacy. He says:

> Love one another, but make not a bond of love:
> Let it rather be a moving sea between the shores
>   of your souls.
> Fill each other's cup but drink not from one cup.
> Give one another of your bread but eat not from
>   the same loaf.
> Sing and dance together and be joyous, but let each
>   one of you be alone,
> Even as the strings of a lute are alone though they
>   quiver with the same music.[48]

Boundaries in relationships and friendships allow each partner to be themselves and love to flow between them.

Real relationships are like our meditation practice. We return back to the present moment, over and over again, to see what, or who, is really there. We drift away into our own scripts and narratives, only to have moments of awakening when we realize we have been missing the being who is in front of us. We have put ourselves or our partner into

48. Kahlil Gibran, *The Prophet* (London: Alfred A. Knopf, 1923), 9.

a box of who they or we are, and, inevitably, our partner breaks the boxes by acting differently than we projected. When this happens, we have to rub our eyes, look again, and decide if we want to come back into relationship with them. If we do, love as complete acceptance has a chance to blossom.

MINDFUL SEX

On the fourth day of a seven-day silent meditation retreat I was attending, one of the teachers, Eliezer Sobel, asked the crowd what types of things they had been thinking about over the course of the week. People volunteered things like "regrets," "my family," and "my job." After all the answers came in, Eliezer looked around the room with a smile on his face and said, "Oh, and I'm sure nobody has been thinking about sex?"

The room burst into laughter. Of course we had all thought about sex. In fact, I noticed that in one week of silence on retreat, I had more sexual thoughts and fantasies than I'd had in several months at home. I was just way too shy and ashamed to admit it in front of a room full of strangers. What *is* the connection between sex, sexual thoughts, and this practice, I wondered? I never found the courage to ask a teacher, but the question persisted.

When I was in college, it was popular for feminist and queer student organizations to host an event where a "sexpert" was brought in to give frank sex advice and answer questions. I attended at least three of these, together with hundreds of others who eagerly packed the room to learn more about the act that most of us were exploring in a major way for the first time in our lives. It felt liberating to hear and talk about everything from positions to protection with no shame or shyness.

Many years later, MindfulNYU, the meditation program that I run at NYU, held two workshops on mindful sex for the student community. Both were filled to capacity, with students spilling out into the hallway and crowding every corner of the room, hungry to hear about sex without shame the same way that my classmates and I had been. In fact, it was not only the most popular meditation session we put on that year, it was the most popular session we had ever had.

So what is mindful sex? Mindful sex education goes beyond pregnancy or STDs (although that is important!). Mindful sex is sex with awareness. It's a journey of exploration, of our own bodies and the bodies of others. Mindfulness can can help us understand desire, intimacy, connection, and energy. Sex as an act isn't terribly complicated, but *mindful* sex, sex with awareness, often takes tremendous courage, patience, and a willingness to hang out in our vulnerability. Mindful sex is about showing up as our whole selves, allowing ourselves to be seen, and being willing to truly see the other person.

SEX AND OURSELVES

Reb Anderson, a Zen Buddhist teacher, writes about sexual energy as a great ball of fire that we must get to know intimately, like other energies in our body. He says:

> If we turn away from our sexual passion, then we freeze and beings are harmed. If we grab it, then we are burned and beings are harmed. But if we just stay close to it, walk around it, always in touch with the fact that we are sexual beings, neither identifying with nor distancing ourselves from our sexuality, then we gradually become intimate with it. From this intimacy, appropriate sexual conduct spontaneously emerges.[49]

In Anderson's view, if we repress the ball of fire that is our sexual energy, we freeze a part of ourselves. Not everyone experiences sexuality in this way—asexual individuals may not identify with this type of "fireball" within. For many, however, when we dim the light of sexuality within us, we dim all of our light and energy, and feel alienated from ourselves and others.

Fully "identifying" with our lust, and trying to satisfy our every sexual whim, is also dangerous. It is a form of

49. Anderson, *Being Upright*, 112.

greed that turns others into objects that we try to possess, in order to escape the discomfort of the fire of lust within us. Trungpa Rimpoche, the Tibetan Buddhist teacher, describes this as a possessive sexual desire rooted in ego. "You see the other person as a kind of juicy steak," he writes, "and you would like to gobble the person up and be done with it—nothing more than that."[50] The Buddha's way has us walk a middle path between these two extremes, making a wide open space to learn about, love, and *be* the sexual energy within us, rather than repress or react to it.

Being with this sexual energy may take different forms. We may choose—as many monks and nuns do—to abstain from sex. I highly recommend you try this, whether or not you are dating someone, at some point in your life. Not releasing sexual energy through orgasm, and yet not repressing it either, can lead some people to feel very focused. Others describe feeling buoyant and energetic. For me, periods of celibacy have often led me to bursts of creativity in writing or art. It can be difficult to do, but sexual energy "repurposed" can be experienced as a powerful and beautiful force.

We can, however, still "be" with the fireball of sexual energy and explore it carefully and mindfully through sex with ourselves or with partners. This practice runs counter

---

50. Chogyam Trungpa, *Work, Sex, Money: Real Life on the Path of Mindfulness* (Boston: Shambhala, 2011), 117.

to so much of our society today, however. Through a constant barrage of images in movies, television, and advertising, young men in our culture are taught that to be a man is to objectify women and to avoid any sign of weakness. According to Brené Brown's research, men absorb the message that emotional vulnerability—particularly in intimate encounters—is coded as weakness, and so they hide their vulnerability through enactments of power, status, domination, and violence.[51] Men and women, Brown says, are responsible for perpetuating this dynamic, as we all fail to provide space for men to be whole, authentic, and vulnerable in intimate encounters.

Young women, on the other hand, learn early and often that they are sexual objects, not subjects of their own sexuality. Sex is something that happens *to* them if their bodies are deemed desirable, and far too often, some form of sexual assault or abuse happens to them without their consent. They are not encouraged to explore and own their sexual wants and needs, especially if they fall outside of a socially permissible norm.

This sexual picture is further complicated if we are a race or size that is sexualized or de-sexualized, and/or if we are lesbian, gay, transgender, bisexual, queer, intersex, asex-

---

51. TED, "The Power of Vulnerability | Brené Brown," 20:49, posted January 3, 2011, https://www.youtube.com/watch?v=iCvmsMzlF7o.

ual, or gender nonconforming. We all come to sex with our unique psychology, personal history, and social messaging.

Navigating the waters of mindful sex and intimacy requires something of us, right off the bat. We must be willing to be real, present, and vulnerable with ourselves, exactly as we are. This means taking a deep breath and accepting our bodies, our wants and desires, and our attractions. It means committing ourselves to healing sexual trauma from our past or from our society in order to come to love ourselves more fully. Sometimes this takes a lot of therapy. Sometimes it is something we practice in loving sexual encounters with ourselves or others. Sometimes, through formal meditation practice, we touch the wounded places within us, and can practice holding those traumas and pains with immense love and light, and gradually begin to heal.

I had a meditation teacher once who shared with us that when she first started meditating, she sat with a very rigid posture on the cushion, her hands in tensed fists underneath her. When she realized she was sitting this way, she would move her hands and try to relax, only to find herself back again in this tense posture, fists underneath her, at the end of each session. This went on for years, until one day, in a long meditation sit, she started to have images of the sexual and physical abuse that she had been through. She had been sitting many years, and had been through a lot of therapy, but she realized that until that moment, her fists were still trying to protect her, and her body didn't feel safe enough to relax. Gradually, through therapy and meditation, she was able to transform and heal her trauma, release her fists from underneath her, and take a stronger, more comfortable seat.

For me, sex between the ages of eighteen and twenty-two was a messy blur of trying to please the other person, trying to hide the parts of my body I was ashamed of, and trying to appear sexy and "liberated"—more like the desirable girls I saw in the movies. I was often drunk and sometimes high. There was some pleasure involved, of course, but I was so insecure, so worried about my partner "getting off" and so removed from my own body that the ratio of getting pleasure to giving pleasure was severely out of whack. Rather than ask for what I wanted, I faked nearly every orgasm I had during those years—much like the faking I was doing in much of my intimate life in an attempt to be liked and accepted. As my therapist said many years later, "As goes in life, goes in the bedroom."

What I loved about the "sexperts" that came to campus is that they urged us to be sexual agents and to take responsibility for our own pleasure, with or without a partner. I remember Betty Dodson, author of *Sex for One*, telling us, "If you love yourself, if you show love to yourself and bring yourself pleasure, then you are never without a sex partner. You are with the best lover you will ever have."

As we sit in meditation and return to our bodies with

love, my experience is that we become increasingly unwilling to let others treat us with disrespect in the bedroom. In my mid-twenties, I was sleeping with someone regularly who did not want a relationship with me. He made it very clear that if someone more desirable came along, we would have to end our arrangement. I pretended that this was fine with me, when in fact it hurt me very deeply. I hoped, during each encounter, that I would be so appealing to him that eventually he would capitulate, like in the many romantic comedies I had seen, and would realize true love was right beneath his nose the whole time.

He was clearly using me for companionship and sex, but the truth was, I was also using him to answer a very deep and scary question about myself: was I loveable? Could I make someone who was ambivalent about me less ambivalent through my charms and sexuality? Those questions kept me ensnared in painful push-and-pull sexual relationships for years.

One day, when explaining my predicament to a friend who is a Tibetan Buddhist practitioner, she told me that there was a saying in Tibet: "Do not use your prize jewels as a begging bowl." Our hearts and bodies are precious, she said, and to use them as a begging bowl is to debase and contort them into objects that only others can fill with value.

Gradually, over several years, I started treating my body and my heart a bit more like jewels. Meditating allowed me to inhabit my body with more gentleness, love, and acceptance. I began to use sex less as a barometer of my own lovability and appeal and more as an opportunity to be fully present with another person. I sharpened my radar for partners who made me feel bad about myself or left me questioning my worth, and began to steer clear of them. I noticed that the more I insisted on my own body being treated with care by my partners, the more my love and acceptance of myself grew.

SEX AND OTHER PEOPLE

My friend is a therapist who specializes in pornography addiction. Most of her clients are young men in their twenties struggling in sexual relationships with real people, due to their exposure to the unrealistic and damaging images of idealized sexual partners/encounters in porn and media. They approach sex with so many assumptions, pressures, and expectations of their partners and themselves that no honest connection is possible. In fact, the way porn addiction most frequently manifests in these patients is through erectile dysfunction—a literal and metaphoric inability to fully show up for the act itself.

Even if we don't find ourselves in this exact predicament, we may relate to the fear of being naked (literally and figuratively) with a partner and completely open to the fullness and authenticity of who they are. It can be terrifying to remove all projections, objectifications, and expectations and to engage with the rawness of this other person. What if you don't like what you see there? What if the person doesn't like what they see? What if it is all too intense or overwhelming?

While it can be scary, that is the real promise and excitement of sex. It offers us the opportunity to go up to the edge of where we are willing to see others and be seen by them, to empty out our expectations, and to dive into the unknown. In this way, sex is not just better when we meditate—sex can be a meditation all on its own.

There is a famous story of a fancy, learned man who comes to a meditation teacher to study. The man sits down in front of the teacher, full of self-importance and entitlement, and says he would like to be enlightened. The man begins to recite facts and history, techniques and stories as the teacher calmly pours the tea . . . and keeps pouring it . . . and keeps pouring it until the tea spills over the side of the cup and all over the table. The man stops his recitations and says, "What are you doing? The tea is spilling everywhere!"

"You are like this overflowing cup of tea," the teacher says. "There is no room for new knowledge, new experiences, or a new way of seeing. If you want to learn from me, you have to empty some of the 'knowing' out of your cup."

When we approach our partners, whether new or old, we have to make room in our cup to be with them as they are. In today's society, that may mean retraining our brain away from unrealistic ideas of "perfect" partners or situations. It may mean committing ourselves again and again to keeping our senses open, just like we do when meditating. We practice taking in what is in front of us, and being present with the unknown in and alongside the other.

HEARTBREAK

Breakups are an inevitable part of relationships. The bad ones are heart-wrenching, crushing, world-destroying periods of time when it feels like life is over. Regardless of who broke up with whom, breakups can bring out our craziest thoughts and behaviors and touch on our most sensitive places.

In one of my most painful breakups, I remember going miles out of my way each time I left the house to walk by the apartment where my ex-boyfriend lived, in the hope that I would run into him. I had no idea what I would say if I did see him. I think I hoped he would suddenly "remember" how beautiful and cool I was and want to be with me. I never found out—despite walking by his apartment over fifty times, we never actually collided. I finally realized that the only thing this behavior would get me was a restraining order. I was living in a haze of denial and delusion, unwilling to face the truth that the relationship was over.

Devastating breakups bring us right up to the edge of

loss, grief, and death. Even though the person is still out there, walking around, what you had together has died. It is over, and now has to be mourned like any other kind of death. Moving out of the kind of denial I was experiencing into real grief was an important stage of that break up, as well as all the ones that followed. I resisted letting go because I knew it would be agonizingly sad to admit the death of the relationship. Once I finally opened to it, however, I was able to let the raw grief wash over me, and carry me slowly toward healing.

The unfortunate part of this process is that it often takes a lot of time. Healing and moving on is rarely fast. In my experience, recovering from heartbreak takes about the same time it takes a huge block of ice to melt on a cold day, drop by tiny little drop. When and if this happens to you, when you find yourself in the middle of this dark night of grief, anger, loss, and fear, try not to run away from it. Try to open up to the rush of emotions, even as they threaten to drown you. It will hurt, but it will hurt more and longer if you push these feelings away. Try to let the cracks and brokenness of your heart soften you and deepen your compassion for the whole world, including yourself. Be very gentle and kind to yourself.

When the heart has been broken, it is our natural tendency to try to protect it the next time around. We build scaffolding and structures so that we aren't vulnerable

again. We put up walls and enact strict screening proce-
dures at the borders.

At some point, however, those walls are no longer protecting us—they are imprisoning us. They are preventing
new love and connections to form. With gentleness, we
can use our meditation practice to soften around our inner
scaffolding and walls. We can forgive life for hurting us,
and forgive ourselves for getting hurt. We can look at that
earlier heartbreak not as a failure to protect, but as a sincere
and brave attempt to love and be loved. Yes, it didn't work
with that person, but you demonstrated that you have the
capacity to love. That is your strength and your power.

The writer Kim Stafford writes about the beauty of
resilience when he recounts watching his daughter play on
the edge of a fountain on a hot summer day. As she wobbles
along the edge, Stafford observes her making it across the
thinnest part, turning around to face him with a smile, and
then slipping into the fountain. A mother sitting nearby
lifts her out:

> She came panting to me across the hot pavement.
> Her dress left a trail of wet, her hair streamed
> down, and her face was bright. She stood stubby
> tall before me. "When I was falling, Dad, I heard
> my little voice. But it didn't say, "Be afraid"—it
> said, "Have fun falling." Her eyebrows went up,
> and her mouth clamped into a line of conviction.

Stafford continues:

> When I live my life now, when I write, when I enter a hard time, in an uncertain way, I want my little voice saying, "Have fun falling." Have fun tumbling into the changes that reign and root and every pair of wings has to carry out—a secret the wind and lightning and sorrow, and love keep making plain. By falling you find the bottom, and without that, no joy.[52]

Have fun falling. Love is born from the willingness to risk our hearts again and again. After we have grieved our losses, can we go back to having a vulnerable heart, and be willing to try again? It may be frightening. It may seem impossible. But surviving a devastating heartbreak can show us our power to return to the surface after hitting the bottom. Without that, no joy.

LONELINESS

I have felt terribly lonely for most of my life. In college, my loneliness hit its peak. Despite having friends, a roommate, and family nearby, I felt alienated, isolated, and deeply

---

52. Kim Robert Stafford, *100 Tricks Every Boy Can Do: How My Brother Disappeared* (San Antonio, TX: Trinity University Press, 2012).

alone. The loneliness went deeper than any of my relationships could touch. At times, it felt physically painful to carry
around.

When I was drowning in loneliness during this time, I
would flail around trying to find a life buoy I could grab.
If I was single, that might be a hasty new crush. If I was in
a relationship, I might decide I needed a better partner, or
more friends, or better friends, or new clothes, or *something
else* to make me complete. It was agonizing. It felt like I
was in a dark cave, all alone, unloved and empty inside.
All I wanted to do was escape, and yet I couldn't find the
path out.

I never spoke to anyone about my feelings of loneliness
and I never heard anyone else talk about it either. People would talk about wanting to be in a relationship, but
nobody admitted they were lonely. It seemed pathetic and
shameful. I wasn't sure what loneliness actually was, but
because it hurt so much, I believed that it was a type of
punishment. It meant that something fundamental about
myself wasn't okay.

The first time I realized that my feelings might not be
unique to me was one afternoon as I was sitting in a conference about something else entirely. The speaker mentioned
that she began her activism in college, where she had been
lonely most of the time. I had a hard time listening to the
rest of her talk as my heart sped up and I felt tears in the
corners of my eyes. She just came out and *admitted* her lone-

liness? How could she be so brave? Something shook free within me as I realized how much shame I was holding about my loneliness—how much extra suffering I was adding to the original pain of feeling alone. If I could peel back the shame and just focus on understanding the loneliness, what would I discover? How could I relate to this feeling in a different way?

Through meditation I started examining my loneliness like a scientist. Of what was this feeling composed? How did I know I was lonely? What were the physical sensations in the body? What were the triggers? What made it worse; what made it better?

It was not an easy task. There was something about loneliness that was hot, itchy, uncomfortable—like a wool sweater in the middle of summer. At first, I would get lost in the story of my being lonely, rather than the feelings themselves. Loneliness would say to me: "What is wrong with you? Why are you alone? This can't be good. You are doing something wrong. You are going to be alone *forever*. Get used to it!" It felt like getting pummeled over and over again. And yet, I realized that the chattering inner voice was trying to stop me from digging deeper into the feeling. With all of its cruelty, it was more afraid of me actually feeling the pain of the loneliness more acutely. It tried to block the way. It would keep me busy with its provocations and while I was there, I was still far away from the darkness at the heart of loneliness itself.

Somehow, I managed to plunge forward. I sat long meditation retreats where there was nowhere to run but into the pain. I breathed. I cried. Finally, from within the thick of the feeling, in a few particularly deep meditation sessions, I started looking around.

It came to me in a series of visions from within the meditation. First I saw a picture of my loneliness as a brick wall around my heart. It cast a long shadow over the most vulnerable part of my heart. It was cold and empty behind the wall. Looking closer, it felt like there were tiny beings holding up the wall, pushing with all their might so that the wall would not collapse. What are you afraid of? I asked the beings. They were frantic, filled with panic, incoherent, pushing with all their might. I was afraid, but as I looked deeper, I caught a glimpse, behind the wall, at my own vulnerable heart. It looked tender and soft and was filled with a powerful longing for love. At this point in the meditation, I burst into tears. I put a hand on my chest. "Poor baby," I said to myself. "All you want is love. All you want is love." It was such a simple, pure wish, and yet so fiercely defended. The pain of loneliness was in the defense, in the separation of the wall and the alienation of myself from others. The wall, trying to keep me safe, was keeping me imprisoned. I wanted out.

And yet, I couldn't knock down the wall all at once. Slowly, I needed to accept and love my loneliness, my defenses, and my fears until my heart grew stronger and less afraid. Through meditation, I came back again and again to the feelings, bringing acceptance and care. Through therapy, I needed to look at the times I was alone and frightened as a child, and how that colored my experience of being alone as an adult. Slowly, somewhere along the way, being alone stopped registering as being lonely. Slowly, I was able to take more risks, let more people in, and find more space within myself for others. Love began appearing in new friendships, relationships, and community. The walls between myself and the world softened, opened, and, at times, disappeared.

When I am able to offer myself love and care in this way, it is almost impossible to feel lonely. The two feelings just don't go together. I can feel desire, I can feel longing, but I don't feel that narrow mindset of "lonely" that depends on me believing I am essentially separate from the world. The Persian poet Hafiz writes, "Don't surrender your loneliness so quickly! Let it ferment and season you as few human or even divine ingredients can."[53] These days I try to see loneliness as this type of gift, "seasoning" me with longing and tenderness, telling me I need to bring love and compassion

53. Shams Al-Din Hafiz, translation by Daniel Ladinsky, *The Subject Tonight Is Love* (New York: Penguin, 2003).

to my experience. Perhaps that means I reach out to a loved one, or exercise, or meditate. Perhaps it means I just sit in the middle of the loneliness and stare out the window. Loneliness is no longer the enemy. It is simply a call from the heart to return home.

6: CHANGING THE WORLD WITHOUT BURNING OUT

OUR TWENTIES can be a prime time for activism and social justice work. Many of us have left home and seen more of the world. We have experienced, seen, and/or learned about structural inequity and deeply feel our responsibility to address it. We have the energy and passion to try to build a better world. The only question that remains is *how* to make change. What should be our approach? How do we remain inspired? How do we keep from burning out? And what does meditation have to do with any of this?

There is a critique of mindfulness from activist communities, arguing that the world is severely broken and does not have time for meditators to stare at their navels, sit on cushions, and retreat from the world. In other words, they believe that a dedication to meditation and mindful living is too selfish for a world that demands that we work for social justice and equity.

Simultaneously, there is a belief of some in meditation and Buddhist circles (most of which are dominated by white and upper-middle-class people) that social justice and politics do not have a place in spiritual communities. Many in these communities do not see that inward transformation is inextricably connected to social transformation. They are busy, stressed out, and are in a privileged place in society that does not require them to think about social problems or inequities, and so they don't.

Fortunately, thanks to the work of several pioneers and leaders at the forefront of social justice causes, Buddhism, and meditation, there seems to be a decreased appetite for both sides of this argument these days. Among growing numbers of young people interested in social justice and meditation, it is becoming increasingly clear that the struggle for self-love, inner freedom, and understanding and the struggle for outer liberation for *all* beings are bound up in one another.

Buddhism doesn't just make a powerful case for the importance of inner and outer freedom (and the deep connections between the two), it also offers a path for how such liberation can be attained.

YOUR LIBERATION IS BOUND UP IN MINE

Why should we concern ourselves with equity and justice? Our twenties and thirties are busy times. We have our personal lives to attend to. We have our school and work life. We have to figure out our careers and our families.

Why must we bother with larger issues like racism, sexism, homophobia, inequality, or environmental destruction?

The truth is, our society is, and always has been, very sick. The diseases of ideologies like racism, extreme capitalism, and homophobia are felt by all of us, whether or not we are in the targeted groups.

Reverend Zenju Earthlyn Manuel writes:

> We must, all of us, openly acknowledge the real norms, desires, biological myths, and practices that fuel racial, sexual, and gender-based hatred. . . . [Society] must say, "Ah, we have willingly hurt ourselves and other people. We have covered up our mess for so long." Society must learn to see. A society that does not examine itself is an unenlightened one.

The more we practice, the more we can identify and understand the ways we perpetuate suffering for ourselves and others, and the more we feel motivated to transform it. Not because it is the "right" or "nice" thing to do, but because our health, our wholeness, and our very life is on the line. We come to see how as a society, we cannot wall ourselves off from one another. We sink or swim together.

There is a quote by an Aboriginal activist group that says, "If you have come here to help me, you are wasting your time. But if you have come because your liberation is bound up with mine, then let us work together."[54] Sometimes it is easy to see how our liberation is bound up in the liberation of others. If there is a neo-Nazi group that spews hatred against Jews and Muslims, for instance, and they commit a crime against someone or damage a temple, community center, or mosque, it strategically makes sense for Jews and Muslims to band together as a stronger force against the hate group. It was a mosque this time, next time it could be a synagogue.

But sometimes the connections are not so clear. For those of us who sit in seats of power and privilege, which have been constructed specifically to define us as against and superior to an "other," it can be hard to see why we should adjust the status quo. Sure, there is a vague sense of "doing the right thing," or "being a good person," but these impulses do not carry the same vitality or longevity as an at-the-core, gut-level, visceral understanding of interconnection and interdependence to which the Aboriginal activists above refer.

On an intellectual level, we can understand our connectivity in terms of science, seeing the multitude of ways our air, water, and food supply depend on the soil, the climate, the farmers, the food packers and transporters, the markets and the other countless forces that bind us to one

54. Aboriginal activists group, Queensland, 1970s, http://unnecessary evils.blogspot.com/2008/11/attributing-words.html.

another and the Earth. We can also understand our interdependence historically, witnessing how hypernationalism,
hypercapitalism, and divisive ideologies have resulted in
widespread trauma and suffering for different groups of
people over time. We can fight for justice by understanding
that it was once our group whose lives were deemed dispos-
able, or by knowing that it one day might be us. All of these
are important entry points into the work of changemaking.

Meditation practice, however, teaches us how to also
understand interdependence *experientially*. It forces us to
take a front-row seat for our own suffering, and see the
ways we perpetuate that suffering on others (consciously
and unconsciously). It urges us to open our eyes even further and see the ways our entire society deems some people
to be inferior and some to be superior. When we live in a
world that divides us in this way, we suffer. These divisions
take time, energy, money, and the spinning of delusion to
maintain. It is unhealthy for everyone. Our hearts are built
naturally to love, to connect, to flourish. The moment we
cast anyone or anything out of our hearts—either as individuals or as a society—it causes pain. Over time, it can
make us spiritually, emotionally, and physically sick.

Dr. Martin Luther King Jr. recognized this:

> I've seen too much hate on the faces of sheriffs
> in the South. I've seen hate on the faces of too
> many Klansmen and too many White Citizens

Councilors in the South to want to hate, myself, because every time I see it, I know that it does something to their faces and their personalities, and I say to myself that hate is too great a burden to bear. I have decided to love.[55]

Deciding to love means we take responsibility for all the social injustice, even if we are not guilty of having created the problem in the first place. We can make change because we see and recognize the pain of others as a part of ourselves. Love drives us to seek freedom from this pain.

In college, although I was committed to social justice and activism, I became confused about my role. I often felt not just responsible for the injustices of the world, but *guilty* of them. Rather than feeling personally invested in the liberation of others as being *tied* to my own liberation, I felt invested in the well-being of others in the hope that it would prove me to be "good" and that it would ease my sense of guilt and shame. I was worried at every turn of saying the wrong thing, of being "called out" for being racist, homophobic, or biased in some way.

Several years ago, I organized an interfaith event led by myself and a friend of mine—a white, Jewish, cisgender

55. Martin Luther King Jr., 1967. "Where Do We Go from Here?" (annual report delivered at the Eleventh Convention of the Southern Christian Leadership Conference, August 16, Atlanta, GA).

man. A woman in the community sent a furious email to myself and several other people, saying that an interfaith event led by two white cisgender Jews was an example of racism and a perpetuation of white supremacy, and needed to be cancelled immediately. I remember my face feeling hot and my palms growing sweaty while reading the email. I wanted to go home and hide. I could not evaluate whether I had anything to learn from what she wrote because I was so deeply ashamed. I felt that she (and, by extension, everyone) could see the dirty secret I was working so hard to hide: that somewhere in the recesses of my mind and heart, I was a racist, ignorant, bad person that did not deserve love. I felt sick to my stomach.

Pretty quickly, that feeling turned into defensiveness. *Who does she think she is?* I vented to my co-organizer. *She doesn't know us! She doesn't know anything about how the meditation will go. How could she jump to such conclusions?* We determined that she must be an angry, sad person. We decided to pity her, rather than hate her. It was a thin defense. I could tell the accusations were still rattling us both.

It took weeks of processing this email with many friends and teachers for me to actually examine the shame I felt about the possibility of my own unconscious bias coming into play in the planning of the event. Thanks to my meditation practice, I knew that I didn't have to cling to these parts of me, and yet the only way I could move past them was through recognizing and accepting that they were there. Once I began to own that truth—that racism and all other systems of power, oppression, and domination were a part of me, like they are a part of everyone else in society—I didn't have to work so hard to deflect, hide, and defend against that accusation. Instead I could listen, examine, and take responsibility for the ways those systems manifested through me, and keep trying harder to learn and live from an awake, heart-centered place.

One of the most beautiful and famous Buddhist texts is the *Metta Sutta*, or lovingkindness sutra. In it, there is the line, "Just as a mother would protect her only child over her own life, even so, let them cultivate a boundless heart toward all beings." I used to chant this line each week at my Zen temple, not really understanding the magnitude of it. *Yes, it is nice to care for all beings,* I would think, and then move on.

Since I have recently become a mother, this line packs a much bigger punch. I would die protecting my son without any question. In a heartbeat. I know this so deeply. I know it with all the force of my whole being. My love for him is so unequivocally large and powerful and beyond my own skin. The Buddha is therefore asking me in this line to cultivate my heart so that I am able to have this level of love *for all beings*. Every last one—the lovely and the annoying, the powerful and the weak. Any child's pain should be like my child's pain. Any adult's—or group's—pain should be like my group's pain. Not theoretically, or intellectually—but in the heart and the gut.

It is a huge charge, and I am certainly not there yet, but I do believe that a love-centered social justice practice comes from this interdependent, interconnected place. I also believe that this type of justice—based on love, understanding and an awareness of our interconnectedness—is the only kind that is sustainable over the long haul.

Go to the Frontlines of Your Struggle

Perhaps it was not a huge surprise that I could not sustain my activism in my early twenties. The activism I engaged in was partly rooted in the fear of being exposed as a bigot, and feelings of being overwhelmed by the injustice I saw all around me. As a result, I slowly retreated from social justice work, telling myself I needed to "go within" and recharge. I was tired of feeling guilty, angry, and powerless to affect change. I barricaded myself away from the suffering and injustice of the world as much as I could.

I remember this coming to a particularly high point during Hurricane Katrina, when I watched the news coverage of the death, destruction, and oppression at the root of such a huge humanitarian disaster. After getting an initial picture of what was happening in New Orleans, my feelings of defensiveness and self-protection kicked in and I immediately tried to turn off the radio or the TV if I saw a glimpse of the story. This went on for weeks, until one day, after sprinting across the room to turn off a story about the hurricane on the news, I realized how much mental and emotional energy it was taking to try and shut out what was happening. Barricading myself within my own ignorance was not making me feel better. It caused me to feel lonely, walled off, and farther away from life. It hurt.

Rabbi Alan Lew, a meditation teacher and advocate for social change, calls this screening out of suffering a "psychic squint" that we do to try and avoid the suffering we see all around us. As we look at the world through this "squinted" lens, we get emotional "headaches" because we can't *just* screen out suffering. When we squint to avoid it, we also screen out joy, love, and our full connection with all beings. We screen out a great deal of life.

The alternative, opening my heart to suffering, meant feeling pain, and it meant I would *have* to make moves towards trying to help transform the situation. It also meant I would have to look at my own suffering and the ways that I cause suffering in myself and others, consciously and unconsciously. It did not mean I needed to beat myself up or take on the guilt (and fragility) that comes with assigning "bad" or "good" to myself in relationship to justice. I had seen how that way of thinking was counterproductive and produced more harm in the world. Instead, I would need to release the question of whether I was bad or good, and dedicate myself to making changes in my spheres of influence. I would need to take steps, even if they were small, to fight for a better world and rectify inequality and injustice. I couldn't "sit this one out"—my life, and the life of those I cared about, was on the line. Breathing into that truth felt like a huge relief. I could handle the pain and the responsibility. It felt like what my heart had wanted to do from the beginning.

In their beautiful book, *Radical Dharma*, Lama Rod Owens, Rev. Angel Kyodo Williams, and Dr. Jasmine Syedullah explore the responsibility and the necessity of understanding one's own suffering through meditation in order to dismantle systems of power that cause suffering in the world—regardless of where one is located socially, racially, economically, or otherwise.

Reverend Angel writes that black people in particular have carried an undue burden in this work, fighting systems of oppression, and yet are in deep need of the healing and repair that Buddhist meditation offers. "We are propelled by the essential human compulsion for freedom, but we can also be driven by centuries of pain and carry a burden greater than people should have ever known. Our healing cannot wait until the structures acquiesce, are dismantled, or come undone. We must take a seat."[56]

56. Angel Kyodo Williams, Rod Owens, and Jasmine Syedullah, *Radical Dharma: Talking Race, Love, and Liberation* (Berkeley, CA: North Atlantic Books, 2016), introduction.

Elsewhere in the book, there is a transcription of a Q&A with the authors at a Zen center in Brooklyn. A white audience member explains that in her community organizing work on behalf of Latino immigrants, she often "makes herself disappear" by standing in the back and remaining silent, in order to make room for the Latinos in the room to speak. She felt uneasy about this, and asked for advice. Lama Rod responded with this suggestion: "Not necessarily to think about being an ally but about getting to the frontlines of your struggle and not just stepping back and saying, 'I can't get in the way of marginalized people.' Go to the frontlines and be there. That's what's going to make me happy. Don't get behind me."[57]

We all have places of power and influence, no matter where we are socially located. For some it might be in our families. For some it might be in a classroom discussion or in a club where we're a member. Lama Rod is asking us to find the frontlines of *our* struggle, the places where we face or see injustice and the places where we find our power. Wherever we are—within places of unearned privilege or within places of unearned discrimination (or both), where can we fully show up? Where can we find a place for the healing we might need, or to offer our unique gifts, our particular voice, joining a larger chorus dedicated to justice?

57. Ibid., 132.

At Soto Zen Buddhist temples, there is a chant that says, "Beings are numberless. I vow to save them." Within that sentence, there is the acknowledgement of a task so large that it is impossible to accomplish: saving every one of an infinite number of beings. And yet, we vow to do it anyway.

There is another Zen proverb along these lines: "In Zen, there are two things: sitting, and sweeping the garden. It doesn't matter how large the garden is." We cannot solve everything. Often our steps are small and humble. Nevertheless, it doesn't matter that beings are numberless. It doesn't matter how big the garden is. All we know is that we have to do *something* to alleviate the suffering. We do not need to be perfect. We just need to show up.

How We Do Anything Is How We Do Everything

When we approach social change work with an unshakable foundation of interconnection, certain *ways* of fighting for justice no longer become an option. We cannot vilify others or rely on the rhetoric of "good" guys and "bad" guys, so popular in politics, when our well-being and their well-being are tied up together.

This is not to say that some people, groups, and governments are not dangerous and do not need to be restrained. It does not mean that we don't fight against oppression or injustice. It does require that we do not reproduce the same division (based on a delusion of separateness) that caused the harm and oppression in the first place, whether in our hearts, our rhetoric, or our goals. We do not fight out of hatred. We do not make certain people into bad guys and good guys. When we are all completely interdependent, nobody can be left out.

This is not easy to do. It requires that we constantly work simultaneously on two fronts at once: the "outside" world and our own hearts. If we are fighting for a world in which certain classes or groups of people are not treated as "other," we have to look inside to see the ways we "other" parts of ourselves. We have to see the seeds of ignorance, hate, and greed (called the "three poisons" in Buddhism) in ourselves so we can recognize and help others transform these seeds in themselves.

I am writing this shortly after Donald Trump was elected president of the US. My intellectual, self-righteous mind tells me that I *should* hate and fear him. He was elected on a platform of racism, islamophobia, xenophobia, and misogyny. As a Jew and a woman, I was a target of his hateful speech, and most of my closest friends and family were as well, for various reasons. I am scared for our future under his presidency and I am committed to resisting and fighting his policies that harm my communities and my friends' communities.

And yet I know deeply that Trump and his supporters are people, not monsters. I know that my well-being is tied

up with theirs, and that carrying around hate and fear for
these people takes up precious space in my heart and uses up
too much of my energy. Maintaining a softer heart doesn't
make me want to embrace the Trump administration or
policies that harm people. It doesn't make me want to stop
fighting. It just transforms the energy of the fight from one
of hate and fear of *them* (Trump and his supporters), to one
of love of and commitment to *us all*, which is a much more
powerful force.

I once heard that the Dalai Lama was asked if there
is anyone he struggles to have compassion for. The inter-
viewer undoubtedly expected the Tibetan leader, known
for living a life of advocacy on behalf of the Tibetan people,
to say that he struggles having compassion for the Chinese
occupiers of Tibet, or at least for the Chinese soldiers who
drove him to exile. The Dalai Lama thought about it for a
little while and then replied, "I still struggle having compassion for mosquitos. I am working on it, though."

The Dalai Lama, who has seen the decimation of his
culture and homeland, who has witnessed so much death
and disappearance, who has spent nearly every day of his
life trying to fight for the Tibetan people, *still* does not carry
vengeance or hatred in his heart for the perpetrators of the
harm inflicted on Tibet. Although a tireless advocate for
justice, the root of his activism is not vengeance, but love.

Thich Nhat Hanh has been advocating for peace, non-
violence, and social transformation for decades. He has

risked his life repeatedly in his efforts to end the Vietnam War and to rescue boatpeople and other refugees fleeing Vietnam. His poem, *Please Call Me by My True Names,* includes the lines:

> I am the twelve-year-old girl,
> refugee on a small boat,
> who throws herself into the ocean
> after being raped by a sea pirate.
> And I am the pirate, my heart
> not yet capable of seeing and loving. . . .
> Please call me by my true names,
> so I can wake up
> and the door of my heart
> could be left open,
> the door of compassion.[58]

Nhat Hanh's poem, his life, and his mission are to keep the door of his heart open in compassion, even for the most vile, evil people among us. His message is not to accept this evil behavior. He has fought against it his entire life. His message is to see the roots of such evil, violence, and hatred in his own heart.

58. Thich Nhat Hanh, "Please Call Me by My True Names," *Call Me by My True Names* (Berkeley, CA: Parallax Press, 1999). Also see Awakin .org. July 13, 2015, accessed April 13, 2017, http://www.awakin.org/ read/view.php?tid=2088.

How we do anything is how we do everything. We can't be peacemakers in our homes and personal lives while speaking a language of hate in our conversations and on our social media. We have to embody the love we hope to see reflected in our politicians, governments, and streets. That means that we have to make peace with our inner enemies and the hatred we have for ourselves in order to properly heal the outside world. We have to find the spark of love and human kindness for all parts of ourselves, including the parts that are power hungry, vain, weak, broken, needy, or whatever our particular inner enemy happens to be.

RADICAL SELF-CARE

For many people who have been marginalized in our society, practices that nourish and sustain us are not a luxury—they are a necessity. Audre Lorde once wrote, "caring for myself is not self-indulgence, it is self-preservation and that is an act of political warfare."[59] When your identity or your body is deemed inferior by the dominant society, then surviving, caring for the body and mind, and thriving is a major act of resistance. Additionally, the work of building a socially just society can be taxing and difficult. It takes a

---

59. Audre Lorde, *A Burst of Light: Essays* (Ann Arbor, MI: Firebrand Books, 1988), 131.

lot of energy and creates the need for spaces to recharge, refuel, and strengthen oneself—alone and in community.

Sangha, or meditation community, is a precious place for this to take place. When the world is painful and we feel lost or alone, we all need a place to call home. Likewise, when we have joy in our lives and want to celebrate with others who will understand us, we need community. Sangha, whether formal, at a meditation center, or informal, with a group of trusted friends, is radical self-care built right into the heart of the practice.

In Buddhism, Sangha is considered one of the "three jewels," alongside the Buddha (teacher, wise one) and the Dharma (teachings and practice). When committing ourselves to the path of the *bodhisattva*, or the one who has awakening and who works for the good of all beings, we say that we "take refuge" in these three jewels. The Buddha knew that doing the work of social transformation will occasionally make us refugees in the wider world. We need real strategies to sustain our hearts, focus our minds, rest and heal our bodies, and remember who we really are. This type of self-care is not about bubble baths, shopping sprees, or other quick-fix strategies frequently suggested by lifestyle blogs. To find the strength to continue, we need to come back to our heart, our practice, and our communities.

Meditation peels back the protective layers around the heart and helps us to be our most authentic self. This creates what feels like an inevitable responsibility and opportunity to push against systems of oppression and bring a new, sustainable, love-focused vision to the table. Our teachers and our communities hold us in this work as we commit for the long haul. The world needs this so badly. The world needs you.

7: YOUR HAIR IS ON FIRE AND EVERYTHING IS OKAY

THE BUDDHA told his students to practice as if their hair were on fire.[60] If *your* hair were on fire, how would you be meditating? How seriously would you be taking your life and your choices? My guess is that you would take up the question of "What now?" with urgency and devotion. Now is now. Now is the only moment. There is so much work we need to do to heal from our wounds, to accept our broken hearts, and to create a more just society. Now is the time to live a life of intention, awakening, and love. Not when we are older, or when we finish college, or when we fall in love or finish this book . . . *now.*

And yet, simultaneously, the teachings repeatedly say that the ultimate truth of everything is that all things are exactly as they should be in the present moment.[61] You, in

60. Theragatha, Ch. 1, "Tissa" (Thag. 1.39), Thanissaro Bhikkhu (translator), Access to Insight, accessed April 24, 2017, http://www.access toinsight.org/tipitaka/kn/thag/thag.01.00x.than.html#passage-39.
61. Thich Nhat Hanh, *Finding Our True Home* (Berkeley, CA: Parallax Press, 2003), 23.

this moment, no matter how distracted you have been or how messed up you feel, are completely perfect. Everything, at the heart of it, is okay. There is nothing we need to do and nowhere we need to go.

How can both of these things be true at the same time? We practice meditation to grow and transform *and* we practice to remember what is already true: at the heart of it, we have everything we need and we are exactly who we should be.

There is a beautiful story in the Platform Sutra that describes this paradox.[62] It takes place in a Chan (Zen) monastery in seventh-century China. The abbot, Hongren, is old enough that he is thinking of appointing his successor. According to tradition, each monk of the monastery writes a poem in which they attempt to describe the ultimate purpose of Buddhist teaching and practice. The inside favorite in this contest is the senior student Shenxiu, who writes:

> The body is the Bodhi tree.
> The mind is like a clear mirror.
> At all times we must strive to polish it
> And must not let the dust collect.

62. "Notes on the Verses by Shen-hsiu and Hui-neng," Darkwing.uor gegon.edu, accessed April 24, 2017. http://darkwing.uoregon.edu/ ~munno/OregonCourses/REL444S05/HuinengVerse.htm.

In Shenxiu's vision, our body is our instrument of enlightenment (the Buddha was enlightened under the Bodhi tree). Our mind holds up a mirror to all that is. When we sit in meditation and live in mindfulness, we are clearing the "dust" of our thoughts and projections in order to reflect life more clearly.

Huineng's poem responds to Shenxiu's:

> Bodhi originally has no tree.
> The bright mirror is always clean and pure.
> Fundamentally there is not a single thing.
> On what can the dust alight?

Huineng is making an equally important point. Even as we clear the mirror and strive to wake up, ultimately, at the heart of things, enlightenment is already here. It never left. It never changes. There is no dust and nothing on which the dust can settle. *Every single thing is just now, just this, just perfect.*

Both Shenxiu and Huineng are correct. We are all broken and in need of healing, and at the same time we are perfectly whole. This is the push and pull of our lives. This is the paradox we all have to live.

This time in your life may feel like an upheaval, when all the old rules go out the window and you have to figure out everything from scratch. Or perhaps you feel pregnant with possibility, scared but exhilarated as you ask big questions and begin to shape your adult life with intention. Or maybe you feel like you've taken a huge hit and been dragged through the mud; or you feel lonely and broken and in need of help. I know that I experienced all of these states fairly regularly in my twenties. I want you to know that in my experience, establishing and following a meditation practice will not only help you manage the stress of this time, but will open up your life and allow you to see and understand the contents of your heart and mind. It will return you to yourself and enable you to know your own preciousness—to remember that no matter who you are, you belong here, and your only job here on Earth is to be yourself and let your unique light shine. This is what it has done for me.

The journey is never over. In order to keep growing, we must all keep practicing. Although practicing mindfulness in all areas of our lives is important, I want to strongly recommend developing a daily sitting meditation practice. Choose a special space in your home or apartment and a comfortable sitting arrangement. It can be as simple as a living room couch, or as fancy as a kneeling stool or cushion you can buy online. Pick a time you can practice every day. It can be easiest to practice either first thing in the morning or last thing at night so you don't lose your intended time in the midst of a busy day. Then choose an amount of time.

It can be as short as five minutes, but I recommend fifteen for beginners. It gives you just enough time to settle the mind and body but doesn't make too much of a dent in your busy schedule. Try to practice every single day. If you miss a day, don't despair! If you missed a day brushing your teeth, would you ditch brushing your teeth from then on? You can always come back to your practice, your breath, and the present moment.

Additionally, to develop and deepen your practice, it helps to find a community with which to practice, a teacher or two you really trust, and some like-minded spiritual friends. Fortunately, there are Buddhist centers and meditation studios popping up all over the country that you can join, and many that have been around for a long time. A quick Internet search will yield these by the thousands. They vary in their affiliations to Buddhism, their racial and age demographics, and their community values. I encourage you to try out a few and see which feels the most like it could be a home for you. I also recommend attending at least one long retreat (three to five days at least) per year, either with your community or with a different retreat group, to sink deeper into silence and to really learn to understand your mind. Many of these retreats offer scholarships for those who cannot afford the full fee or for young people.

To supplement your community practice, there are also many online, mobile, and print resources to support you in deepening your meditation. The more you practice, the more the rewards mentioned in this book will become alive for you, but nobody can do it alone.

Finally, these practices can unearth some very intense, sometimes traumatizing events and emotions for many people. If these arise for you, please seek the support of a licensed therapist to help you process your feelings. Talk therapy is an incredibly valuable "friend" of meditation, and the two can work beautifully together to help you heal, grow, and thrive.

David Whyte wrote a poem called "The House of Belonging," in which he writes:

> This is the bright home
> in which I live,
> this is where
> I ask
> my friends
> to come,
> this is where I want
> to love all the things
> it has taken me so long
> to learn to love.
>
> This is the temple
> of my adult aloneness
> and I belong

to that aloneness
as I belong to my life.

There is no house
like the house of belonging.[63]

Mindfulness in our twenties and thirties is about turning this "temple of adult aloneness" into our "house of belonging." This is our quest. Through practice, we try to live as honestly as we can, being with what is, as it is. We try to understand our emotions and our mind and to use that understanding to be more awake in the world. For me, this awakeness always leads back to love and the importance of giving it, receiving it, and realizing that we are all made of it. When you are at the next "what now?" moment in your life, I hope you can remember this. The journey *always* begins right now.

63. David Whyte, "The House of Belonging," 1996, accessed April 13, 2017. Printed with permission from Many Rivers Press, www.david whyte.com.

APPENDIX:
A BASIC MEDITATION GUIDE

APPENDIX A: SITTING MEDITATION

BEGIN WITH your posture. Find a comfortable, upright position. This can be on a chair, a couch, or a cushion. There is nothing wrong with meditating while lying down (or walking, or running, or rock climbing . . .), but sitting in an upright position is usually the best for beginners as it helps to keep us awake but comfortable. If you are sitting on a chair or sofa, sit so that your back is straight and your feet are planted on the floor (taking into account the needs of your body). If you are sitting on a cushion, it's helpful to have your bottom elevated to be higher above your legs and not to have your legs crossed on top of each other. You can sit in the lotus position if you are very flexible (each foot on the opposite thigh), or the half-lotus if you are less flexible (one foot on the opposite thigh and the other just in front of the opposite leg), or you can sit cross-legged with one shin and foot in front of the other. Both knees should touch the floor or be supported by cushions underneath; this makes for a stable position with three points of the body supported by the earth. You can also be in a kneeling posture, with your knees together and a cushion underneath your bottom, or you can sit on a meditation bench with your knees bent, your shins on the floor, and your feet behind you. No one position is more "spiritual" or more advanced than another. It is purely a personal preference, unique to each person's body.

Once you've chosen a position, allow your body to settle and sink into your seat while also consciously elevating the top of your spine and the crown of your head toward the sky. Open your shoulders and the area around your heart. Let your chin be parallel to the floor or slightly downward, and soften the muscles of the jaw and the face. You can close your eyes or keep them very softly opened at a forty-five-degree angle in front of you. Relax your hands and place them on your thighs, folded in your lap, or wherever they are most comfortable.

Now move your awareness through your body and consciously soften around the areas that are holding tension. Allow the breath to wash through you, softening and opening the body. Notice how your body is feeling. Is there hunger? Is there stress? A pain in the knee? Excitement? Don't spend too much time on *why* you are feeling this way, just notice what is there, like a teacher taking attendance in a classroom. With each breath, gently note what is present (*Anger is here. Calm is here. Distraction is here. . . .*).

Once you have done a general inventory of your body and the physical sensations and emotions that are swirling around, choose a present-moment "anchor" to which you can return over and over again as a concentration object for your meditation. The breath is a fantastic anchor, as it is always there while we are alive. Paying attention to the breath also has ancillary benefits—it calms the nervous system and relaxes the heart, body, and mind. If, for any reason, the breath does not work for you, you can also use the weight of your body in the chair as your anchor, or the rise and fall of your chest or your abdomen (you can put a hand there to feel it, if you like). Some people also use sounds in the room—it doesn't matter, as long as you choose one anchor and remain committed to it during the duration of the meditation.

Paying attention to the breath does not mean *thinking* about the breath. There is nothing wrong with thinking about the breath, but in meditation, we are asked to sink into the *sensations* involved in the act of breathing. What does the breathing actually feel like? Like a doctor listening closely to our own chest with a stethoscope, we become very curious and focused on the texture, the movement of air, the temperature, and the subtle muscle movements involved in each breath. How long is each breath? What is the dynamic between our desire to control the breath and the breath happening of its own accord? Where do we feel the breath most prominently? How does each breath differ from the one before it? In the beginning, to pay attention to the breath is to keep dropping into the wave of our chest and belly as it rises and falls, riding that wave as softly as we can with all of our awareness. As we keep practicing, we may find that we need to exert less effort to stay with the wave. Instead of breathing, we feel life breathing us.

A critical part of the process of meditation is watching our attention fly away from our anchor, despite our best attempts to stay focused. One minute we can be softly paying attention to our breath and then, before we know it, we are planning dinner, analyzing our relationship (or lack thereof), regretting having said something to a friend, or halfway through a wildly imaginative dream. There is nothing wrong with this. Simply give a soft label to the general type of thought (*worrying, memory, imagination, etc.*) and return back to your anchor. This labeling does not have to be precise. It is simply a gentle way to recognize the contents of our mind without getting too involved in the individual stories or ideas the mind produces.

The acronym "DROPS" can help us to be kind and gentle with our thoughts during a period of meditation. Each time we notice we have gotten lost in thought, we can use DROPS: **D**on't **R**esist **or** **P**ush, **S**often. When we notice we are drifting off to sleep or are midway through an intense conversation in our mind, *don't resist or push*. Instead, *soften*, relax your body and mind, and return to your anchor. I also use DROPS when there are outside distractions in the room or coming from the street. (I live in New York City, so this happens a lot!) No need to tense up or find someone to blame. You only need to soften, let go, and start again.

APPENDIX B: MINDFUL WALKING

One simple and profound way we can bring the awareness from sitting meditation into our daily lives is through mindful walking. In fact, the Buddha said that there are four postures for meditation: sitting, standing, walking, and lying down. They are all equal and important! Walking meditation begins by bringing all of your awareness to your steps. First, as you're standing, bring your awareness to the bottom of your feet and their contact with the earth. Try it now. Can you feel them? Feel the snugness of your shoes and/or socks (if you are wearing them). Feel the temperature inside your shoe, or of your foot against the floor, if bare. Feel the pressure and solidity of the ground beneath you. Now, from standing, shift your weight and feel your body as it (slowly) moves to take a step. Feel your body tip forward, the movement of one leg, the lifting and the placing of the foot. As each foot meets the ground, feel the connection. Feel the support of the earth and gravity. Feel the intimacy and connection of walking. Every time your mind wanders, bring your attention back to the connection of your foot with the ground, the movement of your body in space, or some other physical sensation happening at that moment.

If it helps to fine-tune your concentration, try matching your breath to your step. Inhaling, shift your weight to one side. Exhaling, lift up your opposite foot. Inhaling, place

this foot forward. Exhaling, place this foot down. If timing these two things together is distracting to you, let go of
the focus on the breath and simply return the focus to the
sensations in the next step.

Walking meditation is not about where or how far you
go. In meditation centers and on retreats, walking meditation is often done in a circle around the meditation hall, or
on a small stretch of ground on the property. If you actually
do have to go from one place to another, however, it is a
powerful way to center and ground yourself as you walk
between your various destinations. I love to practice walking meditation on my way to and from work. If it is warm
outside, I feel the sunlight on my face. If it is cold or raining,
I pay close attention to the feeling of the air against my
skin. I say "hello" to the world with each meeting of my
foot with the ground. I pay attention to my breath and tell
my thoughts that I'm not going to indulge them during
that walk. I try to leave my phone in my pocket or purse,
and just walk, and breathe, becoming present in my life.
Sometimes, to help my mind stay focused, I use the phrase,
"just this step," allowing all my attention to flood the next
step with awareness and presence. I recommend trying this
practice on your way to and from class, or from your room
to the bathroom, or on your way to lunch. It is the most
portable of all meditation practices! Those who don't walk
because of disability can do this same exercise in a wheelchair or scooter, focusing on your hands and arms moving

the chair/scooter forward, paying attention to the feelings in your palms, to the movement of your body forward, to the support of the chair as you move.

APPENDIX C: MINDFUL EATING

To practice eating meditation, begin by taking a breath and a moment to contemplate your bowl or plate of food. Take a piece of something on your plate and, before gobbling it up, look closely at the food. What is it made of? What forces of nature and human labor brought it to your fork? Does it have a scent? Notice its colors and textures. How does your mouth or your stomach feel as you look at the food? You can say a blessing or a chant before eating if that feels right for you. You can find one of my favorites, written by Zen teacher Norman Fischer, at the end of this meditation.

Once you have examined it, you can gently place the food on your tongue. Are you starting to salivate? Can you feel the temptation to bite and chew? What flavors can you already taste?

Slowly begin chewing, truly experiencing each bite. Notice the feeling of your jaw and teeth working through the food. As you swallow, try to see when the food no longer becomes food and becomes a part of your body. Pause before taking the next bite. Are you eager to eat more? Do you find you enjoy the food more when you eat with this awareness instead of being lost in our thinking, as we often tend to be? At what point do the signals that say "hungry" change to say "full"? Is there a temptation to eat beyond this point? Where does that feeling originate?

Take a moment to feel the sensations after eating. Notice if gratitude rises up. Notice the pause between finishing eating and returning to the rest of the world.

ONE HEART GRACE
By Norman Fischer

As we make ready to eat this food we remember with gratitude the many people, tools, animals and plants, air and water, sky and earth, turned in the wheel of living and dying, whose joyful exertion provide our sustenance this day.

May we with the blessing of this food join our hearts to the one heart of the world in awareness and love, and may we together with everyone realize the path of awakening, and never stop making effort for the benefit of others.[64]

64. Norman Fischer, "One Heart Grace," Institute for Jewish Spirituality, accessed June 21, 2017, http://www.jewishspirituality.org/wp-content/uploads/2015/07/7-One-heart-grace_YIBA-June-2015.pdf.

APPENDIX D: TECHNOLOGY MEDITATION

Begin by choosing one medium of technology with which you usually engage and make it the focus of your meditation for one day, week, or month. Whichever you choose, put a post-it or a big sticker on your computer, TV, or phone to remind yourself to be mindful. If you skip this step, believe me, you will *not* naturally remember. Our favorite technology has a tendency to suck us under into virtual reality very quickly and quietly. The reminder to approach the medium mindfully needs to cut through the habit and addiction in order to have a chance.

I am going to use social media as the example, but any technological medium can be substituted in this meditation.

When you're about to click on the app or open the window of the site on your computer, close your eyes and take a deep breath. Take a few seconds to feel your body in your chair, your feet on the ground, your hands on your device. Feel the air move into and out of your lungs for a few breaths. Notice the feeling and the energy that is causing you to want to check the site. Is it boredom? Loneliness? A desire for escape? Take a few breaths just to notice how you feel with no judgment or rejection of these feelings.

Set an intention for your time on the site. You can say to yourself, *I am going on this site because I need a break from real life right now. My intention is to stay on only for ten minutes and then sign off.* Or you can say, *I am going on this site because I am lonely and want to connect. My intention is to post something that helps me to connect with others, and like others' posts as a means to show appreciation.* One other idea is to say to yourself, *My intention is to give everyone on social media the benefit of the doubt today, and to be kind to myself and others.* Whatever your intention is, spend a few minutes with it before diving into the site.

Once on the site, try to remember to return to your intention every few minutes. Take a minute every now and then to pause and check in with your feelings. Is this engagement fun? Enlightening? Helping you to feel connected? Or is it bringing on comparing mind? Depression? More loneliness? Be honest with yourself, even if you continue to scroll through the site.

Sign off and take a few breaths to reconnect with your physical and emotional body. How are you doing? How is your posture? How are you feeling? Were you able to stay with your intention? If not, or if you forgot to remain mindful at all, forgive yourself. Soften and take the next moment in all its freshness as an opportunity to start again. As long as we have new moments, we can try the next time to bring mindfulness into our technology use.

APPENDIX E: RAIN MEDITATION FOR WORKING WITH EMOTIONS

Begin by settling into your seat. Take a few breaths, relaxing your body and finding your breath. Do your best to bring your attention into your body and your breath and away from the busy mind.

Beginning with the "R" of RAIN, try to "recognize" what you are feeling in your body right now. Begin by being aware of how you physically feel, noticing any prominent sensations in your body. Notice how you are feeling emotionally. Is there a strong emotion that is calling your attention? Or perhaps an emotion with which you want to work? Recognize where in your body you feel this emotion (i.e., chest, stomach, temples), and *how* you know it is this emotion (i.e., a fluttering in the chest, sweaty palms, heat in the head). Breathe and stay with the physical manifestations of this emotion in the body.

Move on to the "A" of RAIN: Acceptance. Whatever you are feeling, can you relax your resistance to it? Try to soften around the emotion. Welcome it in. Say to the emotion: "You are welcome here. I see you. You don't have to leave. You don't have to go away. You can stay here, within me, as long as you need to." Breathe, feel the emotion, and keep releasing resistance.

Once you have sat with the emotion for a while, feeling its contours, allowing it into your body, you can move to the

"I" in RAIN: Inquiry. What is behind this emotion? What does this emotion want to say to me? Don't rush to answer. Allow the questions simply to rest in your consciousness. See if an answer arises. Gently probe the emotion with love and kindness. What is the root of this feeling? What does this emotion look like? If the questions begin to move you too far into thinking or mental machinations, gently release the inquiry and return back to your body and your breath.

Finally, arrive at the "N" in RAIN: Nourish. Ask yourself, "What can I do for myself right now? How can I take care of this emotion? How can I take care of myself feeling this emotion?" With gentleness and love, take care of yourself as you stay with your unpleasant and/or powerful emotion(s).

APPENDIX F: LOVE MEDITATION

Settle into your seat. Take a few deep breaths, releasing all the busyness of your mind and relaxing into your body. Locate the rise and fall of your breath, and ride that wave for a few moments. Relax and settle.

Focus on the area around your chest and heart. Place a hand there if it is hard to feel it. Notice the sensations under your hand—the temperature of your body, the feeling of your clothing, the firmness/softness of your chest. Notice if you feel the rise of the breath, or the beating of your heart.

Anythink Bennett

495 7th Street
Bennett, CO 80102
303-405-3231
Tues and Thurs, 10 AM ▯ 7 PM
Wed, Fri, Sat, 10 AM - 5:30 PM
Sun and Mon, Closed

Date: 12/6/2018 Time: 2:05:25 PM

Items checked out this session: 2

Title: This idea is brilliant : lost, overl
Barcode: 33021030593419
Due Date: 12/27/18

Title: What now? : meditation for your twen
Barcode: 33021030554593
Due Date: 12/27/18

... where anything is possible.

One by one, begin to bring to mind people in your life who have cared for you, starting with the people that cared for you in the earliest part of your life. You may have no memory of these people, or you may have spoken to them yesterday, but imagine these people feeding you, putting on your diaper, ensuring in one way or another that you survived. They may not have loved you or cared for you as well as you would have liked, they may have also hurt you, but for now, just focus on the acts of love and care that were part of your infancy and early childhood.

Now bring to mind the people that loved or cared for you later in your life. Perhaps family members, friends, teachers, doctors, or babysitters. Notice the things they did for you, the ways they taught or played with you or helped you. Can you see their faces? Their hands? The moments when they intervened to help you with something? Check in with your own body when bringing these people to mind. Feel the love. Feel the care. Feel the gratitude, and notice where you feel it in your body.

Now think about the people who love and care for you now. Take a few moments to picture the faces of family, friends, teachers, lovers, classmates, coworkers, doctors, pets, etc. In no particular order, look at the next person's face in your mind, and feel your heart swell in response. Allow the care they give to you, even if it is imperfect, to wash over you.

Take the next few minutes to bring to mind the people

you care for—either happily, or not as happily. Bring to mind their faces, and watch in your mind, what you do for them. Try to tap into the love in your devotion and care for these people/pets. Feel the full range of feelings that come from loving and caring for others.

Finally, pan the camera out to feel the love that the entire world has for you. The care that the clothing gives you in warming and covering your body. The care of gravity, of your cushion, of the air, of trees and nature, of the sun and the moon, of your own body and breath sustaining you, so that you survive another moment. How many of these trillions of forces of life and love can you notice? How do they feel in your body?

Let go of who or what is giving and who or what is receiving love. Just breathe into this moment. Let go and be love. If you would like, keep repeating "love" out loud or in your head. Open up to the feelings that arise and fall in response.

APPENDIX G: METTA (HEARTFULNESS) MEDITATION

Begin by settling into your seat in a comfortable, upright posture. Take a few deep breaths, releasing extra thoughts or busyness in the mind and allowing the nervous system to release and relax as much as you can.

After you have settled into your seat and felt the inhale and exhale of your breath for a little while, call to mind someone in your life whom it is very easy to love. This could be a "benefactor," or someone who has helped you throughout your life, or it could be a pet or a child—someone whose face immediately floods you with feelings of love. Do not spend too much time choosing this person, and only pick one person.

Once you have the person in mind, hold them in your mind's eye. With each inhale, focus on the person's face, and with each exhale, imagine these qualities of safety, ease, and love washing over them.

May [insert person's name] feel safe.
May [insert person's name] feel at ease.
May [insert person's name] feel loved.

Repeat these three wishes (or add/adjust some of your own) for this person over and over again. Try to really open up to the feeling of each word (*safe, at ease, loved*) as you say it. If you get distracted in the meditation and begin to think about other things, do not beat yourself up. Simply soften, let go of the distracting thought, and return back to the meditation.

After you have spent some time wishing these things on your benefactor/loved one, turn the focus around and wish it for yourself. This can be very hard for some people.

Notice if you tense up or have a hard time focusing the wish on yourself. Notice what arises. Do you have a voice that says you are not worth it? Do you feel selfish or self-centered? Soften around the tension or the difficulty without pushing it away. If it helps, put a hand on your heart as you wish these things for yourself.

> *May I feel safe.*
> *May I feel at ease.*
> *May I feel loved.*

Now, bring to mind someone who you don't know very well. Perhaps you like this person, perhaps you have no particular feelings about them whatsoever. Perhaps you know their name, maybe not. Perhaps they are the security guard you pass on the way out of your dorm room or the person who works at your gym. Choose one of these people, and concentrate on sending them the same three wishes, over and over again:

> *May [insert person's name, or say "this person"]*
>   *feel safe.*
> *May [insert person's name] feel at ease.*
> *May [insert person's name] feel loved.*

After several minutes of this, bring into your mind's eye someone in your life with whom you have difficulty. Notice what happens in your body when you bring this person to mind. Do you clench up? Does your heart feel closed? Do you feel afraid or resistant? Even if it is hard, try to breathe and return back to the meditation. You don't need to break down your resistance. Just notice it is there and breathe into it.

May [insert person's name] feel safe.
May [insert person's name] feel at ease.
May [insert person's name] feel loved.

Try to really imagine this difficult person feeling each of these things. Try to bring these qualities of safety, ease, and love into your body as you wish them on this person. Notice how it feels in the pause between wishes.

Finally, expand your mental lens to include all beings, everywhere in the world, including yourself. However you can conceptualize this enormous body of beings, try to picture them *all* experiencing these qualities.

May all beings feel safe.
May all beings feel at ease.
May all beings feel loved.

Repeat this many times over. Rest in the feelings that this meditation elicited, and breathe.

ACKNOWLEDGMENTS

THIS BOOK is the result of so many people's hard work, support, brilliance, and love. Thank you first and foremost to Jennifer Kamenetz, who found me, helped me to plot this book out (a few times) and doula-d this project into existence.

A huge thank you to Hannah Leffingwell, whose sharp editing eye, brilliant mind, and steadfast dedication to this project over multiple drafts helped bring it to life. Her insights are infused throughout the book.

Thank you to all my editors, from my formal editor—Jacob Surpin (who is a GENIUS)—to my informal crack team of proofreaders: Rachel Schiff, Danit Fleischman, Ben Bernstein and Gustie Owens. Critical chapter help came from Allie Shafran, Rachel Brown, Daviel Shy and A'Nisa Megginson. Thanks to Brian Young for the citations. Thanks to Isabel Calkins for my website and so much more!

I'm deeply grateful to the team at Parallax for all your wisdom and support throughout the process and for creating a beautiful community for your authors.

None of this book would have been possible without the crew at New York University's Global Spiritual Life. Deep thanks to Reka Prasad, mindful leader and teacher extraordinaire, Ariel Ennis, an amazing educator and author, the lovely Emily Mervosh, and the wonderful Gerianne Perkins. Thanks to all the GSL chaplains, NYU colleagues, student workers, and to all my students over the years who have enriched my life so deeply. Thanks as well to Dr. Chelsea Clinton, Dr. Marcella Runell Hall, Imam Khalid Latif, and Rabbi Yehuda Sarna, my inspirations in so many things, and to Dr. Marc Wais, for all his support and guidance. A special thanks to one of my heroes and mentors, Dr. Linda G. Mills, who continues to teach me through her extraordinary life what it means to be bold, dream big, and make a difference.

Thanks as well to the whole team at MNDFL for allowing me to teach in your beautiful space and for creating such a warm container for the practice to flourish.

This book was born of thousands of hours of meditation and discussion with the wisest of teachers and beloved spiritual friends. Thank you to Bill Buse, Teah Strozer, Zoketsu Norman Fischer, R. Alan Lew (may his memory be a blessing), R. James Jacobson Maisels, R. Shuli Passow, R. David Cooper, Shoshana Cooper, Eliezer Sobel, Ruth Jacobson, R. Jeff Roth, R. Sheila Peltz Weinberg, Greg Snyder, Laura O'Loughlin, and the Brooklyn Zen Center community, R. Toni Shy, Herb/Tzvi Bilick, Rachel Schiff, Erica Lessem,

Sasha Berger, Rachel Brown, Vanessa Harvill, Jon Hurst, Mira Neshama Niculescu, and Lodro Rinzler. Any mistakes I have made in my understanding of Buddhism or in the teachings and my quotes of these people are entirely mine.

Thank you to my dearest family, Mom, Abba, Tzvi, Rami, Helenka, Trysa, Peter, Daviel, LeCiel, Breetel, Isaac, Leila, Reuben, Michal, Eva, Kay, Iver, Nina, and all my aunts, uncles, nieces, nephews, and cousins. I love you all. Thanks as well to Jennifer Noel, Jen Germain, Evan Parks, Eliana Dotan, and Jana Jett Loeb, whose babysitting gifts helped me to finish this thing (and occasionally get some sleep).

Thank you especially to Zusha, my baby of divine sweetness. Thank you for teaching me every day about life, joy, and what it means to be fully present. I love you beyond words.

And thank you to Ben, my love, my family, my heart.

ABOUT THE AUTHOR

PHOTO © ERIKA SCOTT

YAEL SHY is the founder and director of MindfulNYU (the largest campus-wide meditation initiative in the country) and the senior director of the Center for Global Spiritual Life at New York University. She leads meditation workshops, classes, and retreats around the country and the world, including at NYU Abu Dhabi, NYU Berlin, NYU Tel Aviv, Mindful Life, Princeton University, and elsewhere and teaches weekly at MindfulNYU and at the meditation studio MNDFL in Greenwich Village.

In 2010, Shy was named one of the "36 under 36" change makers transforming the Jewish world by *Jewish Week* newspaper. She has practiced meditation regularly in Jewish, Zen Buddhist, and secular contexts. Yael has been published in the *Harvard Business Review*, the *Huffington Post*, the *Journal of Interreligious Studies,* the *NYU Review of Law and Social Change*, among other publications. Yael Shy lives in Brooklyn with her husband and son.

PARALLAX
PRESS

Parallax Press is a nonprofit publisher, founded and inspired by Zen Master Thich Nhat Hanh. We publish books on mindfulness in daily life and are committed to making these teachings accessible to everyone and preserving them for future generations. We do this work to alleviate suffering and contribute to a more just and joyful world. For a copy of the catalog, please contact:

Parallax Press
P.O. Box 7355
Berkeley, CA 94707
parallax.org